"DON'T EVER GO FROM ME!" SHE WHISPERED

She kissed him. Her tears were wet against his face; her mouth, soft, opened and she bit his lower lip so hard that he raised his right hand part way to protect himself. He held his hand in midair and endured the pain until it blended with the rich pleasure of sexual arousal.

He tried to twist his hips so she would not sense his excitement. Their heads tilted almost at right angles to each other; her left hand squeezed his right and moved it to her left breast and held it there, and they kissed and clung together, until she abruptly drew away and looked down into the nearly dead little fire.

"If you ever leave me, I'll kill myself," she muttered. He could hardly hear her. "I'll kill *you*...."

ARMS BOOK II

THE SEEDS OF FIRE

Kenneth M. Cameron

FAWCETT POPULAR LIBRARY • NEW YORK

THE SEEDS OF FIRE

Published by Fawcett Popular Library, a unit of CBS Publications, the Consumer Publishing Division of CBS Inc.

ISBN: 0-445-04672-4

Printed in the United States of America

First Fawcett Popular Library printing: September 1981

10 9 8 7 6 5 4 3 2 1

For Christian

Chapter One

In the burned-over fields below the palisade, some of the young men were shooting, and the sound drifted up to him like the cracks and pops of a distant fire—as if it were already winter and he were lying in the house by the firepit, dreaming and dozing. He had brought six new guns into the village the day before, and now their owners were proudly firing them. They were young men, almost boys, and it amused him that doing something so utterly foreign as firing a gun should be a show of manhood for them.

"Do I bother you?"

He looked up. "Hello, Weasel." The boy was easily recognized, even silhouetted as he was against the sun. The head was narrower than the heads of the purebred People; this head, after all, was half of his own making—half Seneca, half European.

"Why do you call me that name?"

"You remind me of a weasel I knew once." He had been called Weasel when he had been a boy himself. Skinny and frightened and lonely.

"Did you truly know a weasel?"

"When I was a boy. Smaller than you."

"Did you talk to it?"

"All the time."

"Truly?"

"Truly! I told it all my dreams. It was a very wise old weasel with very strong magic. You remind me of it."

"It is a good name, then." The boy hesitated. He was a very grave little boy and he thought long before he spoke. "Did the weasel give you his magic?"

"Some of it. Some of it."

"And will I have your magic when I'm old enough?"

He was believed to have magic because he fixed the guns and because he brought the guns. No Seneca could make a gun; a scant few of them could replace a cock. Yet they had seen him forge new cocks and springs with his tiny portable anvil.

"A man gets his magic where he can, Weasel. It don't come

7

all of itself." He thought of the child he had been once in Scotland, called Weasel half fondly, half contemptuously by his father; he had hugged himself in a warm corner by the forge and told himself wonderful tales of heroism and romance. Now he wondered if this boy could understand any of that other one. *Can a Seneca dream of heroism? Of course; what is any of them but a dreamer?*

"They have new guns," the boy said needlessly when the sound of shooting reached them again.

"I hear."

"They will make war, they say."

"Not until spring."

"They cannot wait, my mother says."

"Your mother is a very wise woman. That is why she picked me for a husband." Jan grinned; the boy grinned, although Jan sensed that he did not understand the joke. He was simply happy, Jan guessed—happy to be named after a wise old weasel, happy to be talking to his father, who was a man of magic who was seldom home. Only ten, the boy was already muscular; two years more, and he would be ready for the rites that would proclaim him a man-in-the-making.

Jan Morse twisted a tool a quarter-turn and tightened a hand-cut screw. "Where do you think they would go to war, Weasel?"

"Up along the Great Sea-Running River. When the canoes come down with furs."

The boy sounded almost bored.

Jan cocked an eyebrow at him. "It is very convenient, always having a war so handy when a young man gets a new gun," he said dryly.

"Yes. It is the good way to live." The boy did not understand irony. The grown men *did* understand it: many of their jokes and most of the edged humor of their oratory came from their keen—indeed, their bitter—understanding of the irony of existence. Jan wondered at what age such irony became apparent to them. *When they know they are mortal.*

He turned the old gun over in his lap. He had been pushing down on it so hard that it had left creases in the deerskin leggings; they stood out white and fine against the deeper brown of the smoked leather. He shifted his position and the leggings stretched a little, and the creases began to fade.

Jan Morse had taken this gun apart half a hundred times. The screws that he had tightened had been cut by his own hands in a workshop in Leiden, in faraway Holland; the new

8

spring under the lockplate had been forged by him in Inverness. He had cleaned that gun, replaced parts, made new ones, and carried it for more than thirty years. It was his as few guns are ever any man's—his by right of possession and his by care.

"You made that gun," the boy said.

"No." Jan touched the intricate chiseled decoration that surrounded the breech and the central lock mechanism. "No, Weasel, this one I did *not* make." The shallower engraving on the triggerguard was wearing, and in one place the silver of the guard was as thin as the bow of an old, old spoon; the legend that had been engraved into the metal was virtually unreadable. He could make it out, however, because he knew what it said. *I Fecit An. Dom. MCDLXXV Francisco Lazarino Mors.* 1475! The gun was almost 175 years old. Still, it fired as true and as hard as a new one. "No, I did not make this gun," he said again. "One of my father's fathers did—way back. One of my old fathers. Long ago."

"When there were giants?"

"Yes, when there were giants." "Giants" were the Seneca idea of past greatness. Events of legend were ascribed to giants.

"But that gun is broken."

"Only the stock. The wood. I fixed it."

"When one of the People breaks a gun, he throws it away. Unless you are here; then sometimes they bring it to you to heal."

"But their guns are not as good as this one, Weasel. Sometimes, when the People are foolish and trade their guns from somebody else instead of me—one of the damned French, for instance—then they get guns that are no good. Those guns blow up, or the—you have no word for it, but we call it *springge*—their *springgen* break. Then the People throw the gun away because they have nobody with the magic to fix them between here and Nieuw Amsterdam. Because I am always in some village or other, trading and fixing the guns that I bring. But why should I fix the no-good guns that they trade down from the damned French?"

"My mother says you can do anything."

Jan grinned with the pleasure of being adored. He and his Seneca wife truly liked each other; her pleasure in him gave him pleasure.

"My mother says you have magic in your hands."

Jan chuckled.

"My mother says she saw you once make an iron knife from rust."

"She saw me make it from an old lockplate that had lain out in the snow all winter, Weasel; but it was not all rust. Underneath it was good iron."

"If you make knives, why do you not make guns here?"

"Because guns take special tools and much, much metal. The People have no metal, unless they trade it for furs."

"You ought to make magic and create metal. The People would give you all their furs, then. The People always need more guns so they can make war."

"And why do they make war?"

"To get rich. To get rich by capturing furs."

"And what do they do with the furs?"

"They trade them for guns."

Jan sighed. "That they do. That they do."

The old wheel-lock that had been made in 1475 was warm in his hands, as if it did, indeed, contain the living spirit with which the People invested guns; the sun had warmed it as he had worked and now the metal, velvety-smooth from generations of Morse hands (Moors hands, Mors hands) felt like skin. If it had pulsed with the beat of a heart, it would have not astonished him. *I have seen magic,* he thought. A heartbeat would not have astonished him. *I saw the White Beast. I know what the gun and I are to each other.* The old weapon would not last too much longer, however. Even a beautifully made gun cannot last forever. The stock had been badly broken right at the wrist when he had fallen, climbing a shaley glen in the Onayta country; he had repaired the break with rawhide, which had tightened and dried to a metallic hardness, but he would have to replace the stock when the piece of wood that he had curing in the longhouse was ready.

"Have you ever gone to war with this gun?" the boy said.

Jan frowned. "Gunmakers should not go to war," he said quietly. "A man can fight, or he can make the gun; if he does both, he risks his magic."

"Why is that?"

"I do not know. That is the way of things."

"Have you ever gone to war with this gun?"

Jan was silent. Even his oldest crimes made him quiet. "In a way," he said carefully.

"And you did not lose your magic?"

"No." He shot a quick, brutally open look at the boy; satisfied with what he saw, he said quite simply, "I killed a man with this gun. And I did not lose my magic."

"Was it in a war?"

"No. It was..." He tried to think of a Seneca word for "personal." The People were stingy with such words, however; there was little that was personal in a people who had few possessions and no privacy. "It was a thing between him and me."

"Did you pay his family afterward?"

"He was a white-face, like me. We are different from the People. Sometimes, white-faces do not have families."

The boy was bewildered. Every individual among the people had family everywhere, both the immediate family of the mother's house and the more distant relations of the clan, even as far away as the Maaqua country. The boy frowned; in a day or two, Jan knew, he would ask a question about it.

He had told the boy a kind of lie. The man he had murdered so long ago had been his mother's lover; Jan had been only two years older than this muscular child. He had killed other men since—seven, altogether—but never in passion as he had killed that first one. Then he had killed out of red hatred with this same gun. *Raised the gun and shot him in the face. Couldn't do it now. Shouldn't. The gunmaker must take great care in using the gun.*

"Come along, Weasel. I want to eat."

He led the boy along the path into the village; the gunshots faded behind them, blocked now by the palisade and the bulge of the hill on which the village stood. They passed through a grove of beech trees and came out into an almost grassless area as big as the grazing common of a Dutch village; the earth was pounded down by hundreds of feet. Three long-houses framed the area in an uneven U that opened toward the beech grove. Each house had doors in both ends, and outside each door was a garbage heap as high as his shoulder. A rich odor of rot came from the piles. Curiously, the smell excited him. Perhaps the pleasure he took was a perverse one—the melancholic's response to the odor of the privy—but he breathed deeply of it as if to gather the smell into hungry nostrils. This was the smell of the villages—smell of newness, smell of promise, smell of freedom. The odor of cooking overlay the odors from the middens; the odor of autumn—burning cornstalks, turning leaves, earth—tinged its edges, but the one smell dominated, and he loved it. He would have followed that smell to the edge of the world, he knew. He had

11

followed it from Hudson's River when he was only a boy of fourteen, inland to the Maaqua country; he had followed it deeper and deeper into the wondrous wilderness, into this huge mystery that other Europeans called "the desert." He was still following it as a middle-aged man with a Seneca wife and three half-Seneca children, a wanderer led by the nose.

Ishmael. Ishmael the gun trader.

He raised the painted hide that covered the door of the Turtle house and slipped inside, then held the skin so that the boy could follow him.

"Can I go watch them shoot?"

"Of course. Go."

The boy ran off. *My son. And not my son.* Seneca children were the sons of their mothers; fathers did not count for much. Fathers were too often away—or dead. Or divorced. Seneca women got easily disgusted with men who were always at war.

The gun was carried lightly in his right hand; with his left, he touched the soft, plump buttock above his wife's left leg. She squealed softly and caught his hand and laughed. When she turned away at a task, he touched her rump again.

"Quit!"

"I am hungry. My belly hurts."

"Then eat! Is my ass a squash? You meant to get a handful of my ass to chew on, did you?"

"Nice and plump. Very tasty, I bet." The joke was not a very good one; indeed, it skirted a taboo, for at times the People ate human flesh—of their enemies, of course.

"I will give you my hand to taste if you play with my ass like that. You are a randy little runt of a white-face and you have no manners."

"Your rump is too nice. It makes me forget my manners."

"You are a bad man. I should divorce you. Put a squash in your mouth and shut up."

He sat cross-legged by the firepit and ate squash with wood ashes sprinkled over it. There was a little salt in the house— real salt that he had brought her as a gift—but she was saving it. He had been back only four days. It was always the same: his children were shy with him; his wife was flirtatious and mocking.

He heard the rustle of movement behind him. She tickled him lightly along the ribs. "Want to do it?"

"While I eat?"

"No, after, you runty asshole."

"Yes, after. If you did not cook so well, I would do it now."

"I do not understand how such a little man can eat so much. And do it so much. I think you are half rabbit." She pressed herself against his back and whispered, "But I like rabbit."

It was always good to come back to her. And it was always good to go away. Perhaps marriage would not have been tolerable for either of them if he had always been there; the life of the longhouse and of the village was more women's than men's. War and hunting took the men away. Sometimes, they came back. When they came back, they were coddled and treated as guests, but it was expected that they would go away again, and the real life of the village would be left to the women and the wise old men. A younger man who stayed at home was probably a bad husband.

There was movement at the door, and a little breeze blew smoke from the fires as the hanging was raised. His son came quickly down the row of firepits; he dodged one of his aunts and earned a sharp word from his grandmother as he almost collided with her. When he came up to Jan, he was panting, large-eyed. "There is a runner for you!"

Jan looked at his wife. She masked her face with blankness.

"From where?"

"He is from Long Creek, but he kept his message to himself." He moved to his mother. "Can I be a runner on the Trail when I am old enough?"

"Not if you knock down your own grandmother in her house!" an angry voice shouted from the gloom. One of the aunts laughed; Fish-catcher, Jan's wife, grabbed the boy's arm and made a face at him. "See what you have done!" she hissed.

"Can I be a runner?"

"Go and apologize to your grandmother. Go!" She stared at the child, who was about to object. "Do you want me to stop speaking to you?" she said in that slow, dangerous way that mothers always use when they are serious. The threat was the ultimate one to a Seneca child: isolation. The boy slouched off toward his grandmother.

"I must go," Jan said.

"What will the runner want with you? Another trade?"

"How would I know? If I already knew, there would be no

13

need to send messages." He gulped the last of the squash and squeezed her thigh. "Wait for me."

He slitted his eyes against the glare of the outdoor light and followed a path around the house and deeper into the village. The strong, harsh smell of the middens reached him. Four dogs tumbled past him, half-wild, barking. Two hawks sailed, flapped wings, sailed again, woods hawks crossing from grove to grove toward their homes in the forest to the south. Far away, the guns popped.

The messenger was waiting by the men's house. He had already passed his message pouch to another runner, who was gone; his body shiny with sweat, he waited only to speak to Jan before he went in to rest. Tomorrow—even tonight, if there was nobody else—he would run back over the route by which he had come. He was thinner than most of the Seneca men; indeed, he seemed almost emaciated. *The Weasel might be a good runner,* Jan thought. *His body is right. He has my body. I must ask the old men.*

"I am Snow Elk. My son says you have a message for me."

The runner nodded. His temples were coated with a fine white scum of dried sweat—a coating of his own salt, like sand.

"Black Otter of the Turtles will be at Long Creek Village tomorrow and a day. He wants to see you there."

"Why?"

"That is not in my message."

"So. That is all of it?"

"That is all of it."

Jan raised an eyebrow. *But that will not be all of it in the end.* "Thank you." He gave the man a bead that had come from Venice by way of Amsterdam. *Almost my last. Time to replenish.*

"No message to return?"

"Oh. Oh, tell him I will be there. Tomorrow and a day."

He walked more slowly back toward the Turtle house, slowed by thoughts that he wanted to complete before he reached his wife. Black Otter was the most powerful of the Seneca war leaders, a consummate politician with a vision that seemed likely to leap over the traditional borders of the People's land. A generation before, they had been a threatened nation, favorite prey of the Suskeehannocks and frequent victims of the Hurons; now, they were the most aggressive of the Iroquois, less numerous than the Maaquas but more ambitious. *Geography makes them ambitious,* he thought.

14

They were the most exposed of the Iroquois, the most fully surrounded by enemies. Black Otter wanted to put a buffer between the People and their enemies to the west. He wanted to remove the threat of the Hurons. He wanted the furs that came down from the Great Lakes.

He wanted a great deal.

Men sought out Snow Elk—Jan Morse—for one reason: they wanted guns. To fix guns, to trade guns. He had traveled among them for thirty years, disappearing every few years to return to Europe and then come back with more guns, more parts for repairs, more trade goods. In Nieuw Amsterdam, they called him Jan Moors, the White Indian; in all the villages, they called him Snow Elk because of the dream he had had when he first lived among the Maaquas. But Nieuw Amsterdammers and Iroquois alike knew him by the nickname that was a password from the Hudson on the east to the Chenusee on the west: Gun-finder.

Black Otter would want Gun-finder for only one reason. Black Otter would want a new war.

Chapter Two

Black Otter waited for him under the oak tree that marked the center of Long Creek Village, a big, ancient tree that seemed to reach out to embrace the whole hilltop, towering above the palisade so that from a distance it was as recognizable as the steeple of a European town. As Jan walked up the slope toward the tree, Black Otter was murmuring to a man standing next to him, looking down the hill at Jan and going on with some explanation that kept his good hand busy with gesture.

Black Otter had only one sound arm, his right. The other was withered; the People said that he had been blasted by an unhappy spirit before he found wisdom. He had had a different name when he was younger; the change of name had obliterated that earlier, unwise self who had offended a spirit. Now he was a powerful leader and he kept the arm, like his old self, hidden. A great cape of black squirrel skins, into which the red heads of woodpeckers had been sewn, was wrapped around his left shoulder like a toga, and from a distance he looked like a column of black rock with brilliant drops of scarlet blood on it.

Jan moved uphill at an easy pace. There was no good in making the war leader think that he could make the Gunfinder hurry. After all, they were both men of power—and of magic.

Jan carried the old wheel-lock gun in his right hand. Black Otter's long musket was leaning against the oak tree. Jan leaned his own next to it. When he turned, Black Otter had dismissed the other man and was waiting for him.

They made a curious pair. Cultures had crossed so that, although they looked upon each other as European and Senecan, each had adopted so many of the other's characteristics that they made an odd hybrid. Black Otter wore, besides the black robe, silver armbands from Holland and a chain of glass beads from Venice; Jan wore an English shirt and Dutch coat over deerskin leggings and moccasins. When Black Otter offered tobacco, it was the small-leafed, bitter tobacco of the Chenusee country, mixed with the leaves of a small ground

16

plant; when they smoked it, they smoked it in clay pipes molded in a factory in Nieuw Amsterdam.

"Sit," Black Otter commanded. When they were comfortable, he studied Jan for some seconds. They were almost of an age, toughened men in their mid-forties, no longer foolish, sometimes cynical; Black Otter looked huge next to Jan, but there was no condescension from him.

"You are just returned," Black Otter said politely.

"I was in Onayta country, yes."

"And before that, you traveled beyond the borders of the People."

"Yes, south. South and west."

"What did you find?"

"No guns. The Swedes and the Spanish are stingy with their guns—the English, too, but not so bad as the Swedes and the Spanish, who are the worst of all. I saw a man using the spanner for a wheel-lock as a club."

"My Dutch brothers are generous with their guns."

"For furs, yes. Like the French."

Black Otter scowled. "The French want too much for guns. The French want to sell me their little Jesus with every gun. My Dutch brothers are wiser. They keep their Jesus to themselves."

Jan puffed at the little pipe. "Their high mightinesses in Amsterdam are not happy when our Dutch brothers sell you too many guns. I have heard that the French and even the English speak very feelingly to our Dutch brothers over the Big Bitter Water about it." He was trying to move the talk as close as possible to trading so that Black Otter would have an opening if he chose to trade. And now he took it.

"Snow Elk has always been good about selling guns to the People," he said. He called Jan by his Seneca name from the old days of his dream, rather than by his name as a trader. "Even when our Dutch brothers have been stingy with guns, Snow Elk has been good."

"I have been able to bring guns no matter what their high mightinesses said, yes."

"Good guns."

"Very good guns, yes."

"And now I want Snow Elk to bring more guns for the People. I want to buy more guns without troubling their high mightinesses over the Big Bitter Water. Without bothering the French in their castle at Mount Royal."

Jan looked into the hard, shrewd face. *Like a mirror of my own.* He had still the romantic yearnings of a boy, but his face was that of a tough, weathered man. Perhaps, he thought, there was a boy hidden somewhere behind Black Otter's face, too—the boy who had had two good arms. Jan looked away at a bird that perched on an oak twig. The warblers were beginning to move south; they were in the trees now, their nervous movements like a tremor in the huge old tree.

"How many guns?" he asked. When Black Otter did not answer, he looked into his face again. What was there—irony? Black Otter looked as if he were about to spring a joke. "How many guns?" Jan said again. He thought of an impossibly high number. "Fifty?"

"More."

More! It would be impossible for one man to smuggle fifty guns past Nieuw Amsterdam. *More!* "A hundred?"

"More."

Jan hesitated. "Two hundred?"

Black Otter grinned. "More."

It was no good objecting that so many guns had never in the world made their way up the Hudson, much less come west three hundred English miles into the wilderness. It was no use objecting that anybody who was caught bringing so many guns to the Iroquois would be hanged. *If he was caught, that is.* Two hundred guns would instantly create an army in the wilderness. *And make a trader rich.* Jan thought of the enemies of the People—Eries, Hurons, Algonkins—and of how few guns reached them from the French. If the Senecas came with two hundred more guns than they had now, their enemies would flee like dandelion fluff in the wind.

And the trader would be rich.

"I cannot count higher than three hundred," Jan said. He had surprised himself by even seeming to consider Black Otter's request. It was unthinkable, of course. Gun traders brought in half a dozen guns, or ten, or—for a reckless man—a score. But even as he thought of all that, Jan was saying to himself, *Have to get them over here secretly, in the bilge of some old tub, bribe the captain; come ashore someplace, maybe down the Delaware, maybe bribe the Swedes; but getting the guns in Europe, there's a tickler; of course there are my cousins in Holland and there's my own shop, then there's that third cousin in England. I've never tried him, well, three hundred guns, maybe it could be done; Holy Mother of God, what a sale; have to come ashore at night, very tricky—*

18

"So many guns would be an act of magic," he said.

"Of course. Black Otter would pay very high."

"In advance."

"Half. With a bonus on delivery."

"Ten pelts each gun."

"Ten pelts each stand of arms—with horn, half a pound of lead and a pound of powder."

Hundred and fifty pounds of lead, three hundred pounds of powder, Holy Mother, the weight! Still, with three good men, let's see, ten pelts a gun, that would be . . .

Black Otter was drawing in the dirt with a little knobby twig of oak. "On the coast above the mouth of the Delaware," he said. "At night. There are places, behind the sand islands that protect that coast from the Big Bitter Water. I have seen the places. We would build fires. I would have people there expecting you, from first strawberries until the winter gales. One of your winged canoes could come close in."

"Too dangerous. Keep the ship off and come in by longboat. No, a pinnace." Thinking, *What am I saying, this is mad!*

"When, Snow Elk?"

"When must you have the guns?"

Black Otter's face was hard. "The less you know, the better for you."

"Let's say, in the spring, then—when the shadbush blooms along the Delaware. Plum-blossom time here."

"Can you do it, Gun-finder?"

"Give me time to think. It's very big. Very dangerous. Also, very cumbersome. Both going and coming—I can't walk down to Nieuw Amsterdam with three thousand pelts on my back." *Three thousand! He'll have to capture the whole Great Lakes fur fleet!* He knew how Black Otter would get his furs— not by trapping, but by raiding for them, villages to the west, to the north; the canoe route of the Great Sea-Running River. *Not my business.*

Black Otter looked sleepy, as if the cynicism of it all bored him.

"Does Black Otter know Koopman the trader at Fort Orange? Up on Rykerskill?"

Black Otter nodded.

"Maybe the pelts could be sent to him. He'd give me credit for them." Koopman would discount the furs twelve percent, but the profit to Jan would still be huge.

"Give me two days to think it over." He stood. Black Otter

rose more slowly, pulling the glorious robe to conceal his bad arm.

"I'd planned to be in the village all winter," Jan said musingly. "I'd planned to spend it with my wife and my children— an old man deserves a winter of coddling in the village. But if I did this thing, I would have to leave very soon. Very soon. I would want to be sure that my wife did not lack for anything while I was gone."

"Your wife is . . ."

"Fish-catcher. Turtle Egg's daughter."

"I would see to it." They were talking about status, not subsistence.

Jan reached for the gun that leaned against the oak tree, then drew back. Almost sheepishly, he said, "I have a son. By Fish-catcher."

"How old?"

"Ten." *Too young to go to war with you. Too young to use one of the guns I would bring.* "He wants to be a messenger— a runner on the Great Trail."

Black Otter was a seasoned politician. He asked to be reminded of the matter in a year.

Jan stood with the tall war leader for some seconds before they separated. They seemed to be looking down over the village, beyond its palisade to its brown cornfields, but each was looking at a private vision of the future.

"It will be very, very difficult," Jan said.

Black Otter touched his shoulder with his good hand. "I must have guns," he said in almost a whisper. "The People must have guns, or they will perish."

Jan knew already that he would do it. *Why?* he challenged himself. *For the money? For Black Otter's war?* He trudged slowly homeward. The sun was dipping toward the west. *Because of the sign the White Beast gave me. Because I am the Gun-finder.*

When he told her, his wife wailed as if he were dead. His older son wailed and hid in another house; the baby wept. Nonetheless, he told them he was going and he made his preparations. He went away, after only ten days in the village that he loved, the village where he had planned to spend the winter like other men. It would have been the first winter he had spent with them in five years, but he was a wanderer, restless, unpredictable. He told himself that he would spend his winters in the longhouse when he was old.

"Will you come back?" his Seneca wife said to him. Anger made her voice bubble like hot food.

"In the spring."

"For good? Eh—*for good?*"

"Yes."

"Oh, you lie! Go, then—go! And don't expect me to be here when you come back. Or expect some other man to be with me. Go on, then—go—go!" She chased him from the longhouse and threw his bundle after him, but before he had gone a hundred yards he heard the quick pounding of her feet behind him, and there she was, with their baby on her hip and the girl in her left hand, and they clung together and squeezed each other as if they would force themselves to grow together, an animal called Family. "Come back in the spring," she whispered fiercely.

"Tell the Weasel I will come back," he said. His son had not come to tell him farewell.

He took the Great Trail east toward the Maaqua country and the Dutch farms along the Hudson. Above Fort Orange, he stopped to tell Koopman that there would be furs coming for him, and he watched as Koopman marked them on his account; then he caught a little *vlieboot* downriver to Nieuw Amsterdam, which he had not visited in two years. He spent only hours there before he found a ship heading for Holland, because it was autumn and the ships were all heading home rather than face the winter on the Atlantic; he signed on as a common sailor and was gone with the morning tide, shedding America from his shoulders like an old coat.

"How often you make this trip, then?" one of the crew asked him in the stinking crew's quarters up against the stem.

"This is my ninth time back. Eighteen altogether."

"Jesus! And never drownded."

"Not yet. Sick, but never drowned."

Captains were glad to have him, for he was a seasoned deck hand. Back in his twenties, he had sailed for a whole year, down to the slave coast of Africa and back, but he had longed for forest. He had wanted to go inland in Africa, but that coast was already too European, and he knew he would be better off in America, where he had already stayed four years. Ever since, he had shuttled back and forth, Amsterdam to Nieuw Amsterdam, always drawn back to the green paradise beyond the tended Dutch fields.

"What are you, then?" one of the crew said suspiciously. "Some species of trader?"

"Missionary." He grinned. "The Holy Order of St. Musket."

They barely missed the first winter storm. It was bad enough, as the weeks passed, to face the roughness of summer's end. After a week, the bilges stank; the tiny ship stood on its beam ends; the men were bad-tempered. Boredom and fear chased each other in an endless circle. The gray ocean seemed boundless, infinity itself, and their little wooden nutshell was barely a dot on it, a mere chip, a fleck of foam. It seemed impossible that such a speck should dare to make its own way across such heaving space.

Yet they found their landfall, and he left the ship at Scheveningen, his legs rubbery and awkward on the land, which seemed to rise up to slap each step. Still, a night in a tavern put him right again. He had the gift of forgetfulness. The unnecessary seemed never to lodge in his brain; the essential found itself a nest there and bedded down forever. So now with this voyage and its fear of death: forgotten.

He walked inland to 's Gravenhage, bought a proper set of clothes such as would befit a burgher of modest substance and presented himself at the Bank of the West India Company. The clerks there were mostly new and did not know him. *Just as well.* He presented himself to a very fair young man with eyelashes like white insect legs.

"My name is den Moors. I am known here. Meinheer Kordrep knows me."

"On the business of—?"

"I am just back from a venture in Russia. Please tell Meinheer Kordrep that Jan den Moors is here."

Kordrep was fatter than ever. *And older. We're all older.* He saw his own reflection in a rippled windowpane and had to restrain the impulse to flinch away from it, for in his burgherish clothes he looked like anybody. *No magic. Just anybody.* When Kordrep came close to him to shake his hand, he could not keep from taking a step back. *Too long in the woods. Too long in paradise.* He scolded himself that he must act like a Dutchman here, not a Seneca.

"Heer den Moors, yes, yes! Come in, sir, sit—sit! A pipe? Yes? Of course, try this tobacco—from Turkey, with a touch of *chocolat,* yes? Now, let me see—it's been more than a year, I know—"

"Three years, meinheer."

"So long as that! Three years. Yes, let me see." He consulted a list without removing it from a drawer of his desk. While still reading, he murmured, "There's wine by the window—help yourself. Ah, yes—den Moors. From Leiden."

"Just so."

"Leiden, Leiden, Leiden." Kordrep seemed to have misplaced Leiden in his desk drawer. "Aha!" He leaned his head back against his high, stiff chair like a man whose eyesight is bad and who is trying to get as far as possible from his work; he read and then said with satisfaction, "There have been a number of payments into your account from our Nieuw Amsterdam house."

"Confidential ones, I hope."

"Oh, yes—yes! Oh, absolutely confidential!"

"I have been in Russia, you see."

"Ah. I see.. Hmm, Russia. Well, Meinheer den Moors, do you intend to withdraw from your account?"

"No." Kordrep seemed relieved. "In fact, I will be making more payments within the year. For now, I must ask to look into the casket I left with you some years ago. Here is my key."

"Ah, yes, yes! Casket, casket—" Kordrep rang a hand bell, and the young man with the remarkable eyelashes appeared, wiping inky fingers on a bit of rag. After several minutes, Jan's strongbox emerged, slightly dusty and with rime on the brass studs of the base. Alone in a small chamber, he took out as much gold as he thought he would need, locked the box again and called to Kordrep. Within minutes, he was in the street.

Now Snow Elk no longer, and no longer Jan Morse, he wandered the streets of Groszgut as Jan den Moors, traveler from beyond the Baltic, searching for gifts for his return home. In a shop that reeked of spice, he found what he wanted.

"This red leather is from Russia, is it not?"

"Beautiful, ain't they, meinheer? Yes, from Kiev, in fact. Really nice items, suitable for—"

"And the shawl?"

"Persia. Or Samarkand, I ain't quite sure. I have more if the color ain't—"

"They'll do." He chose two necklaces from the Baltic in worked silver and then two tiny lace squares that could be worn by ladies instead of caps.

"Oh, yes, very good, sir—lovely articles, beautiful—such taste, sir!"

Next day, a newly acquired horse took him over a bridge

he knew well into a part of Leiden that he also knew; at his urging the horse clopped up the cobbles of a familiar street.

There was a woman at the door of a house he knew, but not a woman he knew. He stopped the horse, still feeling uneasy perched so high on its rolling bulk. He liked the earth under his feet.

"Is this the house of Jan den Moors?" he said.

"Yes, but master ain't to home. Be off to wandering someplace."

"Master has come home, woman." He tried to get off the beast gracefully, but he started to slide and had to grip the saddle to keep from crashing to the pavement. When he had righted himself and was hoping he did not look utterly ridiculous, he said curtly, "Go tell your mistress her husband's home from Russia. Go along, now!"

It took some seconds for her to take the message into the house. He heard a female screech of astonishment and delight, then other squeals of younger women as they heard the message.

He faced the door with a grin. What man would not grin, leaving one loving wife in America, finding another here in Holland with such joy?

He woke in the night, expecting the uneasy roll of the little ship, and found instead the secure warmth of his Dutch wife's bed. It was high and broad and curtained, and under the feather-filled covers it was as warm as a dream of the tropics, though the air bit like a dog when he put his nose outside.

"Are you awake?" he murmured into the warm mound of her back. Grete was taller than he and she outweighed him by fifty pounds now—a good, big piece of human warmth to share a bed with. Smiling at her in the dark because she had insisted on wearing a nightgown even after they had made love, he squeezed the roll of flesh above her hip and said again, softly, "Are you awake, Grete?"

"I am now." She turned to him, and the bed threatened to bounce him right through the curtains. "I ought to be so angry—but I ain't. It's that good to have you back!" She tried to kiss his mouth and found his nose, instead. He reached toward the cold bottom of the sheets and found the hem of her nightgown.

"Jan—not again!"

"Nah, it's only a loving gesture, Grete—by way of play.

24

Although you move me mightily, you do—make me forget my age."

"The devil I do! All them women you had in Russia, I bet!" She clasped her huge thighs over his hand. "I ought to hate you for leaving me so long alone, but I don't. I ought to have taken some other man, God knows I had the offers if remarks about this and that mean anything, but I didn't, I'm a good woman. But I'm so grateful you've come back! Whatever was you doing in Russia?"

"Trading. How's your cousin Derek?"

"Greedy as ever, and drinks too much. What were you trading in Russia?"

"Guns. I got to see Derek right away. Your cousin Piet, too. And I must go up to Amsterdam to see my cousin Willem if he's still among the living. But everything in good time. Russia? I was buying and selling, you know the trade. Guns. Trying to introduce them to good Dutch guns and not those God-awful *tshinkes* they affect. That's what I want to see Derek about. Some guns to sell in Russia."

"You ain't going back to Russia right off, Jan!"

"Nah. Not right off. We'll see."

"Oh, Jan—!" She pulled his lean body against her comfortable, warm mass. "The girls and me miss you so—can't you stay home and make guns yourself, now? Gallivanting off to Russia and God knows where is for younger men."

"It's my business, Grete."

"You're a good gunmaker, as good as any in Leiden, my cousin Derek hisself says so, and there's none better than him when he's sober. He'd throw you more business in a minute, you know he would."

"Ah, Grete, Grete! What glorious breasts you have! I dreamed of them on cold nights in Russia. When the wolves howled and the white bears roared out on the ice, I dreamed of my Grete and her breasts like warm, soft dumplings."

"Liar! Oh, you terrible liar!"

She rolled on her back. His business was forgotten, at least for the time, and when he woke in the morning he was alone in the bed and the air in the room was as cold as if he were in Russia, after all. He made no fuss about the cold, however; he pushed back the comforters and slipped between the bed curtains, naked as he was born and smelling of sex, to stand on a tiny island of carpet in an ocean of icy tile. He bellowed for hot water and his clothes. Women seemed to rush at him from every direction—one of his daughters, his wife, the round-faced maid who had been in the street. Within minutes, he had hot water for shaving and washing, and Grete pulled clothes from a huge wooden wardrobe in the small, dark room where his belongings were kept from year to year while he was away.

"I got to cut your hair," Grete said firmly. "You look like some savage Indian from America."

"And what does a savage Indian look like, pray?"

"Like the Devil in a church play, for they had two of them here going about just like human beings, all got up in their hellish colors and their feathers and all, and one had hair just like yours, I swear!"

"The style is Russian," he said feebly. Grete sat with him in the cold room while he shaved; now and then she shrieked a command down the steep stairs, then turned back to chatter at Jan about the state of the world since he had left the last time: there was another polder dike going up near Amsterdam, they said; the King of England had lost his crown, they said, and would lose his head as well, which was all right because he was a Papist and his murderers-to-be were Protestants; the war was over in Germany and the trade in matchlock guns was down, Derek said, but gents' pistols were selling well; one of their daughters was spoken for and would marry in the spring if he gave his consent; the cow had died calving twins, and one of the calves had died and the other was a bull and what was she to do for milk?

"Marry the bull to the fellow that wants a wife, and keep Maria at home to give butter," he said, giving her a kiss.

"What a thing to say of your own sweet daughter!"

"She's got the parts for it," he said. "And a certain cowish look about her face that would just set off a bell around her neck."

"Jan! It ain't funny, now! Talking that way of the titties on your own flesh and blood!"

"I'd lie if I said I hadn't noticed them, Grete; they come into view a full minute before you see the darling's face. Her husband will be the happiest man in Leiden, I'm sure. The *second* happiest man," he corrected himself, kissing her again. He skipped down the stairs and ate one of the huge breakfasts that Dutch women seemed to believe were as essential to life as breath: three kinds of bread, and boiled eggs, and four cheeses, and ham, and little sweet rolls that made him think of the flesh above her hips, and dark coffee from Java such as he had not seen for three years. He had missed

26

such food, no doubt about it. He would gain fifteen pounds, living there. *Know when to leave that way. Two notches on the belt, it's time to go.* He regaled them with stories of Russia, which in fact he had never seen; he made each of them show off the gifts he had brought. He felt warm and happy and loved. *Just like the longhouse.* Mother and daughters bound into a female unity; he, the outsider, the guest, the transient god.

He felt a twinge of envy. They were the stable and sane ones; he had nobody to giggle with and no place that he had made his own for all time. *My own choice.* He laughed at something his daughter Maria had said, her enormous bosom bouncing. *Not even a friend.* The thought was a surprise. No friends, even among the Senecas—no enemies, either; only acquaintances, other men as transient as he. *And women are the sane ones, the constant ones; we come and go. That's why sex is so good. Brings us close to them for a bit. Then it's over, and they have each other, and we have—what?* But he knew he had what no woman of his class or his acquaintance could ever have. *Freedom.*

"I'm off to see your cousin Derek. If I can walk, after all that food." He kissed Grete and winked at his older daughter. "Bring your young man around this afternoon—you'd best be quick and marry him while I'm thin enough to give you away. Wait too long, and I'll be so fat you'll have to roll me to the church."

He spent two idyllic weeks with them, weeks like the days in the longhouse with Fish-catcher. He knew that it was some flaw in himself that made him so loved a guest, so incapable a husband. He would have been no good over the long haul, he knew. Adored for a two-week visit, he might have been despised over several years. *Because I can't truly give to them. Only a guest.* At the end of the two weeks, he went up to Amsterdam on the excuse of seeing his cousin Willem about guns, and from Amsterdam he caught a ship to Leith, just above Edinburgh, in Scotland. He sent his horse and a message back to Leiden with a merchant going that way. He would be gone for two weeks, he told them, having heard of an opportunity to conclude a sale in Hamburg.

In Leith, he bought three pearls from a sailor on the docks and waited for a ship heading coastwise for Aberdeen. The day was sunless, dark and rainy, but the wind kept low and a small cog was able to wallow northward through the waves, always in sight of the coast that the drizzle transformed to the shape of low, crouching beast.

In Aberdeen he bought a knife and two little boats carved out of nutshells; he found a horse and rode up to Kildrummie, where he shrouded himself in his cloak and sloshed through the sopped little town along streets that were familiar to him, until he reached the one he knew best, turned down its little slope and came to a bleak, narrow house that seemed, from the street, as devoid of life as the cobbles under his feet. A loud knock brought a light, however, and the light revealed the face of a frightened Scottish farm girl through the crack of the barely open door.

"Don't look so terrified, girl, I ain't a robber. Is this still John Morse's house?"

"Yessir, 'tis, but—"

"Tell your mistress her husband has come home again."

Not waiting to find if the news would be greeted with shrieks in the house, he pushed in after the girl, and he was removing his soaked and heavy cloak when Elizabeth came flying along the passageway toward him. She was in tears but smiling; she said not a word, nor did she make any sound at all, but she clutched him, wet clothes and all, as if she feared he would fly away. Over her shoulder, he saw the silhouette of his twelve-year-old Scottish son in the lighted doorway beyond. Cautiously, the boy came forward, wary, perhaps, of this well-known stranger.

He woke in the night to listen to the wind whistling in from the North Sea like the demon of his wanderlust, as if it meant to blow him right out of the bed and start him on his way again. *Soon enough, demon,* he thought, not unhappily. *Soon enough.*

"Awake are you, Betty?"

"Aye, sweetheart." She sounded contented and warm and drowsy, and he clung to her. For a few nights, she would be more important to him than his demon. He slipped his hand between her legs, and she shivered. "Your hands is like ice."

"Warm heart."

"Warm everything." She was a shy, quiet woman, but she had a frankness toward sex that was as open and fresh as that of the Senecas. She put a hand in his groin. "God, I've missed this fellow so!"

"Not found another, have you?"

"You know better, Johnnie. Where were you this time?"

"India, I told you. Goa and east."

28

"Ach, the moon, ya mean! Might as well be the moon. Poor little Archie don't even believe he's got a father, he sees so little of you."

"Better a father like me than many he might have."

"I know, I know. But a boy needs a father. Anyways—ach, I'm nattering, and you only home a night! I'll shut up. Oh, what a nice fellow this is, John—ain't he grand and huge, though! And you such a runty man, no offense—oh, yes, come into me, Johnnie—"

In the morning, he lazed about the austere little house and tried to be with the boy, but their mutual silences were too long, and they became uncomfortable for him. He knew something about lonely boys—too much, as he knew too much about bad fathers—and he understood well the hopelessness of trying to pierce the wall that such a boy builds. *Maybe, two years ago, when he was ten, I could have done it. Not now.*

"What have you got it in your head to be when you're grown, Archie?" he asked into one of the silences.

"Don't know."

"What is it you like to do, then, Archie?"

"Don't know."

"Why, tell your father, Archie!" his mother cried. Flushed with the pleasure of having the two of them together, pleased with herself and with them, Elizabeth Morse tried to wring joy from her child. "He's mad for music, John!"

"Ach, Ma—!"

"Are you, Archie?"

The boy shrugged. "I like it all right, is all. Listening and singing, and the like." He sneered. "I ain't a *musician* at all."

"What sort of music do you like, boy?"

"Why, church music is all I hear much of." A curious glitter came into his eyes. "Unless them students come down to play their rounds and all."

Jan looked at his wife for explanation. "From St. Andrew's, he means, John. They got some kind of musical instruments, I don't follow it all."

"A consort of viols!" the boy burst out. "One of them has been all the way to Italy and he instructs the others how to play. It's—" He looked at his father. He saw something there that Jan could not keep out of his face—incomprehension, perhaps—and the excitement died from his eyes. "It's just music," the boy said languidly.

"Maybe your da could tell you about the music of India, Archie!"

"Or other places. I heard some pretty strange things, where I been."

"Yes, sir." The boy turned a polite, closed face to him. Jan did not bother to bore him with invented tales of the music of India.

Still, the boy was not unreachable. Jan guessed that he was not so unreachable as he had been himself at that age. Archie was more outgoing: he played with other children at times; he sang in the kirk; he took what seemed to be a genuine interest in the making of guns. Jan—as John Morse—owned half of a small gunshop in the town; the other half was in the hands of the widow of a distant cousin on his mother's side. In effect, the shop was run by the journeyman gunmaker whom the widow had hired, and the guns that came from his hands were mediocre affairs, for all that they bore the old family mark of the skull and the Latin word *Mors*. Jan spent a week trying to improve the man's habits and succeeded only in irritating him. They both knew that he would still be there when Jan moved on again; he could wait out his departure in sullen silence.

Jan went to his distant cousin's widow.

"What's to happen to the little gunworks?" he asked her. She looked angry, as if she had decided they were to have a fight.

"I manage it the best I can," she said stubbornly.

"I didn't say otherwise, Maeve. It's managed very well, in my view. But I'm wondering what's to happen to it. I've got a boy old enough to apprentice soon. You've got boys of your own."

"My Andrew means to go into the trade," she said as if he had already told her that her Andrew was too stupid to be a gunsmith. "I'm putting him apprentice to Mr. Weems at Aberdeen in the spring."

"Well, you're wise not to put him apprentice to that sullen sloth we got in the shop, for he'd learn little but laziness. Halfway measures, that's what he'd learn from our man there!"

"It ain't my fault!" she shrieked. Her voice made his ears hurt. He wondered if she was angry with him for outliving her husband.

"Of course it ain't your fault, Maeve. I only mean that if we intend our own sons to go into the trade, the sooner they can replace that lazy lout, the better." He leaned toward her; she leaned away, as if their bodies were connected by stiff rods so that his forward movement became her move backward. "What would you think of my Archie and your Andrew going off to apprentice together? Give them a chance to find if they can get along well enough to share a business."

"My Andrew can get along with anybody!" she snapped. "He ain't dour like some."

"Aye, Archie's dour. It runs in the family. What do you think, Maeve—could they go off to Aberdeen together?"

"I don't know, I'm sure. Mr. Weems has already accepted my Andrew; whether he'll take another or not, I don't know!"

Jan sighed. "No reason for you to, Maeve. I'll go see the man myself when I go through Aberdeen."

He had been working on a pair of pistols in the shop. Unfinished and forgotten by him, they had lain in a locked drawer since his last visit, three years before. Now he took them out and finished them, while the lazy journeyman pretended not to watch and Archie stood by his shoulder, looking on with genuine interest.

They were pistols of the sort that would become closely associated with Scotland: clean of line and simple of furniture, without trigger guards, equipped with belt hooks for carrying. The straight post triggers needed no protection against accidental firing because the snaphaunce locks had their batteries on long, steel arms that could be swung entirely forward and out of the way of the cocks, so that even if a cock fell through an accidental trigger pull, nothing would happen. The butts and forearms were of red Brazil wood, finished in brass at their caps and their fishtail butts. The barrels, slightly cannon-shaped at their flared muzzles, were an intricate, lovely combination of nine-sided and round cross sections; he had forged them himself during a cool Scottish summer.

"Arms fit for a gentleman, Archie," he said when he had polished the lockplates to his satisfaction.

"Aye, they're fair handsome, sir."

"I'd engrave them more, but I need them. These little guns got to go to work."

"Sir?"

"They're for traveling, Archie. For protection on the road." He held one as if to fire it and let the boy heft one to learn what proper balance was. "Come outside now while I shoot them. They been already proofed; now we shoot them for the sighting." The boy seemed genuinely eager to learn Jan's craft. *Maybe he has the gift,* Jan thought. *Maybe the Senecas would think he was a magician.*

"What would you think of being a gunsmith, Archie?"

"I think I'd like to, sir."

"Better than music, would you?"

The boy hesitated. "I guess music and gunsmithing ain't enemies to each other, sir."

Jan touched his shoulder. "A man can't have two passions, Archie. Nor can he have two crafts. Not the way we make our guns—we ain't like that layabout of a journeyman, who only makes guns because it's something he learned instead of digging privies to earn his keep—for there's genius in our family, you see? Making guns is—" He wanted to tell the boy about how long the Morses had been making guns; he wanted to tell him about the White Beast that had appeared to him when he was a boy in the Maaqua country. *Too soon,* he thought. *When he's older.* "You must look ahead with this much in mind, Archie: you can have a craft and a pastime, but not two crafts. Not a craft that's to be your life, I mean."

A week later, he started for Aberdeen on foot, the two pistols clipped to a belt under his waistcoat. "I'm off to see my third cousin Alan," he said to Elizabeth.

"Ach, Johnnie, when'll you ever be back?"

"Two weeks. Maybe three, Betty. Or it could be more, if I can't find what I need."

"And what's that, then? What is it that you need, that you're always starting out for? Last time you went away, you said you was going for maybe a month and it was *three years!* What is it that's always taking you away from us?"

He looked into the drizzle outside his front door. He thought of the Senecas, the villages in winter, the White Beast pointing him toward the western wilderness. "Guns," he said. He kissed her. "It's always guns."

Chapter Three

He knew the history of the Morse family as no other living member of it did, and as no member had for a century. Most of them—Morses, Moorses, Morrisons and others—were ignorant of their many interrelationships and of the tradition that bound them. He had made the family his study whenever he was in Europe; he had tracked it down as he had traveled. Its puzzles and gaps had filled his idle hours in America. Once, he had scrawled a huge family tree in the forest dirt in an oak opening below Lake Erie, trying with dotted lines and curved loops to make a picture that would explain to him the vast complexity of the people who had made guns and had called themselves by all those names that had begun with Mouers.

Most of them were people who had used the skull as their marque on their guns and gun barrels and gunlocks. Some of them had used a form of their name, too—usually the Latin *Mors,* the same as he used. Some of them, he knew, had no idea what the marque meant or where it had come from, except that they had inherited it from a father or an uncle.

He knew of his cousins Willem and Anders in Holland, who called themselves Moors and who used the skull but not *Mors.*

He knew of a distant relative in England who called himself Morrison (from an Englishman who had called himself Morris and who was descended from the Dutch Moors) and who made swords and tools and, sometimes when there was enough money in it, guns; and his only mark was a circle with three dots in it—the skull reduced to meaninglessness.

He knew of a Duffus in Dundee who was related by marriage and who still used the *Mors* marque, even though he made swords and not guns; and he knew his third cousin Alan in Aberdeen, who made fair-to-middling matchlock long guns and who marked them simply "A. Morse, Scotland"; and he knew his much-removed cousins (third? fourth?) Charlie and Fergus in Dumfries who were the sons of a den Mouers from 's Gravenhage in Holland.

He knew that there ought to be relatives in Italy, but he

33

could not trace them down beyond that Francisco Lazarino Mors whose name was engraved on his old wheel-lock, except that he knew that there were barrels of a superior quality coming out of Italy now with *Lazarino* stamped on them, and he meant to go to Italy one day and find out if those were his relatives who were making them.

He was the historian of the great Mors family, although he did not think of himself so, the only one who could look back toward their obscure origins in eastern Germany. And he might have been the one to bring all these branches of the family together by telling them about each other, but it served him better to keep them apart: he was a man who needed guns for purposes that governments often disapproved, and so it served him to go to this distant cousin or that seeming stranger and surprise him with a relationship he never knew existed, and to plead "family" as a reason for buying guns under the table.

He traveled far. Guns were his passion and his trade, and his family was his secret source.

"Is that Mr. Morrison's house yonder, could you tell me, miss?"

"Why, yes—right opposite. The new one."

"Thank you, miss."

Up here in the iron country of England they had had more war in the last five years than even Black Otter would have liked. King Charles had launched his share of it from Nottingham, and the countryside was still the prey of armies that scurried like groups of ants to find and kill each other. Still, it was Jan's belief that a man who minded his own business (and carried two loaded pistols) could go anywhere, and here he was in Birmingham. He wanted to finish his business quickly and move on, however, for England was a nervous sort of place; men looked at strangers with distrust, and when their eyes met his, they looked away.

War, he thought. *They've had enough of war.* He had been in Germany when the Protestants and the Catholics had been murdering each other. The people had all seemed stunned, and, although they had started their war because of their beliefs, they seemed tired of all that passion and they wanted only to survive.

"Well, sir?"

"I'm here to see Mr. Morrison. I wrote a letter. John Morse, from Kildrummie in Scotland."

The middle-aged maid looked him up and down suspi-

34

ciously. Over her shoulder, he could see a manservant hovering in a doorway. *Bet he's got a pistol, or at least a club. They've had enough war, too.*

"Wait, if you please."

She let him into a little unheated entryway. *Out of the snow, at least.* The manservant stayed in the corridor, ostentatiously polishing brass while he tried not to look too openly at the stranger. Jan pulled his cloak so that the bulges of the pistols would not show.

"This way, if you please, Mr. Morse."

Tom Morrison was so distantly related that Jan could not keep the correct term for their blood tie in his head. He would have to write it down somewhere. *Third cousin something.* On the family tree that he had scratched in the American dirt, Tom Morrison had been a wriggle far off to the side, the termination of a dendrite. Not that it mattered at the moment, for there was no reason to go into great detail with the man himself.

Morrison was a small, rather nervous man whose most noticeable feature was the peculiar slant of his eyes and eyebrows, which peaked in the middle of his face and sloped downward toward the rather high cheekbones. *Slav,* Jan thought. There had been no Slavs in the family for generations, of course, but still...*Not at all the family face—if mine is the family face.* He had seen his own features in a number of Moors and den Moors faces in Holland, as well as on the Scots and on several women with entirely different names who turned out to be relatives with names lost through marriage.

"Good day to you, Mr. Morrison."

"And to you, sir. Difficult times, difficult times—you had no, er, trouble coming down from—was it Dumfries?"

"Kildrummie, sir. If a man is careful, it ain't so bad. The armies are elsewhere."

"The Lord be praised! I hope your religious persuasion, Mr., er, Morse is—"

"Why, the same as your own, Mr. Morrison."

"Hmm? Oh, er, good. Splendid. Well. Your letter said that we are kin, sir. It's gratifying to meet a kinsman, even in such, er, tormented times."

Jan's letter lay under Morrison's hand on the worktable. The room was almost bare except for the table and two chairs and a little chest that sat under a window whose streaked panes gave an unfortunate view of a neglected garden. Mor-

35

rison, recollecting the letter, picked it up and put it down again, cleared his throat and muttered, "Kinsman," again, as if to remind himself of the fact.

"Kinsman, yes, Mr. Morrison." Jan was not fool enough to think the man believed him. In such times, who would believe the letter of a stranger? "Not remarkably close kinsmen, but related. I consider myself, after a fashion, the keeper of the records of our large and very dispersed family, sir. I have discovered branches in England, in Scotland, the Netherlands—in England, sir, the old Keeper of the Royal Munitions under Henry the Eighth was an ancestor of yours, and the son of an ancestor of mine."

The down-turned eyebrows rose in the middle, making them a single, straight line. "Morrice. Henry Morrice?"

"Just so—Firearms Maker to the Gentlemen of the Wardrobe was the official title, I believe."

"I see—Morrice, Morris—Morse. Hmmp! From the Dutch, eh?"

"Moors. Or den Moors, sometimes. But quite the most remarkable thing, Mr. Morrison, is that so many of us have been and are gunmakers, sir. Remarkable. How many of us make guns."

Morrison cleared his throat. He seemed to express guilt in the sound. "I am not, er—I have not made of late any guns."

"But your father did."

"Only for the Africa trade. And the like." Morrison stared out the dirty window. "Knives now. The odd sword. Brush hooks, and so on."

"Yes, sir. More like the Sheffield trade, even though you're a Birmingham man. But surely you made guns, Mr. Morrison?"

"Only while my father was master."

"Yes." *He's frightened,* Jan thought. *Conceives me a spy. Crown spy or Puritan spy, wouldn't matter; either way, he'd suffer.* Jan leaned forward with his hands on his knees, the legs close together like those of a well-bred schoolboy. "I'm here because of family, not because I'm an informer, Mr. Morrison. I've got an opportunity to offer somebody a bit of money for some guns, and I like to keep matters in the family. I'm taking advantage of this opportunity myself and hope to profit handsomely; some of my Dutch cousins are doing the same."

36

Morrison was shaking his head as if he were palsied. "Difficult times for guns," he muttered.

"But times when a man must turn a profit where he can, surely. Not so many opportunities for profit now, are there?"

"Dangerous times," Morrison whispered.

"You mean you don't trust me."

"I don't *know* you, Mr. Morse."

"Of course you don't! And you're right to be suspicious; a man can't be too careful in such times—it's proof of your sagacity, sir! Why, here I am, I could be lying to you; my letter there could be a pile of lies. Why, perhaps there ain't even a John Morse of Kildrummie on the face of this earth! But let me make my proposition, and then I'll show you my *bona fides*—notarized papers, and even one from the Lord Lieutenant for Scotland himself—and then you may judge for yourself of what opportunity for profit I offer to you." Jan smiled. Warily, Morrison smiled back.

"I need guns, kinsman." Jan hooked an arm over the stiff back of the chair. "At least a hundred guns. I've got a source for another hundred in Holland, and some more in Scotland, but what I want now is good English firelocks. Eighty or a hundred good English firelocks, and I can mount them on stout German barrels and have them stocked in a place I know. And keep it all in the family."

Morrison cleared his throat. The outer margins of his eyes sagged as if he might weep. "The gentlemen of the government are very strict."

"Not so strict about locks as they are about whole guns."

"But—the purpose, sir? I need to know the purpose—in these times—"

"Slave trade, sir! Take 'em down to the Gold Coast and turn 'em into fine, black gold! Oh, you're thinking they're to be used on this island, Mr. Morrison! Banish such a thought, sir; I'll give you my affidavit. You can seal the boxes right here in Birmingham and send them by what means you will to an address in Leiden—one of our relatives sir, one Jan den Moors—and this island will never see more of them!"

"Even the shadow of impropriety—dangerous times—current unrest—"

"Indeed, indeed. But there *is* the matter of profit. How is the brush hook and hoe business just now?"

"Very—very slow." Morrison glanced out the window again, hummed a scrap of a low ditty, muttered in a furry voice. "I can make good, plain firelocks, right enough." He

37

drummed his fingers on Jan's letter, and even his fingertips sounded blurred and soft, their sound like the muffled patter of distant hooves. "Pistol or musket?"

"Musket."

Morrison touched the soft fingers to his lips. "I've got the iron. Got a lot from Germany was meant for knives, but trade's all smashed this year, no point in putting a hammer to it. How many locks did you say?"

"A hundred."

"I don't believe I could ever make a hundred. How soon?"

"March at the latest."

"Oh, I could never make a hundred by then. Oh, damn me, no!"

Jan wanted to tell him precisely how he could make them, but he waited for Morrison to puzzle it out by himself. *Hasn't got either the face or the brain of the family. A sheep.*

"One of my girls is married to a fair locksmith," Morrison murmured. The fact. seemed to surprise him. "And his brother's a filer. I could put the parts out to farm, of course. Do you do that in—was it Dumfries, Mr. Morse?"

"Kildrummie. Yes—pass the parts out to cottagers, pick them up and assemble 'em. Oh, yes."

"You are a gunsmith, then."

"Pistols, sir. Pistols." Jan drew one of the Scots pistols from his belt and Morrison flinched back, his big eyes wide with apprehension. "I'm not a highwayman, Mr. Morrison—only showing you some of my work. This here is a good Scots belt pistol—about as good as ever you'll see, I think. Dutch lock on it, from my cousin Jan den Moors; my own barrel and furniture." He held the weapon out, the fishtail butt first. The red Brazil wood caught the dim light, warmed it.

"Lovely," Morrison whispered. "You've got the skill."

"My cousin Willem in Amsterdam makes pistols with ivory stocks. Carved heads at the end of the butt, set in silver—puts them out to a sculptor for that part. A rich man's weapon, of course."

Morrison sucked in his breath. "Oh, yes. Artists, that's what you are."

"A family trait."

"Well, as for that—we've never made but very plain guns here. Not the likes of that pistol, or the Amsterdam ones you spoke of. Not at all."

"Plain locks are what I'm seeking. A hundred by March."

"Well. Er." Morrison handed the pistol back. "Let me offer

you a bed for the night. The inns of this city are drear places at best, and, er, in the morning—if I've slept on your, hum, offer, perhaps—we could come to some—decision—?"

"Your hospitality is most welcome, kinsman."

It was like putting the spring into a lock and making it fit just right. Morrison would supply the locks, he knew; now he had all the pieces for Black Otter's guns, all from members of this far-flung family he had uncovered. There was an elegance to it, as if it were a problem in the mathematick that a geometrist had solved.

When he was leaving next day, with their oral contract sealed with a handshake and a payment in gold, he said to Morrison, "Have you ever seen the White Beast?"

"What? What?"

"It's of no importance. An old family tale, is all."

Ten days later, he was back in Kildrummie with his Scottish wife and his Scottish son. He arrived with a beautiful little viol under his arm, wrapped up in a woolen rug, and he presented it to the delighted boy as he walked in the door. Elizabeth hugged him and made love to him again—but two weeks after that, he was on his way to Holland, braving the rigors of the winter sea because he believed himself to be a man with luck and a mission. And, smiled on by Fortune that time, he arrived safe and dry in 's Gravenhage, as if it were a summer day and he had just been out for a walk; and, after a visit to the West India Company Bank for more of his dwindling supply of gold, he went home to the coddlings and scoldings of his Dutch wife and his two Dutch daughters.

"Don't ever do it again!" they wailed. "Don't ever leave us again!"

"Never, never, never again, loves," he promised them. "Only a trip or two more into Germany, and I'll be at home forever."

He was paying for gun parts and guns and labor out of the gold in his casket, and then he had to dip into his account at the West India Company to pay some bribes to certain representatives of their high mightinesses in Amsterdam, but it was his belief now—his passion, in fact—that Black Otter's guns were a hazard on which he must risk all. It was his task to provide the guns for Black Otter's war—to make history, in a way, although the idea was one he only vaguely grasped. And, if he grew rich in the process, so much the better: his Scottish son could play the viol; his daughters could marry men of substance. *Because it is what I must do.*

Their high mightinesses in Amsterdam would have been appalled to learn that three hundred muskets were being assembled to ship to the westernmost of the always dangerous Iroquois; and the directors of the West India Company would have been enraged to learn that their profits were to be cut by so huge a trade. It was best to keep the whole business a secret, to bring all the pieces of his elegant theorem together quietly and enjoy the mathematick in isolation.

"I've never seen you so happy, Jan," his Dutch wife said. "Is it being home?"

"You know it is."

"But you're ever so quiet sometimes. What do you think of?"

"Guns."

He thought of the Seneca villages in the snow; the wind would be blowing columns of snowdrift over the icy lakes like ghosts now, and in the longhouses the People would be huddled close around the fires, telling stories.

"You won't go away again, will you, Jan?"

"Only one little trip, my love. One last, little trip."

"Not to Russia! Promise me you won't go to Russia!"

"I promise I won't go to Russia."

Inside the longhouse, the smell of woodsmoke and of tightly packed bodies would be rank, touched with the smells of urine and dogs and cooking, yet it would be a smell sweeter to him than the clean and airy brightness of his Dutch wife's kitchen. Holland was everything safe and solid and *white;* the villages were all those things that were secret, dark and dangerous.

He found a ship captain who would carry him and an unspecified cargo to America and to a place he would select down the coast from Nieuw Amsterdam. His craft was tiny, so blunt-ended it looked like a bucket with a couple of masts stuck in it. "She looks older than you and me put together, captain," Jan said.

"What of it? She's sound. Not as pointy-ended as some, so she wallows a little and gives you the pukes, but it's only four weeks or so on the way. I took her up to Iceland on the Norway trade three years ago; she never missed a sailing day, and her so loaded with ice she was nine inches low in the water. There ain't a better little craft on the Zuider Zee."

"Nor none worse in an open sea, I suppose. Well, if you can keep your mouth shut about my business, captain, you've got a commission. I must be off the coast of America by the first of May."

"*Ja, ja.*"

"And I shall have need of a pinnace when I get there."

"Have to tow one over, then."

"So long as it gets there."

"My ship is a swan, my friend—a duck! She will get there!"

"I'll light candles in church."

He exhausted his account to pay for the ship, and he borrowed to pay for the final assembling of the guns, which was being done in a house in 's Gravenhage where the sons of two of his most distant female cousins were working. He kept close watch on them; the Senecas were demanding customers and would stand no shoddy work. Bargaining with the French and the Dutch had made Black Otter as sharp as an army purchasing officer.

One day in March, he found an old English book in a shop and he bought it for his Scottish son. It was an odd sort of impulse; on a whim that evening, he drew a family tree on the first of the leaves and filled it in as best he could. His writing was small and crabbed, but he filled the page, nonetheless. The trunk of the tree ended with a question mark, for he could trace their beginnings only to the Flemish city of Bruges in the fifteenth century. On another page, he drew the marks that the family gunsmiths had put on their guns, even those marks that he had seen on two old cannon in Riga twenty years before. And then, not knowing at all why he did it, he wrote down what he knew of the White Beast. Reading over those words, he knew that they made no sense. *I'll explain to him when he's old enough,* he thought.

Inside the front cover of the book, he wrote, "For my son Archibald from his loving father John Morse, Anno Domini 1648. America is in the mind."

The book was titled *Of Divers Things Founde in the Newe World Called America, with Their Properties and True Descriptions; of the Marvels of that Place; and of the Wilde Folke that Dwell Therin.*

Chapter Four

The wind drove them toward America as if it meant to smash the little ship on the shore there, but when they made a landfall the wind turned sharply about and drove them out to sea again. The captain sailed against it, but, finding it too wild, he steered south, then beat north again while he waited for the gale to subside. It had been Jan's intention to find a sheltered harbor in the sandy islands that protected the marshy bays far south of Nieuw Amsterdam and then to cruise slowly in the protected waters, looking for Black Otter's signal. The tub's captain was a coward, however, and he would not go close to the pounding, dirty surf that made the line of coastal islands noisy.

"Take it in!" Jan bellowed at him over the wind.

The stolid captain, feet spread, hips braced against the after castle, shook his head. The movement was so ponderous and final that it seemed as if a wooden piece of the ship had roused itself to move.

"I paid you good money, you bastard! Take it in!"

The captain shook his head again without looking at Jan, who, dismayed by his own impotence, spun angrily away and looked through the wind-whipped rain at the gray froth that marked the shore.

"There's an opening to the south," he shouted, more in rage than out of any hope of changing the man's mind. "We passed it yesterday."

The captain did not respond.

Black Otter had promised that there would be watchers inside the string of islands who would light fires at night to guide them in. These scouts would take them inland to Black Otter through uninhabited land lying between New Sweden and Nieuw Netherland; then the guns would go up the Delaware and its tributaries to the Seneca country. Time was important now; the weather had delayed the ship, and every night that the signal fires stayed lighted was a night that they might be seen by enemy eyes—Swedish fishermen or hunters, southern tribes friendly to the Swedes or even the English.

42

"What do you intend to do then?" Jan shouted.

The captain gazed north, then south. He made a motion with his hand, palm down. "Ride it out."

"How long?"

"Two days. Three. You had no cause to insult me."

"No cause! You make me sick!"

They sailed north at night and then turned south again until, next day, they were almost in sight of Cape Henlopen. Another ship appeared, too far away to be recognizable; Jan kept the captain from chasing after it to have company. "Keep on your course, captain; if we follow him, we invite questions; if we run, we look like pirates."

The wind dropped the next day; the day after that, there was only a fresh, moist breeze from the land, and the sailors were landsick, for all that the waves remained high and the churning surf was like beaten chocolate. They could see the opening, however, looking a mile wide.

"Take her in."

"I got no chart. My ship will founder."

Jan paced down to the forward castle and back, his shoulder rubbing along the canvas sea cloth that was stretched in the midships to keep the waves off. "Put me into the pinnace, captain. I'm going in."

"You will be drowned like a mouse on a stick."

"That's for me to worry about. Pull in the pinnace; I can't wait longer."

The captain looked as if he would be stubborn, and he made some conventionally stubborn noises, but the truth was that he would be glad to rid himself of Jan and his cargo; without them, he could sail to Nieuw Amsterdam like an honest merchantman and offload his regular cargo and pick up another for home. After a shrug and what seemed to be a fatalistic sigh, he ordered the pinnace drawn in from its position aft. It had ridden the Atlantic under tow; now it had to be hauled in close, its canvas covers stripped away and its mast stepped.

It was hardly bigger than the ship's longboat, but it was normally big enough for six or eight men at oars. Half-decked, it took the waves fairly well, but with the guns and a crew of five, it would be able to carry little food and water.

"Don't miss your opening in the sandspits yonder," the captain said drily. "A gunrunner could starve along this coast."

"What a lovely world, when a Christian captain is so light-hearted about me drowning."

"You're on the Devil's work; what's Christian in the thing? Taking guns to savages is Devil's work."

"Then you've been on the Devil's work, too."

"Nah, nah, I supplied the ship, only. *You* are going to give them the devilish things."

"They ain't devilish, captain! A gun is a gun and no business of either God or the Devil. A gun's got no religion."

"Yah, and a fart has no nose. Goodbye, little gunrunner. Don't drown before your prayers are said."

At the last moment, Jan clapped the captain on the back and shook his hand; and then, grinning, he flung a leg over the rail and scrambled down the rope ladder that hung there. The ship rolled and the pinnace rolled with it; for a moment, he swung free and was looking down over the gunwale of the pinnace at the cheerless ocean, and then the ship rolled back and he slammed against the oak planking. He cursed and went on down, his right hand bleeding.

"Cast off! Cast us off up there!"

He had two sailors from the ship and two lummoxes he had brought from Holland, one of them a distant relative. Jan put himself at the tiller and ordered the others to the oars until he was well away from the ship, when he had the sail unfurled and the pinnace began to pound through the huge waves. Water towered above them, seeming to reach for the mast top before it fell away like a hungry animal that had been disappointed in its prey, to slide under the keel and slink away.

"Row!" he screamed into the wind. The words were whipped away; air blew into his nose and his mouth so that he thought he would choke. He made the gesture of rowing and they looked at him stupidly. The pinnace climbed a wave; the bow went down, the stern came up, and the tiller came free of the water so that the craft yawed. Then it settled back again to climb another wave and he could steer again, though he was soaked through every stitch on him—shivering, angry, wondering if he was about to die.

His third cousin's son was named Olaf—a thick-necked, sweet-tempered boy who had never been farther from home than his grandmother's house in Delft. *Not a Dutch name,* Jan thought every time he saw the boy; still, there were so many odd names in the family, what with wandering and trading, that there was little wonder to it. Now the boy was staring beseechingly at Jan, like an ox ready for slaughter who thought that the man with the sledge might change his mind somehow. Olaf admired Jan; worse than that, he worshiped Jan. He was seventeen and stupid and sweet, and going to America with his tough little relative had seemed like the peak of adventure—back in Amsterdam.

"Now!" Jan bellowed. The wind choked him. But there was sand in the wind now, and he was grateful for the particles that stung like bites. The cannon roar of the surf was all around them, and he was deaf from it. The pinnace shook; it slewed, plunged, seemed to want to slide seaward, and then, like a cork coming from a bottle, it popped through the opening and surged toward the quieter water only fifty yards ahead. The oars were of some good in the calmer water, and the boat moved into the sheltered bay for which she had been intended, no longer a clumsy victim of the wind but a tight, fair, buoyant inland sailor.

"Bail," Jan ordered. His voice was clear, now that he could breathe. The cry of a gull came back to him from overhead; three of the birds circled the masthead. "Two bailing and two rowing, and put your backs into it!"

The pinnace rode the smaller waves inside the islands well, even with the weight of the guns, though he found it a little sluggish to the tiller. *Low in the water,* he thought. He headed southwest toward the wooded mainland. When the pinnace came close enough, he could see that the closest trees were scraggly, many of them dead, because they were growing in water; dead limbs and tops poked up, and the tips of grass were visible above the water.

Not much of a place to have to land.

He anchored in an inlet where a little tidal creek ran in, and he huddled in his canvas sea coat and told the others to do the same. "Sleep," he ordered. "Tonight, we move again."

"At night?" Olaf's breath made a cloud of warm steam like the grassy, sweet steam of cattle.

"Yah, at night, cousin Olaf. Don't ask me questions. Sleep when you get the chance; tonight, you'll have to row."

In the moonlit darkness, they rowed steadily south. The rhythm of the heavy, long oars was like a drumbeat. Now and then one of the men would gasp for air. Otherwise they were silent, and Jan felt for the first time the thrill of actually being on the coast of his wilderness home. Being shipbound and at sea was over; he was *there. America!* He thought of the book he had left for Archie. What would the child make

45

of it—what would his America be? He could smell the wilderness, and with it, in his imagination, the villages and the men and women among whom he was happiest.

He ordered them to rest. There was no wind on the water now; only in the tops of the trees was there sound.

"What happens if we don't find nothing?" somebody said from the darkness.

"Then we look tomorrow night."

"And if we don't find nothing then?"

"Then we keep on looking."

"Why we going south?"

"Because that's where I think we should go."

"But you don't *know*."

"I know more than you. Shut up."

The glow of their pipes pocked the darkness. Tobacco smoke drifted to him.

"Hush."

They rested at the oars. A sound had reached him, high and distant and unmistakable.

"Did you hear?"

"What?"

"Voices. Indians."

"Savages?"

They were afraid. He laughed at them and told them to row slowly. The pinnace rounded a point; beyond it, another—longer, black—thrust into the bay. He thought he could see the glow of a fire behind it.

"Slow and easy."

They hugged the shore to the end of the point, then turned and headed along its south side. There was a fire on the shore ahead of them; minutes later, another came into view around the intervening trees.

"Rest on your oars." He touched the two pistols at his belt and picked up the wheel-lock and unwrapped the oiled leather in which it had ridden over the Atlantic. *Powder, ball, spanner—all there.*

"Not a sound, now."

Under the nudging of a north breeze, the pinnace had bare steerageway, and he turned its stern to the shore and let it drift slowly southward. He rested the wheel-lock on the tiller bar and crouched low to give himself the protection of the stern piece. He made a cup of his hands and shouted into it, "Black Otter!" Behind him, one of his men whimpered, un-

46

prepared for the volume of sound or the savage syllables—the first Seneca the man had ever heard. *Olaf,* he thought.

"Where is Black Otter of the Turtles?"

His voice echoed. Another voice sounded from the shore very low, and a figure passed in front of one of the fires, running.

"Who calls?" a voice said in Seneca. It seemed to come from the wrong direction in the darkness.

"Snow Elk."

"What does Snow Elk want?"

"Snow Elk has gifts for Black Otter of the Turtles."

"Wait!"

The pinnace was slipping too far south. Jan turned his head and muttered, "Two of you take the oars. Push us back up—easy does it, I need to see these people by their firelight—and quiet, my darlings, quiet. If I'd wanted to make my location a proclamation, I'd have brought my trumpeter."

Two lights bobbed on the water. *Two canoes.* They were a good hundred feet apart, a tactic learned from seeing the effects of gunfire on the close-packed canoes of the fur fleet.

"Stop!" he called when they were thirty yards away. Pine knots flamed in their bows, white birch backing them for reflection. He could not see past the dazzle of the burning pitch, and he called to them to shield their lights; the canoes bobbed as men moved forward, and the birch reflectors were turned shoreward.

"Who is there from the Senecas?"

They named themselves. One of them was his wife's nephew, a Turtle from his own village. His heart seemed to grow big; he was happy, hearing the language again, hearing the familiar voice. He called to them to come closer, and a canoe was paddled in until the bow bumped the pinnace's starboard side and he could see the face of his wife's nephew, harsh and dangerous in the strange light—at least to the other Europeans' eyes—but beautiful to him. Jan stood up and took the younger man's hand, held it, felt a great, almost erotic surge of excitement when he caught the man's smell. "Where do we go?"

"Bring your big canoe in with us. Tomorrow we go to Black Otter."

"Is it safe here?"

"All safe. Nobody is here."

"How long have you waited?"

"Since the ice left the Chenusee. Since the first skunk cabbage."

No wonder I heard them talking, he thought. *They're bored.* Patience was not a virtue among the Senecas.

The two fires marked the entrance to a river, one on each bank to guide the ship in and upriver, or so they had intended. Now they had been there so long with their fires that they had got bored and had taken to calling to each other across the river. Jan was worried but said nothing. If they had been seen, there was nothing to be gained by telling them that they had been careless.

Jan slept on the bank among the Senecas; the four Hollanders spent the night in the pinnace. At first light, two Senecas started upriver in a canoe to tell Black Otter that Snow Elk had come with his guns as he had promised.

Jan squatted on the riverbank so that the brown water rippled close to his toes. "What river is this?"

"Muddy River, the Suskeehannocks call it." His wife's nephew jerked his head toward the three Suskeehannocks who were in the party—old enemies now reduced to Seneca tribute payers.

"How far up can my big canoe go?"

"Far up. Far, far up. We meet Black Otter halfway to the Delaware."

Jan was dubious. The Senecas were unlikely to have much idea how deep the draft of the overloaded pinnace was. "This river looks shallow. All swamp through here."

"Very black, lots of stink, yes. But canoes make it easily."

Jan pried a freshwater clamshell from the mud. "Have you seen any other white-face canoes?"

"One. Nine days ago. Way out there." The young man drew a picture in the tidal mud. "Long canoe like this—one small, white wing, like so, square—two big guns on each side."

"A gundalow. Probably the stinking Swedes. Did the canoe come in?"

"No. Way out. Then the storm came. It was a long time ago."

Jan grunted. He wondered why the Swedes would have a gunboat out. *Keeping the Dutch in their place, most likely. Or the English. Not good.* They might have seen the fires by night. Would they have thought that the fires belonged to anything other than a Suskeehannock fishing party? *Risk. It's all a risk.*

"All right, let's go."

They paddled him out to the pinnace in one of the heavy elm-bark canoes; as he clambered aboard, he grinned at Olaf and the other Hollanders, who were staring at the Indians. The Senecas laughed and stared back. One of them pointed at Olaf's sea gown and tried to grab at it, and Olaf swung a clublike hand at the clutching fingers.

"No!" Jan shouted. "No more of that. He only wants to trade."

"He could of had a knife, Uncle!"

Jan guffawed. "A knife. A knife!" He collapsed in the stern, chuckling. "You're a rarity, Olaf, my boy—a wonder! *A knife.*" He wiped his eyes and settled himself at the tiller. "Let's get this bucket moving, darlings! Haul anchor—no sail until we're upriver a bit, so it's oars for now—tide's coming, it ain't so bad—put your backs into it, she's heavy in the water— *pull—!*"

"How did it—how did it—*look,* Uncle?" Olaf's words were grunts timed to his pulling at the oars.

"How did what look, Olaf?"

"The lay of the—*land,* Uncle."

"It looked very good, my boy, very good indeed. Like eating sweet egg bread in your Grannie Katje's kitchen."

His thoughts were on the guns in their stout wood boxes in the bottom of the pinnace—two tons of wood and iron lining the inside of the little boat and slowing it like the burden of worry in an old man's mind. Rowing the boat was like dragging a lifetime of woe; when the tide turned later and ran against them, it would be like rowing uphill. The sail proved to be of little use; the river had broad shallows on each side of a twisting channel, and he could not tack without running aground. After the third grounding, with Senecas and Hollanders straining together to move the boat off the mud, he gave up on the sail and took a turn at the oars; and so they went painfully upriver while the Senecas plied their canoes with obvious indulgence, like young men walking next to an old one.

They slept that night on a muddy bank and were on the water again with first light. Dark swamp hedged them on each side; dead trees rose from the black surface like fingers, like stumps of arms. The sun burned the early mist away and cast a pale, brassy light over them. Jan had to steer standing so that he could look ahead and try to pick the channel out among the wiggly tidal squirmings of the river, through islands and mud bars that poked grass and tangled alders above

49

the surface like feelers. It was a disturbing, hostile landscape, made more so by the scantiness of green on the trees.

At midmorning, when he was resting the men at the oars, he heard a muffled sound behind them. The Seneca canoes had gone ahead to follow the river so that they could pilot him; now, he heard downriver the unmistakable thump of wood on wood and the rhythm of oars.

The Hollanders looked at each other stupidly.

The gundalow!

"Row!"

"We just stopped. We got no rest."

"Shut up and row!"

But it was no good. The gunship had them caught on the river, and they must try to escape it by going upstream; if he could have slipped down to the bay, he knew, he could easily have outsailed the bargelike craft. He bullied his rowers, but within an hour he looked behind and saw a squat sail against the downstream trees, and, below it, the long silhouette of the gundalow. Shallow of draft, it could sail where he could not, and he knew that it would catch him unless he could work miracles. *Make magic.*

"Raise the sail."

"We'll go aground again, Uncle!"

"Raise the bleeding sail and shut your mouth!"

There was a flash of light behind them, and a cannon ball skipped across the water like a playfully flung stone; the sound of the cannon reached them after the ball had passed.

"I think they mean to tell us something. Row, my darlings—row for your lives!"

Chapter Five

Under her dozen sweeps and the little rag of a sail, the gun-dalow came on; her bow gun spat at the pinnace, in whose sluggish bottom the tons of iron and wood dragged like sorrow.

The Senecas, hearing the little cannon, came speeding back. When the Swedish bow gun fired again, they wanted to flee upriver. Jan had to agree with them.

"But you ain't going to!" he muttered in English to himself. In Seneca, he called over the water, "I cannot give up Black Otter's guns! Get up on the banks; shoot the men in the big canoe as they come by you."

The canoes pushed toward the swampy banks. The gun-dalow came on. Jan did not fear the falconet in the other craft's bow; indeed, he preferred that they go on shooting it, for the firing kept two of their men busy. With an inch-and-a-half bore, the gun could do little at the distance; in close, of course, it would be brutally effective with buckshot.

"Mind that oar, Olaf! Catch a crab now and you'll be right out in the river—and I won't stop for you, you great cow!"

A musket volley sounded raggedly behind them. The Indians had fired on the gundalow; Jan saw it seem to hesitate, then slew sideways as the bow and stern guns tried to fire on the banks. They were loaded with ball, however, and they needed shot or chain; the charges splashed harmlessly into the swamp mud. The pinnace was pulling away while the gundalow turned broadside to the current, and Jan thought he might make it if the Indians could pester the Swedes enough. But the gunboat turned bow on and the oars flashed. There was another, more scattered firing of the Seneca muskets.

The canoes would be moving through the swamp now, trying not to offer a target. The Senecas would be wanting to drop downriver out of the fight, and they would be wondering how they could ever explain such an action to Black Otter. They were not cowards, but sensible men whose code of war included the commendable belief that a man should fight when the odds were in his favor. Fear of the war leader

51

and fear of tribal opinion were stronger than common sense, however; they came on up the river, daring the Swedish guns, and they launched another volley from a bend in the river, beyond which the water broadened, allowing Jan to take the wind and sail fast for three hundred yards.

"We're going to make it, darlings!" Jan said with forced cheerfulness.

The gunboat had given all its attention to the Senecas now; its captain knew he had the pinnace trapped. Jan could see men standing as it swung in toward the right bank. They would have abandoned the sweeps for muskets; there was a fierce rattle of firing, the screams of wounded men. They had pinned a canoe against a high bank and poured fire into it.

Now we're for it. He cursed at his men, cursed the sail as it began to luff. *How long till dark? How long till I meet Black Otter?*

For another hour, they managed to keep ahead. The remaining canoe stayed even with them, sometimes firing back at the Swedes. There was no doubt that they were drawing closer. Jan's Hollanders were tiring; they were young, strong men, but they could not keep up so fast a beat for much longer.

The gundalow had given up firing its bow gun. The captain seemed confident he would catch the pinnace.

And then the pinnace ran aground.

One moment, she seemed to be surging along under the desperate oars, and then she shuddered with the impact, and Olaf pitched over backward off his seat, Jan almost following him as the sudden stop lifted him in the stern. Moments before, he had congratulated himself on the expanse of open water he had found ahead; now, they were stuck on a mud bar only ten inches below the surface.

"Damn them! Damn them!" The correct channel was marked by a rippling V against the far bank; seeing it now, he knew that he could have taken the pinnace through it, while the gundalow would have found it too narrow. *We'd have had it won!*

"Out of the bloody goddam boat! Out, out! Olaf, get your ass out of the bilge, you lummox, and get out!" He bellowed at the Senecas in their language. "Get the guns out!"

"Uncle—Uncle Jan—there ain't time, save yourself, not them damned guns!"

"Get the guns out!"

One of the sailors dove overboard into the mud, picked

52

himself up and splashed shoreward, deaf to Jan's orders. The others, however, were cowed by the wheel-lock in his hands and by the terrible ferocity of his face. The long crates began to move shoreward: two men lifted them from the bottom of the pinnace and placed one on the shoulders of a man who stood knee-deep in mud and water and who then splashed off with his burden. Fifteen pounds of wooden box, and fifty pounds of guns, with tools and lead—it made a good load, a load that would not be hurried.

Still, he made them try.

A shot from the falconet skipped past them.

The Senecas were all in the water now, trying to save the guns.

Dear God, give me a one-pounder! The Swedes were inept— civilians, probably, impressed as militia. Four of them were tending the gun, going at it like four bakers trying to get bread into the same oven. But the gundalow was coming on. Jan aimed the wheel-lock at the biggest man in the fumbling gun crew. *Have you ever killed a man with that gun?* his Seneca son had asked. The wheel spun; pyrites rasped against notched steel; the gun spat and the Swedish gunner fell over like a dropped sack of meal.

Reloading in the shelter of the sternboard, he tried to pick out the Swedish steersman. He and all the Swedes were all crouched low now. The sweeps were idle as the rowers tried to hide, and the gundalow swung a little and the sail emptied. They were shaken by seeing one of their own people bleed.

The Senecas had made it to the bank and were firing their muskets. They would not come back for more guns, he thought—nor would the Dutch sailors. Jan looked at Olaf, who was standing stupidly in the waist.

"Get out of it now," Jan said. His voice was kind. "Go on, boy. You did well."

"But, Uncle—"

"Get out of it! And take a box of guns with you."

The pinnace swayed as he went over the side.

The gunboat had turned so that the swivel guns along the gunwale could be brought to bear. He could see men standing near them with muskets—and, behind them, the steersman. Smoke veiled the side of the gunboat as the muskets and one of the swivels fired and he lost sight of the coxswain; there was a despairing shriek behind him and he saw Olaf thrashing in the water, down and dying. The other Amsterdammer

53

had dropped his box of guns and was trying to run through the knee-deep water to shore.

Jan could aim now. He felt quite detached and cool. *Gunmakers should not go to war,* he had told his Seneca son. His sights settled on the Swedish steersman, visible now through the thinning smoke, and the old wheel-lock fired as if it were his eye that controlled the trigger; the steersman went over backward into the water.

The sweeps began to move. The gundalow's progress was uneven, but it began to move closer. Hardly time to load now—only time to stand and draw the Scottish pistols from his belt and aim at the crew that had turned the bow gun on him, face them with a pistol in each hand, aiming, firing, watching a man crumple up—

His world exploded. The top of the sternpiece flew up in splinters and the tiller bar smashed against his hip. His right leg was knocked back as if it had been grabbed from behind, and he was lying in the bottom of the pinnace with his ears ringing and a blinding light in his eyes. He understood that the light was the sun. But he could not turn his head yet, could not move his body. He moved his eyes. There was the stern, chunks blown out of it by buckshot from the falconet; there was the tiller bar, broken. There was his bloody right thigh with two balls in it. There was another ball somewhere in his abdomen.

Gut-shot. Oh, dear Christ.

He whimpered.

He could hear shooting from the bank and the roar of one of the small cannons close by. The gundalow had rowed in very close to him, but apparently the Swedes were afraid to board the grounded pinnace under the fire from the bank; they were probably afraid, too, that they would go aground on the same mud. The two groups were content to fire at each other while he lay in the bottom of the pinnace and sighed and bled.

He wrapped his belt around his thigh and pulled it as tight as he could. He was light-headed, sick, but felt nothing in the leg yet.

He was frightened. *A man can lose his magic.*

It became very important to save the guns. Saving the guns became an act of penance, a reparation, a sacrifice to save his magic. He loaded the wheel-lock and the pistols, smearing blood over the red Brazil wood, gasping for breath and for relief from the pain in his gut.

54

He peeped above the place where the balls had shattered the top edge of the stern piece. The gundalow was five yards away.

He thought he had a good idea. He had a powder horn that had been made in Germany of the butt end of a staghorn. He thought it would make a good grenade to toss at the gundalow. He made a wick for it of a rag torn from his shirt with gunpowder sprinkled over it and twisted up. He meant to light the wick with the flash from the pan of one of his pistols, letting the shot smash into the bulkhead, but when he held the pistol close to the rag and pulled the trigger, the powder burned from the improvised wick like the jet of fire from a Roman candle. He had only an instant to know that he had made a mistake, a terrible, costly mistake—long enough to know that he held the end of his magic in his hand—and then the staghorn grenade exploded in his hand and he was knocked over backward into the bottom of the pinnace, senseless with his head between two crates of his beloved guns.

In the darkness, they were emptying the pinnace of its freight of weapons and pain. He was carried over the dark water by four men at shoulder height. His hands were on fire and he could not see.

Black Otter and forty Senecas had come downriver by canoe, drawn by the noise of the battle. Seeing them, the Swedes had withdrawn. They were only civilians and they thought they had done enough by killing five Senecas and Olaf and by putting a shot into the pinnace.

Black Otter moved the weapons out of the pinnace with the efficiency of an experienced organizer; he sent them off in four lots, two by river and two by land, in case the Swedes came back. Jan was carried upriver in the bottom of a canoe, dreaming and delirious, raving, weeping.

The Senecas knew pain. They were born with pain, grew up with pain. Men and women knew the pain of starvation, the pain of broken limbs, the pain of malignancy. The Senecas had made an art of the toleration of pain. Jan felt their kind of pain now; it invaded him like sexual arousal, like the consuming rush toward climax.

"My hand. My right hand."

"The hand is gone."

"Is there blood?"

"Very little."

"If there is blood, the stump must be burned. To close off the blood. What about the other hand?"

"Two fingers only are gone."

A man can lose his magic.

On the second night, he began to bleed, and they built a fire that blazed high and cast strange shadows up into the pines. He thought it was the sun. They carried him close to the fire and raked out coals near his right arm, then mounded tinder and oily birchbark over the coals until a hot, black-smoked flame shot up, the birch sputtering like fat, roasting meat. His mind cleared.

"Burn it," he whispered.

"Do you wish a stick to bite on?"

"I will sing."

A great Maaqua had taught them about pain. Captured and facing torture, he had squatted in his tormentors' fire until his testicles had burned off. He had sung the whole time, staring at their eyes.

Jan sang an old Scottish song. He could smell his arm roasting. The pain was like an icicle being pushed up the marrow of his bones, up his anus. He sang loud, as if the noise would drown out the remarkable pain.

"It is done. You did well."

He fainted.

They carried him on a litter made of a blue trade blanket and two green ash poles. Ahead of him and behind him, the Senecas walked with guns loaded on their backs. Jan sweated. The burns were infected and the buckshot in his gut and his right leg burned.

A young man who was a healer cut out the shot from his leg. He told Jan that the shot in his gut would heal itself because it was far over against his hip, and in fact it was probably lodged in the big bone there. "But your arms are rotting."

"Yes. I smell it."

"We will let the flies work."

They left his arms exposed so that flies would come and feed and lay their eggs. They put out crystallized maple sap to draw more flies. In three days, maggots hatched in the rotten meat of his stump and on what was left of his left hand, and he looked down one morning and it was like looking at a dead dog that has lain in a field for a long time, with maggots and black beetles crawling in and out of it. The flesh had drawn in on the broken bones. Where the maggots had eaten, the stump looked like lumpy red dough, uneven and obscene, glistening with life, but it was not rotten. By the time they reached Jan's village, most of the maggots had dropped off and the bright, raw flesh had formed scar tissue.

Fish-catcher, his Seneca wife, wailed when she saw him. She already knew, of course; runners had come ahead of them days before. She wailed for sorrow and for joy; she made their children come close to look at him.

"You are a great man," Black Otter told him. Black Otter pushed back his black fur cloak to show Jan his shriveled arm. "They will make stories about you. They will say forever that you were the man who brought the guns that made the People great."

Black Otter sent the furs off to Koopman at Fort Orange. Jan no longer cared much about the furs or about being rich. He was a man with only a thumb and two fingers. He was a man with no magic. He was a cripple. His strength had trickled away from him, and he was so weak that Fish-catcher and one of her sisters had to carry him outside so that he could pass water or excrement, so that he could lie in the sun.

His Seneca children looked at him and said little. His Seneca son sat by him in the sunshine but said nothing.

I will never see those others again, he told himself. *No need to lie about Russia any more.* He tried to look at his life and think of it as over. *I have lived well.*

That winter, Black Otter took the guns and four hundred men and food for five months across the Niagara River and up to the far border of the Huron country, where they hid themselves until spring, four hundred men hiding far from home. When the first warm days came, they swarmed into the Huron villages, every man carrying two muskets, and they destroyed the Huron nation all in a single day—seven villages burned to gray ash on the melting snow, three hundred and seventy-one Hurons dead along with seven Jesuits from France; the Huron nation was finished, broken, a name on the wind. In the final charge, the man next to Black Otter fell and his musket discharged and Black Otter took a load of shot in his face and fell down; and they carried him home three hundred English miles in a blanket, still living, face down so that he would not drown in his own blood. He died in his wife's longhouse, and everybody wailed. They made up songs to tell how he and Snow Elk the Gun-finder were great men.

With his two fingers and his thumb and one good eye, Jan tried to fix the guns that had been damaged in the Huron raid. He could do little. The stump of his right wrist bled sometimes. Then it would get infected and he would have fevers. He never got stronger.

The People were rich. They had so many sewan beads from the Hurons that they threw the beads on the ground like seeds. They had Huron furs, Huron corn, Huron trade goods with French marks. They were secure, because their worst enemy was destroyed. They bought glass Venetian beads and Flemish wool blankets from the Dutch traders at Fort Orange with their new wealth, and they bought alcohol and went crazy. They bought Jew's harps and brass kettles and crosses and rings. War made people rich.

That next winter, influenza came to the villages. The old people said the rich ones had brought it back from the Dutch at Fort Orange. A few of them said it was the ghosts of the Hurons that did it. But people died, whatever the cause; there were so many dead that they buried them five and six to a grave, and often the ones doing the burying were sick themselves and were too weak to dig proper graves. There was enough food, but in some houses there were not enough healthy people to cook it.

Jan Morse died in the middle of that winter, worn out by pain and infection and the heartbreak of having lost his magic. His wife kept his body frozen on the roof of the longhouse with seven others, including her mother's; she drank Dutch alcohol and wailed and pushed her head into the cold ashes of the firepit. In the spring when the ground thawed, she and her sisters and her children buried the dead ones from the Turtle house in a common grave, but they carried Jan's body a hundred yards outside the village and buried him in a solitary grave. Some of the old ones said that he was the cause of their bad luck because he was the Gun-finder, and he had brought the curse of all the ghosts that the guns had ever killed; had he not been cursed, himself, in the loss of his hands? Jan's Seneca son, who was almost as big as a grown man now, broke the stock of the wheel-lock gun against a beech tree to kill the spirit in it and laid the gun in the grave with his father's desiccated body, along with his gun-smithing tools, four extra triggers, three mainsprings, two sears and a smith's hammer.

Fish-catcher threw ashes over her head and got drunk. Jan's Seneca son went off to Long Creek Village to live with the runners on the Long Trail. In the winters, the People told stories about Black Otter and Snow Elk the Gun-finder, but they forgot after a while that one of them had been a European.

Chapter Six

He had always told his wives that when they had not heard from him for two years at a time, they should think him dead. He had said it with a grin, said it as a kind of joke, twitting them about finding younger men with the wealth he would leave them. It was not so much of a joke to them, however, for when he was gone on one of his journeys, his letters might be six or eight months apart, and they worried. Jan was like a strange migratory bird to them, one who was borrowed from some other climate for a season, something whose return could be prayed for but never quite expected.

When two years had gone by, Grete den Moors told her neighbors that she feared she was a widow. She wept angrily. Grief expressed itself as rage: she looked into the mirror in the clean bedroom and saw a woman angry and swollen, and she hated herself and hated Jan den Moors for making her angry. "And who will I marry now?" she asked the mirror. "Who will take me, even with the wealth I am supposed to have? What good were all those years of being faithful?" She was too thrifty to smash the mirror, and she contented herself with breaking an old cup that already had a crack in it.

Her daughter Maria had married before Jan had gone off; now the other daughter was being courted.

"Marry him," Grete told the girl. "Your mother needs a home."

"I ain't sure I like him," the girl said. "He's that silly!"

"Marry him. He's a bird in hand, Katrin."

"Oh, well, but Papa said we was going to be rich. When I'm rich, some better-looking fellow that ain't so silly will see me."

"Marry him, you goose!" Grete screamed at her. "We ain't ever going to be rich, not ever, ever! Them was just stories he told!"

She bullied the girl until she married. Just in time, too, for Jan's creditors took the house and her furniture and their one-third interest in his cousin Anders's gunshop.

"He left no will?" her lean nephew Martin murmured.

"Nyah! Devil a will he ever cared about. You know how

60

he was about the law—worse than the church for trouble, he said."

Martin sucked air between his long front teeth, making a sound that managed to be disapproving and disgusting all at once. "He had money in the West India Company Bank," he whispered.

"He didn't!"

"I beg to differ, Tante Grete. I saw him go in there once, we were in 's Gravenhage together, he made some excuse or other to get away from me. But I saw where he went."

"You followed him, you mean!"

Martin sucked air again. "Better off you'd be if you'd followed him once or twice yourself," he said in the high, thin voice she disliked. It was like the voice of conscience—dry, bloodless, without appeal. "I saw him go in, I saw him come out; that night at dinner, he paid in gold."

"Well, I was sure *you* didn't pay, Martin."

"In gold, Tante Grete. Wherever did he get the gold, but when he was in the West India Company Bank? Go ask."

She asked. Timidly. She was a peasant and the men in the West India House in 's Gravenhage were smooth urban merchants. She was ready to run out the door or fly into a rage, for anger was the peasant's only refuge from authority, except for flight. She was confounded, however, by their treatment, for they behaved as if she were a great lady; weak and dumb with astonishment, she was led into a high-ceilinged room and sat down in a huge, hard chair opposite a very smooth man in a vast amount of white lace collar.

"Are you this man den Moors's lawful wife?"

"Oh, aye, sir! In church!"

"Have you proof?"

"What proof? Everybody knows it! I mean, we got two grown girls, did you think—? Your lordship, I am my man Jan's wife, I swear!"

"Of course you are, goodma'am, but the company requires proof. As their high mightinesses would require proof—as any judge would require proof. I suggest you go to a notary with two witnesses who will swear you are the lawful wife of the man den Moors, or go to the man of God who married you—or to the church, if the man be no longer there, for reasons of age or health or—and so forth—and have the entry in the parish register copied out and notarized. Is the man den Moors deceased?" Seeing her confusion, he said more kindly, "Are you a widow, goodma'am?"

"I believe it, your lordship."

"Have you proof of his death?"

"Why, no, how would I? He's been gone these two years and more."

"How do you know him dead, then?"

"He said it would be so."

The smooth man smiled and stroked his beard, which was as long and brown and shiny as the hair of a lapdog. "In these matters, goodma'am, we must have proof. The affidavit of the physician who tended him at the end, or a deposition from one who was at the bedside, and so forth. Barring those—in such matters, their high mightinesses and common law normally require a delay of seven years—"

"Seven years!" she wailed. *Dear God above, I'll be almost fifty! Who'll ever marry me when I'm fifty?*

Her nephew Martin found a way to declare a man dead after only two years, and after only six months' more delay, he and the West India Company went up to assizes for a judgment and came back with the opinion that they could proceed as if Jan den Moors were dead indeed, at least insofar as the opening of his accounts and his strongbox were concerned.

His account was empty, having all gone to the building of Black Otter's guns. The strongbox was believed to be another matter. Grete and Martin and a half-dozen of Jan's creditors stood about in the company's vast hall while the strongbox was brought up from the vault and opened by the smooth man with considerable ceremony and much signing of papers. To everybody's intense disappointment, it contained one empty leather bag and a very old apple core, and Grete collapsed and had to be carried insensible to a nearby tavern. She came to in an upper room with her bodice unlaced and her skirts hitched up to make her cooler. Standing by the bed was Martin, looking down at her with a wild glaze over his usually fish-flat eyes and a suspicious bulge in his breeches.

"You did all you could," Martin said sullenly when he saw she was awake. "You're a good, sensible woman, Grete."

"Tante Grete," she corrected him.

"That's only a way of speaking," he muttered. He could not keep his eyes off her bare legs. "My mother was your stepfather's child by his first wife. No blood relation."

She remembered the mockery of the empty strongbox. "Oh, Martin," she groaned. She heaved a huge sigh that made her big breasts (*Dumplings, my poor Jan called them*) push against the loosened laces.

"You'd make the right man a good wife," Martin muttered, his Adam's apple bobbing.

She made, without bitterness or sentimentality, an instant calculation. As if putting the two scenes into the two pans of a goldsmith's balance, she weighed the picture of herself growing old in her daughters' houses against one of herself as Martin's wife. *Lesser of two evils,* she thought. *Oh, my poor, lovely Jan!* She looked at Martin's saturnine face, his look of adolescent lust.

"You sure there ain't a blood relation?" she asked in the voice of a child.

"I'll go to judgment on it."

"Oh, Martin," she said, pulling up her skirts and mentally kissing the memory of Jan's eager lovemaking farewell, "let's get on with it, then."

The snow melted on the graves and grass grew from them, waving in summer wind, and then it dried in the frost and vanished under another snow. The cycle of the seasons rolled endlessly ahead, even as it stretched endlessly back. In the villages, Time was, Time is, Time will be, all at once; the present is only a bead on a string.

They marked the years by the names of the great things that had happened: the Year of the Sickness, the Year of the Huron Raid; the Year of No Food All Winter. They called the most recent one the Year of Being Rich because they had reaped the second harvest from the destruction of the Hurons; with the Hurons gone, their place as middlemen in the great trade patterns was taken by the People. The furs that had gone through the Huron country now went through theirs; now it was they who dealt with the French at Mount Royal and the Dutch at Fort Orange. The villages were wealthy beyond imagining, wealthy beyond want. Only the old people and the cynical ones remembered that there had been good years before that had been followed by bad. Most of the People were content with Time Is.

Jan Morse's Seneca wife had been called Fish-catcher since she had passed puberty. In the Year of Being Rich, however, people started to call her Dry Mouth. Names changed as people got older and as they changed themselves. Dry Mouth was a different woman from Fish-catcher; she was sullen, depressed—and usually drunk. She used her part of the Peo-

63

ple's wealth to buy Dutch alcohol. It seemed to her sisters in the longhouse that she never stopped drinking; when she was drunk, she lay in her bed for days, saying nothing, eating nothing. Jan Morse would not have recognized her. But her sisters knew all about such things; she was a different person now.

Toward the end of the Year of Being Rich, she went to Fort Orange on foot because there was no more alcohol in her small village, which was too far from the Dutch traders to keep carrying casks, and she believed that Jan had left wealth with the trader Koopman for her. To her, wealth meant Dutch *aqua vitae*, distilled in the Netherlands and shipped to Nieuw Amsterdam in barrels as big as vats; Koopman would give her Jan's fortune in alcohol, she believed. On the way to Fort Orange she stopped in each village and stayed with relatives in the Turtle longhouse. She was always welcome. If there was alcohol, she stayed a long time; if there was not, she moved on.

Koopman was a stooped, suspicious Netherlander who cursed every day that saw him still in America and who marked off every sundown on a calendar notched into the planking above his bed. He had the days counted right up to when he would be able to afford to leave, and every night when he marked one off with a knife cut, he glared at the remaining notches as if they were his worst enemies in the world. *Three more seasons!* he told himself. He had been there for four years. At first, he had liked it, but he lacked Jan Morse's subrational understanding of the villages. Instead, the villages quickly disgusted him. When he went west into the Iroquois country to trade, he did things that later disgusted him, and he blamed the Indians for the things he did. Because he was a great man among them, bringing them gunpowder and gin and brassware, he could get anything he wanted; he boasted to the sailors who came upriver from Nieuw Amsterdam that he could get anything a Roman emperor could have gotten. His imagination was very limited, and his yearnings were very hemmed in by his puritanical childhood, so when he had had two women at a time, and a girl of ten, and a boy, and had tried both sodomy and fellatio, and he still had trouble with his erections, he was disgusted and he hated the Indians even more than before. He tried things with drunken Indian girls that made him bite down hard and clench his fists when he thought about them afterward. He was Bible-raised, tight, angry. He had come to

America expecting to love the wilderness for all the money it would give him, but he hated it now and he wanted to run away from it because the savages were devils who had seduced him into unspeakable acts for which he would suffer in Hell.

"What is it?" he rasped when the Seneca woman approached him. She was broad-faced and sulky-looking, too old for his taste. "You want gin?"

"Yes, gin. And I want my dead husband's riches."

He stopped with his hand halfway to the brass cup that he used for measuring out the *aqua vitae* before cutting it with water. "What husband is that?"

"Snow Elk. You called him Jan. Morz." Her pronunciation was wrong, but he understood her. He had been waiting for two years for somebody to come and claim the credit for the thousands of furs he had received in Jan den Moors's name; now, just when he had decided nobody would come, here was this ugly old devil! He completed his movement for the cup, and he filled it full of the potent liquid and then poured it into a pewter cup and added water. "A Seneca, was he, your husband?" he said as he pushed the cup across the boards of his counter.

"White-face."

"Never heard of him."

"Hollander."

She raised her hand to drink, but he pointed out the open door. "Your kind drink outside. I don't want no puking in here. Go on, now, this ain't one of your stinking longhouses. I got a rule—white-faces only drink in here."

She put down the cup. "I want my husband's riches."

"You make no sense."

"For the guns! He sent you furs he got for the guns!"

Koopman folded his arms. "Their high mightinesses over the Big Bitter Water would kill any man who brought in guns to you people. Kill me for taking furs he got for guns. You want your husband to be killed, you spreading lies like that?"

"Even the white-face gods over the Big Bitter Water cannot kill a dead man."

Koopman knew that Jan was dead. The Gun-finder was a famous man along the Trail; even as far down as Nieuw Amsterdam, they knew that he was dead. Koopman had allowed himself a little spark of hope when he had heard that Jan was dead, for he thought that there might be a way one

65

day to make those three thousand pelts—or their worth in guilders, for the furs themselves had long since gone to Amsterdam—his own.

"Ah, the man is dead. Too bad. What was his name?"

Snow Elk. Gun-finder. Jan Morse. She took a crumpled paper from her shoulder bag. "On this paper he put—there—his name, your name."

"Can you read, woman?"

"He explained it to me."

He reached for the paper, but she held it away from him. She would not understand anything on a piece of paper, he believed; he could never believe that any savage could understand writing or the abstract ideas that lay behind writing. Still, it was clear that she knew she held something of value. He saw that it was one of his own receipts, made out to Jan den Moors, for "eight hundred best pelts, winter quality, at 3 guilder per peltry, rec'd to his account, to be rendered on demand."

"That paper means nothing," he said as calmly as he was able. "White-faces light fires with such papers."

"This paper is the same as riches!" she screamed at him. "I got more of them!"

"Save them to wipe your fat ass with. Now get out of here."

"This paper is riches! Jan told me so. I can take my papers down to the Hollander Castle at Nieuw Amsterdam!"

"Your head is crazy. Whoever heard of a Seneca woman going to Nieuw Amsterdam?"

"My husband told me just how to do the thing. I go to the sachem of Nieuw Amsterdam and ask for Hollander law. Hollander law will make magic from my papers—soldiers will come here and take back his furs if that must be, and then all my husband's riches will be divided up. I have the paper he wrote before he died. He told me how it will work: one part to me; one part to his house in Hollander nation; one part to his house in Scottish nation."

A will. The stingy little bastard left a will! Koopman tried to hide his terror. He thought of his books, with their carefully corrected pages, their scraped-out entries. The books would stand up to a casual scrutiny—already had, in fact, for the West India Company inspected them twice a year—but they would never pass the eye of a hard lawyer from Nieuw Amsterdam. "No Seneca bitch woman can get Hollander law in Nieuw Amsterdam," he said. "Your head is crazy."

"My husband told me I must do this thing." She looked ndomitable. She glanced at the cup of alcohol and water.

"You go outside and drink your grog," he said, falsely enial now. "You let me look at my papers and see what I an find. White-faces keep lots of paper; maybe I remember our husband, after all."

When she was halfway to the door, he said, "Have you told ll your relatives about this?"

She looked back, the cup halfway to her mouth. "My husand told me no. My husband told me this is a secret thing, ecause of the guns and their high mightinesses. Only me nd you, and the sachem of Nieuw Amsterdam if you were ishonest."

"Your husband was very smart. Go drink your grog."

He watched her all day. Twice he sent out cups of spirit ▶ her; by afternoon, she had drunk eight ounces of pure lcohol and was almost insensible. Next day she was back gain, sick with hangover but convinced that he had a fortune ▶r her; he put her off with the same excuse about examining ne books, but gave her spirit "on account" and let her pick few things from the beads and the bolts of cloth behind the ▶unter. "I have a little bit of riches for you, you are right," e told her. She smiled, showing the places where she had ▶st several teeth. "But I have to add things up and be very xact. The white-faces in Nieuw Amsterdam will look at my apers, and I have to be exact."

He looked at the line of notches that represented the days e must pass before he could leave America; they seemed to tretch the length of the building. Dry Mouth's idea of riches as very modest by European standards; mostly, riches to er meant staying deeply drunk. He was trying to find a way ▶ doctor his books so as to show a very modest sum owed to an den Moors and keep the rest for himself.

She sank into summer lethargy. Perpetually drunk, she eemed contented. She did not want to go to Nieuw Amsteram. She built herself a lean-to high on the bank above the ver, and there she lay or squatted, surrounded by her riches. ometimes at night, other Indians came to the lean-to and rank with her; sometimes they stole her goods, whose abence she hardly noticed. When she did notice, she screamed nd ranted and came down to Koopman's house to get more.

"My riches!" she said drunkenly. "When are you going to ive me all my riches?"

67

"It takes time. When I have all the papers, we will go together to the sachem of Nieuw Amsterdam."

There were fights at her lean-to. The commandant of Fort Orange told Koopman to keep his savages quiet or he would close up the trading post and send Koopman to jail. Koopman said it was not his fault, but the commandant, who was an old soldier now working for the army of the West India Company, waved at him in disgust and told him to put things to rights or face jail. Koopman scored off another angry day on his wall and admitted that he could not go on fooling both Dry Mouth and his books much longer, so two nights later he crept up the riverbank to her lean-to and crushed her skull with a Maaqua war club while she snored. She was sleeping on top of the bag that had her papers in it, and he had to roll her stinking corpse off it to get them; of all the things he had done with women in America, that was the worst. He hated her for making him do it, and he smashed the broken head with the war club again and then crept down the bank and burned all the papers in his fireplace. He burned eight receipts that totaled thirty thousand guilders, and he burned a hand-drawn map that showed where members of the Morse family had made guns all over Europe, and he burned the will that Jan Morse had written as he lay dying in the Turtle longhouse of the faraway villages.

At the end of that summer, Koopman went downriver and found a leaky tub bound for Holland, and he went home and bought a mill and lived quietly and piously, and he never talked about America.

Jan Morse's Scottish wife never did believe that he was dead. Gone forever somehow, but not dead. His son Archie accepted the idea long before the two years of waiting were up, however. As far as he was concerned, his father had always been dead. The stranger who visited them from time to time was a fantastic guest, a bizarre, laughing exotic who brought gifts and made his mother briefly happy and then unhappy for a long time. The behavior of this person who was supposed to be his father had made Archie Morse realize that marriage was a sham, and he vowed that he would never marry and most certainly would never have children. He would not be a torment to another child as his father had been a torment to him.

When his mother came to him in tears two years from the day after his father had gone swinging and grinning up the main street of Kildrummie, bound for God knew where, he knew what she was about to say, and he was bitter because he had no comfort to give her—bitter that his own existence was not enough to make up for his father's absence.

"He's gone, then. Oh, Archie!" she said.

"Who's gone, then?" He pretended not to understand her. He had been apprentice to Weems the gunsmith for two years; he had a man's responsibilities, and he knew that people sometimes laughed at him because he was as serious as a grown man. He was at home, carving a back for a dulcimer he was making.

"Your dad, Archie." Her voice was husky. "It's been two years. He's gone." She wept openly. "I worry about him so!"

"I always think he's gone for good," the boy said. "Then it ain't surprising when he is."

"Nay, Archie, he said it would be the last time! He said this would be the last time he'd go away from us."

"Well, maybe he didn't lie for once. Maybe it was really the last time, eh?"

"Oh, Archie!" She closed her hands over his and over the tool he was using on the wood. His hands were bigger than hers. The curving, thin piece of wood was captured between both pairs of hands like a bird arrested in flight. "Don't be hard, Archie. Your da will come back one day, I know it, and then we'll all be together. Don't be hard!"

"If he comes back, he'll only go off again. It's better to behave like he ain't coming back at all." Weems the gunsmith was sick, and Archie and the widow's son, Andrew, were home in Kildrummie, wondering what would become of them. It was Archie's view that Weems would die and that he and Andrew should take over the gunshop in Kildrummie. That was what he meant by "behaving like he ain't coming back at all"—taking over Jan's share in the gunshop.

"You can't just close up your heart on your own da, Archie!"

"I'm only being practical, Ma." He withdrew his hands and bent over the thin, scraped wood. "I'm only looking at the future and thinking of what we're to do, and him a man that might come back one day but would only go off again, no matter what he told us."

Chapter Seven

Archibald Morse had been a dour child and now he was a dour man, at ease only when he was making music and content only when he was making things to make music with. He made the first viol that most people in Kildrummie ever saw made, a copy of the one his father had brought him, and he made a second so fine that one of the Royal Waits came all the way from Edinburgh to look at it and then to try to buy it, but his very being there made Archie sullen and he would not sell. Most contact with people made him sullen; it was a good thing he was not a drinker, people said, or he'd have killed somebody in one of his black rages.

Even as a young man, he looked bitter and beaten. He scowled all the time as if a black cloud sat just over the black line of his bushy eyebrows and prevented his ever seeing the sun. He earned the name of Dark Archie and he did nothing to lose it, although it had first been given to him simply in order to keep him separate from Archie Duffus, who was fair and blue-eyed and who was called Fair Archie. Curiously, he was a light-hearted man, so the name fit in that way, too, and even after he was killed in a fall down a cliff and there was no longer any need to keep them separate, Archibald Morse was called Dark Archie because of his temperament.

Dark Archie Morse lived in the same house in the same street of narrow houses that climbed the hill toward the distant, gloomy mountains in which his mother had borne him. Six days a week he went to the same shop down by the River Don in which his father had bought a half interest twenty years before; on the seventh day he sat in his front window, where the light was good, and he carved bridges and frets and pegs with the skill and care of a man whose only passion was making the things that would make music. If he had been as good a gunmaker as he was an instrument maker, he could have been making pistols or fine hunting weapons for the great men of the world, but whatever magic he had in his hands was the magic of music. People who saw him as they passed on their way to kirk did not acknowledge him, for he worked on the Sabbath and did not worship; some echo of advice from his ne'er-do-well father still sounded in his mind's ear: *Guns have no religion; neither should gunmakers.* And to this advice he added, *Nor should music makers, neither.*

Dark Archie was a nonconformist in an age of sectarians. He was tolerated because he was the only one of his kind in Kildrummie, harmless in his solitude. Every orthodoxy can tolerate one heretic; if two appear, both have to be burned.

While Dark Archie was growing up and long after he became a man, the kirk was splitting and splintering into more slivers than a dry old piece of pine wood under a hammer: there were New Lights and Old Lights, Covenanters and Assemblers, Episcopalians and Presbyterians and True Believers of the Code of Andrew Melville and outright Papists; and in being a sect of one, Dark Archie was merely pushing the splitting of beliefs to its limit.

"Do you believe in God Almighty?" his partner and friend Andrew asked him as they were hammering out a musket barrel together. They had apprenticed together, as much apprenticing as they had ever done, until Weems had died and they had taken over the gunshop, learning the rest of the trade from journeymen and from their own memories of their fathers. "Do you believe in God?"

"I don't discuss it." The hammers fell like hard words, blow for blow, one, *two!* one, *two!*

"You never come to kirk, Archie. Folk do wonder."

"Let 'em wonder, then." With a jerk of his head, Dark Archie signaled to their little devil of a hireling to plunge the unfinished barrel back into the charcoal of the forge.

"But the law says you got to believe in God Almighty, Archie," Andrew said as he leaned on his hammer. Andrew was older, and he took an older brother's interest; besides, he had genuine affection for Archie Morse.

"Not true, then. The law says I got to swear that I believe in God Almighty, and swearing is a very different thing from believing."

"But that makes you a hypocrite, Archie!"

"Well, then, I'm not so different from the rest of you as you thought."

He made decent guns, it was said, that would shoot where they were aimed if you had a good eye, but he made instruments that would almost play themselves. His and Andrew's guns were plain and solid and heavy, guns to last a lifetime and to do hard service for farmers and herders and the occasional soldier. His instruments, on the other hand—viols, dulcimers, even a lute or two—were light and fragile as music itself, as if melody had been turned to wood for him.

"I wonder we don't put some new mark on the guns, Archie," Andrew said. "Something different from the skull your pa used, for it's morbid, man."

"No point in change for the sake of change."

"Aye, but there is, man! To be *new!* Here we're using this ugly old skull and the word *mors,* that don't make no more sense than a ribbon on a cat's ass—my name's MacPhee and yours is Morse, and where's the skullishness in that, say you?"

Dark Archie shrugged. "It was my da's mark and his before him and so on way back. It's all in a book he give me before he died."

"What, the Morses is in a book?"

"Something he wrote into a book, I mean. Like a family tree, and the gunmarks with the names of the ones that used them."

"Well, I don't care what your da wrote in some book; I think we ought to have our own mark."

"Well, I don't." Dark Archie spoke with such finality that the matter was settled, for, although he was the younger of the two, he was the more forceful. Like many people of dark moods, he often seemed to exert force when he did not mean to, so menacing was his usual manner. And, as if understanding that effect, he said some seconds later, as if in apology, "My da's old mark is known, Andrew—known for the worth of the guns it goes on. But I'll cut a new die, if you like."

"That'd be something, then. The old one's fair round, it's so much used."

Dark Archie cut the new die. Partly out of deference to Andrew, he changed it somewhat, putting the letters of the word *mors* inside the skull shape so that they seemed to form the features—the M for the toothy mouth, the O for the fleshless parture of the nose, the other letters for eyes. The result was a compact little symbol that carried on the tradition of the marks his father had set down in the book about America. Andrew, however, was dubious.

"I don't get it," Andrew said. "I know it means something, Archie, but I don't get it."

Dark Archie sighed. "You'll never be a poet, Andrew. It means enough, believe me."

They made two kinds of guns, he and Andrew, just as their

72

fathers had: long Scots fowlers and delicate Scots pistols. The fowlers were almost five feet long, with heavy walnut stocks whose butts were curved sharply down from the breech; like the pistols, they had no trigger guards, for they used either the snaphaunce locks, as the pistols always had, or a dogged flintlock, whose notched external safety held the cock in place until manually released. A proper, modern flintlock with a good half-cock and a trigger guard would have been more sensible, perhaps, but neither the two young smiths nor their customers believed in moving ahead too quickly. What had been good enough for the older generation was mostly good enough for them.

The pistols were like those that Jan Morse had carried to America and been buried with. In pairs, new guns with the skull and the letters for features could be found on the cross belts of well-to-do Highlanders, along with a heavy-hilted backsword, and sometimes a gralloch knife. Neither of them much liked making pistols, for all that they made them well; their construction bored Dark Archie, and it frustrated Andrew MacPhee, who lacked the patience for the seemingly endless operations needed to finish them. When an order for pistols came in, Andrew would sigh and look beseechingly at Dark Archie like a setting dog that wants to be taken out for a walk, and he would write out the order with groans and the laborious slowness of a lifetime convict. "Now we've got it all to do over again," he would complain, as if making another pair of pistols were an impossible requirement.

"We need the work," Dark Archie would say.

"I know. I know. But how do you stand it, Archie? I go fair mad with all the close work."

"I think of something else."

"Of what? Eh? What else in God's name is there to think about?"

And Dark Archie would allow himself a little smile—a rarity, a genuine rarity, something seen by almost nobody else but Andrew MacPhee in those days, ever. "America," he would say. The first time that he said it, he was thinking of the book that his father had given him and what it might have meant—of the mystery of the gift, which might have been itself a clue that his father wanted him to decipher. *America*. And Andrew, after this answer had been given three or four times, came to understand that "America" was Dark Archie's word for all that was mysterious in the world—a form of secret joke, perhaps, for he always smiled when he

73

said it, but a huge mystery, all the same. The humor of the joke was lost on Andrew, who did not like mysteries of any kind. Yet it seemed to amuse Dark Archie, for he would smile his little smile as he bent to do the drawings of the new pistols, and he would have an odd glitter in his eyes.

There was a real America, they both knew that. America was a place the merchants talked of in Aberdeen; America was a place that real ships sailed to. And after Charles Stewart was restored to his father's throne in England, America was where the new king's brother, the Duke of York, went with his navy to claim the former Dutch lands for England as a prize of war. And America was where some of the regicides who had voted to behead the new king's father had fled. America was where men knew that savages lived, where furs came from, where convicts and freethinkers and Puritans were driven to inhabit.

When Dark Archie was thirty-three years old, his mother began to fail. The change astonished him; he had thought her a constant, a piece of his life as stable as the street of Kildrummie and the stone bridge over the River Don. One day, she said, "I'm poorly, Arch," and after that she said it once a day, quite matter-of-factly—and she slipped away through five years, like a melody being played softer and softer until it could no longer be heard. Dark Archie went on making guns with Andrew and crafting his few, slow, lovely instruments on Sundays, and his mother went on slowly dying—at last beginning to believe that Jan might be dead, because, if he were, she would find him in death. Until her last months, she had no visible symptoms, other than a string of little lumps like a necklace of gristle around her neck. And she had pain, although she made little sign of it, in her breasts and then in her back, and finally in her liver and her kidneys. The lumps ulcerated and she could hardly draw breath enough to live; her eyes closed and mouth hung open; but she lived on. Archie tended her, changed her bed, washed her and dressed her, cooked foods he thought she would like, held her gently and tried to spoon the stuff into her, and threw it out the back for the birds afterward. And then one night she died, and he went to her pastor's house and rapped on the window, and when the man came and said with a fierce, Presbyterian harshness, "What is it at this hour, man?" Archie answered with his tiny smile, "Me mother's gone to America, dominie. I thought you'd like to pray her on her way."

To the astonishment of all Kildrummie, Dark Archie carried one of his fiddles into the church at the funeral, and then he carried it under his arm to the churchyard, and he stood by the open grave with the instrument in his hands like a loaded gun. When the pastor ordered the casket lowered, and the thing was done and the clods of dirt were thrown in, Dark Archie put the wide curve of the viol against his breastbone and coaxed a melody from it that nobody in all of Aberdeenshire had ever heard—a nagging, disharmonious, keening melody that sounded half like a shepherd's sheep-gut bagpipe and half like a cracked old voice, singing. There were snatches of song in it that people thought they knew, and snatches of the God-fearing hymns they sang on Sundays, but it was all woven and patched together into something wild and fanciful and strange.

"Set the dogs to howling all the way over the Brig o' Don," some said long after.

"Fair give me chills," the poacher Tommie Nick said, for he had been luring a salmon from the unwatched waters while the funeral was going on.

"Very—very *passionate*," the dominie said. He shook his head. "And very godless, I fear. Archibald Morse has taken the Devil to be his teacher of music."

The pastor's view became the town's within a year. At night, they could hear Dark Archie playing to himself, and his infinitely lonely, grating music reached the ears of his townsmen on the night wind like the memory of their mortality. His playing could have come to real trouble, in time, no matter how much Andrew MacPhee told them that Archie was a good, good man, but lonely and peculiar because of his worthless father. Those were tense years in Scotland, with the new English king pressing his subjects, and, first, the king's dour brother, and then his bastard son the Duke of Monmouth coming north to bedevil them, and the kirk splitting again and again, with old Covenant men making a government within the kirk and the government trying to make a church outside it, and every man encouraged to turn against every other.

Dark Archie could have been judged too crazy to live, but he found sanity in a woman.

Her name was Catharine Wardlaw, and she was seventeen when he met her. She was a True Believing Christian of the Old Light who was in the kirk at least three times a week, and she knew with all her heart that Papacy was the work of the Devil, and she knew that the English church was no better. She called Episcopy "the worship of Baal and his priests," and when she said "Amalekites," people were supposed to understand that she meant Royalists. Her mind was closed on these issues, as it was closed on the subject of sin and on her election to membership in the Presbyterian community of the godly. Yet she was ready to love somebody. And she met dour, dark, joking Archibald Morse, who was thirty-nine.

She sang, not like an angel, but like a healthy young woman with passion. He had taken his fiddle to Andrew's house for the contract signing of Andrew's oldest daughter, who was sixteen; he was ready to play the antic jigs that folk could dance to, as he sometimes did. She sang, and he played, and he stared at her open-mouthed, as if he had never seen a woman before in his life.

He loved her so deeply that he went to church with her. He never said that he believed in her God, but he never, by word or deed, so much as hinted that her belief was anything less than sacred to him. Other people in town whispered that she, not the church, was his religion, and they said that any room in which he happened to find her was his church, so daft was he. But neither pastor nor deacons could object to his presence in church on Sundays; rather, they thanked the Lord for his conversion—and the parson said privately to one of his more militant parishioners that God was very timely, converting a gunmaker just when things were bad.

The music that flowed from Dark Archie's viol became godly and sweet and utterly unlike the sounds that had leaped from it before.

"You must not play like that no more, Arch," his bride told him, meaning his old music.

"I mustn't?" He had his viol tucked under his arm and his bow in his hand, ready to play; indeed, he had already scraped out the beginning of a tune when she stopped him.

"Nay, love, for you don't know the effect of the music you make. It's like the pipes they play in the mountains—it's something savage, Arch. It hurts my heart to hear it."

"I mean nothing by it."

"It hurts me."

"Then I'll play it no more. I'll sell the viol."

"No, no, Arch! God gave you the gift to make it and to make music with it; you must use your gift. Remember the parable of the talents. Remember Our Lord taught about the talents, Archie. You must play—but it must be God's music that you play, and not wildness. Wherever did you hear such wild music to begin with, sweet?"

He gave her his little glimmer of a smile. "America," he murmured.

She nodded sadly. "Aye, they all be savages there. It shows." She had all the sweetness of youth—and of ignorance.

He never mentioned it again. He played the music of her God and the music that she and other godly people liked. Only once did he seem to hint at the matter, when the pastor of the kirk introduced him to a tall stranger who had sat for the service that Sunday morning.

"This is Mr. MacLean from the west, Archie! Mr. MacLean is here on the business of the true kirk." His strong, lined face lit up with an enthusiasm that seemed unusual for a clergyman as he said to the visitor, "Archie Morse is the gunmaker I was telling you of, sir."

"Ah, the gunmaker!" the stranger said. He squeezed Dark Archie's hand and studied his eyes. "The kirk needs men of your craft, Mr. Morse. And will need more of them very soon."

The clergyman sighed. "Aye—aye!" He seemed to stand on tiptoe in his enthusiasm. "You could be doing God's work soon, Archie!"

"I would have thought that making guns was the Devil's work, dominie," Dark Archie said mildly.

Both men seemed shocked. "A heretical view!" the minister cried. "A wrong-headed view! You must not be misled by kind hearts, Archie! They use the Devil's logic to argue that a pious man daren't shed good blood in the Lord's name. That's lies! When the day for bloodshed comes, the Lord demands bloodshed—He needs the gun just as He needs the sword! I will preach a sermon on this subject very soon. Used in the name of the Lord, the gun is as godly a weapon as the flaming sword of the angel Michael!"

The stranger leaned forward to tower over Archie. "Your guns is not subject to judgment, gunmaker. A man's got a religion and free will, but a gun's got none."

Dark Archie nodded. His glimmer of a smile showed for a moment, and Andrew, had he seen it, would have known that a joke was coming. "I understand, sir. The gun is sane and godly. It's only the viol that's devilish. I see. I see."

Chapter Eight

She made him smile. Correctly, people supposed that she made him happy. The smile, private, slightly baffled, played often over his face after he married Catharine, as if he were happy now but did not quite understand how he had got that way. His partner at the forge made màny jokes about this new Archie and his smiles. Andrew thought him a changed man— as indeed he was, as indeed many men are at different times of their lives. The faraway Senecas were wiser; they gave men and women new names when they changed into new people; in Kildrummie, they kept the same old names and made jokes when people showed signs of alteration.

When Catharine had their baby, the jokes became more common. Good-naturedly, people wanted to share some of Dark Archie's obvious happiness. The idea of the man in bed with a female—especially a much younger, quite handsome female—moved some men to ribald guffaws (but never when he was close enough to hear, for he was strong enough to toss an anvil about like a log of firewood); it made some of the women in Kildrummie look at him differently, too, wondering what it was that they had missed. Neither Catharine nor Archie ever gave any hint of that part of their lives, however, and so the others simply had to go on joking and wondering.

Dark Archie made an undersized gun and a small viol when the baby was born. "He can take his pick when he's big enough," he said proudly. The gun was a boy's fowler, three feet long and very lightly stocked, with a small pistol lock that he had forged himself on the same lines as the snap-haunces that went into his pistols. Somehow, it was the one gun that was most like his instruments, perhaps because of its delicacy, perhaps because it was made with love.

"A lady's gun it is!" Andrew roared at him. Andrew had gotten paunchy and hoarse-voiced. "You've made your infant a lady's long arm, Arch."

"Nay, 'tis a boy's gun. I never yet did see a lady shoot."

"In England, they say, some of them great ladies as is the wives and the you-know-whats of the nobility do shoot like men, they say, tracking after birds and such on horseback with their skirts tucked up to their bottoms."

"Ah, well, what the *English* do..."

"Still, there be a market there, perhaps, Arch. Imagine, if all the women in the world took up the shooting—we'd sell twice as many fowlers, now wouldn't we?"

"We couldn't make twice as many fowlers, Andrew."

"Aye, but we could give up making them cursed pistols!" The pistols continued to gall Andrew. His distaste for them had little to do with their making any more; it was simply a convenient focus for his dislike of work. He had discovered, at forty, that it was work he disliked most of all in the world, and he wanted as little of it in his life as possible.

Dark Archie smiled. He knew Andrew's views. "Customers are asking us for pistols all of steel now, Andrew. They'd be the devil to make, wouldn't they!" He said it to torment his partner, who groaned and wiped his hands over his face. Andrew looked at him with a lugubrious face and said, "Why can't folks let well enough alone? Why must they have things *improved* all the time?"

Dark Archie finished the lovely little fowler and gave it a last polish so that the luster of its superbly grained little stock glowed as if with an inner light. The blued steel of the lock gleamed against the warm wood; the polished brass on ramrod pipes and trigger winked. He had put the new mark into the top flat of the octagonal barrel; below it, in two lines running three inches toward the muzzle, he had engraved, "For my son Duncan from his father Arch. An. Dom. 1679."

Andrew studied the little gun and the small viol. "Well, which is it you want the tyke to reach for, Archie? The gun or the gut box?"

"I will let him decide, I think, Andrew."

The soft Scots cadence of their voices sounded sleepy in the warmth of the room next to the forge. Evening was falling. It was time for them to head home, and Andrew had already put off his leather apron and taken up his plain, worn coat. "But you must want one or the other for him, surely. It's a father's duty to decide for a child."

Dark Archie seemed surprised. "It is?" He seemed never to have considered the idea before. There was so much that was new about fatherhood for him; he had had so little of a father himself, he had no example in most matters. "No, I don't believe I should make up his desires for him." He seemed truly puzzled. "Surely he will make up his own mind, won't he, Andrew?"

And it was just this forthright—and entirely misplaced—fairness that made Archie's child grow into such a spiteful son. "You never gave me ought!" was his constant cry when he was big enough to defy his father's scowl. "You held all back from me—always you held back!" He seemed to be talking of material things, but what he meant was love. Neither of them quite understood that he meant love, for love was never mentioned between them—or, indeed, in that house, except in darkness and secret, when Archie would whisper to Catharine that he loved her, as if the statement were a treasonable act that must be kept hidden—and both would have been acutely embarrassed by the very word. Duncan Morse grew up bitter about the very lack of demands that Archie put on him, as if the father were a careless god who asked for nothing and who could, as a result, never be pleased.

"What've you ever given me but hard words and silence?" the twenty-year-old Duncan hissed.

"Hush now, Duncan," his mother murmured. At thirty-nine, she was beautiful, with the maturity that takes the adolescent softness from a face. She had borne no other children—not for any lack of love from Archie, surely. It was typical of the time. Families were small in that generation after the plague and the cholera that followed it.

"Let him talk if he wants," Dark Archie said mildly. He held a new viol in his lap and he was plucking the strings softly while his son complained. The sounds had no melody, but Catharine frowned at them, as if she heard the echo of the wild music of his old self.

"Aye," Duncan said bitterly, "let the bairn rave, for who listens? Ain't it always the way, though! I could make a roar like the fall of Jericho, and my father would hardly raise his head from those tools of idleness!"

"I hear you well enough, Duncan," Archie said softly.

"Do you, Father? I doubt it! You hear yon music maker, is all. I could speak as a sounding brass, and you'd not hear me."

"Oh, Duncan, what *is* it then?" his mother asked. She had bent toward him in the firelit room. "Why do you go on and on so?"

"Because I want to be listened to!"

"I listen, Duncan," Dark Archie murmured.

"But you don't *care*."

"Aye, I care."

"You wouldn't send me to university when I wanted to go!"

"I couldn't afford it."

"You could! You got money hid enough to send me three times over!"

"And if I had, would that make it your money? No. Besides, you were needed at the forge."

"What's to become of me, then, with no education?"

"Why—whatever you will."

"But what I *will* is to be educated!"

"Then be so." Dark Archie slid a finger up a vibrating string so that it wailed. "I don't stop you, Duncan."

"But you don't help me!"

"No, and I don't hinder you."

"But—! Pastor Lennox says I got it in me to be a powerful preacher and great thinker in the theological curriculum! Pastor Lennox says I should be right now at Edinburgh to the university!"

"He's very powerful in his opinions, Pastor Lennox is." Archie smiled a little. "Maybe he'd like to pay for your expenses."

"At least he cares what becomes of me!"

"Oh, Duncan," his mother murmured.

Archie plucked a string. He supposed he was stingy. He knew that his son thought so. But the gunworks did not produce the income it had ten years before; Archie would never have said so, but he was doing most of the work now, for Andrew liked to sit and talk and rest his gouty feet, and although he took as much money out of the partnership as ever, he put very little work back in. Thinking of these things, Archie said to his son, "Do you have in mind to be a minister of the kirk, then, you and Pastor Lennox?"

The young man blushed. "If I have the call."

"Ah. The call." Dark Archie's little smile flickered, like a lightning bug's flash in the dusk. *Like my call to make music, perhaps he means. Like my own father's call to wander. Like America.* "Well, you tell me if your call comes, then, Duncan."

Exclaiming bitterly that there was no talking with the man, Duncan swept from the room; they could hear his heavy footsteps overhead in the unheated room where he slept, the groan of his rope bed as he threw himself on it.

"Archie—can you not be a little more understanding?"

"Of what, Catharine?"

"Of his desire. He wants to be *somebody*. And he wants to be somebody in your eyes, if only you'd give him some hope."

"Whatever kind of hope could I give?"

"Hope that he could please you, Archie."

Dark Archie stared into the darkness. "I hear people talk of such things and I never understand them. It never crossed my own mind to try to please my father. And when my time came to be something in life, I didn't think so much of getting what I wanted. Not that I've minded for a minute being gunmaker here. Not for a minute—for it's where I met you. But, as for his wanting to please me—" He shook his head. "The most a man can hope for is to please himself—or to learn to be pleased by what life gives him."

"No." She came to him, touched his shoulder and pulled his head to rest it against her. He was nearing sixty, and the black hair was grizzled. His son thought of him as an old man; she could not. She loved him with a deep, constant love that was like her piety. She did not know it, but she loved her husband too well, at least too well for her son to understand. "No," she said again. "Most men can't live with only pleasing themselves. They ain't like you. Duncan ain't like you. You grew up hard, Archie, with no father to help you and no father to smooth the way for you, and you come out right somehow. But Duncan needs the way smoothed a little. He ain't hard in the way you are. Tell him what you want him to be, and he'll be it."

But Dark Archie was wiser than his wife. "Even if I could do it, Catharine, it'd be too late. He's angry now. An angry, spiteful pup." He embraced her, then crossed the room to lay the new viol on the mantel. It would warm there, and before he went to bed he would rub it again with oil and varnish to make it glow. "Tell him he can go to university to study the theology. But he must live like a poor man's son, for that's what he is."

"Tell him yourself, Archie! He'd be so pleased!"

He held her hands away from his face. "I can't. You tell him."

When she had crossed the room, she heard him say, "I can't give what I don't have, Catharine." She thought he meant money, and then, looking at him as he bent over the fire, his face heavy with dark thoughts, she knew that he meant something else. The knowledge was infinitely sad, and she went out with her right fist clenched between her breasts.

Dark Archie sat by his fire like a man dozing. After half an hour, he crossed to a ceiling-high cupboard that almost filled the end of the room. Opening one of its upper doors, he felt along the top shelf and took down the two things that lay there. He carried them back to the fire and removed their wrappings and held them both in his lap—the small viol and the boy's fowler, both as fine and new as the day they had been made. The gun had been proofed, sighted in, and put away, never shot again. He tightened one of the hand-cut ivory pegs on the viol, and the gut string tightened, sighed as if a wind had blown over it, and snapped.

"Old," he said aloud.

He held the body of the little instrument in his left hand and the neck in his right and with a quick pressure broke it where the fingerboard joined the body. With a furtive look behind, he laid the pieces on the fire and poked it up until the thin wood caught. There he crouched until every fragment of it was burned; he scraped out the charred remnants of the ivory pegs.

Next morning, he dropped the burned pegs into the Don, and the same day he put the boy's fowler in the window of the gunshop.

"Is it for sale, then, Archie?" Andrew asked him wheezily. "I ask only in case a customer wants to know."

"Aye, it's for sale."

"How much?"

He named a figure, fair for a boy's gun, absurdly low for one of such workmanship.

Andrew looked the gun over. The engraving had been ground off and the barrel polished. "It's a good buy, for them's daft enough to want a boy's weapon," he said judiciously.

One day, the gun was gone. Archie never asked about it, but the record of sale appeared in the books: *One Gunne per yonge man's Fowling peese: 11 £ 7s. Scots.*

"Is he happy now?"

"Oh, yes, Archie! It's his heart's desire, he says!"

"I only wanted to know."

Duncan was at the university in Edinburgh. Archie had grown accustomed to having him at the forge in place of Andrew; now he had to pay a journeyman to replace him. Andrew seemed more and more like an old man, wheezing when he tried to work, telling endless stories, complaining

83

of being always tired. He had seven children and he believed that it was time for them to take care of him.

"D'you think I'm hard, Archie, expecting them to provide?"

"I think nothing, Andrew."

"I provided for them 'til they were grown."

"So you did."

"It ain't like I'm asking for something for nothing."

"No, Andrew."

"Well, then."

Andrew MacPhee started coming to the gunshop three days a week, then only two. After a few more halfhearted gestures at helping at the forge, he put his hammers in the rack and told the journeyman he was free to use them, and he hung his apron on a hook and never took it down; he sat at the filing bench, polishing small parts and making minor repairs to some of the guns that were brought in. It was left to Archie to instruct the apprentice and oversee the journeyman, to help to weld barrels and forge locks and parts—more time at the forge, more time with the hammer, more heavy labor. Yet he did not complain, and, in truth, he did not mind.

"It gives me time to think," he said to Andrew.

"Think of what, would you tell me?"

Archie grinned. "I never remember."

Andrew grimaced. "The day I put down that hammer was the happiest day of my life," he growled.

The university did not prove the marvel that Duncan had hoped for, and he did not prove the theological wonder that Pastor Lennox had foretold. The pastor's explanation was that Duncan was too fierce in his piety for the worldly scholars of Edinburgh; he would be better understood in Germany. Duncan went off to Gottingen; Pastor Lennox explained that God had called him there. When Duncan returned two years later with the degree of Master of Arts from Zurich, he explained that Gottingen had been disappointingly tolerant of impieties. Pastor Lennox offered up a prayer of gratitude for the narrow minds of Zurich, and Duncan himself preached a sermon on the text "Vengeance is mine, saith the Lord." People who had known him all their lives shook their heads in astonishment.

"Another Andrew Melville!" Lennox said. "Another Knox!"

"Another mouth for Dark Archie to feed," Andrew MacPhee grumbled. "Two, in fact." He was thinking of the lanky Swiss wife whom Duncan had brought home with him.

"Three," his wife corrected him. She bobbed her head toward the young woman's abdomen. "About four months gone, I'd say."

Andrew cackled; the laughter turned to a wheezing cough. "Oh, the men of God was ever fierce fookers," he was able to say some minutes later.

Magdalena Gottshalk—now Morse—was an intense, brilliant woman with impassioned eyes and a high-pitched voice that seemed always to be giving commands. She spoke little English, and what little she knew was of no help to her with the Scots. She wrote both French and German, read those languages and Latin and Greek. Duncan treated her with a remarkable deference, perhaps because she had published two pamphlets in Switzerland before he met her. It seemed to his parents that he was always apologizing to his wife— for them, for their home, for the town—but they could only guess from his tone, for Duncan and Magdalena conversed in German. A trunk full of books had come with them from Switzerland; both of them read constantly.

"She is a professor's daughter," Duncan said proudly.

"A professor! That's very good, a professor."

Duncan's face clouded. "Muddled in his theology, but a member of the faculty. Hasn't had a new idea since he was weaned, but a member of the faculty. Magdalena has ten times his intellect."

"Ah. The father's muddled. I see."

"She should be the one to join the faculty, not he."

"I wonder you didn't think of joining it yourself, Duncan."

His son stared at Archie and then burst into a harsh laugh. "They wouldn't have me! Are you daft?"

Magdalena's baby was born in Archie's and Catharine's house. A girl, it was named Jane Mary. Catharine cooed over it. Duncan seemed withdrawn, Magdalena spent. Two weeks after the birth, the three of them—Duncan, Magdalena, the baby—were gone with only a day's notice. He had been called to a village near Findhorn.

"She'll spoil her milk!" Catharine complained. "Traveling in this weather!"

Duncan's letters came twice a year—never more frequently, never less. He found a congregation near Cawdor; there was some kind of trouble, and he moved on to Aviemore, where, he said, the people were blockheads; he went to Dalmally, which turned out to be populated with heretics and Amalekites; he went to Ballachulish in the Cameron country. There, the Second Agreement was neglected and the Scriptures were not taken with sufficient severity; still, he thought he might stay. Magdalena was hardly ever mentioned; there was a second child, named John. There was news of weather. There was a letter to tell them that Magdalena had died. There was a letter six months later to say that he had a new wife.

"Oh, Archie," Catharine sighed. "Whatever will become of him?"

"Some of it already has," Dark Archie said. He had wondered often if his father's wanderlust had skipped a generation and lodged itself in Duncan; now he was sure of it.

"Don't you care what becomes of him?" Catharine said.

"I can't change his character. And a man's character is his life, I think."

Tears in her eyes, she hung her head, put her hands over her face. "I'd think you would care—for my sake, if not for his!" She sounded bereft. Archie put his arms around her. "I care the world for you," he whispered. "I'd do anything out of caring for you."

"But, Archie!" She wiped the tears from her eyes with the corner of her long apron. "Look at me, weeping like a girl! Oh, ain't I that daft! Archie, Archie, he's your son! Can't you care for *his* sake?"

He held on to her and they rocked back and forth. "A man can't give from a store was never filled," he said without bitterness.

Chapter Nine

At seventy-six, Dark Archie looked sixty. He had a bit of a paunch, and his skin was slack and finely wrinkled with age, but he stood straight and he had muscles like clenched fists; his hair was white, thin so that the wind tousled it easily; his face was lined, but age had seemed to give it roundnesses on the cheeks and the chin, and color, so that he looked cheerier than he ever had in his life. He was vigorous and keen, and when he rolled away from his wife with a pleased sigh in the night after they had made love, he grinned into the darkness and thought that old age was the best time of his life.

Hammering out the glowing metal at the forge while one apprentice turned the work and another hammered with him, he was the very figure of Vulcan—the old artificer, the old creator who has survived Time's blows. He still did not believe in Catharine's God, but he prayed to Him anyway, prayed that she would not be taken from him. They were like two trees that have grown up all twisted together, mutually dependent, each shaping the other.

His life was shaped—hammered and finished. Or so he thought. Duncan was a disappointment to Catharine, but Archie rarely thought of him. He had got through with less heartbreak than he had expected, way back all those years when his father had gone away for the last time, leaving him with a viol and a mysterious book. And now it was almost finished, and it had been better than he had had any reason to expect, and the surprises and the changes were over. Or so he thought.

He was sitting at the filing bench on a rainy day when the shop door opened and Change—in the person of a girl of about twelve—put its head in.

"Please, sir, is this Archibald Morse's shop?" She was eyeing the guns on the walls behind him, as if she had expected to see guns and was confirming that expectation. A little behind and above her on the outside of the door, there was a wooden sign that said, "Morse and MacPhee, Guns and

Angling Tackle," and he supposed she had seen it and was simply being polite.

"It is, then." Dark Archie's voice was very deep now. He had a voice he used for children, so as not to scare them.

"Please, sir, I'm looking for Mr. Morse."

"I'm him."

"Then I'm your granddaughter Jane. And I've brought young John with me."

He saw two huge eyes in a starved-looking face whose intelligence and beauty were unmistakable, despite the dirt and the matted hair and the expression of mixed slyness and terror. There was no question in Dark Archie's mind but that the girl leaning in from the rain was the dead Magdalena's child, for he remembered well that narrow face. Over her shoulder he saw another figure huddled under the eave to escape a little of the wet, though his clothes were so soaked that he could hardly have been wetter than he was.

"Come in, girl."

"And John, too?"

"Why, of course! And don't stand there gawking, girl, get in; well, *pull* him in if he don't want to come! What ails the boy? Is he simple?"

"No, sir. He's scared."

The boy must be ten, was his thought, but this child before him seemed much younger, for he was the size of a six-year-old. Dark Archie looked keenly into the two faces, noting again the girl's extreme thinness. "You two eaten?" he said shrewdly. Both hung back. "You *have* eaten, then?"

"We—oh, sir, we don't know what we're to say!"

"Why, say the truth!"

They looked at each other. There was a strange bond between them, one more powerful than he was accustomed to between children. They were questioning each other silently.

"Come along, let's get you some food and dry clothes," he said. "Can you walk?"

"We been walking all day, sir. Can walk a bit more. Don't you live here, then?"

"No. This is only the shop. Come on, then." He dragged a heavy cloak across his broad shoulders. He was grinning despite himself. "Your grandmama's got a surprise coming."

Catharine was surprised indeed—and frightened, he thought, although he could not guess of what. She bustled the two children into the kitchen and poured out big bowls of soup for them and followed that with the remains of a chicken from the cold room. She sliced dark bread for them and laid out a crock of their own butter from the cow that had been making the trip from their shed to the village common for thirteen years. When they were done eating, both of them looking sleepy and puffed, she took them up to the room that had been Duncan's. Some minutes later, she was down again with her arms full of comforters.

"It's too cold; they can't sleep up there."

"What is it, Catharine?" He stopped her as she bent to improvise a bed in front of the fire. "Come, I know when you're fretting. What is it?"

There were tears in her eyes. "They got marks on them, Archie—both of them. Marks you wouldn't—" She shook her head angrily. "Marks you wouldn't put on a dog had bit you in the road! Them children have been beaten, Archie. They got welts and bruises; the little boy's got a sore that won't heal along his shoulder."

"What do they say about them?"

"They don't say nothing. Won't tell me." She shook her head again and stooped to arrange the bedding. "They just look at each other."

"Aye, they're uncommon close." He took down a viol and plucked its string to see if it was tuned. "Well, ask them no more tonight. We'll see about it tomorrow."

"Archie, I know as well as I know my Bible that those children have been beat! And I ain't sending them out of this place until I know they won't be beat no more!"

His thick fingers plucked a string as he slowly tightened a peg. "We'll see." His smile glimmered. "We're a might old for changes, Catharine."

Even next day, the boy hardly spoke. He was like some small animal that had been caught in the house. The girl, on the other hand, was voluble; Archie sensed that she chattered to protect herself. On the third day, he and Catharine sat with her while the boy dozed in a chair, still worn out. Catharine held the girl's hands.

"Who whipped you, Jane Mary?"

"Ma'am?"

"You got the marks of a flogging on your legs and your bottom, girl; I seen you without your clothes. Who did it?"

The girl looked at them both, glanced at the sleeping boy, and said, very low but very evenly, "My father and his wife, ma'am."

"Why, child?"

"Because I'm bad. I'm very bad."

"What did you do?"

"The last time, I stole milk."

"And John. What did John do?"

"He shat his drawers. When they scolded him for standing up for me. He's so scared of Pa, you see."

"And your father and his wife, where are they? At Ballachulish?"

"No, ma'am. They went away to Holland, I think. Or they said they were going there."

"To Holland!"

"Yes, ma'am. My pa, he was in trouble. Not trouble, for he's God's voice, but the Devil worked in folks to stir them up agin him, and made the constables come to take him."

"What sort of trouble?"

"I don't know!" She looked at them again. "Truly, I don't know! You won't whip me!"

"Of course not," Dark Archie growled. His huge hand touched her skinny shoulder. "But your father is our son, Jane Mary. What you tell us is a troubling thing to us. Now, you say he's in trouble and he's gone away to Holland, and here you are in Kildrummie. Now, how come your father's gone over the water and you ain't?"

"It's—it's all my doing. Not Johnnie's at all. You'll leave Johnnie out of it, won't you? He's ever so much a follower! He does whatever I do. He's not simple, he's not, *really,* but he follows me so! Well, it's because I'm bad. I run off from them. From Pa and his wife. There, now I told you—that's the thing I done, I run off, and poor Johnnie followed me like the little dog that he is. He'd leap in Loch Katrine if I but told him to. Well? Are you going to whip me?"

"We don't whip people in this house, no matter what they do. But whyever did you run away from your own father and mother?"

"She ain't my mother!" Anger flashed from the thin face. Archie wondered if the meekness and the polite chatter were merely a show to hide such rage; if so, she might well be a dangerous child and one who had earned her whippings. The truth, he supposed, lay somewhere in a combination of rage and meekness—the emotions of the weak. He sighed at the eternal, damnable complexity of human nature. *I'm too old,* he thought. *Too old for change.* "Janie," he said very slowly and very carefully, so low in his chest that his voice was like

90

the rumble of a cart going over Brig o' Don, "why did you run off?"

"To excape beating. They was off to Holland in the dead of night; they waked us up and give us tea and said to shush, put on a dress and go outside, we was leaving that hour for Holland. And then—and then—" The girl's smooth chatter seemed to desert her. "Please, I can't say it."

"A body can say anything, child. Saying's only words."

"It's indecent."

"Whisper it, then."

The girl swallowed hard. She clutched Catharine's hands very tight and would look only at her. "Pa's wife said I'd— *bled*—in the bed, and she swore I was a creature of the Devil. She said I was too young for such as that and it was Satan's work and she was going to beat me so I'd stop." She was blushing a purplish red. Catharine looked at her quite steadily and said, "Had you ever bled before, Jane Mary?"

"No, ma'am."

"And it came at night, just like that?"

"Yes, ma'am. On my nightdress and the bedclothes. She said—that Johnnie and I, we was—doing things together in the bed, that's why. *But we wasn't!*"

"And did you bleed more after that night?"

"Some. But when we was walking across country, it stopped."

"So what you did was, you ran away from your father and his wife while they were packing to go to Holland, is that it?"

"Yes, ma'am, because she was going to have Pa birch me, and I know him when he's upset like he was that night, he's very cruel, and I still hurt from the last beating they give me and I was too scared to think—and I dressed like she told me, only when I went outside I just kept a-going. And when I looked back, there come my dog Johnnie, trotting along behind. And here we are. Will you send us back?"

Catharine patted the girl's thin hands. "I won't send anybody to where they'll get a beating, child."

Lying in the bed with her arms around Dark Archie, Catharine murmured, "We'll have to prove the truth of it, Archie. Write to Ballachulish." She sighed. "But, oh, if my Duncan done that to a child—!" Her breath was warm on his neck. "What sort of man did we raise up, Archie?"

His letter to his son at Ballachulish was not answered. His letter to the elders of his church brought a quick reply, however: "Pastor Morse is flown to a place unknown." In its wake came a sheriff's man of Aberdeenshire, who wanted to question Archie very closely about Duncan and who looked suspiciously about the gunshop as if he thought one of the dozen guns hanging near him might be aimed his way.

"Where is your son then, Mr. Morse?"

"He ain't at Ballachulish."

"We know where he *ain't*, Mr. Morse. Where he *is* is what we hope to learn."

"I've had no word from Duncan in four months. What's he done, that you're so after him?"

"Sedition."

"What sort of sedition?"

"Sedition is all I was told. The kind don't matter."

Dark Archie did not need to be told the "kind." In a nation where kirk and government were intertwined, the seditious opportunities offered to a minister were many and varied. Many ministers hated the Act of Union with England; their saying so—and their sometimes open encouragement of violence in opposition to it—made them seditious. And Duncan, he knew, would not have been a man to temper any opinion.

Dark Archie sighed. *Too old. I'm too old for this.*

But he and Catharine made a home for their grandchildren.

Perhaps there was some sort of devil in Jane Mary, he concluded. She had a hidden self that came out in curious, unpredictable ways—an antic wit (a throwback, had he known it, to his own father's childhood wit), a defiant self-destructiveness when she was angry. Most of the time she was an obedient, cheerful girl; her rare, devilish self was the price that they—and she—had to pay.

Johnnie was a different case. Hardly a word came from his mouth in his first weeks with them; nonetheless, they could hear two voices at night from the makeshift bed by the fire. To Archie's surprise, Catharine insisted that the two children sleep separately. "She's a very grown-up girl," she said obliquely. "And he's a very easy-led boy."

"But, Catharine!" Dark Archie pondered what she meant. "They're both too young, surely."

"Maybe they are. And maybe they aren't."

Catharine spoke to Jane Mary, and Jane Mary spoke to John, and after that she slept alone in front of the fire and Johnnie, upset, spent several nights in Archie and Catharine's bed, until Archie, clinging to the sexual desire that was his pride, told Catharine he wanted her to himself. Off went weeping Johnnie to the cold room that had once been Duncan's; they heard him crying for several nights, and then he found some means of dealing with his new solitude. Neither he nor they quite understood it, but in his separation from Jane Mary he saw a hint of independence, and he was drawn by it.

John found a sympathy in Dark Archie that the man's own son never had. So it often is between grandfather and grandchild, no matter what father and son have been: Dark Archie took John with him to the gunshop, kept him by his side while he carved the pieces for yet one more dulcimer—very slowly now, and with the work held close to his eyes. When he played one of his instruments, the boy sat next to him, daring, after the first months, to press himself close to the warm, smelly old body.

"Ye've taken my dog away, I think," Jane Mary said to him. Her eyes had a look he had come to recognize as part of her edged humor. "Dog-napping's a hanging offense in sheep country."

"I've only borrowed him, Janie."

Her face darkened suddenly. "People never come back." It was as if her devil had spoken. Yet, minutes later, she was singing and telling jokes in the kitchen.

Her voice was light, but she was a good singer; she and Catharine made duets while Archie played. Johnnie was interested in the music, but only as a listener; he refused Archie's offer to teach him to play. "Well, Old John," Archie said, "it's a wise man that knows his tastes." The nickname stuck; with his remarkable gravity, he was Old John to everybody. Jane Mary started calling her grandfather Young Archie in response, and he was delighted, although he knew there was a touch of malice in the name.

Old John, though he refused the viol, showed a great interest in the guns. At first the forge had terrified him; later, he admitted that he had thought it was the mouth of Hell, and in the working of the great bellows he had thought he had heard Satan's greedy breathing. He was full of fancies. In time, however, he became accustomed to the forge, and Archie knew he was quite at home when one day he put on a glove and drew a piece of work from the firepit when the apprentice was off in the shop.

"There, sir," he said proudly.

"Why, thankee, Old John! But you must lay it straight on

the anvil, d'you see? No need to hand the tongs to me. Now it's cooled down too much to hammer, you see? For the color's gone to a bruise. But you done it well, boy, you done it well; stand by me and be ready to pull another, will you, while Tom's in the shop?"

Andrew MacPhee tottered down to the shop, as he liked to do now and then. Archie said that Andrew was "far gone," an assessment that was not without vanity because of his own greater health. Andrew wheezed like a chimney and he could not walk ten steps without stopping. He was getting senile, too. Still, he liked to come down and sit in the shop.

"Old John," he would say, looking at the boy. The name amused him mightily. "Old John, Old John." One day he proudly brought a long bundle into the shop. "I've brought Old John a present," he wheezed.

"Now what?" Dark Archie muttered. Andrew was something of a trial to him.

"It's a present for Old John."

"Aye, so you said, Andrew."

"What?"

"I said, 'You said that, Andrew.' What is it?"

"It's a present for Old John."

"Aye, you told me that!"

"What?"

Old strings had to be cut; cloth, which had once been oily, was now stiff and hard and had to be cut away. The layers of cloth stuck together, and when they were pulled apart they made a sound like cracking ice. Still, before the last one came free, Dark Archie knew what was inside them, and he dropped his hand affectionately on Andrew's shoulder.

"It's a present I brought for Old John," Andrew said.

"Aye, Andrew."

It was the gun he had made for Duncan's birth almost forty years before. Hard to imagine that this bright, polished thing had lain virtually unchanged while he was growing old, but there it lay, its wood like a warm pool. Old John hung back from it but stared with fascinated eyes.

"Your grandda made this for your da when he was just a wee thing like a finger," Andrew said. "He didn't know I had it!" Andrew cackled and wheezed. "But I fooled him! I had it all the time—saving it for you!"

"For me, sir?"

"Yes, for you! I knew some boy'd be along. Now, you take this gun. It's the best gun that ever your grandda made, and

I'll tell you how I come to have it. When your da was born—" Andrew grasped one of the small hands and pulled the boy in close and began a long, rambling tale of the making of the gun that was as remarkable for its inventions as for its accuracy. Archie gently took up the gun, sighted down its barrel and rubbed its wood, while the boy stood within the circle of Andrew's arm, licking his lips.

"Spot of rust on the lockplate," Archie murmured. "But you took good care of it, Andrew. You're a sly thing, taking this gun and making out it was sold."

"It was sold! It was sold to me!"

"I'll pay back the money you gave."

"You will not! I bought it, and it's my gift for—for—" Andrew searched for the name. "For this boy here."

"Will you take care of such a gift, John?"

"Oh, yes, Grandda!"

"Will you never point it at no man nor animal, and never raise it even for a joke, and never pull back yon cock until I teach you how to shoot it?"

"Yes, yes, Grandda!"

"And you'll do as I teach you with it?"

"Yes, Grandda!"

The boy handled the gun as if it were a relic. It came close to being too big for him, so undersized was he. To Archie's surprise, John did not try to hoist the gun to his shoulder as most children might, nor did he play with it at soldiers or highwaymen.

"Thank you, sir," he said to Andrew. And all that evening, he sat with it on his lap, asking Archie again and again, *Is it mine? Is it mine to keep?*

In time—almost promptly on his six months' schedule—a letter came from Duncan. He was in Delft. "Driven by envy and the work of Satan," he had moved his family to Holland, he wrote, "except for the two children of Magdalena Gottshalk, who are disobedient and a vexation." He asked that his parents keep alert for news of these two, and, if they heard anything, to notify him at once. Dark Archie thought a long time about the matter, and then, laboriously, he wrote to tell his son that the children were with him and Catharine, "where they will stay until you prove your caring for them better than you dun thus far." Six months later, another letter came from Delft. And another six months after that. And so on, every six months. The children were never mentioned.

When Johnnie Morse was twelve, Andrew MacPhee died. Old John walked behind the coffin next to Dark Archie, all the way to the churchyard. He had tears for the old man, for his own tormented childhood had found a friend in the senile childhood of the aged man.

Jane was fourteen and had the body of a woman. A young man presented himself to Archie as her suitor; he was a farmer in his mid-twenties. Archie was astonished. He sent the man away, telling him to return in four years.

"Too late by then, I fear," Catharine sighed.

"She's only fourteen!" Dark Archie complained.

"I was seventeen when I caught your eye. And not the woman she looks now."

"Aye, but—"

Dark Archie thought it over. "Maybe I should have told that fellow to come back in four months, not four years. Oh, me! I'm too old for all of this, Catharine—too old, too old!"

Chapter Ten

I belong to John Morse of Kildrummie. I was made by Archibald Morse A.D. 1679.

"But it ain't 1679, Grandda. Not by far."

"No, Old John. But that's when I made this gun, you see."

"It don't look so old."

"No, nor ever would, if it's took proper care of. A good gun will last you centuries, I suppose, if it's cared for." He hesitated. "My own da had a gun had been made a century and a half before his time, he said." He had begun to tell his grandson about his father; he took it as a sign of his own aging, for he had never talked to anybody about Jan Morse.

"What happened to your da's gun?"

"I don't know. He took it away with him."

"Where?"

"I don't know. He never said."

"Maybe it's still—someplace, waiting for us to find it."

"Maybe. Maybe."

"Did it have the Morse mark?"

"An old one, yes."

The boy touched the breech of the little gun. "Like this mark."

"Somewhat like that one, yes."

Old John was still a serious child, and he took the matter of the Morse marks and the Morse history seriously, as if he would find in them a substitute for the fatherhood he had lost. Still, he was capable of a perfectly childish delight, as in his response to the actual shooting of the gun.

"What should I aim at?"

"Air."

"Rabbits? Grouse?"

"Air. And when you've learned to hit the air, you'll shoot at stumps. Let the rabbits and the grouse live for another year or three."

The little gun lived above Old John's bed in the unheated upstairs room. In time, other treasures appeared on the wall around it—a hat that had been Archie's once; a crude woodcut of an angler, from a broadside; a raven's skull that he found

97

out on the moor. He could be found often in the outdoors, in good weather and in bad—not with the gun, unless Archie was with him—hunting birds' eggs and odd bits of wood and stone. He returned always with his pockets full, and Catharine always scolded him for his clutter.

"He's a miser, Archie. He hoards everything!"

"He's only making himself at home in the world."

"But I can't clean his room! Piles of this and that everywhere—he'll be bringing rats home in some of the stuff he fills his pockets with."

"He's finding who he is."

And he was growing. Not shooting up—that would come later—but filling out "like a proper boy," as one of the neighbors said. He could lift the hammers at the forge, although he still needed both hands for the biggest ones. He was not yet the right size for his age, but he was catching up.

And Jane Mary was rushing on ahead of him, disappearing into maturity while he tried, unsuccessfully, to stay with her. She was a woman suddenly—at sixteen, the prettiest in Kildrummie (and in Alford and Inverurie, it was said)—and the sooner she married the better was the common wisdom. Her quick, rich laughter invited attention; there was no doubt she liked being courted. Young men surrounded her, but she seemed to favor none. "They're only boys," she said scornfully to her brother, who complained about them, jealous of all.

"Why does she have to do all that carry-on?" Old John complained. "Making a fool of herself for fools."

"People ain't guns, Old John." They were climbing the low hills beyond the town. The boy would run ahead like a dog and then drop back to match his grandfather's slow pace. "People grow up and change. You can't give them a polish and keep them the same as they always was."

"She don't need all that grinning and gawking that goes on." The boy sounded stubborn.

"She does indeed."

"She *don't!* She's got happiness with you and Grandmama and me. What's she need that nonsense for?"

"To be her own self, Old John. She's got to marry and go off someplace and be herself, and you must set that fact in your heart."

But the boy's look was sullen, as if he had been scolded; he strode on ahead of the old man with his head bent. Stubborn, lonely, willful, he slouched against the wind, and Dark Archie thought he was very like any other fourteen-year-old

98

who had been crossed. Trying to keep up with the boy, he heard himself breathing too heavily. His joints hurt. *Too old.* He hated to admit that his body had betrayed him, but he knew it had: the hammers were getting heavier, the slopes steeper. *Too old.*

The boy waited for him.

"When I was young," Dark Archie said between gasps for breath, "the one thing I thought I wanted in all the world—don't start off yet, John, I can't—was for my own da to stay to home. But he never did. He was a fly-by-night man, never in one place for long. I'd think he was there, and then—he was gone."

"Where?"

"America." Dark Archie grinned. "Or maybe that's only a way of speaking. I think that's where he went." Dark Archie's long arm wrapped itself around the boy's thin shoulders. "You mustn't let somebody else make you bitter, Johnnie, wishing for them to be what they ain't. Wishing for a fantasy—to have my da to home—made me dour. It's no way to waste your youth."

The boy seemed not to breathe. He said, so softly that Archie could hardly hear, "It's only that I never been without her."

"Aye. But tell yourself *now* that you're going to spend your life without her. Don't fight, John. Don't eat out your heart for something's going off to America." He squeezed the boy's shoulders, and Old John looked up, in his eyes a haunted understanding that made the old man's chest ache. He squeezed again. "There ought to be a grouse down in yon brambles; go shoot him to please your grandma."

When the Man came into Jane Mary's life, she stopped laughing. One day, she was the witty young woman, seventeen now, always laughing at one of her suitors; suddenly she was quiet, moping in dim corners or rushing off to some unknown place where, Archie supposed, the Man must be. She denied that anything was different, but she could not hide the change.

"What ails her, do you suppose?" Archie said to John. They were at the bench, filing lock parts.

"She don't talk to me no more."

"Can't you guess what ails her, Old John?" Archie was amused. One of the virtues of being eighty was that life seemed more comical than ever. "She's in love, John."

"With who?"

"Why, some fellow, I suppose. You're her brother; ain't you seen her with anybody new?"

"I have not!" John pushed the file angrily over a rough edge. "But I will!"

The Man's name was Matthew Ferguson and he was rich—rich by their standards, at any rate, rich enough to be visiting a great house in the neighborhood and rich enough to be a lawyer in Edinburgh. He had seen her for the first time when he was fishing for salmon in the Don and she had laughed at him for falling in when he had tried to gaff his own fish, his servant being too excited to do it. He had played the fish then, "up to his oxters in cold water," as she told it a hundred times thereafter, always laughing, and she had waited on the bank with the gaff, to thrust it under the white belly and lift the eighteen-pounder from the shallows for him. They had been meeting for some time before any of the rest of them knew of it; John followed her one day and saw her and Ferguson meet.

"Alone, were they?" The old man sighed. His face looked very dour and very tired.

"Aye, sir, but naught—naught happened." The boy blushed. "I was there with my gun to march the bastard straight here if he tried aught."

"Mind your tongue."

"Your pardon, sir."

"Meeting her on the sly, is he?" Dark Archie glowered. "He's ashamed of her, then. The bastard!"

It was easy enough to discover where the young man was staying, and a letter sent in care of his host, poorly spelled and laboriously written, could not be ignored by him; the right, after all, was on Dark Archie's side. He put the matter very plainly: Mr. Ferguson would have the courtesy to present himself at Mr. Morse's house, or Mr. Morse would avail himself of the law.

Mr. Ferguson presented himself.

He was of a type that Kildrummie saw but rarely, the Scottish gentleman cast in the English mold. He wore a sword and carried himself very straight, and he was witty and educated and good-looking in a way that made Johnnie Morse furious. A snob and an aristocrat, he was the very model for all that the boy would come to despise in the class far above him; yet he was as respectful toward Archie and Catharine as anyone could have asked. When, however, Dark Archie ordered Catharine and the weeping Jane Mary from the room,

100

Ferguson looked with obvious disdain at the undersized boy who remained with them.

"John Morse will stay," Archie said. "You're as answerable to him as to me, Mr. Ferguson."

Ferguson might have smiled—"answerable" gentlemen wore swords, after all—but it was to his credit that he did not.

"Mr. Ferguson, you done us an insult." Dark Archie sat, hunched, waiting for an answer.

Ferguson blushed. "Unintentionally, I assure you."

"No, Mr. Ferguson, ye lie, forgive me for saying it—ye lie to yourself or to me and John, it don't matter which. You've insulted us, and if it was not done with intent, it was done at least out of carelessness. I hope you have the wit to be ashamed."

"Why, yes, sir, I am."

"You've caused yon girl to sneak about, a thing she's never done before. You've caused her to set her heart on you—nyah, don't object, man; be honest!—and it's a foolish hope you've inspired in her."

"I encouraged no falseness, sir."

"Oh? What do you intend, then?"

It was put so bluntly that Ferguson, who had been standing, asked if he could sit and then did so, trying to draw words into sensible order. "I made Jane no promises," he was able to say after some seconds. He was, after all, very young—twenty, perhaps.

"Havers to your promises," Dark Archie said brutally. "Don't give me lawyer's talk. You let her run after you—that's enough!"

"There has been no dishonor, I assure you."

"By your standards or mine, Mr. Ferguson?"

Ferguson clambered to his feet, stumbling a little over his sword. "I am a gentleman, sir!" He was breathing very quickly. "It pains me to risk offending an old man, but you—are not—" He quieted himself with a deep breath. "You are not of a position to question my honor."

"Well, if he don't, I will," Old John said. His voice was thin. "Are you going to marry Jane, Ferguson?"

Ferguson turned away. "I'm damned if I'll answer questions from a boy!"

"Be damned then," Dark Archie growled, "for it's a good question. Are you?"

Ferguson sat down again. He licked his lips. "My father

101

would never let me." He sounded more boyish than John. "Marriage is out of the question."

"But you knew that the first time you saw her, Mr. Ferguson." Dark Archie seemed to crouch in his chair like a beast that might spring. "So what were you playing at with the girl? Don't tell me about your honor; your honor ain't worth tuppence! We got a bull in town knows more about honor than you, for he *honors* the fence that keeps him from the cows—*and you don't!* If there's a fence between her and you, then honor it! Now get out of my house."

The young man rose. His face was without color and he was trembling—lips, knee, the hand that touched the sword. "Out of respect for your age, I shall let those words go, Mr. Morse." He turned to the door. "Kindly explain my going to your granddaughter."

"And mind you stay away from her," Dark Archie growled. "Else you'll find what sort of guns I make!"

Jane looked stricken, seemed numb. She did not understand what had happened. Johnnie seemed triumphant. He wanted her to share that sense of triumph; he was as lively, as gay, as she had always been. Now it was she who was the gloomy and quiet one. She sat through supper without speaking, without eating. She was silent when they all sat together afterward. Then, as they all began their goodnights, she looked at the three of them. Her demon was in her face and her voice was hard.

"Couldn't you let be?" she said slowly. "Couldn't you have let happen what would have happened?"

"Janie—it was for your own good—!"

"And what good is that?" She stood up, a fury roused. "Not *my* good—*yours!* Your old man's good! You and Johnnie, it's your good you care about, *man's* good—you don't want another man to have me—ain't that the word you use, *have?* He *had* her? He *took* her? He *possessed* her? Well, I wanted him to, don't you understand that? I wanted him to and I asked him to and he wouldn't! I love him and if I could have done it, I'd have give myself to him—*with all my heart!* And no old men nor little boys would have come between. Ever! *That's* all the good I wanted, and now you've spoiled it all!"

In the morning, she was gone. There was no note. Nothing had been taken. She was simply gone, in the clothes on her back.

John took the little gun from the wall above his bed and stalked off toward the great house where Ferguson was staying; Archie's commands to stay home were ignored. He was gone all day. Late in the afternoon, a farmer brought him home in a cart. He had been beaten, and his hands were broken.

"Oh, God, Johnnie, Johnnie—what happened?"

His lips were swollen and brown with dried blood. He muttered, "Gamekeepers. Said I was poaching. They took—my gun."

The little fowler was returned next day. It had been broken off at the wrist. There was a brief note from Ferguson's host: the gun was being returned "to its maker, who might know where the owner could be found. His lordship must warn Mr. Morse that making poacher's guns was a dangerous business."

Dark Archie burned the letter. He climbed slowly to the boy's room, feeling old and impotent. Johnnie's hands, wrapped in white cloth, lay on the cover like the huge paws of a puppy. He had been tended by a publican who had once learned to set bones in the army.

"You in bad pain, Old John?"

"It don't matter."

"I could fetch a tot of whisky."

"It don't matter." His tongue licked his thick lips. "Three of them. Three big hunkers. Held me down and smashed my hands with their boots." He looked above his head at the vacant space on the wall where the gun had hung. "I'm sorry about the gun."

"His lordship sent the gun back. It'll take a mite of fixing."

"The bastards! I'll shoot them next time!"

"No, Johnnie! It ain't our place to fight with the guns we make. That's wrong, thinking that way."

"And *him,* too!" He licked his swollen lips again. "Now it's too late. Now she's gone and been with him for a night and she must take the consequences." With the terrible righteousness of youth, he judged his sister and pronounced his sentence. "She's dead. Yesterday was the day of my sister's death."

"Ah, Johnnie—"

"She's as dead to me! Now, I don't want to hear of it ever again." He turned his face away and closed his eyes and pretended to sleep.

Chapter Eleven

As if the loss of his sister marked the end of part of his own life as well as of hers, John changed. In the year after, he shot up "like a teasel in the heat," Catharine said, and suddenly he was a tall, slouched youth with narrow shoulders and a spine that seemed to know only curves.

Dark Archie died when he was sixteen. The death was not sudden or violent, but an easy letting go, as if the grip of those huge old hands had wearied, after so long, of holding tight to things. He was sick for a week with what seemed to be the rheum, and then he weakened and fell into longer and longer sleeps. Once, waking to find Old John sitting next to him, he wet his lips and tried to speak and made no sound, and then he tried it all over again and John heard him murmur, "Going, Old John." The dim, distant smile touched his face. "Going to America."

John followed the coffin to the churchyard as he had followed Andrew MacPhee's. He did not weep this time.

Catharine, her lifelong companion gone, was bereft. Her life was locked into Archie's; with Archie dead, her life was locked into his absence. After ten days of near silence, she became short-tempered. Her loss made her nasty; she scolded the boy, banging the food dishes down in front of him as if the noise she made were a complaint to Heaven about her loss.

"Grandmama, what have I done?"

"You done naught."

"I done somewhat, I can tell. You're mispleased with me."

"It ain't you. Let be!"

With Archie gone, there was no natural relationship between them, for they had existed within his presence. After a month of tension, John told her he was going to look for a place as a gunsmith in another town.

"Where? Can't bear me, I suppose."

"There's heaps I got to learn about the craft. There's no gunsmith in Kildrummie now."

"What your grandfather taught you ain't good enough, I suppose."

"None better, Grandmama. But I got more to learn."

"Well, you ain't a fool," she said grudgingly. "And it can't be much for a boy, living with a mean old woman who'd rather be dead." Her clear eyes snapped at him. "Don't deny it; I know I've turned into a mean old woman. I hear myself nattering on, trying to—" Her voice wavered. "I want my Archie back!" she cried. Johnnie stood for a moment in the still room, awkard, embarrassed, helpless; then he slouched away.

He found a gunsmith in Pitlochry who would take him under bond. Catharine lent him the money from a private store of coins. "Old woman's comfort," she said bitterly. "Look at it—that's what you get to keep from a lifetime."

He closed up the shop and took down the battered sign that read, "Morse and MacPhee, Guns and Angling Tackle." She encouraged him to take the tools he would want; the others, and the unfinished guns, the parts, the extra locks and the hand-cut screws and all the leftovers of a shop that had been in the same place for sixty years, he carried back to the house and stored in his own old room. The anvils were put in the cowshed with the dismantled bellows. He had packed one thing with his own tools—the ancient book that Dark Archie had kept in a drawer of his shop table and that he had taken out to show his grandson sometimes, *Of Divers Things Founde in the Newe Worlde Called America.*

When he left at dawn, she clung to him like a young girl and asked him to forgive her.

"Naught to forgive," he blundered. "I ain't him—I can't be. Naught for either of us to forgive in that."

It was October. He walked to Pitlochry with a bundle on his back, like a peddler, and lived in a loft room smaller than the one he had slept in at Dark Archie's. His broken hands were gnarled like an old man's, twisted as tree roots. At night, he read by candlelight when he could afford a candle, and he carefully wrote in a continuation of Jan Morse's family tree that brought the line down to himself.

In April, a coach rumbled up to Catharine's door and a well-dressed woman got out, and a maid with a baby followed her, and when Catharine saw who she was she held out her arms as if Dark Archie himself had come back from the grave by coach. "Jane Mary—Jane Mary!" Her arms could grip like a man's, and the young woman squealed in mock fright.

"You look such a lady, girl!"

"I'm Mistress Ferguson now!"

The maid with the baby hung back, grinning stupidly.

105

Catharine pulled Jane inside and lowered her voice. "Married?"

"Aye! Almost from the day I left."

"Why didn't you tell us, then, girl? Archie would of—"

"I was angry." She shrugged. She was a grown woman now, and the movement seemed to express an adult's regrets. "Don't let's hash it over, Grandmama. It's done. I guess the hurt's been about even all around, so what's the use me going on about it?"

Catharine shook her head. "And you're a great lady!"

"I'm a wife, is all." Jane Mary smiled sadly. "Never a lady, I'm feared."

She told her grandmother that Matthew Ferguson had struck a bargain between his own emotions and his father's snobbery: he had married her, but with a contract that placed her beyond any claim to his inherited position or wealth. She was his wife; neither she nor her child had any claim in law. She lived in a small house in Leith with the maid and her baby; Ferguson lived now in Edinburgh. "I'm a species of secret, d'you see?" she said with forced gaiety. Her old wit had turned inward for its subject. "I'm the wife nobody talks about. How's Johnnie?"

"Why—Johnnie's fine. What d'you mean, the wife nobody talks about?"

"Oh, in Edinburgh they don't know about me. Matthew ain't the eldest son, so there's no great fuss about his primo-what-d'you-call-it; his pa had meant him for an heiress, and now he must make do with me. Which he does. After his fashion. Where's Johnnie, down to the shop?"

"The shop is closed, Jane Mary. Johnnie's gone off another place to learn gunsmithing. Janie, Janie, you don't mean he's making you live like a—"

"I live like a wife, and that's an end of it!" The demon of her childhood looked fiercely from her eyes. "Ach, come, let's not be sharp. I come to take you home with me for a bit—Johnnie, too, I thought, once I'd brought him around." She chuckled. "So, me dog's run off."

Catharine touched her hand. "He's grown up, Jane Mary. Like you."

"Aye." She chuckled again. "When I was a kiddie, I never thought it'd be the best part of my life. Well!" She became brisk. She strode about, touching things she remembered. "You know I'm sorry about Grandpa—you do know that, don't you? But I couldn't—couldn't—"

106

"I understand."

"Will you come home with me?"

"Oh, well—I don't know how I could leave—but—" She cuddled the baby. She scolded the maid and bossed Jane Mary. She cooked for them and made them both eat, and, although she did not treat the maid as an equal, she certainly treated her like a relation. After two days, she went off to Leith with them in the coach, having found with Jane Mary the relationship she could not find with John.

In Pitlochry, Johnnie was finding a quite different world. The currents of the time moved more quickly there, and it was a rare being who could ignore the political feelings of the place. Men spoke openly of the Martyrdom of the Murrays and the Uprising of 'Sixteen—but most of all, they spoke of the Cause.

The Cause!

To see a Stewart back on the Scottish throne, that seemed the goal of every other man he met. No matter that the Stewarts were Catholic; no matter that they had been kings of both Scotland and England and were now deposed; the Cause demanded that a Scottish Stewart sit on the throne of Scotland! To have somebody of the House of Hanover—a German! —usurping that divine right from faraway London was so offensive to these Scotmen that they cursed when they talked of it, and when they pronounced "the Cause," they rolled the words like fine whisky in their mouths.

Dark Archie had been Johnnie's anchor, although he had not known it. Dark Archie had been beyond the contentions of most men. *Guns have no religion.* If these same currents had ever swept through Kildrummie, Dark Archie would have held like a rock, and he would have held Johnnie; now, that anchor gone he was unsteady, and he felt himself rolled one way and another like a stone on a windward shingle. He heard Old Line Covenanters dispute with Stewart Royalists; he watched as Catholics grew hot in their debates with Strong Kirkers. Patriotic Scotsmen confused him by favoring the Hanoverian kings of England, while Episcopalians often favored the Pretender, who was living in Rome and was a Papist. It was all thoroughly confusing, the more so because there were shades of enthusiasm and niceties of passion that were quite beyond his understanding, sects within sects and parties within parties.

His employer was a genial, fat man named Morrie. His genius was engraving and his passion was for the Cause, and he could talk of one while doing the other on the surfaces of the steel pistols that came from his workshop.

"Don't you see, John," he would begin.

"Don't you see, John, why the Duke of Atholl was driven from home...."

"Don't you see, John, why the Stewarts are the rightful rulers of Scotland...."

"Don't you see, John, how the kirk betrayed us...."

The currents moved; Johnnie Morse tumbled. He liked Alec Morrie, who took the place of the father who had beaten him. He filled part of the void that Dark Archie's death had left. "Yes, sir, I do see," was John's ready reply to Alec Morrie. The man's arguments seemed to be like his engraving, beautiful and correct. John surrendered his opinions to his ideas as he had surrendered his twisted hands to his instruction. He learned to express the ideas as if they were his own, and he expressed regret that he had not been there to fight when the Murrays had done battle for the Cause.

"Time enough for that yet," Alec Morrie said mysteriously. "Time enough."

With Alec's ideas, he was taking in the techniques of making steel-butted Highland pistols. Dark Archie had never made but wood-stocked ones; now, new tools and new methods had to be learned—swages for forming the metal barrel groove, new ways of upsetting the metal and forming the butt. Here was the art of working metal indeed—to take a bar of Swedish iron and heat it in charcoal and hammer and shape it until it was a gunstock of soft steel! He admired the warmth of the wood of Dark Archie's guns, but he felt a stronger pull to this burnished metal, which was cold and pure.

In his third year with Morrie, he made his own tools out of the best steel. A complete set of swages and dies came from his hands. They would be his fortune—the extensions of his mind and his fingers.

"You're good, Johnnie, no question of it. As good as any man in Atholl, excepting me. Let's make you better!"

He began the slow process of learning to engrave the steel. At first, it was like working with mittens on; his muscles seemed to have lost all control, and in his broken fingers the gravers seemed to have minds of their own. His scrolls looked spavined, his straight lines palsied. He despaired of ever learning it and wanted to quit, but Alec Morrie drove him.

"It's coming, John—coming, though you don't see it. I do. Yon line there is almost enough to escape hanging with."

Alec Morrie was pleased with him. He hinted at a more attractive arrangement when John's bonded period was up.

108

He smiled approvingly when he heard John lecturing the apprentices: "You see, lads, the injustice of a German on an English throne ruling Scotland is—"

John was sitting at a bench under a many-paned window one afternoon with the graving tools in his hand and a steel pistol on the bench in front of him—the first he had been allowed to touch with the graving tools. Daylight, so necessary to the work, was dimmed by a fine rain that had saturated the town all night and all day. He bent close to the work to study the floral design that had been laid down on the steel with grease and chalk. Wetting his lips, he set the tool to the curving end of a small scroll and raised the small hammer, ready to make his first stroke—when the daylight seemed suddenly to grow dimmer and the work to become obscure.

He looked quickly up. A dark shape had come between the window and the silvered sky, unreal of outline and vaguely threatening through the steamy, rain-spattered glass. As he looked, the shape moved and a lighter place at its center grew bigger and became a distorted spot of flesh flattened against the outside of the pane—a human nose, and, on each side of it, a staring eye that darted back and forth in its socket as if trying to escape. Meeting his own, the eyes narrowed; the nose withdrew and the dark shape receded to a blur—the unclear outline of a cloaked man in a large hat.

The vision disturbed him greatly. Pitlochry was full of secrets, and Alec Morrie's shop was full of mysteries; this shape that spied on him from the rain seemed like the dark realization of a conspiracy.

He shivered. Trying to return to his work, he found that he was distracted by the appearance at the window; like a man sitting in an empty house at night who fears to turn his back on a door, he had to lift his eyes several times to the window to make sure that no one was there. *Only some traveler,* he told himself, trying to concentrate on the work. *Looking for a place for the night.* But the times were uneasy; there were thieves, informers, spies.

A knock on the door made him jump as if he had been touched by the fingers that made it. The graver fell from his hand. He swallowed and cursed softly.

"Wait, can't you?" he said in a voice that was too loud.

The door was bolted, for it opened on an alley next to the shop and was rarely used. He had to use a block of wood to knock the bolt back and then pull hard to free the rain-swollen door.

"Well?"

A man was leaning against the hinge side of the doorjamb to escape the overflow of the gutter. His black slouch hat was hanging, misshapen because of the rain, and the cloak was pulled up over half his face for warmth. The eyes looked boldly at John Morse.

"Well?"

The man pushed himself away from the doorjamb and came closer, putting his left hand on the door as if he meant to push it open and come in. John put his foot behind the door and blocked the opening with his body.

"Don't you know your own father, you arrogant pup?"

The man pulled the cloak down to show the lower half of his face. Without doubt, the man was Duncan Morse, his father; ten years could not wipe out the memory of that cold, passionate face.

"Let me in."

"I—I can't. This ain't my house."

"I'm your *father!* I've walked twenty miles today to find you!" His father's voice had a grating catch in it that he did not remember, as if he had spent the ten years shouting. His face had changed, too; it was lined and creased and folded, as if a large tool had engraved all his disappointments there. "I'm warning you, boy, let me in, or—!"

"Don't threaten me!" His childhood terror of his father had at first conquered him; now it was being driven back by anger at this imposition on his new, grown-up self. "You got no cause to threaten me any more! You dare to raise your hand against me now and you'll regret it—father or no father!"

Duncan pushed against the door, but it held. His nostrils flared and his eyes grew very wide, then narrowed. "The Devil always worked strongest in you, boy. He's found fertile ground now!"

"It ain't your business if he does." Cold rage had taken the place of the old fear. "Now get out of this place. I done without you these ten years; leave it so."

"Ach, that's the way of it! You been suckled and raised up and now you strike at him that raised you! You forget the Commandments."

"The Commandments don't apply between you and me."

Duncan nodded. He grunted to himself, twice; his long, thin hand was splayed on the door to keep it from being closed. He grunted again, still nodding. "You'll rot in Hell for denying me, John Morse. You live in a nest of vipers here

110

and you do the work of Satan for this man—I mean Alec Morrie!" He had raised his voice as if he meant for the whole house to hear. "I bring you the word of God and your only chance for salvation this side of the grave, and you deny me. You'll regret that, if you don't take it back. Now—I come here to do business with you, not waste words. Do my business, and I'll take my curse from off you."

"Your curse is more welcome than any blessing would be. You go to Hell!"

Duncan's eyes grew wide again, then narrow. He grunted. There was sudden pressure on the door as if he had pushed against it, hoping to catch his son off guard; when he failed, he laughed. "Well, the man of God can do business with the Devil if it profit the Almighty. I say it again, boy; I come to do business. Hear me out."

"What sort of business?"

"Why, guns, Johnnikins. That's your business now, ain't it?"

"What do you want guns for?"

"To shoot rabbits with, Johnnikins. Never mind what for."

"Go to Mr. Morrie, if you want to buy guns."

"No, he'd want money, Johnnikins."

"And so do I! What d'ye think, I'd give you guns for free because you had the bad luck to be my father? Nay, I'd say we're both paid back and even, you and me—except for the beatings you give me as a tiny kid, that I'll never forgive you for—but the books is closed between you and me. I do no business with you. Go to Hell."

"Your master's got guns, Johnnikins; he won't miss a few."

"Jesus, you're daft. Get out of it—"

"John, I say you must—you must!"

"Get out!"

The pouchy eyes narrowed as father and son struggled with the door. John heard the hoarse voice whisper, "You ain't twenty-one yet! I can draw you out of this place like a bad tooth. The law is with me!" He thrust an eye to the narrow opening. "I can still whip you—I got those what work with me can help me do it!"

"Try!" John pulled the door open so suddenly that his father half tumbled in, and John thrust him out again and held a shaking, twisted hand in front of his astonished face. "It's already been done, Da! I had me hands broke once by bullies, aye, and had them beat me—and here I am, still alive! You choose to threaten me, well, that clears us of any blood

111

tie, so I threaten you back! You clear off from here and stay away from me and my business, for if you so much as come near me, I swear to God, I'll throw over the one restraint that keeps me from kicking you like a dog at this moment, and I'll give you a drubbing that'll pay you back for every stroke you laid on me! Now get out!"

He saw tiny flecks of foam on his father's lips; he wondered if there were the same on his own. *Two mad dogs.* His father's tongue came out, licked; the foam disappeared. He grunted and nodded. "Almighty God heard every word you uttered, boy." He nodded. "You're cursed. Cursed! I leave you to Heaven's vengeance. I'm through with you!" He made as if to turn away but put his hand on the door again before it could be closed. "But let me give you a piece of news. Your granddam is dying. Ah, that touches you, does it! Aye, she's dying, down where she lives with your harlot of a sister. Maybe she's dead by now. When she goes, yon house in Kildrummie and all that's in it will be mine. You look surprised, Johnnikins! What—did you think it would be yours? Tush, boy, you don't know the law. I'm the *son!*"

John felt breathless. "To Dark Archie's everlasting sorrow."

"I'm a godlier man and a better than he ever dreamed of being! What'd he do, corrupt you into thinking himself a great man, like he done with others?" Duncan shoved his face as close as he dared. "But did he give you aught? I daresay he didn't. For he never gave me aught. Never gave me so much as his sweat!" He drew back and prepared to pull up the cloak. "So much the better; I owe him nothing, alive or dead. A godlier man than he ever was, and with greater things moving about me. But enough! I'll claim my house in Kildrummie. Did the old man keep guns there, Johnnikins?"

John hardly needed to think; the lie came quickly. "We sold them all after he died."

"Did you? Aye, probably you did. But I'll just find out when I take the house over."

"There's things of mine in that house!" John called after the dark figure as it started up the alley. All of his adolescent gatherings were there, some clothes, things on the wall he had once thought valuable. "Things of mine, I say. That's the law!"

He bolted the door with fingers made clumsy by tension. Now that the encounter was over, he was trembling. He found that he was in a rage at the fact that, after a decade, the man
112

could arouse the same childish terrors that had caused him to spoil his breeches as a boy.

He turned to find Alec Morrie standing in the far doorway.

"I heard voices, John."

"Only a man, Mr. Morrie."

"What sort of man?"

"A stranger. Traveler. Made a mistake of the house."

He turned away toward the bench. Morrie's footsteps came up behind him. "In a cloak, was he, and a slouch hat? A tall, lanky fellow?"

"You could say he was, I guess."

"Some of the men have had an eye on him since he come to town, John."

Some of the men! At that moment, Johnnie hated the Cause and "some of the men" and even Alec Morrie; his rage at his father spilled over to include all those who made causes and religions and ideas the excuse for their hatred. *A gun has no religion,* Dark Archie had insisted; he had got the idea from his father, Johnnie knew; the man may have been a wanderer and a poor husband, but he was right in that. *A gun has no religion. And so should the gunmaker be.* Like Dark Archie's beautiful viols and dulcimers, a medium for passionate expression rather than passion itself. *So should a man be.*

"The man's me father," Johnnie Morse said hollowly.

"Holy Jesus!" Morrie's voice sounded shocked. "The man's a Crown spy, Johnnie!"

"I ain't seen him in ten years. I swear it. I thought he was maybe dead, but he ain't, worse luck. And he can't be a Crown spy; he's a preacher of the kirk—he's been in Holland."

"Johnnie, Johnnie! D'you think the boys don't know him? One of our people followed him here from Perth; before that he was in England, we had a letter about him. A preacher he may be, for what better place to spy from than a pulpit? And a sectarian he may be, for there's more confusion in the kirk than anyplace. But a Crown spy he is, for sure. What'd he want?"

Like children at their play! Crown spies and Causes! He had lectured the apprentices on the Cause as Alec Morrie had lectured him; he saw now that he had done it to win the man's approval—to be liked by him. "He wanted guns," he said aloud.

"Aye, that'd be it. For making devilment. How did he expect you to get them?"

113

"Steal them from you."

"So the Crown ain't giving him money for guns; that means he's got some other mischief afoot. One of those double-dealers that thinks himself a great man that'll play the Crown against the Cause and come out the winner some other way. Did you tell him yes or no?"

"Jesus, what d'you take me for? I said no."

"Too bad. We could have caught him if you'd jollied him along. But it's done now. And he's gone? Aye, but suppose you went after him, told him you was wrong, you'll help him—"

"I won't go near him again!" John faced Alec Morrie with the same fury that had cowed his father.

"All right, Johnnie, no need to get in a rage about it! You're very worked up, I see that. Very well, lad, very well! Well, we'll find some other way to stop his bung for him."

John passed grimy hands over his face. "He's going up to Kildrummie to my grandmama's house. There's guns there."

"How many?"

"Upwards of twenty, with parts for more. Some lead. Tools. You could start your own shop with the tools that's there."

"Is he a gunmaker?"

"He worked with my grandda until he was twenty. I suppose he could make a gun, still."

"Jesus. An unlicensed man with tools and a forge could play the devil in Scotland, Johnnie. Where's your grandmother, then?"

"Dying, he says. With my—in Leith. The house is let to an old couple. But they'll not stop him; he'll push in and have 'em out in the street, if he wants."

"Could you get there before him, d'you think? I'm just thinking, John, you knowing the house and all—you got some claim there, if you could move the guns and tools and all away."

"For the Cause?" John said with undisguised bitterness.

"You've always been very strong for the Cause."

"Aye. So I have." John laughed suddenly. "Sure, I'll go to Kildrummie and take the things away. If I go by horse, I'll beat him easy; he's on foot. I'll need another man or two and a cart when I get there." He looked at Alec Morrie. "And I'd like to go on to Leith and see my grandmother. If she's still living."

"That's right and proper. Well, let's see—I can send a couple of the boys—we can maybe slow him down coming through the mountains. Aye, it's a good plan. The men'll think well of you for doing it, Johnnie. They'll be a little shy of you when they find the man's your father, but this'll be a credit to you. Of course, you don't have to do it. You can be what they call neutral if you like."

Neutral as a gun. "Neutrals don't have many customers."

"Well—" Alec Morrie rubbed his stubbly chin. "Well, no. I'd been thinking of bringing you in with me when your bond time is over, but.... Men look to me for a kind of moral leadership, John."

"I'll do it." John laughed again. "I'm sure 'the boys' will think highly of a man who's tricked his own father."

He rode down along the Tay with two men from Morrie's band of loyalists. They were silent and noncommittal in the early-morning darkness, but they all pressed foreward relentlessly. His father would be taking the foot track over the mountains, a challenge to any but the most resolute. His father would not hesitate, he knew; he was a man who could never be faulted for lack of courage, whatever other qualities he might not have. He would take the shortest route to Kildrummie if it meant walking straight up a mountainside and swimming an ice-cold tarn.

By horseback, their route would be longer, but they would move much faster. They crossed the Isal at Meigle Bridge and went on toward Aberdeen, the Sidlaw Hills a dark presence on their left, behind which his father would be making his angry way.

His backside was sore and the insides of his thighs felt like rods that had been heated in a forge fire; still they pushed on, changing horses at Forfar and again at Banchory, where they slept for a few hours and were on their way again before daylight.

The old man and woman to whom Catharine had let the Kildrummie house were flustered by his coming. He handled them badly, he knew; pressured by his sense of his father's approach—as if he were doing something sinful, and his father were his conscience—and aware of Alec Morrie's men pressuring him in a different way, he was not able to be either mannerly or tactful. His old room was locked, but he had the key, to which the rusty metal yielded grudgingly. One of the Jacobites stood behind him while he worked it; he could hear the other down below as he tried to placate the two old people. They were of the kirk, and suspected their sympathy; still, the man was working hard at flattering them.

The long guns were in three boxes, still in the rags in which he had wrapped them three years before. Loose gun parts lay in smaller boxes and in bags; the tools were stacked under the eaves.

"All of it?"

"Aye, the lot. There's anvils and heavy tools in the shed."

"We'll need a cart."

"Get a cart, then!"

"Yah, Alec said you'd want a cart. Jesus, what a day!"

Hours later, they had most of it in a two-wheeled cart that was drawn up behind two sluggish oxen in the damp mire between the house and the cowshed. One of the Jacobites was still jollying the old couple, who seemed to like him because he listened to their grievances and their petty complaints about the town.

"My father'll claim we stole this lot," John said.

"I don't know nothing about it. I was tole to get it out."

"He could have the law. Although he don't know what's here."

"These things ain't truly his, then?"

"Nay, they're my grandmother's, if they're anybody's but mine."

"Get some kind of a paper from her, then, giving them to you."

"What, would it matter? She's dying or dead."

"Matter a good deal. If he's a Crown man, he has influence. But a paper's a paper—even the Crown can't fight paper."

The other man came out of the house. "What's that about the Crown, then?"

"Just giving John Morse here a bit of advice about the law."

"Fook the law. Let's get out o' this. I kept them two ancients busy so they don't know what was took. Is it done?"

"Done."

"Let's get out, then."

He watched them lead the slow-moving oxen to the Dyce road, and he went up to the churchyard and stood first by the grave of Andrew MacPhee and then by the grave of Dark Archie, unable to think of what he should be saying to their spirits or to the god in which Archie, at least, had not believed. He settled at last for dropping a bit of fir branch on each, and saying to himself as he stood again by Archie's, *Well, you was right. You was always right. Causes ain't for gunmakers. Though I don't see how I can keep free of this one.*

116

He rode back to Aberdeen and found a coaster headed for Leith and resigned himself to a day and a night of seasickness.

A maid opened the door to him at the house in Leith. Feeling uncouth and alien, he stood in a sitting room richer than any he had ever entered, not daring to sit on any of the surfaces that presented themselves to him. When Jane Mary came in, he hardly dared look at her. His anger had fled; in its place was awe of her position and a ghastly fear that she would reject him.

"Johnnie!" she cried. "Oh, thank God you've come!" She pressed herself against him, her arms wrapped about his shoulders. He might have parted from her only hours before, so natural was the gesture. "Thank God. She'll be so happy to see you."

"I'm glad I was in time." There were tears in his eyes, a great lump in his throat; he hoped she would think it was for Catharine.

"She's been waiting for you, I think. Or for Dark Archie, for the two of you are all muddled up in her mind." Her hands gripped his shoulders. "Johnnie, before you go in to her—tell me you forgive me. Tell me!"

He had held his body rigid. Now, his hands touched her, joined behind her back as if he meant to crush her. "God, it's you must forgive me. Oh, Janie!"

They wept together. It was like the old, cold nights when they had crossed Scotland as children. In a sense, nothing had changed; they were still renegades in a world where each was the other's best comfort. "Let me go in to her now," he muttered. "We can jabber afterward."

Catharine died at four in the morning the next night but one. They had agreed that he would take her back to Kildrummie for burial, and he made ready to leave with the body that same morning.

"I'd come, Johnnie, but Matthew might come and find me gone."

Strain had etched little lines around her eyes; they were more prominent now because of strain and weeping. He saw her great sadness. They had talked most of the time while Catharine, comatose, had been dying. John knew of Jane's husband's long absences, his mistress in Edinburgh, her isolation.

"You could leave him, Janie. I'd be happy as a king to have you live with me." It was as close to a declaration of love as he was to make; he knew it even as he said it, and the irony of their situation did not escape him. Still, he pressed on. He wanted to speak the truth. "There's nothing in the world means to me what you do. Come live with me, Janie; I'll make a home for you forever."

"Nay. I can't." She tried to smile. "I've cast my lot. I've two children. For their sakes—and because I love him. Oh, Johnnie." She kissed him. "Be off with you."

Back he went by sea to Aberdeen, and then by cart that same slow road to Kildrummie. A pastor he did not know conducted a service, and the neighbors and her old friends and the survivors of her and Dark Archie's time followed them to the burial, where she was placed next to her husband. *Some day it'll be me,* he thought. *And Janie.* He shivered. *What good are Causes, then?*

He spent the night with the MacPhees and left when the sun was only a gray promise behind the mountains. The horse shivered in the chill. Mrs. MacPhee gave him food wrapped up into a bundle, and he put it in an otherwise empty saddlebag, and put two of Dark Archie's old wood-butted pistols, loaded, into the other. He had kept them back from the things that had been packed into the cart, half out of sentiment, half out of fear of the road.

He paused at the fork of the road below the village to look back, but there was no vantage point from which to see the house or the churchyard. *Well, goodbye, then.* It was a silly gesture, bidding stones and dirt goodbye. But he was young, and gestures were still important to him.

Halfway along the Dyce road he saw, far ahead on the road, a dark figure pacing toward him. He knew at once that it was his father. It was surprising that he had been so long; perhaps Morrie's people had delayed him longer than they had planned. The figure came on like Vengeance itself, implacable, hurried, the black cloak flapping about its scissoring legs.

No good running from him. No good letting him make me run. When they were fifty yards apart, he reined in the horse. He felt behind in the saddlebags for one of the pistols, drew it out by the barrel and concealed it in his sleeve. He was trembling.

"You mickle cur!" his father shouted from twenty yards away. He was too angry to wait until they closed. "You dog-shit of the Devil!"

"Stay away from me, Pa."

"You dropping from Satan's ass, you Hell-turd, you Judas!"

"I done nothing to you, Pa!"

"I already talked to them has been to Kildrummie, you thief! You stole from my house!" His father had a long walking staff, and now he swung it high; missing John, he swung again, shorter, and struck the horse across the left ear with a sound like cracking wood. The horse reared, and John, a poor rider at best, felt one leg swing free of the stirrup. Clutching wildly at the horse's mane, at the bridle, the saddle, at anything his grasping fingers could find, he lost his hold on the pistol, and it spun in an arc to the roadside, falling just where the beaten dirt met low grass. He heard his father exclaim; the horse ran several strides and then came up short, almost pitching him off. Man and mount were very still.

"Vengeance is mine, is the Lord's cry!"

He turned his head to see his father only a few feet away, the pistol in his hand. "Now, Judas, give me back what's mine! Then go to your dungpile in Pitlochry and suck up the Devil's offal with the other flies there! Almighty God, that the likes of you should be my son! Now—tell me what you done with them guns and all!"

"I took nothing that's yours."

"Everything in that house is mine!"

"Not yours and never will be! I got a paper, Pa—Grandma signed it for me at Leith before she died. What was took away from that house was mine by her gift. *Mine*. Legal!"

His father was not sane, he believed. The look on the worn face was one of madness, or so he thought it; he knew little of a middle-aged man's lifetime of frustration, of a vanity that was contradicted at every turn in a world that thought nothing of him.

John turned away, ready to set the horse toward home.

"Let be, Pa. It's over. Let be."

He dug his heels into the horse's sides and it began to walk.

He heard the pistol's harsh cough and felt the sting of the shot in his back at the same time, and then pain like hot spikes pounded into his right shoulder; then the horse was running away and he was clinging to it, bent over its neck with a nail of fire in his back.

Chapter Twelve

Causes in Pitlochry, he found, were like hobbies in Kildrum-
mie. What music had been to Dark Archie, rebellion was to
Alec Morrie and his friends. It came as a matter of astonishment to John that they could go on year after year after year,
talking, plotting, organizing—and accomplishing, so far as
he could tell, nothing at all. He began with a young man's
belief in the moment, that audacious Now that is the be-all
of youth; he ended with an almost comfortable, middle-aged
Someday. It was fine with him. He had had enough of causes
although he never dared tell Alec Morrie so.

He had a bullet scar in his back and he had the broken
knuckles of both hands as the badges of his convictions. The
broken hands had not been won while fighting for the Cause
but there was a crossover of sympathy because he had got
them from an aristocratic snob who (it was believed) must
have been an Englishman at heart. Nobody questioned his
entitlement to membership in the Cause any more.

Time seemed to be draining the life out of him and he
could not stop it. He was getting older, almost middle-aged;
he felt hollow, scooped out by Time, as if the very marrow
had been taken from his bones. Jane Mary was getting older;
what might have been between them—*lovers, aye, might a.
well say it, we could have been more to each other than either
of us is to any*—was trickling away, too. He heard from her
twice a year: her children were grown; the boy was wild.
Leith was a quiet place. Between her words, he could read
loneliness and numbness. *Oh, what could have been!* His own
thoughts had no power to shock him. *My sister is a woman.
Let me love her like a woman!* But he did nothing.

He was restless. He wanted to go off somewhere, but all
places seemed alike to him. He had no America; lying alone
at night, he envied Dark Archie's wandering father, whom
he imagined as a big man of great gusto and warmth, a kind
of archetypal sailor. His vision of the man made him seem
small to himself. He let time pass, Now become Someday. He
heard now and then of his father, usually through Alec Morrie
and his "boys"—his father was in France; his father was in

120

prison; his father had been seen, it was believed, in Rome. He tried to shut another door in his mind, but he could never close his father out.

The guns flowed from the workshop. Alec Morrie made him a partner when he was thirty-three. They were a formidable coupling—the two best gunsmiths in Perthshire. It was said that if two gentlemen fought a duel anywhere within a hundred miles of Pitlochry, one was bound to fall with a charge from a Morrie and Morse gun in him, for everybody who was anybody bought from them. Their pairs of steel-stocked pistols rode on the sword belts of the wealthiest men in Scotland; the best blood flowed because of them; exiles like Lord George Murray carried them, fighting for a foreign cause in Sicily, and he carried them again when he was pardoned by the English Crown and came home.

More peace-loving Scotsmen had the perfect kit when they owned a long fowler by Morrie and Morse and a trouting rod by McMurdo of Dunkeld.

It was said that Johnnie Morse was a better gunmaker even than Alec Morrie and that he had magic in his broken hands. John heard it said; he was unmoved. The compliment did not make him happy. He had decided he was one of those people who are not meant for happiness, whether through missing some quality in themselves or through some flaw in the world about them did not matter.

Alec Morrie, on the other hand, was concerned. He wanted his young partner to love life. He wanted him to be cheerful. He thought he knew what he lacked.

"What would you think about marrying my Flora?" he said to John one evening when they had been partners for six years.

"Flora? Marry Flora?"

"Aye. She's going to marry somebody."

"Flora's a baby."

"No, John, she's a woman. And she dotes on you."

Flora was Morrie's youngest daughter. She had been born the year he had completed his bond time; she had tumbled around his legs like a cat when he had worked, a chubby, cheerful infant; she had been a snippy adolescent and a rather sharp-tongued girl. Could she now be a woman?

"Whyever should I marry?" He thought of Jane. He had missed having the one woman whom he had loved; now he had learned to be content with the quick, furtive sex that could be had in certain houses.

"To have a home, man! You're a lonely old bachelor, that's your trouble! People don't entirely trust a man ain't married, John."

Ah, that's it! It's what other folks think—always what others think. "I guess I'm harmless, being a bachelor."

"But it would bind the firm, John. You marrying Flora."

John cast a keen, almost hostile glance at his partner. "Binding the firm" sounded remarkably like "justifying himself to the Cause." Alec seemed to need a great deal of reassurance.

"I'd have thought the firm was bound well enough by the contract," John said slowly.

"It's just a way of speaking, what I said. But Flora dotes on you, Johnnie. And I'll give her a fair dowry—she's my last."

John sighed. "I'll think about it." He knew he would do it. He had no real desire, either way; he would drift, and somebody else's desire would have its way.

He married Flora in the summer. Consummating the marriage was delayed for several weeks, for she was shy and he was fearful; nonetheless she was pregnant by Christmas. He was surprised to find that he rather liked being married. Flora, on the other hand, showed signs of feeling rather the opposite. No matter: they were married in a world where men and women married and stayed married; she would have the children and the house and the kirk, and he would have his work. Of those closest to the marriage, Alec Morrie seemed happiest, and, in time, he forgot that he had arranged the matter with the aim of bringing happiness to his partner.

And there were more important things to think about. The Cause was heating up again: the Pretender had a son, Charles Edward Louis Philippe Casimir Stewart. He wanted to be King of Scotland, and it began to look as if he might actually do something to achieve that goal.

Alec Morrie complained that he would be too old to fight if it came to fighting. "It's true, Johnnie—I'm sixty. Oh, if this had only come twenty years ago!"

"Fighting's for the young," John Morse said slowly. Two broken hands and a bullet in the back had made him cautious. "A man's got to do his fighting while he's still too young to know what he's doing."

"Forty ain't old," Alec said, ignoring the remark.

"I ain't forty. I'm forty-four." John looked his partner in the eye; the other man sighed and shrugged and muttered something about hoping there were enough brave young men about to serve the Cause. The remark stung John, for his wife of five years was given to sly remarks about young men. And John suspected that there was substance behind the remarks, although he could prove nothing. "You've never known me to shirk a responsibility," he said to Alec, who had started to walk away.

"Did I say you had?"

"What you said about young men, it sounded like you meant I was a shirker."

Alec Morrie came back a step. "Nay, Johnnie. Only—I'd feel better if you could make the show for both our sakes."

"Aye, there it is—make a show!" John's tone was bitter. "I made my show, I guess."

"But the Cause will need every man now, John!"

"And won't your daughter need me now? And your grandson Donnie and his little sister? What of them?"

"Well—it'd be a proud thing to say, that your daughter was widowed for the Cause!"

"I'm sure it would. It's an easy thing to be proud for somebody else's doings."

Alec came close to him. "John! I'm shocked, man—you sound so bitter!"

"I'm sick of proving myself over and over, Alec! I proved myself to you; I proved myself to your fellows in the Cause; I proved myself to Flora and hear about my shortcomings after! I'm fair sick of proving myself to you and yours."

"John! Those are harsh words, John!"

"Aye. Harsh words for some harsh feelings." He did not quite understand what he had said himself; the words seemed to leap out from a place he had not known to exist. It rather pleased him to find that there was feeling hidden down there somewhere; might there, then, be feeling enough to make him *act*, to make him more like that legendary swashbuckler his great-grandfather?

Alec Morrie was backing away. "Let's say no more, John. Harsh words lead to—other harsh words, and so on. People would talk if you and me was thought to have argued."

It seemed impossible after all the years of talk, but it did look at last as if the Cause might actually become a war. The resentment he might have felt toward Alec Morrie dissipated; the anger that he had glimpsed subsided. He began to worry about the situation around him, instead: *What if there's war?* He would lie awake at night, fearing the coming of a war. *I*

123

could emigrate. What he meant was that he could run away, leaving Alec and Flora and this whole life he had allowed to build up around him in Pitlochry. But he would not do that. *Must take them with me.* But where? *America.* He remembered Dark Archie's name for everything that was mysterious, irrational and wild. *Would America be better than a war?*

In the evenings, he took down the old book that he had brought from Dark Archie's house. He extended the family tree again to include his two children by Flora. Years before, he had added to the list of marks the one used by Archie; now, below it, he wrote in *Morrie and Morse,* for that was the way they marked their elegant guns. The partnership did not use the skull or *mors.* The partnership was really Morrie's, and a Morse mark was not suitable. John felt ashamed because of that.

On another page, his great-grandfather's tight handwriting had set down the words that he had never been able to understand. They seemed part of the man's legendary quality.

"Watch for the White Beest," he had written.

What White Beest?

"I seen it 1614 in the Maaqua town. Snow Elk, therefore.

"Pierre de Mouers seen it 1511—*la beste blanshe* he said.

"Franc Lazarino Mors, he seen it Brugge 14??.

"The White Beest signifies."

He touched the faded ink as if the meaning of the words would come to him through his fingertips. He had touched an old mark in a cannon once that he had seen in Edinburgh; it had been lying in the moat with several others, ancient guns that had been left there when they had grown obsolete. The mark on that cannon had been one of his family's; looking at old Jan's list afterward, he had found that it must have been made about 1420. *Watch for the White Beest.*

John shook his unimaginative head. It was all *America.*

In August of that summer, Charles Edward Louis Philippe Casimir Stewart set his ambitious foot on the Scottish mainland, and the Cause erupted. He needed troops, guns, and money; there were enthusiasts enough to raise all three for him. By the time he reached Perthshire, four thousand men were following him, as if the Highland valleys flowed rivers of men that poured east and south to join in a sea around him. Tribal, wild, half of them were mere undisciplined brawlers; they would have been easily recognized by Jan Morse as the spiritual kindred of the Senecas who had gone off with Black Otter to destroy the Hurons. They were supposed to be

124

Christians, and therefore moral men, but all that Christianity had given them was self-righteousness and an enthusiasm for blood. Dressed in their shirts and their bonnets, wrapped up in homemade cloth in a hundred meaningless patterns, armed with huge swords and axes and pistols, they were eager to fight, and preferably at close quarters—hand to hand, like cavemen meeting in the dark.

They trickled down through Pitlochry every day. They bought pistols until the shelves were empty. "Join the Cause!" they urged John Morse. He learned to answer, "Lord George Murray ain't in it yet," and they were satisfied, for they understood that a man did not have to move until his chief did. *Though how Lord George became my chief, I don't know, except I married the daughter of one of his kinsmen.*

He lost his excuse when Lord George Murray joined the prince as general of his forces at the end of August. The flow of Highlanders had thinned, however; most of those who were going to join the Cause had already gone. The prince's army had six thousand men now, it was said—and, coming to meet them, an English force that would meet their taste for hand-to-hand fighting with disciplined formations and the bayonet, with the volley firing of the Land Pattern musket and its .79-caliber ball.

"This is a bad place now," John muttered. "A bad place."

"What's that, John?"

"Nothing. Nothing."

Lord George Murray and the prince's wild army met the English at a place below Edinburgh called Prestonpans, and John was astonished to learn a day later that, in a day of dreadful fighting, the Scots had beaten Sir John Cope and his regulars and had captured eighteen cannons. For a wild moment, he thought it would mean the end of the brief war—the end of the Cause, the end of proving himself, the end of all his unrest. But just the opposite happened, for the prince wanted to be King of England as well as Scotland, and his victory decided him to invade England.

A messenger appeared in the shop. He had come direct from the Murray men of Pitlochry who were with Lord George.

"Ye're to come now to the army," the messenger said to John.

"Me?"

"That's the order. They need a man to care for the cannons."

"But I don't know cannons!"

"They believe you do. It's your duty as a loyal follower of the Cause."

He thought of the cannon he had seen at Edinburgh, lying in the tall grass like a fallen tree. Had another Morse been pressed into service as a gunner to it?

He went home and packed a haversack. Numb, fatalistic, he was letting himself be led to his death as he had been led to things all his life.

Flora, however, was delighted. "I'm so proud of you!" she cried. "Folks'll just think the world of you!"

"Better they wait until I come home in one piece."

"Don't be grouchy, John—you're a hero!"

"At my age, being a hero's got no luster to it."

He packed a pair of pistols with their tools, and he hooked another pair to the belt under his coat. They added weight and bulk to his muscled body, which was just beginning to put on fat.

"Take care of the little ones." He thought of taking the boy's fowler that Dark Archie had made, for it was still the best-shooting gun he had ever handled. He wanted his own son to have it, however, and he took another.

"Kill an Englishman for me," Flora whispered when she kissed him. He looked at her as if she were a stranger; she was excited, her color high. As sure as he was standing there looking at her, he knew that she had another man—a *young* man—she would go to as soon as he was gone.

"If I don't come back, you must go to your father's," he said.

"Don't talk so!"

"Your father has my will, in the strongbox at the works. Donnie's to have the little gun that hangs with my books. And the book about America."

He kissed his children and walked to his gate and out into the road, feeling like a parody of a man going off to war. The messenger was waiting there with a horse that looked untrustworthy. John eyed the animal warily.

"Another pair of sore buttocks for the Cause," he muttered.

Chapter Thirteen

The captured English cannons were wheeled six-pounders. The horses and harness to move them had not been taken, so there was some question as to how they would be kept up with the rest of the army; John, upon his arrival, found twelve men loitering about four of the guns, which were to be his to deal with, he having been named to command only a four-gun battery and not the entire eighteen as he had feared. He was to find that it was typical of the disorganized Scottish force that commands were botched and garbled in just this way, even as it was typical of the romantic boastfulness of many of the enthusiasts for the Cause that four guns could grow into eighteen in the time that it took a messenger to ride from one town to another.

"What ye want we should do with this lot of artilleries, now?" a cocky young Highlander who had draped himself across one gun said.

"I wish I knew," was John Morse's answer. They laughed at him. He produced a handful of coins and put them into the young man's hand, telling him to find enough whisky and water for the twelve of them, in hopes that by the time they had drunk it, he would know what to do. They all made approving noises. They would not turn on him, at any rate— not while he could keep them in whisky.

He managed at last to find a sergeant who had once served as a gunner in the English army, and he was able to explain the rudiments of artillery. "Ye ought to have six men to a gun; ye've got three, and the army's strained to spare them. Make do, captain."

"I'm a captain, am I?"

"Well, call yourself one, is my advice. The prince is very liberal with commissions. If ye've no experience of army life, sir, my advice is, put a cockade in your hat and some form of ribbon on your right shoulder, and you'll be an officer."

"For how long?"

The man eyed him shrewdly. "Long enough."

"Well, what should I do with my men?"

"Run 'em dry through the drill, every day of their lives—

load, shoot, swab and load. Make 'em do it till they drop. Teach 'em to swab after every shot, or the idiot bastards'll blow the guns and you to kingdom come with a spark in the bore. Keep the linstock at your side till they're ready to shoot, else they'll blow up the powder keg or set each other's arse on fire. Bury your kegs and cover the tops with wet hide, and, with all them precautions, you may live through a salvo or two."

"What of aiming and sighting?"

The sergeant laughed. "Teach 'em to load and shoot, captain. You ain't going to bombard the English to death with eighteen guns; wait till they come close and give 'em grape. There's no aiming nor sighting to that."

He had to find horses and harness and wagons; then he had to find buckets for water to wet the swabs. There was no organization yet for feeding the newmade artillerymen, who had simply been plucked out of the foot; he had to devise a way of attaching them to the commisary in this make-believe army. Underfed and ill-equipped, his men began their work with ill feeling, for they wanted to be soldiers like their fellows. Whenever they could, they tried to sneak back to be with their kinsmen from their home territories. When they had to stay by the guns, they bickered among themselves, old feuds and disputes flaring. John threatened them with a report to the general.

"Ain't you got no clan feeling, then, captain?"

"None."

"But what clan be you, captain?"

"None. By marriage, Murray."

"Oh, like the general. Oh, well!"

They decided that his Murray connections must give him influence, and so they did as he asked; they even became friendly and tried to console him for his lack of clan. "There's two Poles and a I-talian for officers in the foot. It don't matter that a man ain't a true Scot, so he's with us."

Most of them wore plaids—great lengths of homespun wool in a myriad of patterns, each belted about the wearer's waist and allowed to hang down like a skirt—and, some of them, plaid hose; a few even had plaid waistcoats, but none of the plaids matched any of the others and there was no sense of pattern or uniform to either clan or Cause. The many family groups used sprigs of different greens in their bonnets as a mark of identity; in the mountains of their homes, the leaves were sufficient to keep a man from killing one of his friends. The English would have no trouble recognizing them as the enemy, green sprigs or no.

He ran them through the firing routine every day. He might as well have dressed them up in alb and cassock and tried to run them through the Mass. The only good thing was that they had no gunpowder, or they would all have been maimed.

"Load! I don't care if it ain't real gunpowder, *load!* Duffus, you load that goddam gun when I tell you to or you'll find out what these pistols is for! Now ram. Ram! Oh, shit, put your back into it, man! Ball! What the hell, can't you carry a six-pound ball any better than that? I don't give a shit if it did fall on your toe, load it! Now ram again—oh, Christ, Ainslie, that's the swab you got, not the rammer. Oh, Christ, Christ, Christ!"

They followed the army to Carlisle, having fired only three rounds from the guns. Now they gave over all drills so that they could push and haul the guns over the rutty roads. A carriage broke, and John found himself forging parts at a borrowed forge. His men were wet and sore and hungry, and he felt sorry for them, but he could not let them rest; he threatened them—with the pistols, with General Murray, with God's vengeance—and, sullen, they inched the guns forward.

Carlisle surrendered in November; they had fired half a dozen more rounds, more ceremonial than useful. There was talk of mutiny; the prince, when he was seen, looked angry. Instead of cutting south into England, as it was gossiped that the prince and many of the Highlanders wanted, the army turned back to the north and retreated ahead of an English force coming up to meet it. There was reason to be wary: the English were led by the brilliant young Lord Cumberland, who had already proved his genius and his stamina.

The horses strained and slipped, dragging the guns through mud that was like grease. One fell, its shoulder broken; he had to shoot it. Four of his gunners deserted. Two were found among their kinsmen and were hanged. John Morse was sick for them, for they were only stupid and very young men, but he threatened the rest of his crews with the same end if they deserted. They would not have been alone, by any means; the flow out of the Highlands had been reversed, and there were men leaving the army every day to trek home.

They made a stand in the rain at Falkirk. The cannons could not be fired because of the weather, and even muskets

129

were too soaked to shoot. It came down to broadsword and ax and bayonet; the Highlanders were able to fight their own sort of bloody action, and they had the best of it. John, seeing a bayonet charge by English grenadiers, was sick—exactly the response that the cold steel and the implacable, marching step were meant to inspire.

After the battle, he made himself walk over the field, trying to look at the corpses with brains laid open and bellies ripped. He thought that he might learn the point of it all if he confronted battle instead of putting it from his mind. He learned nothing that was any use to him.

They struggled north again. Lord George Murray was making for Inverness, it was said, to protect his supplies; the prince was sulking because he thought he should be in London by then. John was sick: a cough came up from his belly like a death rattle, and his sinuses seemed ready to burst through his face. Dysentery was universal. His men were weak and dispirited. Whisky kept them going—whisky and habit. And the threat of hanging.

Sick and dispirited, he begged to go home and was given three miserly days, hardly enough to get there and back. He wanted his own bed, comfort, stability. But his house seemed cold and his bed was empty, and his father-in-law (and partner) could not meet his desperate eyes.

"Where is she, then? *Where is she?*"

"She's away just now, John—"

"Where?"

Alec Morrie mumbled something about a friend "over yon mountain," and when John bellowed in his sick and angry voice, Morrie begged him to hush "for the neighbors' sake." John turned and left the house; he hugged his children and glared at his partner and said coldly, "She better be here when I come next, Alec. She better be here—or else." He pulled his son Donnie to him and hugged the boy and then got on his horse and sped back to the army and his cold bed on the winter ground—and a dream.

He dreamed of the White Beast. Or he believed he did; his memory of it was clouded afterward. He was satisfied that he had dreamed of it, however, and the fact gave him confidence. His health improved. He convinced himself that he would survive, whatever happened to the army.

His great-grandfather had been in the dream. It could have been nobody else. He was a huge man, like a bear. There was a field, a lake, flowers. In the very center of the field was a
130

white animal. They were to catch it. It was very important that the animal be caught, and he and his great-grandfather ran around and around it, spiraling in on it—running and running—

John was very vague about the rest of the dream. But it was enough. If the dream meant anything—if the entries in the book meant anything—then he was meant to live.

In the Seneca village below Hanayoya Lake that winter, Fat-eater, fourth in line from Jan Morse on the female side (for it was only by the women that the Iroquois marked descent), set his teeth and waited for the ice to break up. That winter was the latest any man or woman remembered ice on the lake—a hard, hard winter, with a poor harvest before it. The People were starving in the villages. The People were poor, starving, and needy.

"We were very rich once," Ready Hunter muttered. "Once we were so rich we bought good food from the English and the French."

"Once they *gave* us food. Also guns, knives, everything! Now they give us nothing." Fat-eater, Jan Morse's great-great-grandson by his Seneca wife, had a tinge of red in his hair, an inheritance from his European ancestor. But many of the Senecas looked different from the old days; there had been many white traders and black slaves in the villages since those days.

"Now they give us nothing."

"Because they do not need us. When they need us again, they will make us rich again. They will need us when they want to make war. We need a war."

Fat-eater looked into the fire and tried to think of something other than being hungry. "I hate the English," he said. "*And* the French. In the old days, they say, the People made their own wars. The People made themselves rich."

"Well, let us go into the Illinois country and make war, then. We can go out there and make war and the English and the French will not bother us."

"And who would give us gunpowder, then? And guns? You are a fool. If we went so far that we could make our own wars, we would be so far away that we would have no guns to make war with. No, we must stay here and wait until the English and the French make war on each other again. Then they will need us, and we will be rich. We need a war. We need a war."

* * *

131

On April 16, John Morse and what was left of the army of the Cause stood on the right bank of the Nairn River near Dunmossie, at a place that the English would remember as Culloden. Their position was untenable, and Lord George Murray had said so, but the prince had chosen it. They were an army of starvelings, strong with only the courage of desperation.

Coming against them were Cumberland's regulars, well armed, well officered, and in weather that favored their kind of tactics. They had artillery support. With drumroll and measured cadence, they came to take their position on the field like a child's toy soldiers lined up for review.

"I got to pass water something awful," one of John's gunners moaned.

"I got to shit."

"Well, shit!"

"Not me. I ain't et enough since Christmas to pass rabbit turds."

"Is there time to squat, d'ye think?"

"Do it standing, man; d'ye want to die squatting?"

He got the guns to firing, hardly caring where the poorly aimed shots fell. The British came on, firing in volleys, loading as they walked, firing again — an awesome, scary spectacle. To his left and right, Highlanders were dropping from the volley fire; their own return fire was sporadic and futile. Their officers called a charge, and downslope went the Highlanders, swinging their swords, their ragged tartans flapping, unshaven cheeks blown out to screech their battle cries, straight into the face of volley after volley. They crashed against the English line, broke through only to face another line behind the first, and were caught between them. Half of them staggered back to their position on the slope by the guns.

The English came on.

"Give us artillery, for God's sake! Give us support, can't you?"

He ordered the guns loaded with grape and then fired them too soon; he hurried the crews to load again and heard the violent *chuff* of an exploding charge as a spark in an unswabbed barrel went off. The loader, taking the explosion in his face and chest, staggered backward, screaming, hair and plaid afire.

The English were twenty yards away, their terrible bayonets a pointed line before them.

John Morse turned. It was as if his name had been called.

132

He could hear almost nothing of the battle; perhaps the guns had deafened him. In that quiet, he saw them on the slope above him—a man and a white horse, the man big, handsome, in his hands a rope with which he held the horse. As John looked, the man waved, beckoning him to join them. He ran up the slope, away from the cannons. The man beckoned, beckoned; he ran. On each side of him, unseen by him because of his concentration, other men were running, too, a rout, a flood pouring back to the Highlands—running, running—

Mr. Arthur Morrison, senior partner of Morrison and Pittsden, Ironmongers, Birmingham, reined in his horse at a rise above his city and looked with satisfaction at the view that was offered him. He could see the smoke of his own furnace and the smoke of the furnaces of his rivals; in all of them he could imagine that he saw Progress. As a prophet might have read clouds or entrails, he read smoke. As surely as the prophet might have seen a covenant in a rainbow, Morrison saw Progress in coal smoke.

"Glorious," he said aloud. The Morrison and Pittsden furnace was new; the firm was old. Indeed, one of his forerunners had once met Jan Morse in a house that still stood in Birmingham, although nobody remembered either of those long-dead men any more, and nobody would have cared if their family relationship had now been pointed out. It was not the past that interested people like Arthur Morrison. It was the Future. *Glorious.*

Out of fire and iron, wealth. Out of coal smoke, Progress. Empire. Conquest.

An army contract would be nice, he thought. *I might spread a bit of coin about at Woolwich.*

He had heard the news of Culloden, of course. A great victory. It would mean stability, and about time, too. Cumberland, it was said, was pursuing the Highland rebels into their dens and slaughtering them. About time for that, too.

War was inevitable. After internal stability, foreign wars; it was as neat as a geometric theorem. He felt no hypocrisy in understanding the virtues—economic virtues, that is—of war, for he wished no individual any harm and he would have been greatly touched by the sight of a mutilated veteran. But war was inevitable; every sensible man knew that—France was a threat, India and Upper Canada were not secure, the West Indies were always a problem—

War makes custom. Not that I wish anyone harm. But war

is good for business. We must be practical men. If war must come, welcome it, is what I say.

He started down the hill toward his furnace.

England needs a war. A proper war, of course.

Old Duncan Morse lay on the floor of his tiny church with blood seeping from the gash in his head. He could see his pulpit above him, much foreshortened, and, hanging from it, the broken-spined Bible he had let fall when he had been hit.

"May the wrath of God fall on England," he muttered.

"Nay, Da, it's only a crease."

He was seventy. A spiteful, cruel seventy. Hard as iron. "An English soldier did it. With a musket butt."

"I know, I know, Da—"

"We got to get out of it, Nathan. We'll take yer brothers and their wives and flee this place. Cumberland's butchers will be through again, and they'll find ye next time. They'll use worse than a musket butt on you younger ones."

They had burst open the church door while he was preaching and had dragged him from his pulpit. Two men in the church had been bayonetted, another had been shot. It was said that Cumberland had recruited the scum of the English army for this task of sweeping the Highlands clean; it was even true that he had signed up deserters from the army of the Cause to kill their fellows now that the Cause was lost. Some of Cumberland's words had even preceded his men into the Highlands: "If you don't want cowshit in a pasture, you drive out the cows," he was reported to have said. And now his soldiers were at work, driving man, woman and child from valley after valley.

Duncan Morse sat up. "We're getting out of it," he said.

"Yes, Da."

"God means for me to go to America. Cumberland is God's scourge in Scotland; it all works out for the best."

Lord George Murray gathered the futile remnant of his force at Ruthven and sent them home. He had lost a thousand men to the English, three thousand to desertions; half of the remnant were sick or wounded. No cannons, no food, no supplies; many of them had left their weapons on the field when they had run.

"Go to your homes now," Murray told them.

John Morse had run, and everybody had run; so many had run that day that there was hardly shame in it. Now their

134

prince was running all over Scotland, and the Highlands were full of English troops.

John Morse knew that he had found himself at Culloden—found himself, paradoxically, in flight. *I ran—and found my destiny!* He had seen the White Beast, and nothing else was half so great a thing as that.

He came to Pitlochry early in the morning, expecting English soldiers, but they had been before him already and had gone on. The gunshop had been dismantled; tools were smashed, the bellows ripped, the forge knocked apart. Alec Morrie had been bayonneted in his own doorway, hoping to reason with one of Cumberland's grenadiers.

"Where's your mother?" he asked his son sternly.

The boy shook his head. He stared wide-eyed at his father, who had changed somehow and no longer seemed like his dour, numb Da.

"Did she ever come back, Donnie?"

The boy shook his head again; his small mouth breathed the single, damning word. *No.*

"Let her love her man, then. For she's seen the last of John Morse!" He packed what he could find of his tools and their clothes, and he took his children to a nearby farm to hide them, and then he rode Hell-bent for Leith by night and roused Jane Mary from her sleep—and her numbed unhappiness—with a word.

"Come!" He cried. She was in a nightgown, he in a mudstained cloak; he did not look like her brother, but like some mad-eyed preacher from the mountains. "Come with me!" It was a command.

"Where?"

"I love you, Jane Mary!"

"My children—"

He snorted. Her daughter was married and living in Edinburgh; her son was a little snob who was living in London and never mentioned her. John grasped her hands; they were cold and dry and she trembled. "There ain't much time left, Jane Mary. We must grab what there is. I *know* we must—I know it!"

"But—I don't know—"

"Come with me!"

"Where?"

"*America.*" He began to laugh. He folded her in his arms and laughed with his head back, unlike the John Morse she had always known—a man who had been freed.

America!

135

Chapter Fourteen

In 'forty-five, when I was young.

Thus did his stories begin, as if the rhythmic phrase were the beginning of a ballad of romance.

"In 'forty-five, when I was young—"

Yet they all knew he had not been young in 1745; he had been only a few months short of thirty-nine, in fact. But now, in the dimmed sight of his early seventies, perhaps being forty seemed as zesty and full of sap as being twenty had seemed to a man of thirty-nine.

All of the family had heard all of his stories—all the bitter, ugly tales that the splenetic old man had told over and over until he had embellished and nurtured and polished them into small wonders of acidity, object lessons in the morality of cynicism. How the twenty-five-year-old Duke of Cumberland had earned himself the title of "the Butcher" at Culloden and after, breaking the Highland Scots and satisfying at last their yearning for self-sacrifice. *Moral: Young men make good murderers; poor men make good corpses.*

How Lord George Murray had doomed himself to perpetual exile by leading the armies of the Stewart popinjay, Charles Edward. *Moral: Idealism is only for those who have nothing to lose.*

How the pretty young prince had been hidden and protected in Scotland even after the defeat that he had brought upon them. *Moral: Folly is a well that has no bottom.*

"You put your faith in an idea, and the thing will bite you like a mad dog," he said. He swung his massive hammer and repeated the final words, "A mad *dog!*" striking the red tongue of metal as if it were an idea that had dared to suggest that he believe in it. He plunged the iron back into the forge.

"Pump!" he barked.

David Morse leaned on the bellows handle and air gushed over the charcoal like the breath of a great animal. The coals brightened. David thought of dragons, of dragons' fiery breath; the vision carried him to other pictures from romance—knights, ladies, men engaged in formal combat over a lofty principle, a quest.

136

"When Lord George Murray went out in 'forty-five," his grandfather rasped as he watched the iron rod, waiting to pluck it again from the coals, "I was one of the fools who went with him." He shook his head. His lower lip curled out and he spat expertly into the forge, his spittle hissing back at him like an angry cat.

He took the rod out and studied it. In the dim light of the shed, the color glowed like the dragon's tongue. "Now, you see, that ain't ready yet—do y'see, David? You muckle-brained jackass, can you hear me?"

"Yes, sir, I hear you."

"Well, can you see that color? Do y'see it, not quite sunset orange? Well?"

"Yes, I see it, though it's faded now."

"Aye." The old man thrust the rod back into the coals. "Pump." He stepped away from the forge and raised a great quantity of phlegm from his throat and spat it out into the rotten snow that still lay by the shadowed side of the shed. In the colder air, his breath came out as steam. Old John Morse had a belly and a stoop, but his arms were huge and strong, despite the fat that had spread and softened him. Lackluster hair thinly framed the great bays that time had worn back from his forehead, and only a vestige of the dark curls that had once dropped there remained. His eyes were red as if he wept sometimes, and he rubbed them hard with his right thumb and third finger.

"Now," he said. He took up the rod again and placed it on the anvil, and with four strokes enlarged a six-inch length into a flat rectangle. "Now, it is upset enough, you see. Do you hear me, you numskull?"

"Yes, Grandfather."

"Always dreaming, you're like a dog by a fire! What is it I just did?"

"You upset it, sir."

"Aye, so I did." He returned the metal to the fire. "When I make the curves for the buttstock, I will do it on the bick; but now, the groove for the barrel, that I will make on a swage." From a wooden box that he had carried out from some hiding place in the house he took a steel swage and dropped its shank into the square hole on the anvil's top. David could still read the name in black letters on the dark-red box: "J. Morse Pitlochry." The old man's name was cut into the shank of the swage, too. These were the tools that had come out with him from Scotland in 1746—from Oban to Halifax, Nova Scotia; from Halifax four years later to Ipswich, Massachusetts; and three years after that, from Ipswich to this isolated farm above the Connecticut River. Nobody had seen the box opened in all that time.

"Time was when I could forge a pistol stock so clean that other smiths thought a filer had been at work on it. I forged a pair of pistols that Lord George Murray gave to the pretty prince for a gift." He laughed nastily. "And the royal pisshead lost them running from the field!" The laughter ended in a drawn-out growl and another discharge of spittle on the coals. "What did I say that tool is, David?"

The young man sighed. "A barrel-channel swage, sir."

"Aye."

David was eighteen. He had been around forges and blacksmithing all his life; he could shoe horses and weld ax heads; he could make coopering hoops and even make the tools with which to do his work. Yet he had little love for the work but preferred wood and cabinetry, finding in the unpredictable and lovely graining of a burl the same exotic texture as that of his dreaming.

"I tried to teach your father to make a pistol once," Old John muttered. He wiped his chin and unshaven silver stubble rasped against his hand. "It didn't take." He laughed again but not so loud, the sound an echo of the other. "Not enough money in it, I suppose. It's a wonder to me that your father took the time to engender you, as there was no money in it."

David said nothing. His grandfather's contempt was such a constant of his life that he hardly marked it. His father did worry about money, it was true, but he was not the grasper that Old John pretended; he was a good churchman and a good husband, it was said, a good provider to his wife and his five children.

"There's no money in the pistols," the old man muttered.

"No, sir."

"Too hard to make. Nobody cares. I suppose I'm wasting my time, teaching you to make them."

"Oh, no, sir!"

"Huh." The old man looked at him with his head down, bull-like, his shaggy eyebrows arched. The light cast upward from the forge cast ugly shadows around his mouth and forehead. "Maybe I am. I don't care. I'll make one pair to please myself, d'you follow me? That's the secret of life, David—

please yourself, and never care too much for anything. D'you understand that, you blockhead?"

"Yes, sir."

Old John Morse began to swage the glowing rectangle of iron into what would become the barrel channel of an all-metal pistol. Another story of the old days began to form as the metal turned, this one something about a blood feud; David only half heard it through the murmur of his own romantic thoughts.

"And who are they when they're home, now?" he heard the old man say suddenly. He looked up from the bellows to see that the old man had left the anvil and was standing in the shed's open mouth. Beyond him, two horsemen were coming slowly up the road.

"Strangers," he murmured as he joined his grandfather. The cool outside air was momentarily welcome, and then his sweat chilled and he shivered.

The old man turned abruptly to the anvil and took up a pair of tongs, with which he moved the unfinished pistol stock deep into the dark coals along the side of the forge. It had begun to take on its final shape, if only roughly, the butt curved down, the beginnings of a fishtail upset at the end of the curve. Buried in the cooler part of the forge, it was invisible, and Old John took down an unfinished iron hinge from a nail on the shed wall and thrust it into the orange coals.

"We're making a hinge for the new barn," he growled. "D'you understand me?"

"Yes, sir. A hinge."

"Aye. It don't do to let strangers see a gun in the making. It upsets them rather fierce."

The two riders came on steadily. They must have known they were being watched, but they maintained at least the appearance of casual conversation. One of the men was very young and rather plump, his clothes of a quality and cut that meant he had money or at least the expectation of it; the other was leaner and rougher and looked as if his expectations had already been pretty well disappointed.

"Come a distance," his grandfather said. David noted the full saddlebags. "One's a Boston man, from the clothes," he said.

"Have I the honor of addressing myself to Mr. Morse?" the younger man said as he turned his horse in front of the shed.

"Who wants to know, then?" His grandfather's voice was not quite rude.

"I was told that I would find Donald Morse the smith up here."

"I ain't Donald Morse, sir."

The plump young man giggled as if to show that his own good nature could not be troubled with an old man's surliness. "Well, may I take it that you are a smith at least, sir?" He peered into the shed. "I'm a trifle chilled from riding up your mountain; the wind's honed itself an edge this morning. May I warm my hands?"

"Ain't going to stop you, then."

Once inside, the two men huddled near the forge. They seemed intent on warming themselves; yet, when their eyes had grown accustomed to the gloom, they looked about carefully.

"Been making hinges," Old John said when the rougher one's glance went to the forge. "New barn yonder."

"Ah, indeed, indeed!" the young man said. He perched one haunch on the anvil, and then, finding some obstruction to perfect comfort there, he moved and looked down at the barrel-channel swage that was still in place. Lifting it with the same care he might have used in handling a stemmed glass, he looked at each of its faces and then at the shank where the name was marked. He leaned against the now smooth anvil and began to pack tobacco into a short pipe.

"My name is Cotton Emory." He picked up a coal with the tongs and held it over the pipe. "This is Mr. Flynn of Greenfield. We're traveling on a matter of business. We lay last night at Mr. Dickson's at Shelburne Falls." He puffed mightily. "You may ascertain the truth of that, if you send."

"And why would I care to, sir?"

"These are restless times."

"Aye." The old man looked first at the plump one and then at his silent companion. He spat on the fire. "I am John Morse," he said grudgingly. "If it's a matter of business, you'll be wanting my son Donald. He's a great man for business."

"And where will I find him, sir?"

"He'll be over to the new barn. He's setting up a cooperage in there, and a bigger forge, too. It's just over yon hill, on the far side of our orange house there."

Emory swung around to David. "And are you a Morse, too, young fellow?"

"Yes, sir—David by name."

Emory nodded. "Maybe you'd lead us to where your father's working then, David. Unless you're needed here—?"

"Nay, I can make a hinge alone." The old man jerked his head. "Be mannerly and take these gentlemen to your father."

It grieved David to be treated like a boy, but more often than not he was; small for his age and too delicately featured, he looked more fifteen than eighteen. He made a movement to follow the two men out of the shed, but his grandfather's heavy hand drew him back.

"Don't do nothing daft with those two," the old man whispered fiercely. David tried to twist away, but the grip tightened. "They're bad cess, those two."

"Why?"

"Ah!" The old man's breath was fetid. He had only his front teeth left and it always seemed that he had been chewing on wet earth. "I know their kind. I know that look. Take care, you hear me? You understand, you jackass?"

"Yes, sir."

"No, you don't! You don't understand nothing!" The hand tightened still more. "Let your damned fool of a father listen to them if he likes; if he's greedy enough or fool enough, let him! But not you. You stay away. Let 'em haver, but pay no heed."

"Who are they?"

The old man chuckled. "The worst kind in the world," he said. "Men with a mission!" He laughed again and pushed his grandson out into the weak sunlight toward the two strangers who wanted to be led to his father on a matter of business.

He watched David move away with the strangers. Old John had hopes for David—astonishing as it seemed, he still had hopes. Small, wizened hopes, the hopes of a bitter old man who had married badly and wasted his essence on the Cause; it surprised him that he had any hopes at all left. Still, his grandson David seemed to him a young man who might yet be taught what sort of place the earth was, and so he had hopes for him.

Old John Morse moved back to the forge. The coals shifted, their everchanging orange glow like the light of memory: all his bitterness, his lost hope was there. Yet his remembered joy was there, too—the years with Jane Mary when they had lived as man and wife in this new world, happy at last in each other's love. They had had eighteen years together, and he dared ask for no more.

The family's moves had come about because of fear that they would be recognized. He had brought them this far west to try to escape people altogether. Now there were other people near the Morse farm, but it no longer mattered. Jane Mary had died in her sixtieth year of influenza. Old John was alone again, but it was a different loneliness now, one colored by the memory of happiness.

He stirred the forge fire and watched the red patterns change. He smiled. He was thinking of a joke. *Thank God for the Cause*, he was thinking. *If I hadn't gone off to fight for the Cause, my wife would never have left me. Now, there's the only good thing I ever heard to come from the Cause at all!*

He stirred the fire again and stood musing over it, an old man for whom the shifting glow was a tapestry of remembered pictures: the White Beast, Jane Mary, self-discovery and brief but poignant happiness.

"It was worth it," he said aloud. He looked around the dim shed defiantly, as if he expected a voice to contradict him.

Chapter Fifteen

The spring mud was sticky in the road and he had to keep to the higher bank above the ruts; still, there were places where he had to veer into the track and his boots became heavy with the sodden earth.

"Good soil out here," the plump man said amiably. In fact, it was not particularly good soil. "Good soil if you don't carry it off on your boots, I mean."

"Yes, sir."

"Your father farms as well as blacksmiths, does he?"

"Yes, sir." The wind was blowing from the south, warm and wet-smelling like his grandfather's breath. The apple trees along the road were tightly budded still, without a hint of green; yet in five weeks they would be joyous in their full bloom, and his grandfather would walk along the road with a blooming branch in his hand like a wand, striking the blooms as high as he could reach on every tree. Out of this barren landscape, that life; between the two, more rain, more mud, more labor. Spring.

"Your grandfather is a Scot, from his voice."

"He is."

"I never knew Morse to be a Scots name."

The plump man had dismounted to walk next to David; his plump face seemed cheerful and interested. "My grandfather fought in the 'forty-five with Lord George Murray," David said, giving that event a coloration far different from his grandfather's.

"Did he!" Emory, too, was trying to keep to the edge of the road while he led the horse up the ruts, but when the animal pulled a little aside he stepped into the mud, and, perhaps to convince David that he was not merely a townsman with no control of animals, he swore and yanked the horse's head around. "Did he," he said again. "Then he's no great friend to England, I suppose."

"Why—no, I suppose not. No great friend." There was a safe thing to say. His grandfather was not a great friend to anything.

"Then your father is not, neither, I guess."

143

"Well…" He shrugged. Perhaps Emory took the gesture for an excusable caution, and he did not press further; in fact, David was not so much cautious as confused. He knew of the controversies on the coast; he had heard of the tax troubles and the massacre and the tea protests in Boston; he had listened to excited gossip of the tarring of a governor's man and of the threatening of Loyalists. Yet he felt no thrill of sympathy for the Americans. England remained to him a place of legend and fantasy, obscured by the same intensity of emotion that colored his grandfather's stories of Scotland. Too, loyalty was a virtue, rebelliousness a heinous vice; obedience—to his father most of all, who was not the penny-pinching miser his grandfather grumbled about, but a sober, God-fearing, utterly humorless man weighed down with a too heavy sense of responsibility—was law. How, then, was he to feel sympathy for the disloyalty and disobedience of a few coastal people (who were in it anyway, his grandfather had hinted, to make money)? And how could he balance his own image of England—grand, lovely, civilized—against the rough and muddy place in which he lived?

"Well—"

"And you, young fellow, how do you feel about the king that's trying to put his heel on our necks, hey?"

People seemed to think that Scotsmen should hate England as a gift of birth. Yet, he had an uncle who had died at Fort Carillon, wearing a Highland uniform and fighting for the English army; he had a second cousin who was one of Sir William Johnson's enforcers at Johnstown in New York; he had other cousins in Halifax who once every two or three or five years wrote his father a letter, and they seemed quite happy in that garrison city. Still, it was always best to tell people what they wanted to hear, and he said, with a counterfeit modesty, "The English Crown ain't exactly *loved* by me, if you get my meaning, sir."

That made Mr. Emory happy, and he turned his talk to birds, which seemed a subject he had a special interest in, the birds of the Connecticut Valley being different from those of Boston. David could give all the birds there their local name and tell him which had wintered over and which were passing through, for he was enough of a countryman to note almost unconsciously these signals of the season's progress.

Then they came up to the new barn and David showed them where to tether their horses away from the work. The smell of new-cut lumber was in the soft air, piny and domestic.

Fifty yards down the slope there was a pile of it, brought here from his father's sawmill on the river. Twenty yards n the other direction, a man was chiseling a mortise in a beam, while on a crosspiece of the new barn itself, his father was balancing so that he could look out through the rafters at the newcomers. Seeing David wave to him, he disappeared inside the structure and appeared a minute later on the ground outside, ducking under a piece of sheathing that one of his workmen was raising into place.

"These two gentlemen come to the old forge, Father," David murmured, intercepting him before he had reached the two men. "Looking for you, they say. The fat one's from Boston."

And then they came up, Emory smiling pleasantly and the other one looking as grim as a minister; and his father shook hands with each slowly.

"Your father directed us to you, sir, and your son was good enough to show us the way. I'm Cotton Emory and this is Mr. Flynn. Mr. Flynn is from Greenfield. Perhaps you know Mr. Flynn."

His father studied Flynn, who looked back insolently.

"I believe I've heard of Mr. Flynn," he said.

Emory grinned. "You just may have, sir! Mr. Flynn's made a name for himself in a way, I think. Yes, a definite name. Mr. Flynn's a man of powerful views."

His father folded his arms. "Go help your grandfather, David." His voice was always heavy and sad; now, it was faintly angry.

"Might he stay, sir?" Emory's tone was light and his educated accent was comical next to Donald Morse's, which was a harsh mix of Scots and New England nasality. "I think the young fellow is old enough to know what's what in the world. And your workmen will be less curious if he stays with us."

"Well—I ought to go, I guess." Reluctantly, David made a movement away. He was stopped by his father's voice. "Well, stay, then." Donald Morse looked at Flynn, then at Emory. "You'll want to go somewheres private, I suppose."

"Not at all, not at all! The very worst thing we could do!" Emory turned his back on the barn and gazed out over the valley. "We've only come to admire your new barn and to discuss buying some timbers, you understand." He pointed down the valley. "What a pleasing prospect is here, Mr. Morse! Many an English nobleman would pay dear to have such a vista from his palace. But of course many an English

145

nobleman has the money to pay for one, eh?" He started toward a clump of trees thirty yards away. "We will just stroll down to this pleasant grove and back—come on, Flynn; smile if you can, Flynn, we ain't attending a hanging—Mr. Morse, we can talk as we walk, I guess; David, on the other side of me, if you please—good...."

Emory stopped the group halfway to the trees and turned back toward the barn. From that vantage point, they might have been studying its construction.

"I'm looking for a gunmaker, Mr. Morse." Emory looked at Donald Morse, who remained as stolid as one of his own cattle. "Not for m'self, of course. For the Committee of Safety. You know what that is, I guess?"

Donald Morse nodded. The skin of his face had long ago settled into furrows and pouches, aged by sun and wind into a mask of worried resignation. Now when he frowned, the expression was mostly lost in the permanent lines.

"You've made guns, I know, Mr. Morse."

"One or two."

"More than that, I think. I've seen a fowler of Dr. Benn's in Dorchester that is as good a shooting gun as anything that comes out of London. And most beautifully stocked—a thing of art!"

David's heart pounded. It was he who had stocked that gun, two years before, deep-checkering the cherry wrist and carving a scallop shell at the tang. His father did not so much as look at him, however, and he took the cue and kept quiet. Donald Morse looked down and began to chip caked mud off the sole of his right boot with the edge of the sole of his left. "I didn't make the lock for that gun," he growled. "I never made no locks."

"But your father has, I think. Your father has made whole guns."

"Not for donkey's years."

"No matter; he could teach it. Why, he could probably teach it to this young fellow here."

David wondered if Emory knew enough to have guessed what they were doing at the old forge. It seemed unlikely.

His father went on chipping, chipping at the mud, his hands deep in his waistcoat pockets. "I haven't the steel," he said at last. "Steel for springs. No proper steel for the battery. That's why I use London locks on my fowlers. The few I've made."

146

"But if we found you the steel, then you could make the locks, couldn't you? Well, sir?"

His father's look of stubbornness was familiar to him, but a stranger might not have recognized it, might have taken it instead for some look of peasant shrewdness—the puffing of the lower lip as if he had a cud tucked there, the slitting-up of the eyes. David thought that his father had the same ideas about loyalty and obedience as he.

"The Committee of Safety are ready to pay you seven dollars a musket, completed and delivered ready to fire, Mr. Morse. And we'll arrange for the steel. Arrange for Salisbury iron if you need it. I'm offering you a prime bargain in a seller's market, sir—a unique opportunity, Mr. Morse!"

His father went on chipping away at the mud, which seemed to be as stubborn and slow to yield as he. "Going to fight the English army, are you?"

"If attacked, we will fight, yes, sir."

"Going to fight the English regulars?"

"The British army have invested Boston, sir; if they march out to impose more tyranny on the countryside, yes, we will fight them."

"With my muskets."

"Only out of necessity, Mr. Morse. As a *defensive* show of force."

"Yes, and then one of my muskets gets found, what does the English army make of that? What do they make of me, then?"

Emory chuckled; even the dour Flynn smiled. "The British ain't marching out to the Connecticut Valley, and you may take a note upon that, sir! The British army don't dare budge west of Cambridge without making out its will and taking up a collection for the widows, sir. If they come west of Worcester they'll be cut into little pieces and fed to the hogs for slops."

Donald Morse looked at his fine new barn, whose unpainted sides were clean and golden in a sudden shaft of sunlight, the building itself a hopeful and domestic sign raised against the dark background of uncleared woods. "In Queen Anne's War," he muttered, "the French come down out of Canada to this place with their Indians. Why not the British now?"

"Because we ain't going to let them! Because we're organized! Because the Committee of Safety can guarantee the peaceful lives of godly citizens like yourself that come to the aid of the cause of liberty. For seven dollars a musket." Emory's voice was the soft voice of a tempter. "We'd like to give you a contract for three hundred muskets, Mr. Morse. To be paid in gold."

"Psha, how would I ever make three hundred muskets?"

Flynn spoke up for the first time. He had an oddly thin, high-pitched voice that was entirely at odds with his physical self. "I got two barrel forgers ready to come to you, and forty-seven German and Dutch locks we got in storage. Take on a man or two for stockmakers, you can make three hundred guns easy."

The word "easy" made Donald Morse look aside at Flynn. "What seems easy to you maybe ain't so easy to them who has to do it, sir."

"Seven dollars a musket—in gold, Mr. Morse!" Emory cried. "You'll never make that in wagon-wheel rims and horseshoes! A deal of money, sir—a deal of money! And honestly earned in the service of a great cause!"

"I don't know about causes much," his father said. "I got a farm to keep up, as well as that smithy."

"Ah, but besides the money—which will more than pay for that barn, sir—there's other benefits! Other than the satisfaction of helping the cause of liberty, I mean. Now, take your son here—you have other boys, have you?"

"Two." Donald Morse looked defiantly at Emory. "One of them ain't quite right."

"Ah." Emory nodded as if he understood all about Samuel, who was thirteen and who had to haul up his words as if by main force, with his face twisted into a stammering, embarrassing horror that his sisters sometimes mocked most cruelly. "Well, sir, if you take on the musket contract, I can assure you that the committee will excuse you and all of your family from all service with the militia. Or with the army, if it came to that. If the British won't see reason and give us justice."

"Well, I got to finish my barn—and then there's planting time will be right on me without let-up, and every other man in the valley pestering me to make this and mend that and patch that wagon tire and—"

"Morse, you stand to *gain* by making muskets!" Flynn took a step closer to Donald Morse. "You stand to *lose* by not. You ain't the only smith hereabouts; there's Ben Tosten at Charlemont, we got our eye on him, too. Now, if you say no and he says yes, then what choice have we got but to warn other loyal Americans that you got no sympathy for the cause they fight for and are no better than a Britisher yourself? What choice would we have but to warn off honest people from you and send them down to Ben Tosten? Just as we'd send them *to* you if you show your sympathy to us?"

In the silence after Flynn spoke, David could hear one of the workmen laughing from the barn. The wind had shifted—colder now, with rain coming.

"Flynn's a guiding spirit in the Sons of Liberty," Emory murmured.

"I know that; I know that!" his father said.

Flynn nodded briskly. "The Sons look at it this way: a man is either a friend or he's an enemy. A friend we protect and take care of, guard his place and send him business; an enemy we can't do nothing for, we couldn't save even if we heard somebody had took it into his head to burn down his new barn or his house."

"I'm not your enemy," Donald Morse said cautiously. His voice was almost inaudible and he seemed fearful, almost whining. "But you know, I don't give these things much thought. A man can be right-thinking and—and still see the right on both sides of a thing, can't he? Must he come down hard on one side or the other?"

"Whoever ain't with us is our enemy."

For the first time, Donald Morse looked at his son directly, as if he meant to communicate some of his own anguish. *Understand me,* he seemed to ask. "I got the farm and the new forge and—"

Emory cut him off. "I think you understand the situation, Mr. Morse. We don't care to flog a dead horse; you know where we stand and what we've offered. I daresay you want a little time to think the matter over—perhaps discuss it with your good wife."

No doubt Emory had learned the gossip of the valley, perhaps from Flynn: *Donnie Morse is a fish that can be caught with a single hair—if the hair is his wife's.* "Her head on his shoulders makes a good man," some said.

So Donald Morse looked relieved, and he thanked Emory and Flynn and said he would think it over.

"Good, then!" Emory's wide face split like a pumpkin into a wide smile. "Mr. Flynn will stay close to your thoughts, sir; you can expect to see him in a week, let us say, to save you any inconvenience in communicating with us. In the meantime, if you have other questions, you may seek him out at

149

Greenfield or even reach me in Dorchester." His hand rested quickly on Donald's shoulder. "I hope you will join us in this work, Mr. Morse. I see that you are a man of qualities, and I would wish you well in the world." He beamed, first at Donald and then at David, and with a burst of laughter, as at some joke that had just been told, he turned back toward the barn and led them up the hill, pointing as he went at this thing or that—a tree of peculiar shape, a bird whose flight was strange to him, a huge rock that had been pried from the reluctant Berkshire earth by Morse strength—so that muskets and rebellion seemed the farthest thing from his mind and from his world.

David rode behind him to the old forge, half listening to the same prattle and replying with what he hoped was enthusiasm that would satisfy both him and Flynn. At the old forge, he slipped off the horse and joined his grandfather in the shed.

"Returned safe and sound, sir," Emory said, touching his hat to the old man.

"Aye. This time." The old man did not smile. There was a smudge of dark soot across his nose and below one eye like some ghost of battle paint.

"You were at Culloden, I'm told. You've left your grandson a mighty legacy."

The old man spat. "Old sins cast long shadows, they say."

Emory laughed. "Come, sir, the Scots are famous for their courage. The greatest fighters for their cause in the world, they say, hey? Why is that, now?"

Old John Morse looked at him shrewdly and then turned back to his work. "We bleed good," he said dourly. "Our blood is very pretty in the paintings that they do make afterward."

Chapter Sixteen

In May, Old John Morse came up the rows of apple trees along the valley road, swinging a blossom-laden apple branch into the blooming trees, "forging the seed," he said, striking the pollen of one tree on the blossoms of those others that he had raised from grafting stock brought from Ipswich twenty years before. In the same month, the first of the Committee of Safety's barrel forgers came, and he was pitiful enough to make the old man laugh. The other one came in July, and he made him both laugh and spit; watching one of the two at the forge, he would shake his head and make rude noises and finally stamp out of the new barn. The first barrel that came from their anvils caused him to spit and then to pick up his own hammer and smash the one weak spot along the weld with a single accurate blow.

Yet by August of that year the Morse gun works was more or less in operation. David supposed that everybody from Atholl to Charlemont, rebel and Loyalist alike, knew what they were doing, yet his father scurried about to keep up the appearance of a fully working rural forge: horses were still shod, wagons repaired, latches and toasters and weather cocks made, just as if there were no new smiths forging the parts that would become three hundred muskets to be shot at English soldiers. His father grew more haggard with the work and the worry of it and he seemed perpetually exhausted at trying to do the work of Morse the farmer and Morse the smith and Morse the master gunmaker. It was no Crown nor the local roughneck law of Flynn and the Sons of Liberty was going to come after him. Old John tried to tell him that; his wife tried to tell him that; but it did no good. He was a dour man born, made to worry and work hard. The Crown had stout cudgels in Boston and Hartford and Albany, but not so much as a pithy willow switch to wield in Greenfield and the upper Connecticut Valley, while at that dawning point of the American Revolution the noisy mob around Sam Adams and his country counterparts had only formed themselves into a gang of street propagandists that, at best, might have come

151

to his aid in an hour of need and defended his forge with the last drop of whiskey in their veins.

So the barrel forgers came in May and July, two untalented men whose claims to ability were not borne out by the barrels they made, which were fit "to shoot at privies with, and then hit naught but shit," as Old John said. He aimed the second barrel that was made at a window and put a taut string down the bore and showed David where the string's shadow rippled like a snake, with every slightest curve a flaw in the bore, the whole foreshortened into a seeming inch of errors. Taking his hammer then and marking the exterior of the barrel with chalk at each ripple, he cold-hammered the wretched thing straight or as straight as such work could be made; and then, never content to have bad work done anywhere around him, he went to the smiths' anvil and stood over the man until he found how the fellow had managed to do such a dreadful thing to soft iron; and then he bullied him and shouted at him until he understood how a gunsmith does a proper job of forging a musket barrel.

The man stayed surly until Old John made a barrel for the two of them—alone and with only poor half-addled Samuel for a helper to hold the mandrel—and made it straighter and cleaner and with a stronger weld than either of them could make on his best day and with two helpers.

"Now *that* will shoot mickle straight!" the old man said. "Straight enough for fifty paces, at the least. Now do you the same!"

They never did learn to make barrels as good as that one, but they got careful enough, he said, "to cobble up an iron tube I'd dare to let my grandson put a stock to."

With the second barrel forger came a succession of so-called forgers' helpers, laggards and no-goods and life-losers dredged up by Flynn and Emory and pumped full of a gassy fervor that leaked out through the cuts and tears in their enthusiasm with each working day. The local ones lasted a few weeks or months, the strange ones not so long; their comings and goings constantly broke into the flow of the work, each arrival meaning new training and new accommodation to new idiosyncrasies, and the quality of the Morse product stayed low. Still, they had to be borne with, too, because gunmaking took labor, and something was better than nothing.

In November, a reputed whitesmith and finisher came to their part of the valley and was moved into a little old log house three miles from the Morse farm that had served over twenty years for tenant house, chicken coop and tool storage. The man was a wiry Irishman named Sullivan who announced, half belligerently and half mockingly, that he had worked for the great Dalton of Dublin; and it was true he had certainly seen a pair of Dalton's pistols, for he could describe them in detail and even spell Dalton's name.

David Morse first saw Sara Sullivan in late September. He had ridden over to the little house—the Barnes house it was called, although nobody named Barnes had lived in the county in David's short lifetime—on a plowhorse with twenty-eight gunlocks and a great lot of screws in a leather seedbag behind him. Eleven of the locks had been made in the new barn, six by his father and four by his grandfather (the best by far, and too good for such guns, but too time-consuming in the way the old man made them, though it was the only way he knew) and one made by David himself, who was learning the craft, learning it his grandfather's way from the pair of Highland pistols they were still working at in odd hours; the rest of the locks had been sent out from Boston by Emory, a conglomeration of English and Dutch locks, half of them rusty and inoperative, three with broken cocks and five with ruined springs, locks collected from citizens here and there who remembered the useless guns their fathers had left in the barn or the cellar. These had been reconditioned and fitted with handmade springs and hand-forged cocks where they were needed, and now they were being sent to Sullivan to be filed and finished and to have slots cut in the heads of screws that had already been rough-fitted.

The Barnes house was in a hollow three miles east of the Morse farm, an unhealthy place with a spongy sort of tract behind that seemed undecided for half its width whether to be a swamp or a muckland, with dead trees sticking out of its wet bottoms like weary hands, and thin green scum over its open pools, until, content at last to admit what it really was, it gave way entirely to water and became a greasy pond that might have made a decent skating place in winter if it hadn't been so hard to reach and that was no earthly good in summer except for breeding insects and the snapping turtles that ate whatever ducklings hatched around it. Even the Sullivan cow would not go near it, but had to be watered from the well like one of the family. (It was said that somebody's child had fallen down that well and drowned once upon a time. Nobody was sure just when. Perhaps it was when the aboriginal Barnes was there. The well water was not very tasty, whatever its history.)

David was riding along, his thoughts as always upon what he would become when he got his opportunity—living, in fact, through a drama of which he was the hero, this one something about a complex lawsuit in London that saw him arguing before the House of Lords, wearing a blue brocaded suit of the latest cut, but with a sash of plaid—when he saw Sara Sullivan at the well. The house was behind her, unpainted and bleak; the swamp was behind that, unhealthy and dank. Yet she, in the foreground, sprang away from them as if through some painter's trick that makes one figure leap from a landscape, as if she had been caught in a single shaft of light while the rest of the scene was in clouded gloom. It was not her dress, for that was a faded and sometimes dirty yellow; it was not any ladylike bearing, for she was bent over the well, which had no winch, to pull up a bucket by a rope; it was not any elegance about her, for her hair was a jumble and her feet were bare. It was beauty, certainly; and rarity, for he saw few girls other than his sisters; and sex.

Her sleeves were pushed up over brown arms, and one white leg showed above the knee where the rope had pulled up the skirt in the hauling of the bucket; her breasts were visible almost to the nipples as she bent forward. There was an ease about her he didn't understand and was aroused by, and a glare from her eyes when she saw him looking at her that seemed almost crazed and reminded him oddly of Samuel when he was trying to speak some very hard word.

"Don't miss nothing!" she said. She held onto the rope, but straightened and pushed back her dark hair from her neck.

His heroic dream dropped away, forgotten; he moved entirely in her world. He reined in the horse, which fell immediately to browsing along the roadside. Words, which came so nimbly to him in his fantasies, all scuttled off. His ears felt hot.

"Imbecile," she said, and she bent over the well again and began to haul on the rope. He, speechless and delighted, watched her as if watching women pull up buckets of water were a high point of courtesy. When the bucket came to the level of the stones, she leaned farther forward to grasp the bail and swing it up, and the movement splashed water over the stones and her feet.

"Ah, the bastard!" she cried. She looked up at David. "It's

154

as cold as your stepmother's breath, that water! Look at it, all over me feet and me dress, the bastard!"

He was suddenly down from the horse and standing next to her as she wrung out the sopped skirt, trying not to look down her bosom and yet unable to keep from looking there.

"Can I help?" he said numbly.

"Aye, a load o' help you'd be up me wet skirt," she said. She stood up suddenly with the twisted skirt still in her hands, and the motion made her stagger back a step. "Who're you?"

"I'm David Morse. I'm looking for Sullivan the whitesmith."

"Oh." She shrugged. "Morse, is it. I heard of yous."

"My father's the blacksmith."

"Oh, aye, who don't know that?"

"I've brought the—the work for Sullivan."

"What, them gunlocks? Aye, I heard about them."

"Can I help you?"

"Aye, you can carry that bastard that spilled on me; I hope it breaks on the hard ground."

He grinned. No woman he had ever met or read about talked like this. It delighted him, as if she were a visitor from Paris or London, bringing the latest and most sophisticated fashion in talk to him. "If I spill it," he said, "you'd just have to get more from the well."

"Oh, well, aye, you'd like that." She shrugged again. "Then you could look down me dress some more." She straightened herself, tugging at her waist with the thumbs and index fingers of both hands opened around her hip bones; the gesture seemed to make her grow taller, emerging from the calyx of her hands like an exotic bloom. "But don't yous get any funny thought about me, thank you; I'm as honest as any lady in Boston is this minute. Mind where your thoughts go, you hear?"

"Of course!" He found he was smiling and blushing at the same time. "I wouldn't think of you—in any—I wouldn't think of you."

She laughed, and again he was reminded of Samuel. "Je-sus, if your eyes had hands I'd be black and blue." She grasped the reins of the horse and pulled the animal's head roughly away from the roadside grass. "Bring the water and don't spill none; I'll take your horse. My name's Sara and I'm Sullivan's daughter."

She put the horse between them. Normally, this would have been the opportunity for him to slip into some inner soliloquy—he had left much to be said to the House of Lords—but he could not do it now, did not want to. He was acutely aware of the smell of the horse, of her reddened hand on the greasy bridle, of her bare feet that seemed endangered by the animal's big hooves.

Her father, whom he had seen only once at the farm, was a thin, balding man with a dry cough and a grand manner who had somewhere lost two fingers from his left hand; David's eyes strayed back to this mutilation with a perverse fascination as Sullivan explored the bag of gunlocks, shaking his head and sucking on his teeth and exploding with exasperated sounds of "Ecch!" and "Tsha!" and "Ah!" as if the contents were too poor for his attention.

Of the three downstairs rooms in the little house, two were roughly furnished and the third held only a broken churn and cobwebs. Sullivan's daughter disappeared moments after David went in, and a minute or two later her mother entered, a plump, surprisingly (in that atmosphere) cheerful woman who said, "Well now!" when David introduced himself. She offered him tea—the Loyalist drink, it was said, but she made no politics out of it—and led him into the kitchen and sat him down on one of the two chairs there.

"He's a good man, your father," she said.

"Why, yes. Yes, I believe he is. Thank you."

"I was that pleased, when we come, it was nighttime and he had a man waiting for us with a lantern."

"Oh, yes, one of the new helpers, I think."

"And your mother, she'd sent a pot supper and a loaf; I think that's more than kind, it's Christian."

"That's like her, yes."

"Tsha!" Sullivan said. He pushed the locks from him and glanced scornfully at David, and then, with a pair of tiny eyeglasses pushed up on his pate, he leaned back in his chair, causing it to creak dangerously.

"They're a wretched lot," he said.

"They're all we've got," David said. His tone was defensive. "We must make do, they say."

"In Dublin," Sullivan said, and then he belched and scowled down into the palm that had covered his mouth, "in Dublin, they'd cut those up for scrap iron."

"You must listen to thunder," Mrs. Sullivan said cheerfully.

"What's that?"

"I said, you're a great talker, Sullivan; this ain't Dublin

and you're full of wind and whiskers, like the barber's cat."
She winked at David. "Pay him no mind." She poked a plump
finger through the pile of gunlocks, moving one or two as if
to make some distinction between one kind and another; then,
picking up one that Old John had made, she held it up and
said, "Now, there's a piece of work that Dalton hisself could
put on a gun! Look here, Sullivan—is that a piece of work or
ain't it?"

Sullivan looked at it and waved it away. "Pitiful, that's
what it is." He groaned.

She beamed at David. "Y'must listen to thunder," she said
again and she went for the tea. Overhead, footsteps sounded
on an uncertain floor whose squeaks were as ominous as those
of Sullivan's chair. He looked up and shook his head mourn-
fully again and then picked up another of the locks and held
it close to his eyes. The glasses were still up on his skull,
forgotten or simply useless.

"That's an English lock," he said. It was a pronouncement,
the serious and detached judgment of an astronomer iden-
tifying Betelgeuse for a layman. As there were a large crown
and the word "Tower" engraved on the lockplate, the discovery did not seem particularly remarkable.

"English." Sullivan nodded as if his worst fears had been
confirmed, put the lock down, and rubbed his eyes so hard
he might have been punishing them. "This lot will take donkey's years to finish," he said. "Terrible work it'll be, finishing
these." He took off the neglected glasses and peered through
them at the only window. "You'll tell your father that they're
such a lot as Sullivan has never in his life seen, and he'll be
very lucky if they can be brought into any condition as will
satisfy Sullivan hisself."

"Yes, sir."

"It could take weeks, filing a lot like these." He put the
glasses back on his forehead and passed his hand down his
bald skull to his neck. "A man should be paid extra for filing
these sort of firelocks."

"You'll have to take that up with my father."

"Well, you'll tell him what Sullivan said."

"Yes, sir."

"Because, see, I feel that your father, being only a blacksmith, don't perfectly understand the subtleties of the lock
finisher's art."

David wanted to tell the man he was an arrogant coxcomb,
which was what his grandfather would have said, or some-

157

thing worse; but he was too acutely aware that this sniveler was the father of the glorious creature he had seen at the well. Still, some of the eloquence of his fantasies came back to him, and with that rhetorical skill that he normally reserved for addressing the House of Lords, he said loftily, "My father, and his father before him, and his before that, have been making guns of a quality equal to any you have seen, Mr. Sullivan. I believe the Morses know their business, sir."

Sullivan looked at him. Sullivan was a coward, and he looked away. "Pish, toosh," he said childishly. "Stand up, missus, it's the King of Rome come to call."

Blushing, David stared at his tea while Sullivan excused himself to perform an errand in the decrepit barn. The room was pleasanter without him; for all that there were a short-haired bitch and five pups on an ancient scrap of cloth in one corner, and a hen that wandered in and out through the open door, it was a pleasant room, and David sat in a pool of warm sunshine and became almost drowsy, eating Mrs. Sullivan's soda bread with fresh butter and drinking inky tea. He was brought awake by the sudden intrusion of the daughter, who stopped when she saw him, with one hand gripping the door-post and her face distorted. "Still here, are you?" she said in a loud voice.

"Sara, Sara," her mother cautioned.

"Well, I thought he'd gone, is all, Ma."

"Where's your manners, you brute girl? He's a guest, and the son of your father's employer."

Sara grinned. "L'am Sullivan's as free as King George hisself, and calls no man his better!" she bellowed, slurring the words to sound drunk. David smiled.

"Stop it now!" Her mother seemed shocked, although he suspected it was not the first time she had seen this performance.

"I have to go," he said to spare her more embarrassment—and to spare himself. "My father will be waiting for me to do the milking."

"I thought you was a blacksmith, then," the girl said.

"Oh, aye, but there's the farm, too."

She leaned against the doorpost. "Gentlemen of property," she said sarcastically.

"Sara!" Mrs. Sullivan's voice was sharp now, and the girl turned away, kicking at the hen as she went out. A glance around that clean kitchen, that pathetic oasis in a near-ruin, would tell why the mother's voice was edged with real anger, would show her fear of losing even such a fragile hold on comfort as this. David smiled and thanked her and said he would carry her message to his mother. Pointing at the gunlocks, Mrs. Sullivan said in a lower voice, "Don't worry about this lot, now; they'll get done, never fear—there's more than one pair of hands in this house." Smiling, holding up her apron with twisted hands, she watched him retrieve the horse and walk it up the road, and he, looking back at her, saw that she must have been a pretty woman once, though such a fact meant nothing to him. *She must be almost forty now.*

The girl was at the well. She made no attempt to pretend she had not been waiting for him, sitting on the stone rim until he led the horse past her and then rising gracefully.

"Will you come back?"

He forced the bridle down to stop the horse; holding it behind him, he rubbed the animal's long nose, feeling the stiff, short hairs rise against his palm as he brushed them. "When the locks is done, I mean," she said.

"Yes, I'd like to."

"You can come back to see me, if you like."

He blushed again. "Thank you."

"If you come as you would to any decent girl. I'll not be treated like any trollop, you hear me? I'm decent."

"Of course! I'd have as much respect, Miss Sullivan, as for any of my sisters."

She laughed, a raucous, almost masculine sound. "Devil a sister I'd make!" She took a step toward him. "You ain't been in the world, have you?"

"I've been to Greenfield."

She laughed at him again. "Greenfield! Two privies and a pigsty! I been to Dublin! I been to Calais and Cherbourg; I seen the Solent when our ship lay off of Southampton. I was to Quebec when we come through Canada. I spent a month at Boston in the winter." She frowned. "But that don't mean nothing, none of it. Just seeing places ain't nothing. You might as well be a corpse in a casket and say, 'I got meself carried through Paris, France.' Do you follow me?"

"That's just what I think! You got to live in places, to be alive in them, be a part of them—do great things in them! When I get to London, it will be to—well, I mean to be somebody."

"Like what?" Her voice was suspicious, derisive. "What would the likes of you do at London?"

159

"I thought of being a lawyer, maybe. Or a member of Parliament."

"What—from Greenfield, Massachusetts?" The laughter was raucous again, the crude bellow of a man hearing a dirty story.

"There *will* be members of the Parliament from here, you can believe that! They'll give Massachusetts representation; that's what all the fuss is about. It'll all be settled and men like me, young men with ideas, will go to London and plead the case of Massachusetts and the rest! This talk of rebellion, that's all daft, that's the wild ones like Flynn and his drunkards that call themselves the Sons of Liberty and all they mean by rebellion is not paying their share of taxes; when it comes down to cases, when these brawlers are put in their place and the loudmouths are shut up, then men of sense will have their day and the Crown will give us our due. Then we'll be in Parliament—you'll see!"

She looked at him in silence. It occurred to him that she had not listened, that she had been bored. "Ah, I don't care about all that," she murmured sadly. She rubbed her nose. "That's all nonsense. Grown-up men's games. Anyway, what are you making muskets for if it's going to end peaceable?"

"So that it *will* end peaceably, don't you see?" He had heard his father rationalize it a dozen times. "It ain't the musket that's rebellious; it's the hand that holds it." She was not listening again, but he went on more heatedly, a little angry with her. "The guns we make ain't to use; they're only to show that we could use them if we wanted to! It's a way of backing up an idea, don't you see?"

"When you come back to see me," she said almost dreamily, "come in the early evening, like any proper man. I ain't some farm girl to be waylaid at chores."

"No, Sara."

"And wear proper clothes."

"All right."

"And don't try to take no liberties."

"Of course not."

"And don't expect no kissing nor none of that right off."

"No, of course!"

"Well, go on, then. Get out of this."

"Yes, Sara."

Chapter Seventeen

By December, when the first snow drifted against the barns and the house was banked for warmth with horse manure along the foundations, the gun works was operating. Like an old horse that cannot pull well on all slopes, it went forward haltingly, now at an even and rapid pace and now not at all, most often because of a lack of the raw materials that had been promised, sometimes because of a change in the laborers who were sent. The finished locks and barrels were stored in the loft of the new barn, waiting for wood to stock them with.

Up to that time, Donald Morse had made no trigger guards or buttplates or end caps for his muskets, hoping that Emory would find him enough, but in November Emory came with more rigid specifications from the committee, demanding that the guns be of a military type as much like that carried by the British army as possible; and after that, the Morses had to undertake the casting in brass of the smaller pieces of hardware with which the guns were to be completed.

"I shall never finish them. Never, never, never!" Donald Morse groaned. "How will I ever finish them?"

"Ah, havers," his father said unkindly. "You'll do it by taking one thing at a time, same way as you do anything." He was finishing the locks for the pair of Highland pistols he had begun to make that day when Emory and Flynn had first come, and their laboriously forged metal stocks and barrels seemed like bright proofs of his words. "One thing at a time," he said again.

Donald Morse looked at the disassembled military musket that had been sent out by Emory, at all the parts that the Morses had not yet begun to make—trigger, swivels, nosecap, ramrod, buttplate. "I will never do it. Why did I let myself be trapped into such a thing?"

"Havers."

The old man was right. Piece by piece, step by step, the Morse muskets were built. Donald Morse never believed they would be finished; he was an anxious, dour man. But the guns were built, however slowly.

"Ah, how shall I ever do it all?" Donald Morse groaned;

he groaned it to himself, plodding down his road; he groaned it in his wife's arms, feeling without sexual excitement the comfortable warm valleys and mountains of her body; he probably groaned it even in his dreams, which were always of enormous tasks left unfinished, of schooldays when lessons were unlearned and tests were utterly unprepared for.

"One step at a time," Old John said as he pointed out how, when there was a shortage of iron, the smiths could be put to cleaning and rebuilding the forge or how, when the axle of the grindstone broke, David and Jonathan could use their time in melting swaff iron from the barrel ends and nail stubs and screw cuttings and breechplug bits that had been collected from the floors by Samuel.

"This won't last," David Morse said, dreaming over the spinning grindstone or the forge and waiting for evening, when he would see her again. From the day that he first saw her, she became a wedge driven between him and the life around him, isolating him from it, forcing him into himself, into his fantasies of her.

"Mrs. Sullivan says thank you for setting her house right when they moved in," he had said to his mother that first day.

"I'm sure she'd do the same for me."

"Well, she was very grateful."

"What opinion did you form of Sullivan?" his father had asked around a mouthful of bread and ham.

David had hesitated. "He was very critical of the gunlocks," he had said slowly. "Though his wife assured me the work would be done."

His father had frowned at this.

"What is it?"

"Eat your supper."

"Was it your opinion," his father had asked slowly, gazing now at a piece of boiled potato on his fork as he continued to chew, "that Sullivan is a *steady* man?"

"Well, sir—"

"What your father means," Old John growled, "was he drunk?"

David pretended to be astonished. "Oh, no, sir! He was very acute—very picky about the quality of the locks."

"Aye, he's Irish."

David had looked around the table, suddenly defensive, finding himself siding with strangers against his family for a reason he did not yet understand. His sister Nora, moving

162

the handle of her empty cup in a circle on the oiled tabletop, had murmured with disarming casualness, "I hear the Sullivans got a daughter." Her face had been carefully bland.

"I guess there was some girl about the place."

"I hear she's very bold."

"Nora!" His mother had been scandalized.

"They say she looks like a gypsy."

"Gypsy!" David had tried to laugh, feeling choked. "What do you know about gypsies?"

"Well, I know when my brother's blushing, anyways."

His mother had scolded the girl, but she had grinned mockingly at him when the adults' talk turned to other things.

When, next day, his mother had found him alone in the cowbarn, she had been hesitant and embarrassed, but she had managed to say quietly, "Is it true about the Sullivan girl?"

"Is what true, ma'am?"

"Is she—bold?"

He had shrugged. "No more than Nora, I guess."

"How old is she?"

"Maybe seventeen. I didn't ask."

She had frowned. He was shoveling cow manure into a cart, and she had reached out to rest a hand on the cart, and she had seen the manure and had stopped with her hand halfway there. "You got to remember, Davie, they're Irish."

"Ma'am? I don't follow."

"It means they ain't like us."

He had forced himself to laugh. "They got two eyes and one mouth, same as everybody I see about this place. They ain't Negroes or red Indians or nothing."

"Well." His mother had sniffed. "I wouldn't advise you to let them get familiar." She had looked at him then as if she had hoped for a reply—some sign of willing submission, of gratitude for her caring, something indicating a son's love—but nothing had come. He had turned back to the cow manure and she had stood there, a strong-bodied woman of forty-six who had borne eight children and raised six of them, her hands grimed with soot from the bake oven and her face red from heat and work, and for an instant she had been as vulnerable as a child. He had heard her sniffling as she had hurried away, and, unkind as sons must be, he had hated her sniffling and her advice.

Three days after that, he rode over to the Sullivans' on the pretext of taking two more locks. There was no sign of Sara and none of her father, but Mrs. Sullivan was in the kitchen, a file in her hand and one of the gunlocks in a patch of sunlight on the table.

"I, ah—well, Mrs. Sullivan—" He felt both foolish and elated, doing something he had never done before. "I'd hoped to see your daughter, ma'am."

"Oh, she'll be that sorry! She and her pa ain't about the place today." She smiled at him, apparently the most cheerful woman in the county.

"Well, ma'am, I also wanted to ask, also, if, ah, if it would be, ah, acceptable—to you and Mr. Sullivan, I mean—if I, ah, called on Sara. Once in a way. Once or twice. Of an evening, I mean. Now and then."

"You may come whenever you like!" Taking the two new locks, she went out of the room, and he thought he heard her talking, but in seconds she was back to offer him tea.

The house looked a little more scrubbed than the first time, and part of the yard had been scythed down. "You're settling in, I see," he said to be polite. "The place looks capital." In fact, he disliked it intensely.

"Oh, it's coming along," she said. "Sullivan's so busy, of course."

So he took his tea and was polite and went home, frustrated in his hope of seeing her and wondering where she was.

Two days later, his father had paused in his work at the forge and had looked at him.

"I hear you went to the Sullivans' again, David."

"I took some more locks, sir."

"Is it Sullivan's girl?"

"I don't even know her, sir! I only said a few words to her."

"But she struck you as—comely, did she?"

"Yes, sir."

"Well..."

"Mrs. Sullivan seems very pleasant, Dad."

"Aye." His father moved the iron, and the charcoal rustled like chunks of ice. "They're not Catholic, at any rate."

"Sir?"

"I stipulated that only Protestants of good character would be taken here. Some things are more important than this rebellion, as you'll learn. Sullivan purports to be a Presbyterian." The light from the forge threw his face into a deep shadow. "Make it clear to the girl that you expect to see her in church on Sundays, or you'll not call on her."

"But, Dad—"

164

"You heard what I said, David! It's little enough to ask! A girl like her, and a fellow of your—well, a fellow like you, noticing her in an honorable way—she'd best be meek as cream, for her own good."

As he turned to the bellows, his father called him back. "And David."

"Sir?"

"You understand how to behave with a young woman, do you?"

"I think so, sir."

"I don't know how much the Sullivans understand our ways, but I expect you to remember our reputation—and the girl's, to be sure. I would not have the two of you left alone by the parents, do you understand?"

David sighed. Embarking on what was to have been a great adventure, he felt cheated, as if he were being told to set sail on a cowpond.

"I will speak to Sullivan myself, first chance I get. You're young, she's young; the blood is easily heated. I will not be disgraced."

"Yes, sir." With difficulty, he kept anger from his voice. "Will I pump now?"

"When I tell you." He stirred the iron again in the coals. "You must not fling yourself at life so, David. Slow and steady, that's the way. Anything good is well worth going slow for."

Chapter Eighteen

Under the steady tapping of the hammer, the graving tool moved in tiny arcs across the metal surface, a hard steel plow cutting through the field of softer iron, its furrows lines that became pictures in the way that the lines of woodcuts and engravings did. Each time the hammer rose, it almost touched the right lens of the old man's spectacles, so low was his head bent over his work. Even so close as that, however, he could not see it as well as he once had, and he blinked his eyes often and squinted at the picture that would not quite come clear. He had owned the same spectacles—small lozenges of glass in wire frames—for more than twenty years; if he needed stronger ones now, it did not matter, because there was no one close by who knew how to make such things.

Old John Morse moved the eyeglasses up his forehead with a motion of his blunt middle finger. The fingertip massaged the left eyeball and then the right and then pulled the glasses back into place. He bent over the work again and moved so close that he seemed about to kiss it.

Both stocks of the Highland pistols were complete. The barrel of one lay near them, its breech end a fluted octagon in cross section, the forward two-thirds round, with a slightly flared muzzle and rings at three-inch intervals along it. The steel stocks were graceful and slender, the butts widened at the bottom to swell easily into the inturned scrolls that carried their lines back upon themselves in ram's-horn curves. The flat sides invited the engraver's hand, and already the lower third of one of the butts had been worked. A thin frame of conventional scrollwork enclosed the first of the weapon's scenes.

"Achilles's shield," the old man said to David. "When Thetis went to Hephaestus for armor for her son, he covered a great shield with all the scenes of life. That's what I'll do with these pistols. I'll make them unlike any pair of pistols that's ever come out of Scotland."

"It's a terrible lot of work, Grandfather."

"Aye. Most decent things are."

He had scribbled drawings before he began to cut, but

these he would show to no one. Still, the pictures remained in his head; to David, they seemed to be in the old hands themselves, in the dirty, cracked, big-knuckled fingers that tilted and aimed the graver and caused it to leave behind a minuscule track that became part of a vibrant, two-dimensional reality. In the trapezoid at the bottom of the buttstock on the right side, a hollow-eyed skull appeared, and on each side of it, blunt wings—the Angel of Death, the figure that hovered over so many New England tombstones. In the oval cartouche farther up the curve of the butt, an open coffin stood tilted against a wall; a skeleton, wearing the tattered remnant of the shroud it had been wrapped in, stepped out of it. Around the cartouche, the broken old hands had begun to shape a weeping willow that seemed to embrace it.

"Is it all going to be like that?"

"Aye, this one. Not the other." He squinted and twisted the tool to shape a fragment of the tree, then began quoting from the translation of the *Iliad* that he read almost nightly while Donald Morse read his Bible and his wife sewed:

> "'Two cities radiant on the shield appear,
> The image one of peace, and one of
> war.'

"Mine ain't of peace and war, but death and life. Death first." He smiled.

The boy frowned but said nothing. The old man had retired to a downstairs room to work on the pistols; contemptuous now of the barrel forgers and the muskets they were making, he would share the same forge with them only in a constant mutter of complaints. David's father said that the old man was getting odd, but he said it without rancor or fear, said it almost casually as he might describe any natural thing—the appearance of apple buds in April, the lowering of the river in summer. Old people, he seemed to say, inevitably got odd; just now, it was Old John's turn. But David was frightened by the idea, which seemed to threaten him because it suggested that he, too, was part of that dreadful inevitability, that his flesh and Sara's were fallible.

"Time," he said softly.

"What's that?" The graving hammer stopped, the old man never risking a stroke if he was distracted.

"It's all Time," David said. "It's Time brings death and all the rest. I hate it."

"Time brings death, yes; it brings life, too. Maybe Time should be on the pistols." He put the hammer down and rubbed his eyes. "Maybe Time is God." He peered down at the work as if it were new to him and he were trying to understand what it meant. "Time giveth, and Time taketh away. Time makes you young and me old." He picked up the graving hammer. "Yes, Time should be on them. Maybe I'll give my rattle-bones here an hourglass. Or put a clock on my church steeple when I do the funeral. And on the other, I'll have an old man mowing—life, with the harvest. Summer. Plenty and happiness, but somewhere, the old man, mowing. A reminder." Old John looked up at David. "Like I'm a reminder to you, boy, much as you hate it."

He could say nothing to that, not even deny it. Now that Sara had come into his world, he wanted less than ever to be with the old man. Impatient of him, he sought out other work to stay away from him.

"Dad's getting odd," his father said when David told him about the pictures on the pistols. "But he don't mean any harm."

"No, sir." He couldn't understand his father's patience with oddness. It seemed to give his father positive satisfaction, as if some rightness in the scheme of things were being illustrated for him. Old people got odd, and later on they died; then the next generation came along and got old and odd in its turn, the process logical and bittersweet. Yet Donald could not confide in his son his terror that the rightness of things was spinning out of order and that he was beginning to see chaos where all his life he had thought he saw order. The gunmaking was part of the disorder, something he did not want to do; the rebellion and the talk of war was part of it; his own lack of control over his life and over his sons' lives was in it, too.

"After all, David, everything works out for the best." He said it as if he believed it, but that night he lay awake long after his wife was snoring, his arms around her from the back, his hands cupped over her breasts even after his right arm had gone numb from the weight of her.

Then he delivered the first part of the Committee of Safety's musket order, and chaos seemed to take a long step nearer. The guns were sent off, complete and made to specifications, after being proofed out behind the Morse barn and stocked by David with the help of his brother Jonathan, as good as good, plain muskets could be, and Donald Morse smiled with the relief of it and made a joke to his wife and waited for the money that was due him. Flynn showed up five days later with money, all right, but it was only a third of what had been promised, and Donald was red-faced and angry after Flynn rode off. Flynn had filled the parlor with gassy talk of patriotism and sacrifice, and Donald had tried to thrust his own voice in to talk of expenses and the promises that had been made, but he hadn't been able to make it clear. He would get all his money in good time, Flynn said. Telling his wife that, Donald Morse held his head and groaned.

"They're just driving me betwixt the rock and the hard place!" he whispered to her. He wanted to hide his anguish from his father and his children. "I can't stop making the guns for fear of Flynn and his rowdies, and yet I got to go on paying the smiths and that Sullivan and the workmen, and who will ever pay *me?*"

"It'll all work out for the best," she said. "It always does. Often and often you've said that to me."

His anxiety was too much for him to hold in, and he told David about it the next day. "That—that *damned* Flynn didn't pay me half of what's due us!" he blurted out when David brought fresh charcoal to the forge.

"Aye, but he'll pay, won't he, Dad?"

"Oh, aye, when the people see the light of freedom, he says." Donald let his hammer drop end-down on the anvil. "When money begins to flow from the patriots, he says. He brings me this letter from Emory saying what a grand thing it is I'm doing for the cause of liberty! Well, liberty ain't going to feed your brothers and your sisters or pay them workmen's wages! Nor it ain't going to help set you up in a household when the time comes."

David blushed. "Ah, don't think of that. That's years off."

"But I should be able to plan for that! A father should be able to give his sons a help when they start out, like my father done me. One day, maybe sooner than you think, you'll be married and independent, David. But you got a right to expect something from me. But how am I to provide it if I go into debt's own hellhole making muskets for a lot of rabble-rousing devils—" He let the hammer fall again. "Making muskets for people who won't pay me what's owed."

"It'll all be over soon, Dad. All this talk is just haverin'.

Let Flynn bully; in six months, he'll be a flash in the pan, you'll see."

"Six months! Oh, it's easy for a young man to be cheerful. But I ain't got the time ahead of me that you have."

Time. It was like an enemy, like an Indian in the old Greenfield settlers' stories, something that crept up and threatened from behind with a vicious, spiked club. Only with Sara did Time seem to turn a kindly face, and time with Sara seemed harder and harder to find, as the work at the gun-making increased and his own responsibilites in stocking the completed muskets became greater, as spring approached and the farm chores began to multiply, and as, maddeningly, he had to join the local company of militia and drill with them far more often than he ever wanted to.

"Keep time, there!" the self-appointed sergeant bullied.

Captain Speke's company of Greenfield militia were not yet armed with anything so good as Morse muskets, nor were they equipped with military cartridge boxes and hangers, nor did they have anything approaching a uniform, yet they drilled with an enormous gusto and they drank afterward with a thirst and an appreciation that would have done credit to any company of the British line. Many of them were Scots, and so they fixed on the Scots device of putting green leaves in their hats for a quasi-military cockade—elm for preference, because it was a native American tree. Their officers wore green sashes and every man had a green bit of cloth that he tied around his left arm, and thus they were a uniform body.

The Morses supplied five men to the militia—Donald, his sons David and Jonathan, one barrel forger and one helper. To be sure, they had been excused from such duty by the promise of Emory and Flynn, but Donald Morse saw in his dour way that insisting on that privilege would only make resentment among his neighbors, and so he had bent the other way and insisted that his older sons and his healthy workmen all drill until they were as good as any in the company. He even tried to get Sullivan to join, but the lock filer pleaded age and superior social status; it would be a shame, he implied, to take away Captain Speke's command from him.

"But you could join as a gentleman volunteer and be a private soldier," said Jonathan Morse, who read books about such things and knew more about the army than anybody in the company.

Sullivan shook his head sadly. "It breaks my heart to turn

170

you down, lads, but I'd be untrue to me parentage if I accepted anything less than the captaincy."

Some of the militiamen had fought in the French and Indian War under Speke, and they had been at Quebec; but many of the others were raw—as raw as a fresh-plucked hen, Speke said, and so they had to drill and drill and drill some more. They learned to march in a ragged line and to stand at something like attention and to go through the manual of arms with great ardor.

"Poise your firelocks!" Speke would bellow, and muskets would point in every direction and Speke would shut his eyes and swear quietly and think about what the whisky would taste like afterward.

Jonathan, standing at attention next to David, with a fowling piece at his shoulder and a scrap of green petticoat bound around his left arm, whispered with fierce delight, "God, I love it when he swears, Davie! I feel like a real soldier then!"

But David was thinking of Sara.

"Davie! Oh, by Jay! He's thinking of *her!*" Jonathan spat. "Can't you ever think of anything but your woman, Davie?"

"Quiet in the ranks!" Speke shouted, and he gave the order for a forward march and a to the rear march, and the company walked off in several directions.

Yet, David sometimes thought of other things. Watching his grandfather engrave the pistol, he became engrossed in the scenes that were coming into being there, and then he would return abruptly, and almost with a gasp he would realize he had not been thinking of her. Or he would listen to his father's bitter complaints about the workmen and would try to offer some advice or comfort, and he would forget her for the time that those words were being spoken.

But everybody around him knew he was infatuated.

"Have you made yourself clear to her yet?" his father asked.

"Not for marrying, if you mean that. Not yet."

"But she welcomes your attentions, does she?"

"Oh, well—" Oh, well, there was the difficulty. Sometimes she welcomed his attentions with a smothering delight, and sometimes she seemed indifferent to him. Once she had even refused to see him and she had stayed in an upstairs room until he had left the Sullivans' wretched house, and then the next time she had been gay and talkative and clutched his hand and wrapped it around her waist and held it there all the time her mother was gone from the room.

"Oh, well—she don't discourage me from going there."

His father shook his head. "Maybe you'd best see less of her, Davie. Give you both a chance to think about it all."

The idea appalled him. "I don't see her all that much, Dad."

"So you think. Your mother's properly scandalized; if it was any decent girl, she says, you'd have been married or sent packing by this time. Of course, she's very low on the Irish, your mother is."

"Well, I don't think I see her all that much." David sounded angry and stubborn. "We can't do nothing till this stupid rebellion is over; and I won't stop seeing her just because Ma has notions."

"Don't you ever speak to me like that!" They glared at each other. Donald was ready to strike his son. It was a test for both of them, and Donald—or, perhaps, the training of a young lifetime—won. David looked away. "I'm sorry, Dad. I misspoke myself."

Donald Morse nodded. "Aye, and don't you dare ever to do it again. If I had taken that tone to my father, he'd have thrashed me, no matter what my age!" And then, himself repentant, he put a hand on the young man's shoulder and shook it roughly. "I won't say you no, David; I know how it is, I guess. I couldn't live without seeing your mother every day when I was young, but—the times is so different. Maybe, like you say, when the rebel talk is over, something must be done. Pray God it be soon, Davie."

"Amen to that."

But in April came the news of Lexington and the triumph at Concord, a massacre to create martyrs and a victory to create heroes. Flynn called a meeting of the Sons and burned a lobsterback in effigy on Greenfield common, and Jonathan Morse wore his green ribbon and his cockade to do his farm chores. The news threw Donald Morse even deeper into his black mood, preoccupied and short-tempered and almost unable to work. He even took to his bed for a day when he should have been out plowing.

"Whatever will I do?" he said to his wife. He was lying on his back with the pillows pushed aside, laid out like a dead man with his hands crossed over his chest under the blankets. "Whatever will I do if there's war? The English will find my muskets—they got my mark on the underside of the barrels. They'll come here and they'll—"

"No, they won't! That don't make sense. Nobody will come

172

here at all. What would they be looking at the underside of gun barrels for, and they bottled up in Boston, as the news has it? Now you sleep, Donald; everything will look better tomorrow." The platitudes poured from her like sweet oil, and by and by, he slept.

Captain Speke rode through the countryside on his bay plowhorse to mobilize his troops, and the day after the news had come he took half of the company away—in farm carts, on farm horses and on foot—and left half behind to defend the valley. After all had been to a dawn service at the Presbyterian church, where the minister prayed and exhorted them to be quick and make the English learn what Hell had in store for them, the ones who had been chosen went off very gaily, thinking themselves the lucky ones, and those who were left behind cursed loudly and told their neighbors how unfortunate they were.

Jonathan Morse went with Speke; David stayed behind. One of them had to go, their father said, for the sake of the family, and Jonathan volunteered eagerly. David was glad to stay. He wanted no part of rebellion or fighting; he wanted things as they had been, with dreams of great things and London, and the reality of Sara.

"I'm so glad you didn't go!" Sara's whisper was like the fierce hissing of a burning log. She held him so tight that his neck hurt; his hands, pressed to her ribs, felt the bones and the thin layer of fat and the first outcurve of her breasts. They were in the Sullivan sitting room with the door ajar an inch; her parents sat in the kitchen, giving them nominal supervision. Another month, a sign of an intent to marry from him, and they would be allowed the privacy of a closed door.

"Don't ever go away from me!" she whispered. She kissed him. Her tears were wet against his face; her mouth, soft, almost pulpy, opened, and she bit his lower lip so hard that he raised his right hand partway to protect himself. He held his hand in midair and endured the pain until it blended with the rich pleasure of sexual arousal. Tumescent, he tried to twist his hips away so she would not sense it. She forced her teeth against his, their heads tilted almost at right angles to each other; her left hand squeezed his right and moved it up to her left breast and held it there, and they kissed and squeezed and clung together for thirty minutes, until she abruptly drew away and stood up, looking down into the nearly dead little fire.

"If you ever leave me, I'll kill myself," she muttered. He could hardly hear her. "I'll kill *you!*" she said angrily.

He moved behind her, put his hands on her upper arms and kneaded them. "Sara—"

"Oh, leave me be!" She pulled away and knelt to poke at the fire with a piece of iron rod as if she were jabbing an enemy.

"I love you, Sara," he whispered. His voice was trembling. It was the first time he had ever said it.

"Oh, I suppose you do." She sat on a stool by the fireplace and hugged herself.

There were other such nights. Her moods swung from one passion to its opposite—from sexual arousal to frightened revulsion, from amorous statement to bored denial. He was confused to find that he was exhilarated by her instability, which seemed to make her rarer and more desirable for him. For the bad times, he learned patience and what he thought of as forgiveness; for the good times, he learned to value them. He took a few tentative steps toward finding how to bring her out of her black moods, and in such small successes he was fool enough to think that love made him a better man. It gave him, at least, an idea of himself that made him happy, and being happy, he wanted everything around him to be happy.

"Death, it's still death!" he cried as Old John moved the graver over the steel. "Why not do something gay for once in a way?"

The old man put his spectacles down. He pressed his thumbs into his eyes. "I'll get to the gaiety," he said.

"I'd think you'd like the change."

"Would you, now? Ain't it grand to be nineteen, though!" He squinted at the pistol. "Anyway, death makes some quite gay enough—rich widows, and heirs to property, and old friends who're gay because it ain't them as has died." He put the pistol down and took up his spectacles again. "Go on, now; I'm making a very bloody murder."

He tried to make his mother happy by joking with her and by assuring her that Jonnie would be all right. She had had one letter from him, a skimpy, ill-spelled tale of boredom and dirt. The British were inside Boston, the rebels were around it; nobody seemed to know if anything would ever happen.

"Jonnie'll be all right," David said. "They ain't going to *fight* the British army!" He put his arm around her shoulders, less clumsy and shy now than before he had begun embracing

174

Sara, and she stiffened a little. She was thinking of Sara, too. The girl had been several times to supper, and all the Morse women disliked her, thought her lazy and willful and too full of herself.

"My tea water's boiling," she said briskly, and she moved out of his arm. "Anyways, it ain't Jonnie so much I'm worried about, now he's been gone awhile and I'm used to the idea. It's your father. He's worried sick."

"Ah, it's them muskets. But we'll finish with them and be done, Ma. I been working evenings after chores to take them off Pa's mind."

"Not every evening, you ain't."

"Now, Ma—"

"I'm just stating a fact, David."

"Yes, Ma. Your pardon, I'm sure."

"Well, then. I'm sure you could stay home to help your poor worried father for two weeks or so. Miss Sullivan won't age too much to appreciate you in that time, I guess."

"No, Ma."

"And some time apart would be good for both of you. Indeed, I think it might be all for the best if you'd see some other girl for a change. Now, if all Jonnie's doing is sitting outside Boston in dirty clothes learning foul language from the soldiers, I think it might as well be you sitting there and giving him a spell off, let him live like a Christian for a month or two while you saw some new faces. Have you thought of that?"

"Well, it hadn't occurred to me. I'm the one that stocks the muskets, see, and I'm needed."

She looked hard at him, the way she might have looked at a stranger—an appraising, chilly look. She made some decision and snapped her mouth shut, but he thought he knew what she had seen in his face and he knew she was angry.

It was a late spring that year, and it was not until the first week in May that the old man walked slowly along the row of apple trees, striking their blossoms with his blossoming wand. David had usually gone with him, but this year he was too busy, trying to store up time to be with Sara. Half-crazy Samuel went instead, his face twisted as he tried to pronounce some word that the old man could barely understand. That night, Sara was listless and would hardly speak to him; yet five days later when he could break away from the forge, she was so ebullient that she frightened him; talk poured from her and she jumped up and danced alone and flung herself

175

down again. He quieted her by grabbing her arm and dragging her down on his lap and mashing her mouth with his own, and suddenly the energy that had gone into her wildness went into passion. She bit him; she kissed him so long that they panted like wrestlers struggling in some taxing hold. He dared to put his hand on her breast and then under her bodice against her skin for the first time, marveling at the softness there and the erect nipple. His own arousal was fierce, and his long-sustained erection made his testicles ache up into his abdomen and down into his thighs.

"Sara—Sara—" He had no idea what he meant to say. Did he want to say he loved her? Did he want to ask her for sexual release? She gave him no chance to decide, but pressed her mouth against his and reached behind herself to undo the ties of her dress until she was bare to the waist.

She was sitting on his lap in a shaky little armchair whose wooden slats were a torment to his back. When he tried to shift his position, she pulled her head back from his and relaxed a little the fierce hold she had on his neck; and thus bent a little back from him with her dark hair tumbled down around her face, she looked down at her bare breasts as if she understood for the first time that she was half naked; and she put her hands over them and swung off his lap to stand at the far side of the little room with her back to him.

"Sara," he said weakly, afraid that in another swing of her mood she might cry out to her parents, "I'm sorry!"

"For what?"

"That I—that I went beyond—what I should have."

"How? How did you go beyond?" She turned back to face him, her arms crossed over her breasts.

"I'm sorry."

"For what?"

"For, for, you know—touching you—your—"

"What, *these* is it?" She took her arms away. She laughed, looking down at herself. *"They* ain't so much. Well, take a good look, Davie—it's what you wanted, ain't it? Ain't it? Ain't it for these and the other that you been coming over here all this time?"

"No, Sara, you know better than that."

"Have yourself a real gaze, Davie! They ain't so much. I seen lots better; one o' your sisters has a pair on her would do credit to a milking cow; maybe you should have a gaze at those. Well, come on, look, Davie! Or would you rather see the other now? And put your hand there, so you can rub it

176

good with your great rough smith's hands that feel like a grindstone going over my flesh? Do you want that part tonight, or was you planning that for next time, or what?"

"I said I was sorry, Sara!"

"Oh, it's *sorry* you are. Oh!" She shrugged and wriggled back into her dress. "Well, it's true, they ain't much, so you got something to be sorry for." Then she laughed and fastened herself and ran out to the kitchen, where David, some minutes later, tried to chat calmly with Mrs. Sullivan and to make sense with Mr. Sullivan, who was getting drunk and wanted to discuss the end of the world.

When he left the house, Sara pulled the front door closed behind her and stood in the dark with him. He started to reach for her but was stopped by the coldness of her voice.

"I never want to see you again," she said calmly. "I ain't that kind of girl."

"Sara, I promise, I swear, it will never happen again!"

"Indeed it won't, for I'll not see you, never."

But a week later he was back and she was glad to see him, and when he asked if she had forgiven him, she looked blank and said vaguely, "For what?" But it was some time before he dared to do more than kiss her.

Chapter Nineteen

On the 17th of June, 1775, Jonathan Morse saw the British line march three times up the grassy slope of Breed's Hill, their backs straight, their lines dressed as if for a parade until the broken terrain began to make unsightly curves and bumps, their bayonets fixed like rows of gleaming fence pickets in the sunlight. They came up three times, and they went back twice, and the third time, he saw them use their bayonets—angry men whose discipline had turned their rage over the Concord defeat and those two first bloody marches up the hill into ruthlessness.

Positioned behind a stone wall, Speke's militia watched them come, a little awed the first time because they were countrymen looking down over the city of Boston as if it were a toy town set out for a rich child's game, while toy ships sailed in a puddle of water and lobbed real shells into nearby Charlestown and set it aflame. On command, the militia fired, loaded, fired again; the advancing lines showed gaps; the picket rows of bayonets had spaces, as if they were a fence around a neglected house.

One officer out of every British eight who were to fall in the entire war fell in that one engagement. Jonnie Morse saw eleven of them die, saw them close enough so that he understood too quickly and too horribly what soldiering was really like. With the chest crushed, the lungs opened, blood rushed in and drowned a towheaded ensign who, in his agony not twenty yards from their stone wall, was not a hated lobsterback any more, but a boy who had walked too far and died too young. Another was knocked sideways directly in front of Jonnie, his lower jaw and nose carried off by a blast of buckshot from farther up the wall, and Jonnie Morse, in the act of loading his fowling piece with his own load of buck, said a rushed, silent prayer that the poor man would die quickly, *Oh dear God give him peace, don't let him live like that, please God,* but the legs moved and one hand rose slowly upward as if to grasp something in the sky—a hand reaching down for him, it looked like to Jonnie—and the poor creature moved and twitched until young Jonnie Morse, who was not a very good shot but who prayed that his Presbyterian God might this time make him accurate, put four lead balls into him, one of which entered his sternum because he was lying on his back with his legs toward the wall, and tore through his left lung and his heart and gave him his rest.

When the first British line marched back down the slope, uneven and gaping now and with a quarter of those still standing moving lamely or leaning on a comrade or staggering drunkenly at an angle to their fellows, the rebels cheered—cheered, some of them (Jonnie Morse was one), because they thought the terrible business was over. But they came again, like figures in a nightmare, unhurried, disciplined beyond terror, company by company, regiment by regiment, battalion company at center, light and grenadier companies flanking, and the country boys and small-town, part-time soldiers swallowed hard and fired again, mostly hitting nothing. Some shot ball, mostly ten and twelve gauge; some shot buck-and-ball in the same caliber, one ball and two buckshot; many shot plain buck or swanshot or even the birdshot that happened to be in the pouch from last year's hunt, and as a group they fired thirty times for every man they hit— but they fired a lot and hit a lot, and the British turned and staggered down the slope again. When they came up that last time, they came in perfect disorder, all regimental organization gone, lights and grenadiers and battalion soldiers mixed, green coats next to red, colored lace next to plain, cocked hat next to peaked—and they came up raging.

The third time that they came, they made it all the way to the stone wall and over it, and then they got their own back, for they were skilled and then some with the long, triangular bayonets. The militias, as if they had been engaged in a harmless game that ended when the British reached the wall, turned and ran. Jonnie Morse ran. He had seen the man next to him, a farm laborer from Turners Falls, get a bayonet right through his neck, a British regular reaching over the wall with the practiced sureness of a man stabbing into a haymow to pitch the hay up on a cart.

Jonnie ran.

He heard Captain Speke swearing, and, as afraid of his captain as he was of the British, he turned back, only to see Speke, who was standing with one foot up on the wall and his sword raised as if he expected to have his picture painted, get a bayonet in the belly from another regular. To Jonnie's astonishment, the soldier had a broad Scots accent: "Rebel

179

bastard!" he shouted, and then, bellowing, "Up, Glenannin!" he clambered up the wall.

That night, walking with a hundred other hungry and disconsolate militiamen, he was ashamed of having left his captain to die while he ran. Other men around him showed the same sense of shame, neither looking at each other nor speaking much. Many had lost their guns, some their packs and gunpowder as well—whatever would have slowed them down had been thrown away.

Speke lived, as it turned out. A British doctor said he was beyond help and would not bother to operate, a failure that saved Speke's life, military surgery being what it was; and ten months later, with an abdomen that gave him pain for the remaining twenty years of his life, he came groaning home to Greenfield after Washington's cannon had liberated Boston.

When he got home to the Morse farm, Jonnie said very little about Breed's Hill, unless he was in the Bunch of Grapes with the other militiamen who had been there, when they swapped stories and lies and built up a fabric of comfort for each other about having run. Some of his father's dour and nervous nature began to appear, young as he was, though he seemed much older now than the boy who had gone off six weeks before—as if, in Boston, Time had marched with a quicker step.

"Jonnie's gone dour," his mother said.

"The Morse men are like that," Donald answered. He did not raise his eyes from his Bible.

"You wasn't, until this gun business started. At least you wasn't *strong* dour. And Davie ain't."

"Davie's mad for that girl; you can't judge by now. All the Morse men are dour."

"Davie's notional. But he ain't dour."

Jonnie sought out his grandfather in the little room on the sunny side of the house where a table had been moved to serve him as a bench. Much of his time, Old John sat without moving; then, when his eyes and his patience would bear it, he worked on the pistol. Cloud-weakened sunlight cast watery shadows over his head and arms. The graving tool moved; death made its careful progress over the pistol stock.

"There was a Scot among the British," Jonnie said.

"Aye, there would be."

"I saw him stab Captain Speke in the gut. He was mad, like."

"Aye, he would be."

The boy chewed his lower lip on one side. "I saw an officer shot. Right in front of me. It took off half his head, but he was still alive. So I prayed for him to die."

"Did he die?"

"Yes, sir."

"God answers some prayers, you see."

Jonnie did not tell him that he had shot the officer himself.

Coming into the cowbarn that evening, he found David finishing the milking, the barn warm and heavy with the grassy smell of cow and the mixed stink of manure and sharp urine. On an ordinary day, he would have helped, but today he was forgiven work because it was his first day back. Together, they would have milked the animals and carried the pails into the stone half-cellar nearby where a dripping spring kept the stones cold and the milk fresh. The barn cats would gather, and together they would pour the milk from their oak pails into crocks submerged in the cold water, straining the milk through copper sieves and then tipping the milky foam out for the cats. In a circle around the pan, tails out like the spokes of a wheel, the cats would lap until the pan was empty.

But this evening he had no part. He might as well have been still on Breed's Hill, separated from that comfortable ritual. The thought made him angry, and, seeing David, he stopped.

"Jonnie," David said shyly, his forehead resting against the cow's plump side. Milk spurted in regular thrusts under the coaxing of his fingers. Reverting to boyhood, he turned one teat and shot a stream of milk over Jonnie's stockings.

"That's a daft thing to do," Jonnie said bitterly. They were the first clean stockings he had worn in weeks.

"I'm sorry, Jonnie." The sound of the milk in the pail faded. "We're all glad you're back, Jonnie." He pushed the three-legged stool back a little. "Want to help?"

"I got good clothes on."

"Oh. Well, it don't matter. Like to get done, is all."

He moved the stool to a black cow and leaned close to her, her tail pinned against her leg so it could not swat him.

"Can't wait to get to your woman, can you, Davie?"

"She ain't mine."

"Just can't wait to get to her! Ma told me how she'd begged

you to come and take my place. But you couldn't, I guess. Had to get to your woman, ain't that right?"

David raised his head. "I'd have gone instead of you if you'd asked me."

Jonathan laughed unpleasantly, but said nothing.

"What's that mean? That laughing? I'd have gone, I surely would have!"

The black cow began to drop excrement on the stone floor. Jonathan watched it as if it were the most remarkable thing he had ever seen. "I seen Captain Speke get the bayonet. Right in the belly. I seen a man get his face shot off." The cow's tail arched and more dark-green mud oozed from under it. "I shot a man. And all you got to worry about is how quick you can get to your woman."

David kept on milking. "I got other things to worry about."

"I run, did you know that? We all run! I guess you would have, too. Not as fast as you run after your slut, o' course."

"Don't talk like that. Don't use that word."

"Oh, she's a slut, right enough. I seen them around Boston. Them Irish sluts. Have one for a shilling—less, some of them. I had one. Up against a house there in Cambridge, me and some of the Greenfield boys went turn about with her. So don't lord it over me, Davie. You been with a slut and I been with a slut, and the only difference is, while I was watching men get their face shot off, you was playing titties in the Sullivans' front room!"

David was on his feet, the three-legged stool knocked over behind him. "Take it back! Take it back, take it back!"

"I won't! It ain't fair, Davie! You should have gone to take my place, that would have been fair! But it wasn't fair, me soldiering while you was—"

They had faced each other angrily many times in their lives—natural companions, natural enemies. Before, they had fought like boys, slapping, swinging wildly, throwing each other to the ground until the winner sat astradde of the other and demanded a surrender.

Now they fought like men. Both were strong; both were angry. Jonnie bulled into David, who swung a fist that cracked on his brother's cheekbone. They punched with short, hard blows. David's right foot mushed into the cow manure and began to slide, and while he was off balance he took a blow high on his left shoulder, then righted himself and swung first one hand and then the other, a short, hard left hand that knocked Jonnie down.

182

"Take it back!"

The juvenile demand made the adult fight ugly and pathetic, for they were no longer in that world where things could be taken back and all made right again. Jonnie kicked and squirmed away and David, following, took up the three-legged stool and held it high behind him, one hand poised over Jonnie's legs in case he kicked.

"Take it back or I'll kill you!"

He rolled his shoulder back still farther, ready to deliver the blow.

"David!"

With his head ducked low like a guilty animal's, he turned to look over his shoulder at the cowbarn door.

"Put that thing down, David."

It was their grandfather. Even his poor eyes could see what was happening in the lanternlight.

"Now let him up, David."

He relaxed his hold and rolled backward on his heels, the stool held low at his side. Jonnie scrambled away from the cows into the aisle between the stanchions and lay there for several seconds, torso raised on one arm, head low, his breathing harsh. There was cowdung on his stockings and his breeches and old straw on the back of his waistcoat.

"You go on out of this, Jonnie. You go on up to the house and ask your sisters to make you cleanly. Don't let your ma see you filthy like that."

Jonathan pushed himself up without looking at David. When he had stumbled out into the dusk, David put the stool down next to the black cow and righted the pail, which had been knocked over so that its milk had run over the boards and the stone troughs like thin whitewash, blue on the edge of the puddles.

"Waste like that is a sin," the old man said.

"I'm sorry, sir."

The old man stuck out his flaccid lips. "I suppose it was about him soldiering. Hey? Aye, I suppose it was. Well, don't tell your father about it. I won't. He's a great fretter, your father." He came closer to David. "You might have killed your brother. Do you remember why Cain killed Abel?"

After some seconds, David murmured, "Because his sacrifice was better in the eyes of the Lord."

"Aye, just so. I think you're jealous because Jonnie's sacrifice is better—not in the eyes of the Lord, maybe, but in the eyes of the Sons of Liberty and the almighty Greenfield

183

militia. Now, if you can't bear his sacrifice, Davie, why, get out of it—go away, I'm telling you. You and your dad, you keep saying it's going to end. Well, it ain't! Any sensible man would have known the day your dad started making guns for them that it wouldn't end. You make a gun, somebody got to use it—guns are like that. If you can't stand that fact, why, get out of it."

"He called Sara Sullivan a name."

"Aye, I'm sure he did. And who wouldn't, with him off seeing horrors while you're at home courting? There'll be more namecalling, I think. If you can't bear it, Davie, get out of it."

"I can't."

"Because of her? Why, take her with you! She'd go. That girl'd do just about anything that was foolish and contrary, I guess."

For a moment, David thought quite seriously about running away, and then he shook his head. Under all his dreams, all his conscious fantasies, was the reality of the Morse farm and the Morse family—the timbers that shored up his inner life. It was unthinkable that he should run away from them.

"Now I suppose I'll have to marry you." Her voice was sterile with bitterness. She rolled away from him and lay on her left side with her back to him, and when he shifted and his bare hip brushed her buttock, she pulled farther away so that there could not be contact.

"I'll marry you, Sara. I want to marry you."

"Aye." She made it sound hopeless.

Minutes before, he had been elated—on the verge of one of the great adventures, being clutched by a naked Sara, nearing orgasm. Now he was resentful, but he could not say of what—dared not say of what. If he felt revulsion, he repressed it, and to show himself (and her) that his passion was simple and consistent he put his right hand on her hip and squeezed. "I *want* to marry you."

"Oh, take your great coarse hand off me."

He scratched an insect bite on one leg and found that it had become a considerable lump, and he wondered how many others had raised welts while he had been lost with Sara. They lay in deep grass a hundred yards from the Sullivans' miserable house. It was night, warm, the air faintly threatening rain.

"You'll be sorry," she said. It was a flat statement of fact.

184

"No, I won't."

"Yes, you will." She seemed to be warming to the idea of his being sorry. "By God, you'll be sorry!"

"I love you, Sara."

"Oh, I know that! How wouldn't I, with you telling me ten times of every day of my life?" She sat up. He smelled the grass that she had bruised under her body, smelled her body itself and his own, and he was aroused again. "Well, I'll marry you," she said sadly. "Nobody's going to say Sara Sullivan's any slut you can do it to and forget. I'll marry you, all right."

"I'll try to be a good husband, Sara."

"Sure, you will. By your lights. Working in your pa's gun works and driving a plow betimes and telling me what a great man you're going to be when you're about a hundred years old. Just the kind of husband every woman wants!"

"Why do we always come to this?"

"To what?"

"To this bickering and discontent and all! No matter how warm, we always come to this."

"Aye." She was silent. Absently, she passed her right hand over her left shoulder and paused to scratch a bite on her upper arm. "Aye, we always come to this. So get used to it."

"But it'd be so easy to be content!" Her shoulders were warm under his hands, his thumbs just touching her throat on each side, as if he might slide them together and strangle her.

"I thought you wasn't going to be content until you got to London and the Houses of Parliament."

"Well—" He moved his hands up her neck until the thumbs lay just behind her earlobes. "I'd rather have you than any House of Parliament."

"Oh, you're mad," she said. "Don't you ever have any sense at all?"

He went on trying to convince her, and she went on being sour and sad; they made love again, and afterward she was bitter and said that she would have to marry him and there was no way out of it, and she made it sound like a death sentence.

"I'll speak to your parents tonight," he said.

"No, you won't! You'll wait until my pa's sober."

"Well, tomorrow, then. Tell him to wait here for me and I'll ride over after supper."

"He ain't your lackey, to wait on you, just because he works for your pa!"

"Oh, Sara, you know what I mean!" He held her. Her naked body was like a warm corpse. "When will we be married?" he whispered.

"Not too soon, I hope."

Still, she kissed him warmly outside the door before he left, and she whispered that she would die if he didn't marry her, and he rode off savoring the memory of her body and spinning fantastic stories of what his life as a husband would be like.

Chapter Twenty

It was raining in England. It was raining all over Britain, in fact—had been raining for a week, would go on raining, some said, until there were no crops left and no dry ground to plant new ones in and England would starve. All the jokes about the Flood had been made and grown stale; all the mundane remarks about the weather had been uttered, agreed with, and forgotten. Farmers gathered in village markets and exchanged sad stories of their losses—fields lost, cows drowned, newly planted crops washed out. Fishermen raged at the bank-high rivers, even in Hampshire, where the mayfly was on and for once the meadows were too flooded for anybody to get near the fish. Rain and more rain was all that any Briton knew, except in a few places in the Highlands, where it was snowing.

Woolwich Arsenal looked as if it had been built out of wet sponge. Water seemed to ooze out of the very stones. Water from downpipes no longer followed its old courses to the drains, but poured across flagged walks and down cellar stairs, carrying with it thinned mud that was now tramped everywhere through the dank old buildings.

Yet, Captain Patrick Ferguson of His Majesty's Seventieth Regiment of Foot was happy with the weather. He had been waiting for such a rain; delays had kept him away from Woolwich for the first part of the week, and he had feared that the weather would change before his opportunity came; however, the rain had persisted and now he was crossing to the Woolwich firing range in an excellent humor, while a private stumbled along after him with two wooden gun cases, silently cursing the climate and the army and this tall, dour young captain who went splashing on so resolutely.

Patrick Ferguson was thirty-two years old. His lean face had been tanned by the hot sun of Tobago and weathered by the cold of Nova Scotia; a career soldier, he, like many others, was grateful for the rebellion in America because it would offer rare opportunities for advancement. In such a war, a man could distinguish himself, could stand out from the pack—and to get ahead in his majesty's army, one had to stand out.

Patrick Ferguson approached this problem of career as he approached the rain and the puddles that day at Woolwich Arsenal, without humor, without regard for anybody else. The man who followed him with the gun cases was utterly forgotten, an underling not worth his attention; Ferguson had an eye only for his own goals. He was not a popular man, this severe Captain Ferguson, for all that he came from a good Scots family and for all that his father was wealthy.

Least of all did he care that he was related to the Morses. As yet, the Morses meant nothing to him; the fact that he was an expert in the field of firearms and the inventor of a new rifle could hardly give him anything in common with a family of Massachusetts gunmakers. He was happily oblivious to the fact that his grandmother was old John Morse's sister Jane Mary, and he was far too snobbish even to consider that he might have so close a relative in common with a family of rebels.

Crossing a paved yard, Ferguson headed for a stone building, along whose wall he walked so as to avoid the sheet of water that poured from an overloaded gutter overhead. The private, both hands busy with the gun cases, stomped disconsolately through puddles and then walked directly under the water sheet to demonstrate the extent of his martyrdom. Ferguson never noticed.

A vaulted archway under a bridge between two buildings gave some shelter. One cloaked officer was already standing there, apparently hesitant to leave it for the unprotected world beyond. Ferguson glanced at him and looked away. Coming under the bridge, he shook his cloak and took off his hat to swing it groundward and shower the wet stones with heavy drops. The cloaked man moved, and Ferguson glanced again at him, not much surprised to see that he wore the uniform of one of the German regiments of Hesse-Cassel; since April, the German troops headed for America had been gathering in British ports to convoy with British troops. German officers were no longer an unusual sight.

The man smiled at him. Ferguson frowned.

"Hullo, Ferguson." The German spoke excellent English, with just a touch of an Irish accent.

"Is it—Hanger? It is, by Heaven!"

"By Heaven, Hell, and everything in between, it is George

188

Hanger, yes. *Captain* Hanger, if you please." He swept the cloak off one shoulder to reveal an epaulette.

"I'd heard you'd left the Foot Guards."

"Left it after a great row, yes! The ass of a colonel wouldn't give me a company; old George wouldn't put up with that and he resigned, by God! Never liked the Guards much anyway. Damned snobs or utter boobies, the lot of them—most of them are both, in fact."

Ferguson nodded to the private to put the gun cases down. "But what are you doing in Woolwich, Hanger?"

"Watching Captain Ferguson demonstrate his new rifle, I hope." Seeing Ferguson's surprise, he said quickly, "An old friend in the Ordnance told me about it. Couldn't pass it up, Patrick—hope you won't mind my nodding in."

"No." Ferguson smiled. "Not if the gods of Ordnance don't object."

"Oh, they'll positively love me! Everybody does; I've been translating all manner of nonsense from one general to another—half the British staff think I'm an English officer on special detachment, and the other half think I'm a very witty German who's on detachment to them. Between the two, I am in Jove's lap, Patrick, a very Ganymede who is welcome everywhere! Even at sopping Woolwich, which is the dreariest place I've been since I left Bremen."

Hearing a clock strike, Ferguson signaled for the soldier to take the gun cases up again, and they stepped out into the rain. Hanger fell in beside Ferguson, holding closed his cloak and trying to leap over puddles in his black jackboots.

"Actually, I should be in America now, Patrick, but for fate and a drunken Dutchman. We made Bremen with von Heister's division, but they put my jaegers into a tiny coracle of a boat with a Dutch captain so far gone in genever I wonder to this day that the fool could stand, and when I saw that they meant to send us to England in that hulk, I balked—absolutely balked! Put a pistol to the Dutchman's head and said that if his boat shipped one drop of water I'd pull the trigger. My troops cheered and thought I was a capital fellow—still do, in fact—and the Dutchman wept and hiccuped and shat his britches, and the end of it was that we were put back ashore and so didn't sail for a month. Now we won't be out of England until mid-July, which gives me time to call on a lady who cared something for me when I was an ensign and thinks even more of me now I'm a captain. And, of course,

189

to watch Captain Ferguson demonstrate his amazing patent rifle."

"Not patented yet."

"When shall I see the marvel?"

"On the range, when everybody else does."

"You won't even tell me about it?"

"Nothing to tell. Seeing it is everything. Tell me about your jaegers, instead—are they good?"

"Well—" Hanger grinned. "The German soldier's not the English soldier, Patrick—only two things he really cares about, his mustache and his pizzle—likes size in both of them. If a fellow's got a Gargantua in either department, he's a capital fellow; if he's colossal in both, they make him an officer." Hanger grinned and twirled his own brown mustache. "I'm a captain, as you know."

Ferguson grunted, but said nothing.

Hanger guffawed and clutched his cloak more tightly. They turned from a stone walk and began to pick their way over a field so sodden that water was squeezed up around their boots with each step.

"Dear God!" exclaimed Hanger. "But for the calendar, it could be January!"

"Ideal weather for my purposes." He strode resolutely forward. Hanger kept up his leaping for another few strides, a ludicrous figure in his flapping cloak with his booted legs twitching in a frantic dance. "Oh, Hell!" he muttered after three more jumps, and, falling in beside Ferguson, he began to walk with more dignity but with wetter feet.

A rather miserable junior officer was waiting for them at the range. At a word from Ferguson, he dashed into a small house twenty yards away, and, some minutes later, a reluctant procession of graver and older officers began to trickle out. Each paused almost ritually just outside the door, looked upward, shook his head dolefully, and shrugged himself deeper into greatcoat or cloak. Only one man ignored this pattern, a tall fifty-year-old who popped straight through the door and made some joke that caused the younger ones to laugh.

"Jeff Amherst," Hanger murmured.

"Aye. One on my side, I think."

At the last, an overweight and red-faced general waddled out, an aide bustling in front of him with an umbrella while a black servant followed with a folding chair and another came behind with a bucket full of hot coals that sizzled and spat in the rain.

"Lord Townshend?"

"The same."

"The hero of Culloden! No friend to a Scot, I think—his face is not a friendly one, God knows."

"No friend to anybody these days, the old pudding."

Lord Townshend stopped. The umbrella stopped. The chair was placed so that it just touched his lordship's legs; he sat, and an aide raised the skirts of his greatcoat so that the bucket of coals could be placed between the lordly feet and the coat dropped over it like a tent. Ferguson grunted in disgust. Hanger, chuckling, muttered, "Better he'd put one of Mother Betty's chicks down there, Patrick. They do say he warms to that touch sometimes."

A captain detached himself from the group around Townshend and splashed up to Ferguson. "Are you ready, Captain Ferguson?"

"Entirely, sir."

"Then pray do begin. Their lordships are waiting." The officer had a very long nose, high-bridged and pinched, that gave him an equine look.

"Ass," Ferguson murmured. He signaled to the private, who opened a gun case and brought out a rifle, then closed the case up again and wrapped it with the other box in a painted canvas for protection.

Ferguson walked toward the group of ordnance officers and stopped a few feet from them while Hanger moved around them and joined the junior officers at the rear.

"My lords!" Ferguson began. "General Harvey, fellow officers—I must thank you for coming out on this desperate day, which the Almighty has provided especially for the testing of weapons." One or two of the younger men tittered, and Amherst smiled. Ferguson rested the rifle in the crook of his left arm. "Knowing that the officers of His Majesty's Ordnance would overlook any discomfort to themselves, I did not hesitate to pray for just such weather as this." Amherst went on smiling, and even hid his lips for a moment with his hand, perhaps because he was watching the large drop of water that was collecting on the end of Townshend's nose.

"I will demonstrate, as I have said in letter and in papers of application to the Ordnance, a rifle embodying improvements of my own design, which is intended to give its user advantage of any troops to be met in any field in any weather.

191

I need not mention, I think, the unrest in America, to which we have seen ten thousand men dispatched to suppress a heinous rebellion and for which another transport of thousands is soon to depart. These men have gone and will go with the musket of the Land Pattern, a sturdy, dependable and time-honored weapon; yet, could a single corps of them go armed with my rifle, I do believe that they could materially shorten the struggle and cut off the heads of the Hydra of disloyalty before it can strike back, and bring the loyal hearts of the great majority of the Americans back to his majesty's governance. Of the shooting of rifles of their own making by some of the rebels, particularly those of the southern and western settlements, I need not speak, for who has not heard of the 'widow-makers' that have been described in letters to the London newspapers?

"There are no riflemen in the regular British army establishment. There are a few excellent riflemen among the German troops of Hesse-Cassel and Hanau—one of whose officers I am flattered to see present today as an observer." He nodded at Hanger, who did not smile but who bowed gravely and accepted a supercilious nod from Townshend with a lifting of his hat. His captain's epaulette hidden under his cloak, he was quite willing to pass for a colonel if anyone cared to make that mistake.

"I will delay little longer, my lords and gentlemen—but I will say only this on the subject of the rifle as against the smooth bore musket: a trained, properly equipped rifleman will hit one of every three man-sized targets at two hundred yards under field conditions; one of our regular soldiers, equipped with the Land Pattern musket and given our regular annual allotment of twenty cartridges as his yearly training shots, will do well to hit one man-sized target out of six at *fifty* yards under field conditions. And to the objection that the rifle, because of the tightness of the ball, is too slow to load, I offer the weapon I shall now demonstrate for you, with which I will prove that I can load faster and shoot better than any musketman in Europe.

"Let me now proceed to the demonstration."

"Thank God," Townshend was heard to say. The equine captain snorted.

"I will load in the rain. I will fire five shots a minute at that target two hundred yards downrange." He pointed at the distant rectangle. "I will move forward at the infantryman's pace, loading and firing as I go. If I am successful, I hope to convince you that this rifle"—he held up a gun custom-made for him in London—"will make one man into a squad, and a corps into an army.

"Will someone serve as timekeeper?"

"Here." The horse-faced officer raised one gloved hand, in which he held a cased watch.

"Signal when I am to begin, please, captain."

The officer stared at the watch. His hand came up slowly, then dropped and he shouted, "Now!"

Ferguson wore a regulation cartridge box at his right side, from which he now drew a paper cartridge seemingly identical to those used by men of the line. There was a murmur from the group, however, when he transferred the cartridge to his left hand, whose wrist pressed the rifle butt against his body, and with a single twist rotated the weapon's trigger guard a full turn, thus lowering the breech screw and exposing it for loading. Ripping the cartridge paper above the ball with his teeth, he spat the ball into the breech and shoved it forward with a finger, then tipped in the powder; a full twist back with the trigger bow and the breech closed, pushing excess grains of powder up to the top of the barrel. With the movement of a single finger, this powder was swept into the flintlock pan; the frizzen was swung down, and the gun was loaded, primed and ready to fire.

Ferguson sighted quickly and fired. Downrange, a soldier popped into view as the range officer's safety flag waved.

Ferguson was already extracting another cartridge as a paper circle was pasted over the hole in the target.

"A hit!" cried a lieutenant colonel standing next to Amherst, a telescope at his eye.

"So I see," Amherst murmured drily.

Ten seconds later, Ferguson fired again and scored a second hit; fourteen seconds after that, he scored a third time; and, three seconds short of the allotted minute, he had put five balls into the target.

"Remarkable," Amherst exclaimed.

"I think he's on to something," Hanger said to the group.

"I want some brandy," Lord Townshend growled, and an aide handed him a bottle from a hamper.

"Loading and firing while moving forward!" Ferguson announced, and began to walk at infantryman's pace toward the target, firing five more rounds into the target as he went forward, the last going in from forty yards out.

Returned to the group with perspiration now joining the

water that streamed down his face, for his hat had been discarded as he had started to shoot, Ferguson smiled boyishly at Amherst and held the rifle up for them all to see. "Perhaps the rain is not enough to convince you of the gun's resistance to the elements!" he cried. "Witness!" His enthusiasm and his showman's flourish caused Hanger to smile and look away.

Ferguson held up a wine bottle, which the private filled from a canteen, and Ferguson then loaded the rifle and proceeded to pour the water down the barrel and into the pan.

"No problem at all!" he announced cheerfully as he took out a cleaning rod and thrust it down the barrel. Opening the breech, he tipped out most of the powder there and then gave the cleaning rod a tap and the ball rolled out; he flipped open the pan cover and wiped out the pan. Half a dozen strokes with the rod, followed by another pass with a clean twist of tow, and he pronounced the rifle ready to fire. He loaded in another cartridge and fired the charge on the first try.

A colonel near Lord Townshend leaned close to the uncomfortable chief of ordnance. "You must admit, my lord, you won't see that done with the regulation musket."

"'Course not. Regular soldiers have too much wit to pour water down their barrels."

But Hanger was frowning. He thought he had missed something or that the others were inattentive, and he watched carefully as Ferguson demonstrated the loading process again. Never having to use a ramrod, he could load quickly and efficiently, standing, walking or sitting. He fired four more shots and then took up a second rifle and fired it while lying on his back.

"This shows us, I gather," Lord Townshend drawled, "that even a weary soldier may fire the Ferguson patent." His aides laughed and he helped himself to more brandy.

Later, there was a lunch in the little house for the senior officers and Ferguson, and Hanger simply went along as if it were his due. Questions were fired at the inventor, and he easily dealt with them all—accuracy, range, size of powder charge, cost (four times the regulation musket, he estimated).

"How do you think a corps of men armed with my rifle might do in America?" the dour Ferguson asked Amherst.

Amherst had been Governor-General of North America, and he had seen Rogers's Rangers at Quebec. "Superb country for light infantry," he said. "Heavily wooded, quite broken, often presenting desperate terrain for heavy cavalry but offering a superior advantage to a mobile and agile force. Your riflemen should do well, captain."

The private had cleaned the guns that had been fired, and Hanger examined them with the greatest care now, feeling into the recess behind the breech screw and pushing his index finger forward to the point where the rifling began and then looking to see if grease or fouling had clung to his finger. The rifles were sparkling clean, however, and there was no residue. Catching Ferguson's eyes across the now hot and boisterous room, he winked.

Lord Townshend, complaining loudly of the lateness of his coachman and the foulness of the weather, was the first to leave; but, fortified with ham and oysters and brandy, he was at last pushed into his coach. Amherst, who had been murmuring something to Ferguson at a window, made some remark that made Ferguson smile as the coach clattered off; and Amherst, gripping his hand as if to reassure him, left him and quickly made the rounds of the other senior officers, shaking hands and exchanging goodbyes. Twenty minutes later, the ordnance observers were gone, and only Ferguson, Hanger and a junior officer who had sidled in and got almost instantly drunk were left.

Hanger ordered a corporal to have the young man conveyed by carriage to his quarters. Ferguson was shrugging himself into his greatcoat; stewards were clearing away the food; and Hanger, wrapping himself again in the wet cloak that he had worn on the range, joined Ferguson at the door.

"Can't imagine a more successful trial, Patrick."

"You thought it went well?"

"Like thick cream, Patrick! Very smooth."

"Townshend hated it."

"Townshend hates everything. That's his job. He's lost his reputation, lost his wife, lost his command; all he has left is his disapproval. Amherst is on your side, clearly."

"He was kind, to be sure."

The rain had lessened and the wind had dropped altogether, and instead of the former gale, there was now a fine, drenching mist.

"A good Scots day," Hanger mused. They started to walk over the grass; reaching another walk, they turned to the left and headed for the arsenal buildings. Hanger pulled up under the arched bridge and put his hand on Ferguson's arm. "See here, Patrick." He glanced up, then looked away as if embarrassed. "About pouring that water down the barrel."

195

"Well?"

"Patrick, I'm not a man to spoil another's triumph, but—" Hanger looked almost miserable. "Was there soap in that water, Patrick? I thought I saw a bubble."

"What if there was?"

"That gun was too fouled to be loaded again, wasn't it?"

Ferguson pulled away. "That's nonsense."

"Patrick, there ain't a rifle made that don't foul a tight ball after five shots. Why didn't you tell them that?"

"I fired ten shots."

"Oh, blather! Good God, Patrick, you can tell that to Townshend but you can't tell it to me. I know rifles, man!" Hanger stepped in front of him. "Does that gun foul too much to be fired properly after five shots?"

"You saw me fire ten in succession."

"Aye, that I did. And I looked into your cartridge box while their lordships were at the trough—you'd some cartridges in there a full bore size smaller than the others, Patrick. Balls you could put in past the fouling and still hit the target when you walked up close, ain't I right?"

Ferguson gazed at him and then nodded jerkily. "There may be a minor flaw or two that I will eliminate in the final model."

"Yes. Well, you were right to show off the thing to its best advantage." Hanger stepped aside and then fell in step with Ferguson; suddenly, he stopped the other man again by stepping in front of him. "But promise me, you won't take a company into the field with it until it's perfected."

"I owe you no promises, Hanger."

"Promise yourself then, eh?"

"Jeff Amherst is anxious to see it proven in America."

Hanger shook his head. Careless though he might be, he was a man still capable of worry and compassion. "Patrick, don't put a lot of men into a position where they'll stand with their backs to the wall and have to depend for their lives on a rifle that can betray them. You're an idealist, the most valuable kind of fellow there is in some circumstances, and I'm only a rakehell who don't give piffle for most things in the world, but I'd never hang up myself and the men under me out of eagerness to prove something—and don't you do it, either. I wouldn't let that drunken Dutchman drown them, anxious as I was to get to America before the sports are over, and I don't think you should rush to get there just because you're passionate about the rifle. Go slow, man, I beg you."

"I am sensitive of your concern, Hanger, though I take it as a remarkable piece of rudeness on your part to suggest that I would be thoughtless of the men under my command. I shan't challenge you over it, because I don't care to waste my time on fripperies, but I'd prefer that you say no more to me, if you please."

Hanger looked at him, his dissolute face puckered with concern. Abruptly, he shrugged and smiled carelessly. "So be it, then. I ain't cut out to be a preacher, clearly."

They walked on to the arsenal gate, where Ferguson called for his horse.

"Will you dine with me, Patrick?"

"Certainly not. I'm amazed you have the gall to ask."

Hanger laughed. "Patrick, Patrick! Come along, man, I won't be put out of countenance just because you think I'm rude; telling Hanger that he's rude is like telling milady's lapdog that he barks." When Ferguson did not smile, Hanger took off his hat. "My apologies, Captain Ferguson! Forgive me for insulting you, sir."

Ferguson swung himself up into the saddle. "I'll accept your apology, Hanger, but I'll not dine with you."

"Next time, then! In America."

It was Ferguson's turn to smile. "You are incorrigible! Well, so be it, then—in America!"

He clucked to the horse and moved off through the soft rain.

Chapter Twenty-one

David Morse had been married for five months.

And Sara had been right: he was sorry.

His whole life seemed to have turned around, as if he had gone at one stroke from the hopefulness of youth into maturity at its most dismaying. He blamed the change on marrying.

His brother Jonathan hardly spoke to him now, and then only in as few words as were absolutely necessary; they could hammer at the forge together, their strokes as cunningly intertwined as lovers, and never speak or look at each other. The fight had been made up, more or less, but they were enemies still, and their mother looked at them and shook her head. At the Sunday before David's marriage, she had insisted that they kneel together and pray for the return of brotherly love, but they had stood up as bitter as they had knelt down. Some prayers are not answered.

Their father seemed distressed only because their hostility added to his worries. "Why can't you get along?" he whined. The martyr's tone had got into his voice over the winter and spring, and it could be heard now whether he was complaining about the weather, which was always wrong for his crops; or the failure to pay for the muskets that came out of his works; or the madness of the Boston men and Southern hotheads who were pushing the colonies into independency; or the coldness of his sons to each other. "Why can't you pretend to get along, at least," he groaned, "to please your mother and stop her forever complaining at me?"

"I mistrust Jonnie could ever hide his feeling," David said. He could not speak for his own feeling, which he thought was more numbness than dislike but which he could not seem to change.

And of that realization of one of his dreams, his marriage, he was most bitterly disillusioned. In church or among their neighbors, he found it pleasurable still to have with him a woman whom he could show off as *his;* Sara herself, however, was not so pleased, and she let him know it.

"We never do things just for our pleasure any more," he said.

"Like what?" She was in her dull mood and her tone was flat.

"Like walking out or singing together or just talking of—"

"Of what?"

"Of London, and all like that."

"London!" One of her hands made a little motion as if to wave a fly away. "We'll never get to London."

"But we took such pleasure in talking, Sara!"

"You talked. I listened." She made the motion again. "Talk's easy."

"I thought you believed me," he said bitterly.

"So did I."

He tried to take her hands, but she clenched them into fists, and all he held between his hands was two hard lumps. "Sara, when the rebellion is over, I promise you—"

Her mouth opened and closed and an impatient little sound came out.

"Well, it *will* end! Then you'll see."

"I don't want to *see*," she said. She pulled her fists away and hugged herself. "All I want is my own place."

"Oh, God, Sara! We been over that and over it!"

They lived in a room in his parents' house. It had been Samuel's room, because he was the only Morse child who slept alone, nobody else being able to bear his thrashings and his bizarre nighttime talk; now, however, Samuel spent many of his days in bed, and his mother had moved him downstairs into the birthing room so she could be near to him, and the room that had been his had become David's and his new wife's. David had thought it a pretty room, a room he had been happy to bring her to—bright in the morning sun, cozily low-ceilinged and snug to make love in.

"It's a cold place," she had said. Waking on their second night in that room to hear her sobbing, he had heard her whisper, "What am I doing in this cold place?"

David got up every day at four o'clock. He needed no one to wake him. His body woke like an animal's, and he pulled on breeches and stockings and went downstairs to warm his hands at the dull ashes of the kitchen fire until the new sticks caught and fire flared up enough for him to see his breath going out in the cold room. He would call his father then, and his father would call Jonathan and the three of them would go outside to chores—David to the cows, Jonathan to the forge

199

fires, his father to the horses or to prepare for some task that he had planned for the day. By six, David would be back in the house; his mother and sisters would be up, the girls' eyes puffy and their words few and interrupted by yawns, but the kitchen would be warm and sweet with the smells of cooking food. Then David would go upstairs with warm cider or milk—no tea now, not since Jonathan had come back from a meeting of the Sons with the edict that no loyal American would drink tea—to wake Sara.

One morning, she did not get up. "I got to lie in the bed a while," she said.

"Are you sick?"

"I guess maybe I am. You let me lie here."

His mother sniffed when he told her. His sister Nora grinned slyly and said something to Bet that made her giggle. Too late to stop them, David realized that they were making some joke about Sara's being pregnant. *Could she be?* Their lovemaking was erratic now, an up-and-down line that paralleled her moods and his efforts to keep up with them. He decided that she could be pregnant and that he liked the idea; *father* was a new role, one that he could surround with the same glow as he had the role of husband before he had actually become one.

But she denied it. "Oh, you're an idiot! Of course I ain't that way!"

He hung his head. "You could be, I guess."

"Not through any famous effort you ever made."

"Why, Sara—why—"

"Oh, let me be!"

So the family had to accustom itself to the fact that on some days, Sara would simply not get out of bed. She stayed in the little room, and the rest of the family had no clear idea of what she did, though David understood—often lying asleep for hours in a way that the work-driven Morses could not conceive of, but sometimes restlessly awake, or, vacuous and numb, gazing stupidly at the sky beyond the dormer window.

"Can I get you something?" he would ask when he came back from work at noon.

"No. Nothing."

His mother frowned. His sisters whispered. His father complained. "Can't you get that wife of yours to be some help to your mother?" The whining tone was in his voice. "She ain't the almighty Queen of Sheba to get on without doing her share, David!"

200

"I've asked her, Pa. What more can I do?"

"I hear about it and hear about it from your mother, and it's just what I don't need, one more burden put on my shoulders at a time when I'm already heavy laden with enough worries to break the heart of any mortal man. And now money's going all to flinders, they say in Greenfield, and what am I to do about that? Money won't be worth air, they say, and I ain't been paid half of what I'm owed on these damnable guns!" Donald Morse shook his head. His face had become that of a disappointed old woman. He sighed. "I guess I see what they're about. I'll never see the gold that was promised. They mean to wait until the money they print ain't worth air, and then they'll pay me when it costs them nothing but paper!"

But David had no interest in the currency decline and the galloping inflation; he was watching, instead, the astronomical rise in the price of happiness. In April, he watched Old John touch the apple trees with his wand, but the sight gave him no pleasure and only reminded him of what seemed to be better days; in May and June, he worked next to his brother and neither of them said as much, or said it as kindly, as he would have to a stranger. By midsummer, it seemed to him that his heart was cracking from the pressure of unrelieved misery, and he did not understand why that had to happen to him.

"It's these damned guns!" he said to Old John. "I hate those guns! It all started with them." He did not say that meeting Sara had started with the guns, too.

"It ain't the guns, Davie. It's youth going, is all." The old man brought the stock of the second pistol close to his eyes, ready to make the first cut on it. Death was finished and lying in a drawer of his worktable, wrapped in an oily flannel cloth; now he was ready, after a winter of not working at them, to begin Life. "Youth is all wanting—everything's bright and pretty in the wanting of it. It's the having that begins to hurt." He selected a tool and studied its edge with slitted eyes. "It's the having that breaks your heart. And after, when your heart is good and broke, then you grow up and you begin to understand a little."

"It don't have to be that way. It's a daft way to live your life."

"Aye, maybe. But the only way we have. 'Wisdom comes through suffering,' that's what the antique Greeks said."

"I don't care if I'm wise! I want a little happiness, is all!"

Old John laid the graving tool against the steel and took up the hammer, and a curved line like part of a parenthesis appeared. It would form one curve of the underlip of a newborn child, held aloft in its father's hands. He could see it already in his mind, the vision there sharper and more far-seeing than his eyes could ever be.

"Well, you can be wise or you can be foolish. Them's the choices. Happiness ain't one of the things being offered."

He came in from milking on a hot July evening and found that Sara was gone, their room still and empty except for the flies that batted against the window glass. Frightened, he looked in their chest of drawers and found her clothes still there, and he tumbled down the stairs to the kitchen, red-faced. "Where's Sara?"

"I wouldn't know, I'm sure." His mother plunged her floured fists, to which scraps of dough clung like burned skin, into a wooden bowl. "I ain't got the staple of news, I'm sure."

"She's went out." Nora's voice was nasty. "She said she was going 'home,' if you please." Nora began to hum; she made a great show of lifting a heavy iron kettle from its place next to the water bucket and carrying it to the fire.

"I guess she can visit her folks if she likes."

"Well, who said she couldn't? Why, she can visit all she likes, I'm sure! Although I would have said, if I'd been asked, that I thought her *home* was with her husband."

"Well, maybe if you ever marry yourself, Nora, you'll find that you want to visit back here sometimes, and not find it so odd." The stroke hit home; Nora, who wore her own heart a little too visibly and who had not been proposed to when she'd hoped for it, was hurt and angry and turned her back to him.

He rode the swaybacked old gray horse through the dusk to the Sullivans' mean little house. The irony of the journey was keen to him, making the same trip he had so many times before they had married, but with such a different spirit then. Angry and dispirited now, he wondered if he dared to strike her. There was a discipline that husbands were supposed to exercise over their wives, a discipline that the church and the law took account of and said was justified.

Sara's mother was standing in the high grass in front of the house, almost as if she had been waiting for him, and he, dropping from the old horse and striding through the uncut weeds, hardly acknowledged her.

"Please don't go in there, Davie."

"I'll do what I got to do!" he gripped her arm and found that she was shaking. "Where is she?"

"Don't go in there."

"I will go in! She's mine, I got a right to take her back! You know she run off without a word to me, her husband? I won't have her running back here like I'm some dirt she takes no notice of, some dirt she can humiliate with my family!" The words had run through and through his mind as he had ridden over, and now they staggered and stumbled out, tripped up by his anger. He found that he was shaking, too, and it was hard to control his voice. "Her place is with me!"

"Yes." Even in his rage he understood that she was trying to protect him. "Come back in the morning, Davie."

But he could not. He could not let go of his anger so easily. "Hell wouldn't keep me from her," he muttered. "She's going to know that she's my wife!"

The weeds were like thin fingers that tried to catch his legs as he passed, the big, tough leaves of burdocks slapping against his stockings as he passed. In the light of the little hallway, he saw that they were pasted with green burrs.

"Sara?" He sounded like Captain Speke when he was bellowing orders. *"Sara!"*

A sound came from the kitchen.

Four angry strides took him to the kitchen doorway.

"Oh, dear God."

He knew the look of her father when he was drunk, knew the ferret look that came into his mouth and around his eyes, knew the meanness that crept into the face. But he had never seen Sullivan's daughter like that before, and now he could not believe what he was seeing.

Her face looked swollen. She coughed slightly, a ladylike cough that was exaggerated and foolish; one strand of hair was loose and trailed across her forehead and her left eye, and her right hand, which was trying to pick up a blue mug in front of it, missed and fell clumsily on the table and then began to move slowly toward the mug again as if it were a creature with its own will.

She slewed her eyes toward him. "Oh. It's you."

Her eyes drooped sleepily. Her hand found the mug and raised it, and slowly, slowly, her head went down and the mug and her mouth met.

"Sara, you're to come home now."

"Go to Hell."

"Sara!" His right hand shot forward to point at her. "You will obey me! You're my wife!"

She shrugged one shoulder as her head tipped to one side and the hand raised the mug again. Her neck seemed boneless, a doll's cloth neck, and the mug tipped and some of the liquid spilled down her dress. Sullivan, coming in the kitchen door from the barn then with a jug in his hand, saw David and stopped, and a slow, mindless chuckle came from him.

"Shut up!" David swung to face him. "You worthless sot, shut up!"

Sullivan looked mean. He spat; the main charge of spittle landed on David's right calf, and a little of it ran down Sullivan's chin. David swung his left hand and struck Sullivan just beside the nose and knocked him backward, and Sullivan, trying to catch himself, backed out the doorway and fell on all fours in the chicken-scratched dirt outside.

"Now you're coming home!" He reached across the table to pull her up.

"Never! Never, never, never!" She stood up. She did not behave as drunks were supposed to—did not sway, did not stagger. She seemed to have sobered.

"I'm never going back to that nest of sanctimonious females. You all make me puke!" She straightened. For the first time, she seemed to notice that her father was just outside the door on all fours, dripping blood among the chicken droppings. "We could have the authorities on you for that." She was very grand. "You could face jail. Or worse." She looked down at her father, then up at David. "Assault. I was a witness."

"Sara, come home with me."

"Never. Never, never, never, never, never—"

"Sara—"

"Get out of it."

"Sara, please—"

"Get out!"

He reached for her wrist. She flinched back and began to move away from him, the mug held out of his reach. He had thought she was afraid of his striking her; now, bitterly, he realized that she was afraid he would take the mug away. Some of it spilled, and she moaned, "No, no—" and he was furious again, furious because all she cared about was the whisky, and with a quick movement he caught the mug and threw it away from him and heard it smash against the wall.

He looked around at the broken pottery, and when he looked back she was swinging the fireplace poker in front of her.

He remembered the poker. He had made it himself as a gift for Mrs. Sullivan. It was heavy and well made, and now it came swinging toward him and he could not quite duck aside or block it with his arm, and it came smashing against his wrist and his right ear and mastoid and the shock of the blow stupefied him.

"Get out!"

She raised the poker again. In that moment, he understood what Mrs. Sullivan had been trying to protect him from— this creature who was loosed when Sara was drunk.

Dear God, how many times has she been like this before?

He spun to his left and rushed out of the room. Mrs. Sullivan was not in the hallway, not in the dark yard. He threw himself on the old horse and urged it away from that horrible house, his head beginning to ache fiercely now, tears filling his nose and making him hiccup with sobs. He stopped at a little brook to cup water in his hands and try to pour it over his ear, and then he stripped off his shirt and soaked it and rode on home with the cold cloth held to the side of his head as if it were a seashell in which he heard some distant, magic music.

Two days later, she came back. His mother and his sisters were silent. Sara came in the back door of the Morse house and went up the stairs to their room and their bed, and he found her there at noon.

"I'm sorry, Davie. Oh, God help me, I'm so sorry," she whispered.

"You're all right now." He knelt beside her with his cheek against hers. She looked middle-aged and her breath was foul, yet he loved her repentance. He could tell himself that everything would be better now and that such a thing— ghastly, unbelievable, not even to be talked of—could never happen again.

He kissed her forehead. "You ought to eat." He brought up bread and hot soup, ignoring his mother's anger and his sisters' astonishment.

"Eat." He stroked the hair back from her face. He spooned up the broth and held the spoon to her lips.

"What happened to your ear?" She touched the swollen flesh.

He loved his own generosity. "Nothing," he said. "Eat."

That night they made love, and for three days she was

205

penitent and cowed, and she helped his mother and sisters and was cheerful with them, singing songs they didn't know and telling stories that weren't quite racy but that women could giggle at when there were no men about.

"She's a changed girl," his mother said to her husband, half meaning what she said because she thought any good news would be good for him. "Maybe Davie gave her what for."

"Pray God it's true." Donald sighed.

She went to church with the family and prayed and knelt, her hand in David's, her face young and pretty again. Then one day she stayed in bed; and early in August, she was gone for three days and came back, shaken and puffy and unable to eat.

"Oh, God help me! I'm so sorry, Davie."

"It's all right; eat."

"Say you forgive me."

"Yes, I forgive you. Eat."

"You're too good for me, Davie. I'm bad. I'm a horrible creature. You'd be happier without me."

"Don't talk foolish, Sara. Here, eat."

She sipped from the spoon. Her head rolled on the pillow so that she was looking away from him. "Maybe if I had my own little house, I wouldn't be like this. I get so miserable, living here. Always being reminded what a horror I am."

"Nobody says that, Sara."

"They don't have to say it. They mean well, I guess. But I know what they think. Maybe if I was in my own little place, I'd not be so cursed."

"Well—" He dipped the spoon again. "If I say I'll look for a place, would you promise me you wouldn't do it again?"

"Oh, yes, Davie! Oh, dear God in Heaven, yes! I promise!"

Lying in their bed that night, his right hand on her warm hip, he prayed into the darkness, *Oh Heavenly Father, make her well; lift this curse from her and make her like other women; please, dear God, Almighty God, take away this burden from her and make her whole.*

But only some prayers are answered.

Chapter Twenty-two

In the bitter February of 1777, David Morse and his wife
moved from his parents' house and went to live in the tawdry
little house where Sara had lived with her parents. The Sullivans went twenty miles away to live in rented rooms in
Orange, the reason given being that Sullivan could no longer
work under the oppressive employ of the Morses and wanted
to show his talents elsewhere.

"But you were just getting the place fixed nice," David
protested to Mrs. Sullivan.

"It's for the best, really, David."

"But—"

Sara was firm. "Shut up, David. My father wants it this
way."

He looked at the two women. Mrs. Sullivan was serene in
her sadness, entirely without anger; Sara, buoyant, swung
between talkativeness and angry impatience. "Oh, I can't
wait to move out of that cold house!" she cried, hugging him
from behind as they rode home on the old horse.

"My mother won't like it much, I guess."

"Ah, she'll be glad to get rid of the Irish witch that stole
her son."

"She liked your mother. She'll think we put her up to
leaving."

"What business is that of hers, at all? They're my parents,
ain't they? Ain't I the one to suffer, having them live to Hell
and gone in Orange town?" She hugged him again. "Oh,
Davie, it'll be so fine! You'll see."

His mother did not understand, and, if she felt secretly
that she was glad to get rid of the woman who had given her
son such obvious grief, she said nothing. Perhaps she was
growing a little callused to such shocks, now that she had
had Jonnie off to war and Samuel getting worse and her
husband always worrying.

"She wants her own house is all," David said with more
cheer than he felt. "And her parents were going anyways.
She wants to be a real wife, she says."

"Well, that's as it should be." Neither of them sounded quite convinced.

"She can cook very hearty, you know. We'll be quite snug there."

"Well..."

Sara was happy in the first weeks. The very smallness of the house, which made him restless, pleased her; even its crumbling condition seemed to be an opportunity, and she scrubbed and polished and even carpentered when she had to, and the house that had been neglected by her father and merely maintained by her mother became almost pretty, though every night when he trudged home and saw it first from the hillside he felt a pang of regret and dislike.

Her parents had sold the cow that had been pastured along the edge of the poisonous swamp. One day in March, Sara brought home three hens she had bartered for, full of herself because she had got the better of a Massachusetts farmer in a trade. Under her nagging, he turned the half-fallen barn into a henhouse, and when the weather turned warm early the hens began to lay, little pullet eggs at first and then good, big, proper hens' eggs. Winter, drawing away from the ugly little house like a gloomy shadow as the snow receded, seemed to be taking his unhappiness with it.

He thought that he needed only the end of the war to be quite content. David began woodworking again and talked of the cabinetry he would do "when the foolishness was over"; he took a few tools home and made a makeshift shop in the barn and began, during the half hour that he could spare in the morning, to make a box for her to hold tea in when that Loyalist leaf could be safely owned again. The box would have ball feet and sides that sloped slightly from top to bottom and an inlaid top with a pattern in brass wire, like the decoration on a gunstock. It would be the most elegant thing they owned, and he would have made it.

While the war went on, however, his few free moments were like a dream of peace. His father went on complaining and worrying, and though he got new contracts and hired a third barrel maker and ordered more Salisbury iron than ever, the Committee of Safety's payments lagged behind and he said he was even further in debt than before. Jonnie talked only of "independency" and carried a copy of *Common Sense* everywhere with him and was a popular member of the Sons of Liberty, who had now become so identical with the militia that David gave up the drills and gratefully spent the time at home.

"My married brother's got too grand to march with us," Jonnie said at the Bunch of Grapes one Saturday when David had stopped in on his way home with a rooster to keep the hens company. David stared back at the cluster of half a dozen men around his brother.

"I'm forgiven duty because I'm a gunsmith, and you all know it," he said.

"Jonnie's forgiven, too, but he drills all the same!" one insisted. "Jonnie was to Bunker Hill!"

"Yes, and I'm proud of him for being there. But you wouldn't have much of a rebellion if your gunsmiths all got themselves shot."

"Not much chance of that happening to you," another said.

David looked at him. He did not want to fight with anybody, especially these rowdy louts he secretly thought his inferiors. "So long as I make muskets," he said, "you got no quarrel. If you want to fistfight me for the sake of saying you done it, why, I can't prevent it. But it seems a daft waste of time."

"Ah, leave him be," Jonnie said. "He don't know no better. Anyways, he's wore out from fighting with his wife." They all laughed with him, and David was forgotten. Now nineteen, Jonnie was very much a man, insisting upon a man's perquisities, coming in late from the tavern on Saturday night but still doing a man's work six days a week. He was courting a girl, too, a broad-faced giggler named Felicity Gough whose family had two farms and a mill. He was no dreamer, but in his leaden way he had his own visions, and he was setting about to make them reality.

"We could have the biggest gun works in the Connecticut Valley," David heard him say to their father.

"And when'll that be, Jonnie?"

"In a year or three, Pa, you'll see. We could be rich, you'll see. We could serve the cause of independency and make ourselves rich to boot. There ain't nothing wrong with that."

"And how are we going to be rich, when they don't pay us what they owe us, and I go further into debt just trying to stay even?"

"Pa, if we *win*, then the debts'll be paid, with interest! Can't you see that? Can't you see how much we got to gain by winning?"

David leaned against a partition around the forge and

209

said, "We got more to gain by living peaceful than by fighting any war."

"Have you read *Common Sense?*" Jonnie demanded angrily.

"No, Jonnie, I ain't."

"Well, you read it! It's all writ out there. It's all in there. Paine knows a thing or two; he's got old King George down pretty good, all right. You read *Common Sense.*"

David took the pamphlet his brother urged on him and put it on a shelf in his makeshift workshop and went back to his own work on the tea box. But Jonnie was persistent.

"Did you read *Common Sense* yet?"

"I've been much busied, Jonnie."

"Yah, busied! You don't dare to read it. You're like some old man; you're afraid to read it. I heard a talk about your sort, Davie, down to the Sons. 'Privy Tories,' they call your sort—afraid to fart for fear you'll spoil your breeches. Afraid to read the truth for fear you'll upset your smooth life."

"I ain't afraid, Jonnie."

"Then read Tom Paine!"

"Oh, who's Tom Paine but a renegade Englishman who ain't lived in America long enough to find his way to the shithouse in the dark?"

Jonathan's face stiffened in anger. "The Sons'd give you a ride on a fence rail if they knew you said that. That's the way traitors talk!"

"No, Jonnie! *Common Sense* is the way traitors talk."

Jonnie was pale. "My God, what a position you put me in! My own brother—by God—don't ever say that around me again. I ought to report you, don't you know that? Don't say it ever. Don't speak to me!"

David trudged home the three miles to his little house. The walk, morning and evening, made his long day still longer, but he found pleasure in the solitude and the face that nature turned to him. The days were nearing their longest and the light lasted and he had time to think. There were rumors that the rebellion was going badly and might soon be over, and on an early summer evening, tired from labor, it was possible to think of peace restored and of things returning to what they once had been.

He was well down the hill to the house before he noticed that there were no lights. Sometimes, when she could bear the mosquitoes and the little flies, Sara waited for him in a crude chair he had made out under a tree. Tonight she was

210

not there, and the door was closed. He walked around the house, reluctant to go in, fearing what he might find. He did not call to her, but stepped into the barn and lit the lantern that was there and in its feeble light he moved to the hen coop. The door was open. A hen rushed past him, clucking madly; another moved nervously in the dark.

He paused and lifted the lantern.

The rooster lay dead on the littered floor; a hen hung half out of a nesting box. He could find none of the chicks.

A fox or a weasel, he thought. The weasel was the likelier, perhaps a pair of them; they were wanton killers, going mad in an undefended chicken coop.

He went back to the house and got another lantern, not daring to call Sara's name or look for her, and in the barn again he picked up the dead ones and carried them out to the swamp, moving from tussock to tussock until he stood on the edge of a black expanse of quickmud and black water, and he heaved them in and the white blurs of their bodies disappeared as the rotten-egg stench of the mud welled up; and then he went back to the coop and cleaned away the signs of carnage, bloodied feathers and a nest of smashed eggs and two dead chicks that had had their heads bitten off. When he was done with his sad, futile work he went back to the house and right up to their bedroom and found her in their bed, a bottle on the floor beside her. Her deep breathing was like the gasps of somebody drowning in the viscous mud of the swamp, and he did not wake her.

He waited near the hen coop most of the night, a musket that he had made himself beside him loaded with shot. When the squawking of a hen waked him, he tiptoed inside and was in time to flash the dark lantern at a hen that was trying to fly while blood gushed from its neck, and a weasel, caught in the light, blinked once and flowed away like a thick brown snake. He fired, and he missed.

In the morning, he went wearily around the barn, nailing boards over the holes the killers might have come in by, but the barn was all holes and he threw the hammer against the wall in frustration, thinking, *This is my life, trying to stop up a million holes with a handful of boards,* and in his anger he almost went for the ax to butcher the rest of the hens, but he conquered the anger and gulped down two of the eggs that were left, raw in a little milk, and went off without waking Sara. That evening, he walked two miles out of his way to borrow a vicious little brute of a dog that was part bull and part bobcat, from the look of it, and he tied it to the hen-coop wall, and after that there were no weasels for as long as the dog was there.

"Why did it matter so much?" he said to her when she was sober again. Weeping, penitent, she lay in their bed and would not look at him.

"I don't know," she moaned. "Them hens—I seen them, and it was like—all my plans, my work—oh, God, I don't know! I ain't no good!"

He sighed and rubbed his eyes. "Where did you get the whisky?"

"I had it hid. I always got some hid, don't you know that? I ain't no good!"

"And have you got some hid now?"

"No. I drank it all."

"All right, let that be the end, then. Do you hear me? Not another drop comes into my house, or by God—!"

"I'm no good. I'm no good to anybody."

"Oh, talk sense!" His anger, as at a child's slowness to learn, was futile. "Just promise me you'll never do it again."

"Will you forgive me?"

With his hands covering his face, he might have been weeping, but in fact he was dry-eyed and trying to keep from destroying her fragile penitence with his rage. "I guess I'm pretty well out of forgiveness by now, Sara."

"Oh, say you forgive me! Say it! I promise I'll never do it again. I promise. Just say it!"

Not looking at her, he picked at his lower lip with restless fingers. "I forgive you, Sara."

Ten days later, it happened all over again, but this time she was wakeful and venomous. When he tried to frighten her with his anger, she laughed at him, and when he raised his fist to strike her she laughed even more, and he hit her as he would have hit a man, with his closed fist on the side of the face, and the next day she had a swollen cheek and a tooth with a piece chipped away from the inside. When she was sober again, they clung together and they begged each other's forgiveness, but he knew that there was something utterly false and self-indulgent about the scene, and he began to go about like a man who wears his troubles like an iron coat.

"What is it, Davie?" his father said at the forge.

"Sir?"

"I see you chewing away at worries, Davie. I know what worries are. What's troubling you?"

David shifted the iron on the anvil and struck it once. "I guess you got enough of your own without I tell you mine, Dad."

"Aye, worries enough for twenty; but sometimes it helps to speak out." His father put the iron back into the coals and shook it lightly as if it were a mess of Indian popping corn in a basket. "It's that wife of yours, ain't it?"

"Yes, sir, I guess it is."

"Does she drink, Davie?"

"Yes, sir."

His father nodded gloomily. "Aye, that's what your mother said." He shook his head as if unable to believe that so many vexations could have fallen on one man. "What a piece of folly you committed, Davie!"

"Yes, sir."

"Which can't be undone, you understand!" His father looked at him shrewdly across the anvil. "You swore an oath in the church. You made a grown man's vow; now you have to suffer the grown man's consequence."

"Aye, I understand that," David said heavily.

"Is it—so bad?"

"Sometimes. Sometimes it's pretty bad. Sometimes it's good. But I just feel like I been—put into a box and closed up, sir."

His father nodded. "Well, we told you. Your mother told you, and I told you." He struck the metal. "Now you'll learn!" He struck again. "But there's never no telling you, boy, oh no!" He tapped the darkening iron once more and thrust it into the fire. "When will you ever learn, do you think? When will you ever learn to think of some other creature but yourself? Do you know what troubles you put on all of us with this cursed marriage of yours? No, you don't, because you never think." His father spat bitterly; and then, in one of those twists away from anger and hatred toward affection that David was beginning to recognize as part of his father's way with his sons (and part of Old John's way with *his* son, and part, even, of David's way with Sara—*Is this love? Is it always this, both the fist and the kiss?*), his father's voice softened almost to a husky murmur and he said gruffly, "My heart goes out to you, Davie," and he patted his son's shoulder once and dropped his big hand, embarrassed. They hammered

213

on the iron together until they had finished shaping it into a new shaft for the grinding wheel, neither speaking.

When they were done and the piece was put aside, Donald gave his son the same shrewd look as before and said abruptly, "What would you think of going away for two weeks or three?"

"Why—" David frowned. "Where to?"

"Philadelphia." His father spat again. "Emory's gone to stay at Philadelphia." He wiped his streaming face. His fingers left black streaks on the glistening skin like a child's idea of warpaint. "He writes a letter to me, it come yesterday, he says, 'Mr. Morse, if you will have your monies, come after me.' That's what he writes. 'Follow me to Philadelphia, and the Congress will supply you handsomely.' Ain't that canny of him, now?"

"Mr. Emory's in the Congress?"

"No, he's gone off to be aide to some fool who is." He looked at his son with a smile of shared conspiracy. "Don't tell Jonnie I said that; he'd have me riding on a rail for sure." Donald put his hammer down and moved his arms up and down, elbows bent, in a movement of the sort a rooster makes before he crows. "I'm just sticky with this heat, I am! Now, I can't take the time to callus my bottom on the chair of some prim ass while my work here waits; and sure I can't send Jonnie, who's eager but outspoken, and besides, he's got that Gough girl near to the point of saying yes. Pump up that fire a little, Davie. But you, you're somewhat a talker, and I guess you wouldn't object to getting away for a little time, would you?"

Happiness bubbled in him as he pumped the bellows, absurdly glad to have such intimacy from his father. It was likely that his mother had put Donald up to this, and he would already have talked it over with her. Still, when he spoke, it was very cautiously. "I guess a respite wouldn't harm Sara nor me, sir."

"That may be." His father's weary face turned toward him. "Can you demand our money from some jobbing clerk that thinks he's twenty times too grand for you?"

"Why, I guess so, sir. It can't be too different from trading horses. And we're in the right—the money's truly owed us, I mean—so I can stand up for what's ours."

His father looked gloomy again. "I guess being in the right don't count for everything. So far, it ain't counted for *nothing!*" He wiped his face again; stubble rasped under the calluses of his hand. "Where's the *right* in any of this? Where'll
214

the *right* be if the British beat them, and Emory and his Congress are pitched up on the hayrick for all time, and I'm left to whistle for my money? Where'll the *right* be if I'm branded a traitor and left unpaid by those that owe me, driven from our home and..." His voice returned to its complaining whine and became an unrelenting keen, wind nipping at the corner of a house. David pumped the bellows and thought of Philadelphia. *Three weeks! Three weeks alone, away from Sara! Three weeks in the biggest city in America....*

Chapter Twenty-three

The little gig moved among the New York water traffic with the quick movements of an insect, the two pairs of oars flashing like a water boatman's legs, while in the stern the coxswain one-handed the tiller and stared almost languidly at the wharves of the garrison city. The harbor was crowded with transports and gunships; on the docks, the colors of uniforms flashed among the workmen and the lookers-on.

"Looks rather like Portsmouth," a major of grenadiers said.

"Not enough poxed whores for Portsmouth," a Guards captain drawled.

"There will be, now you're here, Jack."

The Guards captain acknowledged the compliment with a smile.

"Does anybody know the way to headquarters?" Patrick Ferguson was entirely businesslike in the midst of the joking.

"Any female between fifteen and fifty will know where General Howe has set himself up." There were snickers, and the captain raised his hat gravely. "Well may you titter, gentlemen, but Sir William has more conquests off the field than on it, I assure you; under his command, you may always look forward to snug winter quarters in some place where the ladies are extremely handsome."

The coxswain ran the gig under the bow of a merchantman and ordered the oars shipped as they slid cleanly along a wharf. Moments later, one oarsman was monkey-climbing a ladder while another threw up a line.

Ferguson fell in with the Guards captain and kept pace with him through the crowded streets. New York struck him as no more prepossessing than a provincial English town, certainly poorer than many and hardly credible as a great city. He wore now the green coat of an officer of rangers, distinguished by the old-gold facings of his riflemen, but nobody much marked his colors in a place where most of the uniforms of the British army could be seen, mingled with those of Hesse-Hanau and Brunswick.

"Captain Ferguson, His Majesty's Rifles. My orders."

"Yes, sir." The sergeant hardly looked at him, but reached up to take his papers with one hand while with the other he groped for the orderly book. "I'll send you on directly I log these in, sir."

Ferguson was aware of a figure in a doorway to his left but did not turn; his attention was already on problems of quartering his company and finding a proper shooting range for them. If he could, he wanted to get them out of the city and give them some taste of the infamous American woods.

"And here you are at last, Patrick."

He turned. "Hullo, Hanger." It was the same irrepressible young rakehell whom he'd met at Woolwich Arsenal.

"It's been—God in Heaven, is it a year?"

"A year and a bit." Ferguson grinned suddenly and clasped Hanger's hand. "Good! I'm *glad* to see you here." He sounded as if most sensible people would have felt otherwise. "I've brought *my* riflemen, you know."

"So I'd heard; rumor reaches even here, you know. She's a slow bitch, but persistent. Come into my room, Patrick." He waved toward a doorway. "Sergeant, Captain Ferguson will be with me; send his papers up to the colonel, will you? Tell him he's studying tactics with the Hessian liaison."

In the small, bright room, which had been a little back sitting room until the army had taken over the house, Hanger pulled out a chair with one booted foot and moved a tray with decanter and glasses an inch across his table. "How many have you brought?"

"A hundred and forty-seven, plus officers. All armed with my patent rifle."

Hanger poured wine into two glasses. "Teach 'em to shoot by pairs, Patrick—one to load while the other stands ready. I got eighteen of my men butchered in a skirmish by not doing that; the bastard rebels come in close while you're loading."

"Not with my rifle. They won't have the time—or the stomach."

Hanger looked into his glass. He was smiling. He was a wearier and an older man than he had seemed at Woolwich. "I was at Trenton, you know. Have you heard about Trenton?"

"We heard that the Germans surrendered."

Hanger smiled still more. *"We Germans,"* he said carefully, "had our breeches set afire."

"Tell me what the Americans are like," Ferguson said intently.

Hanger glanced at him. Somber now, he thrust his lips

out in a truculent, wary pout. "Like tripe," he said. "Ever eat tripe from some old cow, Patrick? You chew and chew all evening, and it's still as tough and tasteless at the end as at the beginning. That's what the Americans are like—we chew and chew, and they just won't be swallowed. They're a very tasteless lot, I fear."

"Superb riflemen, they say in London."

"Pah, they say! Of course *they say;* what have they got to do but talk? Most of them are armed with fowling pieces you wouldn't give your cook to shoot at crows in the kitchen garden with. It ain't their shooting has given them the reputation, it's our blundering! We lose a battle, what shall we blame it on? Why, the American riflemen. We sustain terrible losses, how shall we account for them? Why, the withering fire of the rebel rifles. My dear Patrick! The British soldier shudders in his gaiters at the mere thought of American rifles; and in the meanwhile, for every man who actually falls to a rebel rifle ball, five fall from massed musket fire and ten are incapacitated in camp by disease, while a hundred are lost to stupidity and hesitation."

"You mean you've lost faith?"

"I've lost faith in London and my lords North and Germain, and I've lost faith in dunderheaded generals who have a genius for mismanagement."

With a poor attempt at casualness, Ferguson asked, "Any idea what my orders are to be?"

Hanger poured himself more wine. "Let me see what I can do. Howe's in New Jersey, trying to draw Washington out; I'm to join him there in five days with my company. Any objections on your part to serving under a German?"

"You?" Ferguson's neck was stiff.

"No, no—von Knyphausen. Decent enough fellow, able officer. He needs a skirmish line."

"I'd serve under the Bey of Calicut if he'd employ my rifles properly."

"Capital! I'll see what I can wangle." Hanger stood up and opened the door. "Now you must go up and be very formal with the colonel, who lives in the illusion that he makes the decisions here. Suffer him gladly, Patrick; he'll sign anything if he's sure his rear is covered. And welcome to America."

"Why are you so miserable?"

"I don't know. I don't know, truly."

"You can't sit here without lights, night after night."

"Stop forever tormenting me about it."

"I ain't tormenting you, Sara, I—oh, God, stop your eternal weeping, will you! In the name of God Almighty, stop!"

"I can't stop."

"Of course you can!"

"Let me weep if I want."

"You've got no backbone, is all! Put on some lights; do something—it ain't like there's nothing to be done around here, God knows. There's cooking and cleaning you could do like any other woman. You can't sit here forever weeping!"

"Leave me be."

"Sara, my God—please—"

Please what? His fists were clenched. His voice trailed off before he could put the hazy thought into words: *Please stop making me hate you.*

He had told her about his father's idea that he go to Philadelphia. For a day, she had been cheerful and loving and had said the change would be good for him, for both of them; then she had slumped into her dull mood and had sat listlessly without doing her work, and he would find her still there in the dark when he came home at night. Trying to shake her from this state, he only made her weep.

"Is it me going away, Sara?"

"Why would it be that?"

"I won't go, if you mind so much."

"Go! I'm that happy to be rid of you, you and your pious advice. Go and be damned to you."

Jonnie was sullen that it was not he who had been chosen, but when news came of a British strike down Lake Champlain, he was cheered because the milita might be mobilized. He was a sergeant now and was very pleased with himself, and if his memory of Breed's Hill ever haunted him, he gave no sign of it. Still, he was jealous of his brother and did not try to hide it when they were alone.

"Jesus, I wonder Pa'd trust a Tory to take his affairs to Philadelphia," he said.

"Easier than to trust me to fight the British," David said, "for I wouldn't. Anyways, I'm a better argufier than you, Jonnie."

"Jesus, we might as well be sending a Tory spy."

"Oh, Jonnie, Jonnie! Let's not fight, these last weeks before I go."

"Do as you like. I got principles."

Yet Jonnie had the good grace still to carry a message to

219

him, however jealous it made him. "Yon old man wants to see you now," he said at noon one day.

"Who's that? Grandfather?"

"Aye, who else? It's something about them pistols he's always hunkered over. Damned toys for gentlemen, if you ask me!"

David went through the house to the small room where his grandfather still sat every day, though he had not touched his tools in months.

"You wanted to see me, Grandfather?"

"Aye, I do—if I could see, that is. I'm gravel-blind these days—you're just a shape like a ghost, boy."

"I'm sorry, sir. Maybe the doctor—"

"A waste of good money! Maybe I seen enough, who knows? Anyways, that's havering; I· hear your pa's sending you to the capital of fools."

"To Philadelphia, yes."

"That's what I said. It's where they got their Congress, ain't it? The wise men of Gotham, all gathered to build a fence to keep cuckoos in." He slowly opened the wire bows of his spectacles and looped one over his right ear, turning his head a little to the side, then put on the other with the same movement. Without touching the pistols, he bent over them.

"I'll never finish these two, Davie."

There was nothing to be said to that.

"I finished Death all right. Life is mostly a blank still." He lifted his head and slowly removed the spectacles. "You'll have to carry them to Philadelphia as they are."

"Me, sir?"

"Oh, aye, they're for you. They've always been for you. You're the only one as understands this kind of workmanship, for all that your age makes you a damned fool most of the time. They'll shoot right good as they are; maybe you'll finish the engravings when your hand is trained."

"I don't—I could never know what you meant to go there."

"No, I daresay not; but you'll learn, you'll learn. Any old ox like me can do scenes of death, that's easy! Celebrating life, that's something you'll learn."

"But—well, I shan't *need* them, surely."

"What, going amidst that great gang of patriots? I'd as soon go into a madhouse unarmed. Take them, boy; they're yours."

He felt over the tabletop until his fingers found the barrels

220

nd then he held the pistols out, steel butts first. "Only prom-
se me you won't finish the engraving until your hand is fine."

"I promise, sir." He smiled, delighted to have the old man's
ompliment even more than he was pleased to own the pistols
hemselves. "They're beautiful," he said.

When he went back to the new barn, he carried the pistols
olled in a cloth, and Jonnie, passing through the stocking
oom, saw the bundle and stopped. "So he give them to you,
lid he?" Embarrassed, David said nothing, and Jonnie mut-
ered, "You even tried to hide them from me."

"No, I didn't, Jonnie. I don't want them scratched."

"Damned toys! But it's a rich thing, that that daft old man
vould give a pair of pistols to a fellow that wouldn't shoot
ne if some damned Englishman was raping his sisters before
is very eyes!"

"Oh, Jonnie—"

"Yah, to Hell with you!"

David hid the pistols in his rolled-up coat the rest of the
lay, and carried them home that way. For once his house
vas lighted and Sara was in the kitchen. She had cooked a
linner, but he knew she had been drinking.

"Oh, it's you," she said.

"Yes, it's me. Who else?" He tried to kiss her, did barely
kiss her cheek as she moved her head away. "How have you
een?"

"Oh, like the queen in London, how else would I be, alone
n this place?"

"Well, that's good, then."

He moved to the little sitting room with a lighted candle
nd unrolled his coat.

"What's them?" Her voice was hard and suspicious. She
ooked over his shoulder with her head tilted back in a way
hat suggested she thought she was acting like a lady.

"The Highland pistols my grandfather made. He gave
hem to me."

"Ugly damned things." She reached past him to pick one up.

"You'd better not, Sara."

"Oh, to Hell with you."

She picked up Death and balanced it in her hand, then
retended to aim it at a mirror; turning like a duelist, she
imed it at him. "How I'd like to do it!" she cried; and then,
ointing the muzzle at her own temple, she said, "Or this!"

"Don't do that!" He pushed her hand aside. "Don't ever
oint a gun, even in play!"

221

"Play! *Play!*" She laughed. "You're such a stick, David. God, how glad I'll be when you're gone! How glad I'll be!" She threw the pistol to the floor and swept out of the room, swooping through the doorway by catching the jamb with her fingers and swinging around it. He retrieved the pistol and found it unmarred, and wrapped both weapons in the cloth again and hid them in the decrepit barn where she could not find them. On an impulse, he picked up the tea chest he had made for her and carried it inside, but she had gone upstairs and he knew she would be drinking there. He sat and ate the food she had prepared and then took the tea chest into the sitting room and rubbed and rubbed it with oil until the rich wood glowed and he could see the dim outline of himself reflected in its reddish depths, a dark shape like a ghost of himself.

In the morning, his father led him into the dark little room that served as an office. There, for an hour, he listened to his father ramble through the grievances he must try to find justice for in Philadelphia—contracts made, money not paid, rising costs and expensive labor and unobtainable materials. Together they made a list of the demands he was to make and the people he was to see. With his father leaning over his shoulder, he went through the sheafs of papers that marked the progress of the Morse gun works from the beginning of its first weapon three years before up to the present.

> Compl^d to date A.D. Jul 27
>   1777:
> Muskets, plain 347
> Stands of arms, full 229
> Trench pikes 413
> Swords, hangers, & cutlasses per
> order of Greenv^le militia 22
> Fascene knives, brush hooks &
> sickles per order 128
> Axes, belt, Indian type 417
> Also divers knives, pistols &c.
> under various charges.

Of the lot, less than half had been paid for, many of those by private funds and sales to the militia.

"You'll need the contracts and letters," his father said.

"They could be lost, traveling like I'll be. I'll make copies f you'll permit it; we can have them notarized in Greenville. The judge is one of the Sons."

"Aye, copies are good. Though even they'll be enough to hang me if ever the British find them." His father went away shaking his head. For three days, David copied documents in the hot little room, cursing the Boston and Philadelphia men who wrote such hard fists and who were so prolix as to take three pages to say what a few sentences would have said far better. One day his grandfather wandered in, and David complained to him of their paralyzing wordiness.

"They're lawyers," the old man said contemptuously. "What more could you expect? Still, it could be worse." He winked. "They could have been clergymen."

His mother appeared another day with tears in her eyes, but all she had to say was, "Have you any clothes need mending?"

"No, Ma, I done them. Sara, I mean. I done buttons, is all." She sniffed.

His sisters were quiet around him. Even Nora had no mockery for him; and in turn, each of them but Jonnie brought him some small thing to carry along, as if he were setting out on a long sea voyage and not simply riding down through two colonies to Philadelphia. The old man's pistols remained his prize, but he had a new waistcoat from his mother, fully suited for city wear; and a neckcloth from one sister and a little embroidered bag from the other; and even Samuel, confined now to his downstairs bedroom, called him in, and, drawing up his words like heavy buckets from a well, his head twisted down to his chest, handed over a drawing he had made of David arriving in Philadelphia, a shaky, crude sketch that a child of five might have managed.

The last night before he was to leave, Sara did not meet him at the door and the house was dark.

"Oh, God," he sighed. *Dear God, keep her asleep until I'm gone. Keep us from hating each other.*

His clothes were packed in two saddlebags, and the papers were tied with ribbons and stored in a wallet, to be carried inside his waistcoat. One of his father's horses was tethered in the barn. At daylight, he would ride to his father's house and say his goodbyes, and then he would be off.

He wiped down the Highland pistols and laid them in front of him. Measuring the powder carefully, as his grandfather had taught him, he loaded each with powder and ball and a paper wad and set them on the edge of the table, away from the candle. Using the right side of his thumb as a sweep, he brushed the black crumbs of gunpowder into his left palm and threw them into the fire, where they blazed and snapped and the odor of sulfur spread in the little room.

"Aye, you're a devil. You're a devil!"

She stood in the doorway. The fingers of both hands were wrapped around the doorframe to support her; her long hair hung down both sides of her swollen face like rags.

"Get out of my house, you devil!"

Dear God, why did you let her wake?

"I'm going soon enough, Sara."

"Aye, so you say."

"I'm going to Philadelphia tomorrow. Don't you remember?"

"You're lying. Liar. Get out of my house!"

He shrugged and turned away. The pistols glinted on the table.

"You're going to leave me, ain't you?"

"I'm going away for three weeks, you know that."

"You're never coming back. Never! *Never, never!* You're leaving me!"

"Don't shout, Sara."

"Why are you leaving me?"

"Please, Sara, don't start. Just don't start. I want to get a night's sleep."

"Why are you leaving me?"

The tea box he had made for her was in the very center of the table. She lurched out of the doorway and stood over the table, staring down at it with her eyes widened as if in horror; then, a childish voice full of astonishment, she said slowly, "You're. Going. To. Leave. Me."

"Sara, I'm going to Philadelphia on my father's business."

She moved, as if to reach over the table, and he quickly put his hands on the pistols. She picked up the tea box.

"Take your trash with you," she said. "I don't want your trash!" She threw the box to the floor. One foot broke off and skidded to the hearth; the sound of the box hitting the floor told him that the wood had split.

"Now get out!" She kicked the box and it bounced toward the fire.

"Now get out! Get out, get out, get out!"

"Sara—!"

"Get out!" She tipped the table over and swayed above it.

"Damn you, Sara!"

224

"Get out of my house!"

The pistol in his right hand came up. She stood five feet from him, lips parted, face distorted. The slight concavity of the upper surface of the barrel served as a sight, and he brought it just to the bridge of her nose—

What had he meant? He would ask himself forever afterward. *To scare her, was all. To frighten the drunken wits out of her. To show her what I'd held back—to show her I wasn't a weakling that didn't know any better, a milksop couldn't stop her from what she was doing—*

Many men love war. They find their best selves in it, or think they do. They find that they are able to hate more deeply, kill more bloodily, stand more courageously than they had ever dreamed. In such amoral and ultimate surroundings, they find what sort of creatures they really are.

David Morse was in a separate war. He found that he was a hater.

His finger tightened, and the finely tuned trigger tripped the sear and the cock fell; sparks leaped to their work. In the instant when the gun went off, he knew that he hated her and wanted her dead; even as his conscience was denying that he could do such a thing, he knew that he had done what he wanted. In this separate war called love, he had found himself.

She swung to the left and back and knocked a cup from a small table as she fell. He was shaking. Nauseated. Vomit rose in his throat, and he staggered to the front door only in time to void the contents of his belly over the step, and then he leaned on the doorpost panting, the sour smell of it in his nose, tears of pain and tears of horror running down his cheeks. "God, no," he moaned over and over. "Please God, no." But when he came back into the room, her body was there on the floor. There were flecks of blood on the wall behind where she had stood and a puddle of thickening blood under the back of her head.

David wept. He wrapped his head in his arms and leaned against a wall to weep. He hid in the dark cave of his arms. If he had still been a little boy, somebody would have come and punished him and that would have been an end to it. But nobody would come and make things right with a punishment. He would be found out, jailed. Hanged. *Hanged.*

He walked through the house in the darkness.

Nobody.

He looked into the decrepit barn, out by the well, in the little fenced-in field where the horse stood, silent.

Nobody. Nothing.

A hope stirred. It was the beckoning of a finger. *Make me a bargain,* it seemed to say. *A lifetime of guilt for escape from punishment.*

It took him a long time to work out how he could do it. He wrapped her body in a sheet and tied the bundle with rope, and he carried it out through the slimy dark to the edge of the swamp, far out on the tussocks of teetering grass that stuck up above the black water like hands, and he laid her down and went back for the rusty anvil that was in the barn, and then he carried it out and tied it to her body with the rope. He was wet to the crotch when he was done; his scrotum was small and tight against him from the wet cold; he was as muddy as a hog in a wallow, but he could not see himself. When the moon slid from behind a cloud, he looked at it over his shoulder like a creature caught eating carrion. When the moon was masked again, he waded out to his chin in the stinking water, with her body half floating, dragging the anvil, and he launched her ahead of him, pushing off with his feet so he went in over his head and started down with her, as if she wanted him with her yet, dead as she was. He let go at last and floated to the surface, breaking the oily water like a dark bubble from the mud. She did not rise with him. She was gone.

He changed out of the wet clothes. He wrung them out and hung them to dry; naked, he went all over the room and the hall through which he had carried her corpse and wiped up every telltale drop of red. The bullet was still in her head, so there was no mark of it in the room.

Finished with the nauseating task, he put on dry clothes and went through the house with a lighted candle, looking for some sign of her, of the crime. In a corner of the table he had used for a desk, in a small drawer, he found a note she had left for him weeks before. *Gone to my pa's.* It had infuriated him then, and he had kept it out of hatred, to challenge her with one day. Now it became a proof of his innocence. *She wasn't at home when I got there; she's gone off to her pa's, she said. See the note she left? You know how she is when she drinks.*

He saddled the horse and led it out into the darkness and rode away from the miserable little house, praying that she would never float to the surface of the pond to haunt him, praying that he would never have to think of her again, praying that he could go back to the young man he had been before she had ever appeared and start his life over from there.

He fell asleep in the woods, praying.

Chapter Twenty-four

Sick with the terror of discovery, he rode to his father's house at first light. His mother and sisters were dressed and busy in the kitchen, and his father and grandfather came from the barn as he rode in. The early meal was silent, broken only by feeble jokes and habitual exchanges. David ached to seem natural—and so was unnatural.

"Where's Jonnie?" he murmured to his father.

"Why, I guess—I guess he's down to the barn."

"I'll just say goodbye to him, then."

He picked up a saddlebag and walked out of the house and along the woodshed and the summer kitchen to the L where the barns began; he went through them one after another until he found Jonnie in the cowbarn.

"Jonnie."

His brother did not look up.

"Jonnie, I come to say—Jonnie, won't you look at me?" His brother went on milking. They had few enough cows that had to be milked twice a day, but he was making a great thing of it. It had not been so long ago that they had fought in this barn. David found himself choking; he wanted to put things back to where they had been, back before Sara— Tears stung his eyes; without knowing that he was about to do it, he heard himself cry out, "Jonnie, you're my brother! For God's sake, don't let me leave like this!"

Jonathan turned his head. His face was angry, but it changed so quickly he might have removed a mask. He was on his feet, and the two of them were holding each other in their powerful arms—and both were weeping. "Jesus, Jonnie—Jesus—"

"Holy Christ." Jonnie gulped. He stepped back, his hands still on his brother's upper arms. His eyes were icy with tears. "Holy Christ."

"Jonnie—Jesus, don't ever hate me, Jonnie. No matter what!"

"Hate you! Holy Christ, Davie!"

"Don't hate me. Promise you won't hate me."

"I never hated you, Davie." Jonathan's voice was soft, as

if with wonder at a discovery. "You only made me so goddam mad with all your—never mind. It don't matter, Davie—*it don't matter!*"

"You won't hate me? No matter what?"

Jonnie hugged him again, aware that his brother was on the very edge of reason, not guessing why. He chuckled, meaning to cheer them both. Whether he matured, all in that moment, or whether he had run ahead since their first fight and was now waiting for his brother to come even with him, did not matter. Both felt a surge of feeling—somber in David, joyous in Jonathan. "You make me so goddam mad, I got no time to hate you, you ape."

David backed away. He fumbled in the saddlebags. "Jonnie, I want you to have—something of what I—we got to share these." He took out the pistols and unwrapped the cloth that covered them. "We ought each to have one."

He tried not to think of one of them as the weapon that had killed Sara. They were things made by his grandfather. It seemed important to share them with Jonnie; he ignored the fact that he was sharing his guilt, as well. "Take one."

"Aw, I can't, Davie."

"You can. Pick."

"It's breaking up the pair."

"Well, we're a pair was almost broke up. They'll come together again."

Jonnie chuckled. "Well, then." His hand hovered over one of the weapons, then settled on the other. *Life.* He had chosen the unfinished one. Not the one that had killed Sara.

"Take the other if you want it. It's got the engraving."

"No, this suits me fine. Maybe the old man'll finish it for me. Or you will, when you come back."

"Aye, that's what I'll do. When I come back."

"I love you, Jonnie."

Jonathan blushed. He looked at the cows, the gun, the floor—anywhere but at his brother. "Right," he said. "Right."

David flung his right arm around his brother's neck and squeezed it, and then he was gone. Within minutes, he had made his other goodbyes and thrown the saddlebag over the horse's rump.

He climbed the hill past the apple trees and turned at the top to wave at the distant line of figures, who still waited dutifully to return his last salute. Beyond them, no rider came pounding from the wretched little house; no constable came with a warrant for his arrest; no hangman came hurrying. He had gotten away with it.

He followed the Connecticut Valley south as far as Northampton and turned west and south, crossing the Hudson above Catskill on the third day and trading his jaded horse for a fresh one another day's journey beyond that. Once in the Hudson Valley, he was in the midst of the war. It was real there, imminent, and he was glad of it, glad to be distracted from his guilt, glad for the gossip of a British army to the south and another rushing down from Canada; if the two could join, the travelers opined, the rebellious colonies would be cut in two.

"No comin' back here from Philadelphia, then!" a merchant said cheerfully. David smiled hollowly, thinking, *No coming back for me at all*. Sara's ghost was more powerful than any British army.

He lived like a sick animal, with his eyes cast always over his shoulder. His awareness of his companions was so heightened that he noted the tiniest details of their clothes, their habits, their cleanliness or lack of it; he studied them for some sign of knowledge of his crime. When one of them mentioned a murder that had been committed, he felt himself start to tremble, and his sphincter constricted painfully. It was some other murder—*somebody else did a murder, imagine!*—but their talk frightened him and he fell behind on the excuse that his horse was lame. Thereafter, he rode alone, looking for paths and little-used roads, avoiding towns. He met militiamen who were moving northward to join Benedict Arnold above Albany; when they challenged him, he showed them his papers and they let him go with thanks, as if he were going to Philadelphia to make more guns to supply them.

He dreamed of Sara. The brutal sexuality of these dreams frightened him as much as fear of discovery did; tumescent, he would wake from them in the dark summer night to groan aloud and seek with a hand for the warm, so often drunken body that should have lain beside him. In fields and haymows, in a barn near the Delaware, he dreamed of a sexuality more intense than any they had known, and he woke to disgust. Turning aside from his course of flight, he found a whore in Easton and brutalized her, degraded her; after he had paid her, he beat her unconscious and then fled again, crime now piled on crime as he scuttled down toward Philadelphia with

230

his head turned always back to watch for enemies, like a dog with a stolen bit of meat.

He reached the city during the second week of August and took half of a bed in a small tavern room with three other men. Two of them were there on commissary contracts; the other was a printer, drawn by the presence of so many men who used so many words. David shunned them all. When he came into the room, they fell silent or ignored him.

Philadelphia was full of whores. David spent his father's money on them, seeking he knew not what from them. Absolution, perhaps. Coupled with them, he hated them and he wanted to smash their insipid faces with his hands; he was too frightened, however, and he slunk away as soon as he was done, still fastening his breeches. He could not risk committing another crime in Philadelphia, for the city was his last resort: he did not know where to flee beyond it. It was a corner into which he had driven himself.

On a sweltering day, he sought out Emory's lodging to pursue his father's business. Emory's clerk told him to wait.

He waited, in fact, for three days.

"I ain't even seen the man at a distance!" he complained to others who, like him, were waiting. "What is a Massachusetts man to do in this place?"

"Why, you are a green sprig," one of them said. "Ain't you given him his sugar titty yet?"

David looked from one man to another.

"He don't follow you, Rafe."

"His sugar, man." Rafe rubbed a forefinger and thumb together. "Money, man!"

"What—*bribe* him, do you mean?"

They laughed. It was not only the word, but the grieved tone in which he spoke it as well.

"But Emory was the one who come to us, back in 'seventy-four. He was all ideals and great words!"

"I'm sure he still is," one of them said drily. "Try some money on him, Morse; you might find he'd be a very hospitable patriot."

"Devil a patriot if he does!"

"Now, now, don't gainsay honest greed, youngster! What's the rebellion about, if it ain't about money? Taxation! Free trade! Export rights! If them things ain't *money*, what are they?"

One of them chuckled. "You know what sound they say Sam Adams's ballocks do make when they swing together?"

231

They looked at him expectantly. He half rose from his chair with a loosely closed hand held in front of his groin; when he shook his hand, the sound of clinking coins came from it. Even David laughed.

"Money, Morse, money! Send your man in some sugar, and he'll see you. But mind"—the man held up a hand—"don't be crudish about it. You got to send it in with a sweetheart's letter, reminding the dear man that here's the money he lent you when last you met. He'll understand."

"How much?"

"Five pounds. If it's in gold; if it ain't gold, don't bother."

"Five pounds!" He had only twenty pounds in all, and that seemed a fortune, though his father had given him a letter on a Philadelphia bank so that he could draw more if he had to. But he had planned that the money would more than last him and that he would buy presents for them all and come back with most of the money intact; now he could see it vanishing in a few days, if he would have to see many such patriots.

As he quickly learned, there was a black market in gold in Philadelphia, in case he had the bad luck to have his father's debts paid off in Continentals. In the City of Brotherly Love, few officers of the Congressional government wanted to be paid in their own currency.

And Emory did see him—and on the same day that the five pounds was sent in. Emory sent him to an assistant of commissary, who sent him to a lieutenant of ordnance, who sent him to a thin gentleman who seemed to have no direct connection with the Congress but who knew everybody and who understood best how everything was to be done. It took twenty-five pounds in gold (bought for double that in dollars) to see the fellow; but, as David was told, the man's usual price had risen now that the British had been sighted on the Elk River in Maryland, where they had leisurely disembarked and turned their horses loose to recruit on fresh grass.

"You have done the cause good service," the thin gentleman said, reading over the papers that David had brought.

"Indeed we have, and not been paid for half of it."

"Which amount will be—?" The gentleman peered at the bottom of a page.

"Something more than four thousand dollars, sir—which I mean to have—in gold—before I leave Philadelphia."

The gentleman smiled. "Unless General Howe arrives before your gold does. Yes, yes." He leaned back. "Four thousand. That is not a very large sum, of course. Still—just now, the Congress are somewhat embarrassed for gold. Not utterly embarrassed, you understand—they eat, they drink, they pay their tailors—but that part of their monies that is meant to go for guns and weapons is near exhausted. Would you demand *your* money, and so deprive the army of its gunpowder or its food?"

"Well, sir, I guess I'd take my money if it meant depriving the army of its ears and little fingers; for all I've seen in Philadelphia is people scrambling for money, and 'Me first' is the motto on their flag."

The gentleman made a high-pitched sound like a squeal. "Sparks, sparks! Well, Mr. Morse, you have your head about you, I will say that; but you must understand, you cannot get blood from a stone, no matter how you squeeze it. There *ain't* any gold."

"Are you telling me that in your official capacity, sir?"

"My capacity, sir! What capacity is that? I have no official capacity that I know of." The gentleman contrived to look astonished. "I am—a honeybee; the Congress and the army and the commissaries and all the little clerks and officers are an orchard in full bloom. I buzz; I fly. I know the orchard and I know where the honey lies. But I have no official capacity."

Frustrated, David banged his hand on the arm of his chair and said angrily, "Then I guess I don't see why I spent good money to talk to you, sir."

The gentleman tapped the list of Morse contracts. "Because you want some honey." He leaned in his chair languidly with the index finger of his right hand laid along his cheek, an attitude that made him seem a little pensive and almost coy. "Do you keep bees up in—is it Massachusetts, Mr. Morse?"

"We chop down a bee tree when we can."

The man's eyebrows rose. "Indeed! How close to nature you must live! When one keeps bees, Mr. Morse, he quickly learns that to get honey, one must give honey first—it inspires the winged honeybee and provides for him through the winter. Do you understand me, Mr. Morse?"

David swallowed. The gentleman, for all his delicacy of body and gesture, had a very steady gaze, and it was David who looked away. "I guess you want more money."

"I! Why would I want more money? No, Mr. Morse, but I shall need some honey to spread among the hives—the little clerks and commissaries, I mean. A little here, a little there,

233

and we may find where there is a forgotten comb from which we can extract your father's gold."

David locked his fingers together and moved his palms back and forth over each other. "Can you give me assurances, sir?"

"I can give you my word—and the word of General Howe, who should be at the city gates by then."

"How can you be sure of that?"

The honeybee fondled the lace on his neckcloth and smiled slowly. "I am the very Mercury of intelligence, Mr. Morse— that is my lifeblood. Howe's army has left Elk River and is marching north; unless we want to spend the winter with him, we must conclude your business and be gone within three weeks. Will you trust me in the matter?"

Shifting uneasily and locking his hands together again, David mumbled unhappily, "Well, I guess I will have to."

"Good!" The gentleman bounced from his chair and stood elegantly on a little Turkey carpet, pulling down his long, figured waistcoat so it fit without wrinkles over his flat torso. "I will begin at once." An almost loving smile touched his face as he looked down at David. "I will need another hundred dollars to start."

David drew more money on his father's credit and took it back to his new guide through the labyrinth of government; the man himself not being there, the money was taken by a gruff secretary, who gave him in return a receipt that had already been made out and signed by the honeybee:

Rec^d in payment on past account one hun^d dollars,
Resolution Gamble.

"Call back in a week," the secretary said, and tried to shut the door.

"But how am I to know what's happening?"

"You'll know—in a week."

He walked angrily back toward his tavern, hating it and hating Philadelphia. Work would have been welcome to him; accustomed to labor, to the constant activity of the farm and the forge, where there was always more work than there were hours in the day, he was miserable without it.

Dear God, is this what my dreams of London would come to—wishing I was back home with a hammer in my hand?

Unable to bear the filthy tavern any longer, he found a room in the house of a Quaker couple named Warren.

He unpacked quickly. His dirty clothes had been collecting since he had reached the city, and he was ashamed to see them tumble in a filthy pile from one bag, their odor musty and bitter. At the bottom of that bag, all but forgotten, was the pistol, and he pushed it guiltily to the bottom again and covered it with his father's papers, ashamed to have brought it into that quiet and peaceful house.

The summer was hot in Massachusetts. In the forge, it was hot as Hell. Donald Morse and his laborers worked half naked and sweated as if water had been poured over them from a pail. At night, the house seemed airless and unforgiving. Donald Morse slept only for minutes at a time; he would wake and throw the rough sheet from him like a man in a fever.

"Ain't you sleeping, Donnie?"

"I can't. Don't fret over me."

"Come close."

"It's too hot."

"What is it? Is it Davie and that money?"

"It's everything! Yes, it's Davie and the money—Davie and his slut of a wife and where in the wide world she's gone to; how can I tell him she ain't with Sullivan after all? Run off with somebody else, I suppose."

"Don't even say it!"

"Well, where is she, then?" Her silence seemed to prove him right. He nodded into the darkness. "We're sorely tried. What *ain't* wrong, these days?"

His world was like a bag whose drawstring was untied: things were tumbling out, willy-nilly. The bag had once been right and tight; now it was loosed, upended; everything was rolling away in all directions.

"Now it's Jonnie," he said.

She did not answer. She was asleep.

Jonnie had left the day before with Speke's company to join the rebels near Stillwater. Donald found reason to be grateful, for once, that Samuel was afflicted. He could not go to war.

"But Jonnie can take care of himself," he said aloud. He did not really believe what he had said. He said it to try to give order to things, even if the only order was that of the words, fitting together into the sentence. It was as if things

235

had tumbled out of the bag and he had said that they would roll back uphill and jump into the bag again.

"Both my sons can take care of themselves," he said into the hot darkness.

"It's as I said before, Mr. Morse—there ain't any gold." Mr. Resolution Gamble, professional honeybee, shook his head sadly; like good lawyers and good procurers, he had that quality of feeling deeply the woes of his clients. "It's become the very devil to get money in Continental paper, much less gold!" He giggled. "For gold, I fear we shall have to go to London." Taking his cue from David's frown, he became serious again. "Take my advice, Mr. Morse. It is the best advice you will get in Philadelphia. *Take a note.* Take a note for all these debts—Committee of Safety debts, Congressional debts, militia debts—the entire amount. Take a note of—let us say five years, at twelve percent?"

"More paper."

"No, sir—money."

"Not if Howe takes Philadelphia and the Congress are arrested."

"I think that will not happen. And if it does, the people will elect another Congress; the countryside is filled with ambitious men. Even if the rebellion fails, Mr. Morse, some— many—debts will be honored. The economy of these colonies would be broken if such debts were ignored, and the economy was a burden to London long before! Do you think his majesty's government are mad? The king is a mediocre buffoon, to be sure; Lord North is a weary timeserver; Germain is war-obsessed; but there are sane and knowledgeable men in London, Mr. Morse. I tell you, sir, take a note and I assure you that you will sell it—*in London*—for at least two-thirds of its value in gold! Could do it today! Why, I'd buy such a note myself at those terms, if I had the gold. Would that satisfy you, Mr. Morse—two-thirds of the total in gold?"

"It ain't mine to say. It's my father's money."

"But you must say; you're his agent in the matter."

The day was humid and sweat glistened on David's wrists, to which a fine film of dust that drifted through the open windows clung. "Farmers don't trust paper."

Gamble sighed. "I know. Farmers like things they can touch, like dirt and sweat." Gamble crossed his legs, fanned his face idly with one of David's papers. "I have it in mind to get another contract for you. Three hundred stands of
236

arms—perhaps five, though the French muskets coming in now may make the Ordnance overconfident—at quite an exorbitant price. Twenty dollars a stand was the figure I asked, though it's ridiculously high. Perhaps we shall get eighteen. Ninety-five pence per stand will be returned to me as commission. In addition, there will be another contract for the purchase of iron and the haulage of materials with"—he waved his hand in a small circle—"certain other interests I represent."

"But my father don't want more contracts!"

Gamble nodded as if he already knew this and the knowledge saddened him. "Y-e-e-s. Shall I have the contracts drawn?"

"But—I feel like I'm shut up in a box, Mr. Gamble!"

"Yes, yes. But everything works out for the best. Shall I have the contracts drawn?"

He shook his head and sighed bitterly. "My father won't like taking more paper."

"Mr. Morse, in this life, what we like and what we accept are often two quite different beasts."

"You mean you got us between the rock and the hard place."

"*I* have! I?" The honeybee was astonished. "It is not *I*, Mr. Morse; it is the Congress and the rebellion and the times. If I had *my* wishes, you would all be happily farming up in Massachusetts and never in your vilest fantasies dream of having to gather honey in this orchard. *I* am trying to help you, Mr. Morse." Gamble looked hurt, seemed to conquer his wounds, and became brisk. "Shall we simply call the matter closed? Shall I cease to represent you?"

"No. No. I must take what I can get, I guess."

"A profound sentiment, Mr. Morse. An excellent sentiment! Always take what you can get."

He sat in Gamble's back sitting room to write a letter to his father and to try to explain this new complication. No matter how he tried to put it, the situation came out sounding like a new lot of worries to add to Donald Morse's store; yet he had to inform his father and ask his permission to accept the note. Bitterly, he folded the letter and gave it to Gamble's secretary to add to Mr. Gamble's packet going north; which traveled much faster and more safely then the post in troubled times.

It was a bright, hot day, very hot for Vermont. Jonnie had

conquered the memory of Breed's Hill with two tots of rum and a brief prayer; now, his Morse-made musket in his hands, he waited for a British force that was supposed to be marching toward them from the far side of the mountain. They had been listening to the sounds of firing for two hours. He had been thinking of all those guns, all that powder and shot. *Somebody's getting rich,* he thought. It amused him that he could think of such a thing when he might be facing another bayonet charge like the one that had terrified him at Breed's Hill.

Somebody's getting rich. Why shouldn't it be us?

Most soldiers know by instinct that somebody—probably somebody older, fatter and already richer—is getting rich with their blood. Jonnie Morse was trying to work out how to do something about it.

Why shouldn't the Morses get rich from it?

He heard a faraway drum, then saw a regimental pennon and the dark colors of German uniforms. Burgoyne had sent a force of Brunswickers over to subdue the Vermont town of Bennington; it was said that he had not sent English soldiers because he had such contempt for the militiamen who would be the enemy. He had sent hirelings—so-called Hessians from Brunswick and Hesse-Cassel.

Now they're going to get their asses wiped.

Jonnie watched them come along the narrow road into the ambush. He could not help thinking of all the money that had been spent to outfit them—money for uniforms, money for brass helmet plates and cross-belt buckles, money for muskets and shoes and cartridge boxes.

Somebody gets rich while they march. Why shouldn't it be us?

At a murmured command, he raised the heavy weapon and aimed at a grenadier in the front rank. A sword flashed; smoke drifted around him, drifted from the trees across the road. He cut down the grenadier with a pull of the trigger.

There's three sides to war, he discovered, *Me, him—and the one is getting rich.*

They called him Message-bringer, and he was the fifth in the line from the man they had called Snow Elk, although he did not know his own ancestry back that far. He knew his mother's line and his mother's clan. He knew that his grandmother had been a black woman, and he knew that he had a white ancestor somewhere because of the color of his eyes,

238

but he did not know that he was descended from Snow Elk, whom the Dutch had called Jan Morse.

But he did know the legend of the Gun-finder.

"Let me tell you a story," he said in his harsh voice. Everybody listened to him.

"This is a story of what the white-faces have done to us. We think they made us rich. But they made us poor. Listen to this story:

"One year, a giant named Gun-finder came to the villages. He had the first gun that the People had ever seen. They did not dare to fight with him, and they gave him a place to live outside the village. And they said, What is that in your hand? And Gun-finder said, This is my magic. This makes men rich. This makes men giants!

"And the giant, Gun-finder, gave them a gun. And another gun. And another gun. And the People said, Look, we are rich, we are giants. And they forgot how they had been before Gun-finder came: they forgot how to grow corn, and they forgot how to make houses, and they forgot how to shoot the bow. And one day they looked around and they said, We are not the People any more. Who are we? And they went to Gun-finder to tell him to take back his guns, but Gun-finder was dead. He had died from all the bad magic in him. And he had all their houses and all their fields and all their bows, and the People were poor! And they wailed and threw ashes on their heads, saying, Give us back our riches! Give us back ourselves! But Gun-finder was dead.

"And they buried him outside Kanadaque in a big grave, and you can see the mound of it, still, for it had to be made big to hold the ghosts of all their things."

Message-bringer looked around at all the intense faces. He let his voice drop very low so that they would have to strain to hear him.

"We cannot undo what is done. We cannot give back all the knives and the guns and all the silver medals that the English gave us. We cannot buy ourselves back from the English king. We cannot walk down to Kanadaque and tell Gun-finder to go home over the water."

He shook his head. "The English want us to fight for them against their own people. They want to give us more guns. They want to make us English soldiers."

He shook his head again. "I wish Gun-finder had never come this way."

Chapter Twenty-five

For David, Philadelphia in that hot summer and early autumn was like a city under a spell, in which ghosts and spirits moved uneasily and he walked like a man bewitched. His dreams were less uneasy, but his days were more like one long, tormented dream: the frustration of his attempts to get his father's money left him idle, restless, and the city had a bizarre and unhealthy air of siege that was a fitting background for his own anguish. Rumors had the British army closer and closer, like oncoming death from some horrid disease; yet, unlike the others in the endangered city, he had no refuge to which he could flee if the worst ever happened. He was a man without a home—without a soul.

He thought he was in love with the Quaker wife in whose house he lived, Mrs. Warren. It was a love that could be neither spoken nor returned, he thought, and so it seemed pure and fine to him—a single bright spot of pure metal among the dross of the city. Her husband was a Free Quaker and a grain merchant; he supplied the army, unburdened by the conscience that made more conservative Quakers turn their backs on the soldiers and shun all work that might support the war.

David rode out with Mr. Warren to look at the rear units of the rebel army as they formed up to stand off the slowly approaching British. The sight of the soldiers agitated Warren, who was a patriot for all his religion; excitedly, he pointed out new cannons and scurrying messengers and the masses of poorly uniformed men who seethed among the tents and ramshackle huts.

"It tempts me, David—tempts me fiercely!" Warren shook his head resignedly. "Were it not that Mistress Warren keeps me true to my faith—!" He shook his head again, but his face was serene. "Is it not a moving scene, David?"

Because he thought he loved the man's wife, David wanted to utter some pleasant lie; abruptly seized with disgust at himself and the scene before him, however, he said hoarsely, "I don't care for it."

It was as if Warren had not heard him. "I see greatness

at work here, David. I see liberty put to the test and emerging triumphant!"

Alone with Mrs. Warren at home, David allowed himself to show his bitterness. "I seem to be more a man of peace than your husband, ma'am," he said acidly. He was in the habit now of seeking her out. At that moment, she was sewing up bits of quilt, her hands always kept busy like his mother's.

"William thinks the soldiers very noble. For their sacrifices, I mean. You don't, David?"

"Maybe I know soldiers too well, ma'am." His voice sounded childishly petulant to even his own ears. "These soldiers look a very bedraggled lot to me."

"Oh. And does their being bedraggled make you more a man of peace, then?"

"No, but—" She was four or five years older than he and sometimes took advantage of the difference to tease him. Angrily, he said, "They disgust me! A man should look worthy of his ideals!"

She smiled. To many men, she would have seemed something less than beautiful, for her face was too long and her mouth was too wide, yet she had such intelligence and serenity in her face that she caused more than one man to stop and look at her. The smile was radiant, somehow secret and generous all at once. He could not see her smile without thinking of being in bed with her—without thinking of Warren's being in bed with her, for there, too, was secrecy and generosity. "Thee are very young, David," she said sweetly.

He stood abruptly, setting his rocking chair to swinging wildly; its shadow pitched against the wall like a frightened horse. "I ain't so much younger than you! Why do you throw that up to me?"

He wanted to grab her, kiss her, crush her; he wanted to show her that he was a man of passion, unlike (as he thought) her tepid husband. *I've given up the whores for you!* he wanted to shout. She would only have smiled, he knew, and told him that he deserved no praise for what he should have done anyway.

David muttered angrily that he would have a walk for himself before the light was quite gone, and he hurried toward the door; before he reached it, she spoke.

"I think thee are no fighter, David, and that is why the soldiers disgust you. I think thee are no rebel, neither. Thee must search thy conscience and find out what truth is there."

"You mean to say you think I am a Tory, then?"

241

"That is not for me to say. But I think it is better to be a Tory in good conscience than to be a poor tormented thing that does not know itself."

He hesitated. His heart was beating wildly; the conversation, although held across the distance of a room, seemed intimate, almost amorous. "Could you—feel affection for me if I was Tory?"

"Neither William nor I would feel anything but affection for thee under any circumstances, David. We have come to like thee. But I grieve for thee, seeing a man much troubled and never at peace with himself."

Her inclusion of her husband made him bitter. "Save your grief, then. I ain't asked you for it!"

"No. Nor need you. I feel grief for all who are not at peace."

He was swept by dizziness. The room seemed to darken and to fade; he was short of breath. "I'd give anything to be at peace!"

"Ask God to help thee, then. It is He that brings us peace."

"Help me. Help me!"

She was only a silhouette against a window. He could not tell even if she was looking at him. "Pray to God, David. Not to me. I can give thee nothing but my compassion."

He waited. He supposed that he was invisible to her, as she was to him. He hated to shatter the intimacy of the moment. "I would to God I had met you—in time," he said softly.

There was silence. Her voice seemed to come to him from a different part of the room, even from some place beyond it. "We must not pray for what God cannot give. Neither of us. Go on now. Go, David. Please, go."

In the second week of September, he called at Gamble's house and was told that a note for the money owed his father would be forthcoming in a day or two and the new contracts were being issued. He had not heard from his father, and dispirited and frustrated, he accepted Gamble's terms.

"It's a pitiful thing to take a piece of paper," he said.

"But as I told you, Mr. Morse!" the honeybee cried. "I will buy the note at half its value the moment you wish to sell!"

"Two-thirds, you said."

"Did I? How remiss of me...."

While he waited he wandered like one of the lost souls of the enchanted city, watching the preparations for the flight from the place: in every street, houses were being shuttered; carts passed him constantly, loaded down with household goods. The havens that might have existed for him—house, wife, parents—were a mockery; bitterly, he acknowledged the power of Sara's ghost in its revenge. He walked through a downpour, angry and hopeless. At the Warrens', he shook the water from his hat and flounced out his coat to shake the water from it.

Mrs. Warren, a basket of apples beside her and a knife in her hand, called to him. They had hardly been alone together since the afternoon when he had gone to look at the troops with her husband; now, she called him to her almost shyly. "David? You must be fair drenched."

"I shall dry."

"Would you sit by the kitchen fire with me?"

"I—" Fear that her husband was in the house made him bitter. "I thought you'd be getting ready to flee, like the others."

"Well, so we are. William has already gone to the country with his wagons."

David wiped his damp face with his hand. "Do you leave tonight, then?" The imminence of it shocked him; although he had a little put aside his romantic hankerings for her, he had hardly stopped thinking about her.

"We dare not stay long, William says, after the British reach the river. We will close the house."

"The British will open it again."

"Mr. Warren thinks not. We have friends who would see to it. But we must not be here to antagonize them." Her hand moved quickly around an apple, the skin coming off in a single spiral like a long green caterpillar. "I have an uncle, Dr. Lamb, who will stay, however. He will see to our property. He would take you in if you stayed."

"But I'm not staying!"

"Is that what your conscience says?"

His wry laughter sounded hollow; distant thunder rumbled like an echo. "I guess I will just do what's expected of me."

"Then thee will never be a free man, patriot or Tory." Her hands rested motionless in her lap. Lightning from far away flickered dully and made the window glow like metal. "Whichever, I will hold thee in my heart and pray for thee."

He cleared his throat. "I'll always be grateful for that. You took me in; you've been good to me." An impulsive step carried him close to her. "Tell me what to do! For God's sake, tell me what to do!"

She shook her head. Some thought began to form itself into words, but she swallowed them, and, taking up her basket, she hurried from the room.

The next day, he accepted the five-year note and carried it about with him like a guilty secret as he prowled the streets. The thunderstorms of the day before had given way to steady rain, and the street orators were gone—probably packed to flee with the rest of them, he told himself sardonically. He was relieved there were no letters for him, and he went slowly homeward, dragging his steps so he would not have to see the Warrens at supper and talk of his affairs. When he came in the door, however, she was waiting for him, stepping into the hall at the far end as he had seen her the first day, a ghostly figure in plain gray in the shadows.

"There is a letter come for thee."

It struck him like a blow; he could not say why. "Here?"

"A man came from Reading with it; it hasn't come the regular post."

His hands were trembling when he broke the seal, for he had recognized his father's crabbed writing on the outside. As he read, his gut tightened and he thought he would be sick.

David,

> *I cannot believe you mean this about a note on the Congress. I will not take it, I will see them in H. first. You have failed me and your mother & yourself. Come home at once, do no more.*
>
> *What are you about, spending money like a drunkard and ruining us? You was set a simple task could have been completed in a week, now it is over a month & you are such a fool as to think of taking paper.*
>
> *Come home at once & tend to your own affairs. A son should be a sharer of his father's burdens at your age, not a greater burden still.*

Donald Morse.

He ran from the house, over the wet streets that were empty now of carts and people, slipping once on a cobbled lane and falling on his back to land dazed and stunned; he scrambled up and ran on, impelled by a passion to find Gamble and sell back the note at any price. If he could get rid of it, if he could go home with at least some of the money his father seemed to prize so, he might redeem himself, he thought; sobbing, cursing himself and the wet streets and his father's cruel letter, he staggered on until he pulled up in front of the handsome hive where the honeybee had lived.

The house was dark. He looked along one side, expecting to see lights at the back and finding only deeper darkness. Almost hysterical, he pounded on the door and shouted, a frightened child locked out of comfort; but when he had knocked and called and wept, and circled the house once in the rain and had no answer, he leaned again on the front door and pushed against it once with his shoulder as if he might force it open.

"You won't find nobody," a voice said behind him.

It was a man with a lantern and a gun. He hung back near the gate as if he expected David to rush at him.

"They're all gone off," the man said.

"Where? Where have they gone?"

"They didn't say." The man lifted the lantern a little. "Best you come out of there, now; they're shooting housebreakers."

"But how will I find him?"

"You come out of there, now. I don't know you. Just come out of there."

Back at the Warrens' an hour later, he moved dazedly down the hallway. He thought the house was empty; in his confusion and his clumsiness, he stumbled against a long bench in the hall, and when he heard a low voice from the sitting room, he cried out. "Who's there?"

"David?"

For an instant, no longer than it takes to click a door shut or cock a pistol, he thought the voice was Sara's. *She's here!* Terror seized him; his hair seemed to have a cold, ghostly hand running over it from the back, brushing it upward; his heart raced; nausea surged into his throat.

"David, is it you?"

It was Mrs. Warren. She was dressed for travel and carried a heavy cloak over her arm. Even in silhouette, she was clearly not Sara, and the relief at that knowledge, coupled with the feeling that had grown in him for her, caused him to say her name aloud; abruptly, he took the two steps that brought him close to her and wrapped his powerful arms around her. This was not romance, nor was it mere adolescent love; this was pain and need and desire. His arms closed over hers, pinning her arms between her body and his own; press-

245

ing her tight to him, he raised his face toward the ceiling. Tears ran down his cheeks, and an inarticulate sound like the attempt of some brute animal to form speech came from his mouth.

With a shuddering breath, he knelt, still holding her; his arms now clutched her thighs. His face was pressed into the fabric of her dress just at her belly. "Don't leave me—don't leave me—!" he begged.

"Oh, David—oh, David, David—!"

"Don't leave me! I've got nothing—nothing!"

"I must not—I must not—!"

"Stay with me!"

They made love in the darkness of his bedroom—silent, somber, passionate. Their joy in each other was intense and almost desperate, as if something in her responded to his own anguish and was satisfied by it. Then they lay together without speaking, until she got up wordlessly and led him to the candlelit sitting room where her bundled clothes were, and she took out a dark, smocklike garment that she put on.

"Thee are hungry."

"No. Yes. Ah, it don't matter!"

"Come."

They were like the only ones left alive in the deserted city. If there were ghosts, they did not come inside that house that night. It was as if they had escaped whatever black enchantment lay on the place.

"I love you," he said, lying with his head in her lap.

"Nay. Thee do not know me. Nay, do not speak." She put a finger against his lips. "This is not love, David. This is—I don't know; it is something different. Something sad and wonderful. And brief."

There was no question, even in his own mind, that she would stay with him past the morning. Yet it seemed enough.

"If only I had met you—soon enough!" He sighed.

"Don't waste thy breath on follies. Take what is."

He touched her face. "Forgive me. I know you'll suffer for this. Forgive me."

She smiled. "Thee must learn to forgive thyself, David. Nobody else can do it for thee."

Toward morning, he told her that he had killed Sara. They had talked, been silent, made love again, talked; it was a lifetime compressed into a night, and, toward the end of it, telling her seemed as natural as breathing.

She cupped his face. "Poor soul," she said.

246

"What shall I do?"

"Make thyself right."

"Shall I go back? Give myself up?"

"If that will make thee right with thyself. But only if it will make thee right. Man's law is only man's way, David— not God's. Make thyself right."

"How?"

Slowly, slowly she shook her head, her eyes on a dying candle. The room was bleak; the first light of day was washing it. "Give thyself away. Give away thy youth, thy hopes, thy vanity. Thee hast taken a life, David; give thine own away, then."

"How? Where?"

Again she shook her head. She was thinking of herself, of her own sin. "The way don't matter. Only do it. And be at peace."

She slipped away half an hour later, leaving him with a kiss like a sister's. He was spent, calm, resigned at last.

Chapter Twenty-six

The battle for control of Philadelphia began on the hills over-looking Brandywine Creek. From the top of one, Captain Patrick Ferguson heard a rebel attack begin in the early morning as the American skirmishers, followed by heavy troops in support, moved out from positions on the south side of the river and began to poke at the British forward line as a city man might poke at a wasp's nest with a cane to see what it contained. Ferguson, commanding his own riflemen as well as a company of Queen's Rangers on his right flank, and able to communicate with the Hessian dragoons on his left, was eager for the opportunity to engage his men. He listened in vain, however, for the telltale crack of rifles from the American line. There was only musket fire.

Far to his left, he knew, Hanger's jaegers were waiting with von Donop, but he could not know if Hanger was being fired on, too.

Impatient, peremptory in his commands, Ferguson paced nervously and showed his annoyance with his situation. It was not his employment as a diversion that disturbed him; he accepted that as a sound military tactic. The main British army was marching north and east, hoping to encircle the Americans while he and the Germans under von Knyphausen distracted the rebels along their main front. It was inaction that disgusted him—holding a position while he could hear the firing to the east. He watched the British dragoons sweep in and out again, and the Americans came on.

The day before, Ferguson had skulked down to the river with a squad of his men and some of the rangers. Three of them had crossed the river at dusk and had returned with a sketch of the American order of battle, and now, hearing the firing, Ferguson could picture the rebels coming on, their temporary triumph speeding them as they took the wooded heights above the river and came down the hill toward the road that separated his troops from them.

Then he could see the first men coming over the hill toward him. They kept good order and they moved with decision, and

248

he was pleased that he had not been positioned opposite some ragtag militia.

"Tell General von Knyphausen that I will engage the enemy at once and that I hope to recover the slope above Chadd's Ford." Moments after the messenger went off, another was sent to alert the flanking company of rangers. Ferguson himself moved with his two companies down the wooded hill, but halfway to the bottom a breathless runner told him that additional Americans had crossed the river to the east and were coming fast along the road. He ordered the rangers to hold; running forward with his men, firing, dropping prone to load and fire again, he began to pour aimed fire into the oncoming troops of Maxwell's American Brigade. The effect was awesome: at two hundred yards, occasional rebels began to fall; at one hundred, they were dropping as if pulled down by greedy hands, new gaps opening constantly in their line. By the time they were within their own shooting range of eighty yards, they were raggedly ordered, and in some places so broken that their mass firing by platoons was impossible. The British riflemen offered few targets, loading while lying flat or kneeling.

"Under heavy attack on the right, captain."

The Americans were pressing in along the road from the east despite the fire from the Queen's Rangers on the height above. Ferguson sent to von Knyphausen for support, but none came; overextended from his hilltop position, he was in danger of being flanked or overrun. The Hessian dragoons charged along the American line and sheared off the rebels attacking from the east and the advance was slowed; Ferguson hurried his men back up the hill when the dragoons had passed, and from the vantage point they were able to pour fire downslope at the attackers.

"Any trouble with the rifles?"

"The usual jamming, sir. We're down to three in five in some platoons."

"Provide hot water where you can. Every man to clean, one each five in order. Sustain fire where you can."

Ferguson had become resigned to the fouling that jammed the threads of his patent breech. In the custom-made officers' rifles, the fouling was not significant, and a charge of saliva on the threads every third or fourth shot freed them. In the rifles manufactured in Birmingham by Morrison, however, the problem was often severe. By that morning's end, eighteen of the manufactured guns were inoperative and had to

249

be sent back to reserve, where an armorer would strip them down and try to put them back into action. Of the remaining rifles, thirty-three were in danger of soon reaching the same state.

"Clean them, damn you!" Ferguson roared at his sergeants.

"Beg pardon, captain, but they've got to be boiled almost."

"Then boil them! I want those rifles clean!"

The men grumbled. Water was boiled in a cooking kettle and the breech screws were scrubbed with brushes; by two o'clock, most of them were serviceable again. Ferguson was ordered forward with his company and the rangers; placing the less reliable rifles in the rear, he started downslope again. The Americans had withdrawn; crossing straight north below the hill that they had occupied, Ferguson moved against rebel troops who had not yet confronted aimed fire and who had braced themselves for a conventional assault from the British line. Choosing their targets, moving like hunters through the heavy brush and the tilled fields, the riflemen cut like a sickle through ripe grain, their effect so deadly that the main body of von Knyphausen's troops had little more to do than walk and mop up in their wake.

At the river, Ferguson pulled up and wrote an immodestly curt note to his commander: "Have reached the ford and await your arrival."

"Rifles into those woods!" he ordered. "Resist any attempt to recross the river. Queen's Rangers into support with bayonets. Lieutenant Collins!"

"Sir!"

Ferguson took a step forward to face the lieutenant across two fallen trees. From the far side of the river and up the opposite hill, puffs of smoke marked the futile musket fire that the Americans were using to cover their withdrawal.

"Lieutenant, place your men so that—"

Ferguson gave a grunt of shock and surprise. His right elbow had been slammed against his body and his rifle fell to the ground from numb fingers.

"Dammit. Dammit, dammit!"

The word swept up and down the line of his men. "Ferguson's been hit!" Some raised their heads to look at him, not believing the rumor; others knelt to aim across the river, and their rifles cracked.

"Get down, sir. Get down! In the name of God, get down!"

He was trying to see where the shot had come from. It had

o be a rifle, he knew; there was a perverse satisfaction in
that. He allowed himself to be led behind a tree and sat down
with his back against it, his strongest feeling one of annoyance that they were babying him so. With his left hand grip-
ing the right arm above the elbow, he looked at the lieutenant, who was bent over him with the intensity of a mother
whose child has been injured.

"Tell General von Knyphausen that I have received a
small hurt and am temporarily delayed. Lieutenant, if need
be, you will command."

A soldier cut off the sleeve of his green jacket and pulled
back his bloody shirt. The bullet had hit just at the elbow,
and the joint was smashed; dark blood welled from the wound
and dripped on the dirt and leaves around him.

"I can't move my hand, I'm afraid."

"We'll carry you to the rear, sir."

"No, no! I am not to be moved! I can bleed here as well as
anywhere. Lieutenant, one man of every five is to clean his
rifle, then the next and—and so on. Provide hot water where
you can. Water from the river. Jammed rifles are to be posted
to the—to the—"

Someone had tried to straighten his arm to begin band-
aging it, and the end of his order was lost in a burst of pain,
and he fainted.

"What if Washington gets his ass whipped by Howe at
Philadelphia?"

"Let Philadelphia fret about it. What's Washington done
for us?"

"He done plenty! Didn't he send Morgan and his troop up
here?"

"Morgan—shit!" The angry militiamen spat. "Pennsylvania riflemen—loudmouthed turkey shooters is all they
are."

Jonnie Morse stretched, shifted his weight, nodded in
agreement. "I'd like to see them riflemen face a bayonet
charge before I thought very highly of them," he said quietly.
Men listened to him. He was an old hand—Breed's Hill and
Bennington made him a veteran in their eyes.

"Jonnie Morse has been there and back," somebody muttered. "Listen to what he says, now."

"Well." Flattered, Jonnie spat. "I seen men who had to be
as good as Morgan's run from British bayonets, that's for
sure. I say nothing against them; all I say is, they load *very*

slow, and when there's a charge coming at them, what ca
they do but turn and run?"

Other heads nodded.

Jonnie spat again. "Rifles is slow to load, and they're slo
to make. Give me buck and ball any day, and a good muske
from my father's works."

"Now you're talking straight sense."

A lot of muskets from my father's works, he thought. *There
money in lots of muskets.*

They were waiting in reserve on the American right; ahea
of them, a force under Benedict Arnold was pummeling th
British redoubts.

"Check your powder," he said. He had seen a messenge
come up to Captain Speke. "Check your powder and get read
to move." He grinned at another Greenfield man. "Time f
the gents back home to get rich."

Dr. Lamb's house was a small, spare one, dirtier than th
Warrens' and cramped with books and instruments. The do
tor put him to work as his helper when the wounded bega
to trickle back into the city, asking no questions after he ha
read the note that David Morse had brought from Mrs. Wa
ren. The work was dirty and disgusting and he hated it, b
he went through it as a form of penance, vomiting when I
had to and tormenting himself with the knowledge that th
same kinds of wounds that he now saw were also caused k
guns that he had made.

"I shall try to get used to it, sir," he said.

"No, that is what you must never do! That is what genera
do; that is how they can perpetrate this butchery. I'd f
prefer you spew ten times a day than that you 'get used
it.'"

After Brandywine, the American wounded came back ar
Dr. Lamb helped with them, forgetting his politics; after Ge
mantown, the first British troops and the first Britis
wounded began to appear, and he tended them in turn. Th
patriots had fled; the Congress was gone. Lamb, walking ba
through the somber streets with David and his black servar
shook his head morosely as a squad of Hessian soldiers cla
tered by.

"God help Philadelphia," he murmured. "First the Crown
enemies, and now its friends. We shall find out which is wors
I suppose."

At suppertime, there was a loud knock on the outer do

A frightened maid hung back without answering it, and, at a nod from Lamb, David went to the door instead, his right hand hovering near the pistol whose belt hook was clipped to the waistband of his breeches.

A Hessian officer stood on the step. David expected seizure or arrest, some form of violence, and so he was astonished when the officer removed his hat and bowed and said in excellent English, "I am looking for Dr. Lamb."

"This is Dr. Lamb's house."

"I know that. Show me to him, if you please."

David looked over his shoulder; at the bottom of the stairs, Lamb looked at him and nodded.

"This way, please."

Two German soldiers stood guard at the end of the walk; a cart with another soldier in it waited in the street. He led the officer to the doctor's study and hung back as the officer went in; crossing the threshold, he bowed again. "Dr. Lamb."

"The same, sir."

"Captain Hanger, von Donop regiment of Hesse-Cassel. I have a wounded English officer, doctor."

"How bad?"

"The wound itself, not so bad; only an arm. But it's gone septic, y'see. Caught one at the Brandywine and he won't let the butchers cut it off. I'd like to leave him with a decent civilian doctor and not let him die of his own poisons in hospital."

"I will be working in the hospitals myself, captain."

"Yes, but it ain't the same. You can give him a little extra attention, yes? And your people will be about; you can tell 'em what to do. If it ain't him, it will be somebody else, doctor—better one wounded officer than a brace of healthy grenadiers for the winter, don't you think?"

Lamb's sympathies were clearly with the Crown, but he had the pious man's distrust of the military and the private man's hatred of intrusion. Finally, he said, "Bring him in. I'll do what I can for him."

"Good enough; that's all any of us can do." Hanger turned to David Morse. "You, fellow, lend a hand."

His boots clacked on the wood floor. "Quaker, are you?"

"No, sir. Scots Presbyterian."

"Are you, by God! And not a servant neither, now that I get a look at you. Not a rebel, I hope."

"No, sir."

"Good. Well, you and your doctor take care of my friend,

and I'll see that you eat as well as anybody in Philadelphia this winter. Understand me?"

"Yes, sir."

"Capital! Help with his shoulders, will you—these square-heads handle a man like a damned side of beef—that's better—can you get his shoulders alone? Damn me if you can't; you're strong, ain't you! Watch the gatepost there—careful on the step, now—"

The maid held the door open, her body flattened against it as if she feared even the touch of one of the Germans' coats.

"This way," Dr. Lamb said from the stairs.

The two soldiers started up the stairs with the feet, and one boot banged against a spindle.

"I think I could take him better alone, sir."

"What? Oh, can ye! By God, I believe the boy can, at that. All right, up he goes—take him careful, boy, we mean to have him fight again—"

David stepped slowly up the stairs, his back erect under the weight. It was very much like carrying his brother Samuel.

"Absolutely capital! Why, he ain't been so comfortable since he was carried by his nanny. Up you go, up you go—Valor carried in the arms of Youth, by God! It's a perfect allegory!"

David put the officer on a bed and stood back, rubbing his spine where the strain had been greatest. As Dr. Lamb bent over the injured man, Hanger ordered the soldiers out of the house; coming to the top of the stairs, he pulled David's arm and led him a step along the upstairs hall.

"Blacksmith?" he said.

"And a farmer, sir."

"Yes, your hands look it." Hanger's fingers hovered on David's left arm, then moved deftly and raised his waistcoat as the other hand took the pistol from his waistband.

"Beautiful work. I saw it while you were lifting him." Hanger stepped back and studied the weapon. "Much too expensive a piece for a farmer, even if it ain't finished." He looked up shrewdly. "Where'd you get it?"

David looked at him, disliking him for his easy superiority and his swagger. He understood that he could well be in trouble, but he could see no good way to lie. "It was a gift."

"From Bonnie Prince Charlie, I'm sure. Where'd you get it?"

"My grandfather made it. It's one of a pair."

254

"Where's the other?"

"My brother has it."

"And where's he when he's home?"

"In Massachusetts, sir."

"Loyal or rebel?"

David said nothing; then, bitterly, he murmured, "Rebel."

Hanger nodded. Without giving the pistol back, he went quickly down the stairs and into the front room, and no more than a minute later, David could hear him calling. "You, there! Blacksmith!"

"Yes, sir?"

"Don't hang over the rail and yessir me; come down when I call to you, dammit!"

He hurried down, to find Hanger seated at a writing desk, a paper and ink in front of him, a pen in his hand. Blowing on the paper and waving it in the air, he handed it to David.

"There's a receipt for your pistol. If you're caught with that, with an English officer in the house, you could be shot. You'll get it back, don't worry—if you're reputable, I mean—I ain't a thief. Now, are there any more weapons in the house?"

"None that I know of, sir."

"Lie to me and I'll have you whipped."

"None that I *know* of. I'm a guest here."

Hanger wiped the pen and threw it on the desk as if it had offended him. With his hands resting palms down on the desk in front of him, he said, "Have you taken an oath of loyalty, blacksmith?"

"No, sir."

"Well, you'd damned well better. You'll get the pistol back when you do and not before, do you follow me?"

Sadly, bitterly, as if he were playing some dismal scene he had been through before, David murmured, "Yes, sir. I understand."

Chapter Twenty-seven

David Morse had never been close to a man like Ferguson before. His own old fantasies of London and Parliament had been peopled with vague faces; he had not imagined the hard face of aristocracy. The man's assumption of his own innate authority—his own innate superiority—was shocking to David. In the Connecticut Valley, men were well-to-do or they were poor, but they all worked for what they had. Men earned authority with work and with moral power and with persuasion.

Ferguson was an aristocrat. (Hanger was an aristocrat too, but he was the sort of aristocrat one could understand—a bit of a bully, a bit of a snob, a bit of a comedian.) Severe, even ascetic, Ferguson puzzled and fascinated David. There was something diabolically attractive in his arrogance.

"Tea, sir?"

"Put it down, Morse." Ferguson had designed a lap desk that David had made; it was over his legs now on the bed with sheets of paper spread on it; with his bandaged arm swung out of the way, Ferguson was laboriously making ink drawings of improvements to his rifle.

"Could you make that part if you had the tools, Morse?" He knew that David was a gunsmith.

"I—*believe* I could, sir. From your drawings." David had learned a good deal from Ferguson about drawings and design.

"How long would it take you?"

David pursed his lips. "Without dies or swages, sir?" He hesitated. Whatever he said, it would be a guess. "At least two days, sir."

Ferguson frowned. One of Ferguson's failings was his assumption that every man around him was as serious about his own obsession as he was himself; thus, if somebody said "two days" to him, he took it as seriously as if he had said it himself.

"Pour my tea, Morse."

"Yes, sir."

Ferguson put down his pen. He looked at David. *Tryin*

to be pleasant. He had heard Hanger urge Ferguson to be "a bit more of a human being."

"You said you're a Scot, Morse."

"Not quite, sir. My grandfather came from Scotland after the 'Forty-five."

"Odd."

"Sir?"

"Morse isn't a Scots name." Ferguson sipped the tea. He was exhausted. Loss of blood had weakened him; infection and fever had weakened him still further. He looked emaciated and unhealthy, with spots of color on his nose and his cheekbones as if they had been marked there with rouge. "Quite odd, Morse. There's a Morse in my family somewhere. Never been quite clear about it. Step-grandmother, or some such."

"Scottish, sir?"

"What? Oh, I suppose so. We're Scots, yes."

David knew better than to suggest that there could be any relationship between them because of the coincidence of names. It was a farfetched notion, and Ferguson would have been offended by the suggestion.

"Have you written to your father, Morse?"

"Yes, sir."

"In years to come, you both will be glad of it." Ferguson's intelligent eyes seemed very large in his sickly face. "To ourselves, we owe absolute honesty and total commitment, Morse. To our parents, we owe honor."

"Yes, sir."

"This rebellion will end soon. Then you will be able to go home. Such wounds heal in time." Ferguson glanced at his wounded arm. As if the sight angered him, he snarled, "Clear these things away!"

David hurried to obey. He felt almost comfortable—almost *safe*—as Ferguson's servant. His guilt was kept at bay; discovery seemed impossible, so long as he was here as the servant of this English aristocrat. It was not London, but it was safe.

October, 1777

My dear father and mother,

    You know by now I am nott coming back but I must write these few words by way of explanation. I cannot say how sorry I am to have failed you both, and Grandfather and the others, and I think it is the best thing that I do not come back to trouble you now.

This Philadelphia, which was a Place of nothing but Greed and argument, has become more peaceful since the British Army entered. There is good order and some good fellowship, I have made a friend or two and am not discontent.

Trust nott but I shall be well. I pray for you all and think of you with the greatest affection, and maybe one day if it is God's will I will come back to you. Until then, believe that I am y^r loving and respectful son,

David Morse

Flynn and Jonathan Morse and another zealous Son of Liberty stood in Donald Morse's kitchen, their faces set like those of men who have achieved some long-desired prize. They stood close by the table while Flynn spread out the paper and smoothed the wrinkles where it had been creased by many hands, and Donald Morse, reading his Bible by candlelight, rubbed his eyes and asked what the matter was.

"The matter is this letter," Flynn said in his graveled voice. "The matter is sedition. The matter is your son Davie!"

"What letter is that, Mr. Flynn?"

"A letter your son writ from Philadelphia in October."

"And how did you get it?" Old John asked. Nobody paid any attention to him.

"My David's no seditioner," Mrs. Morse whispered. Jonnie looked at her, his jaw stuck out and his nostrils flared, his righteousness and his anger overstated because of Flynn. His mother looked at him and she was frightened, frightened that he could be her son and behave so.

"How do you explain this letter, Mr. Morse?"

"How can I explain it when I ain't read it yet?"

"How'd you get it?" Old John bellowed again, and when nobody looked at him he shouted at Donald, "Send them packing, Donnie! This is wonderful talk, and a sweet way for a brother to act—you skulkers creep about in the dark of night stealing letters and—"

"Shut up, Grandfather!" Jonathan's face was flushed.

The old man's head came up jerkily. "Don't you dare ever to speak to me like that again! You greedy little pup, I know how they come by that letter—*you* give it to 'em, didn't you?

God help you, Jonnie Morse, you was given that letter for your dad and you took it to that great jackass Flynn, and now—"

"Desist, old man!"

"Desist yourself! Why, you no-good, Flynn, I remember when your ma was on the town rolls for a beggar, and you and your sisters was fed by the parish or you'd've starved! And better we'd let you, but Donald Morse and his wife and some like them give food—and money, too, aye, and clothes to put on your skinny back—and now you're puffed up like a hog snake, puffed up with wind! Oh, ain't it some rebellion that puffs up beggars the likes of you!"

Flynn's head was down as if he was reading; his voice tried to be level and threatening. "I read sedition and treason here, and I hear it in this room. Maybe it's common to this here family."

"I'll sedition you, you puffed-up—!"

"Father!" It was Jonnie's mother, her face tense with fright. "Let it go, please." She looked at him. "Please."

And the old man looked from her to Jonathan, whose hands were trembling and whose lower lip was caught between his teeth so tight it looked as if he might bite right through it, and to Donald Morse, who went on looking at his own big hands where they rested on the open Bible; and Donald's shoulders sagged and his head came forward, and when he spoke, his voice was tired and wheezy. "I mourn the day I ever brought this family to this cursed place," he said.

"Aye, and I mourn the day you ever whelped that mean-eyed pup there," Old John said, jerking his head toward Jonathan, and the old man turned and shuffled out of the room, pushing angrily through the girls, who were trying to listen from the other side of the door.

Flynn cleared his throat. "Now, about this letter—"

"I'm sure Davie didn't mean no treason!" his mother said.

"He was upset." Donald Morse's voice was a whine. "His wife left him; I—I was harsh with him about—about the business he went down there on—"

"That don't explain treason!"

"My Davie ain't a traitor!" she cried.

"Ma, he was never one of us!"

"Aye, he was never strong for the rebellion."

The third man spoke up. "He didn't go to Boston when Jonnie and the rest did. He didn't go to Saratoga."

"And the first day I come here," Flynn growled, "back in

'seventy-four, he was very indifferent. Him and the old man, they was both indifferent."

Donald Morse kept his hands flat on his Bible and would not look up. "What are you saying, Flynn?"

"Saying? I'm saying your son is guilty of seditious writing!"

"Well, now you said it. What else are you here for? You must want something, or you'd not have come here with two of your bullies—one of them my own son."

Flynn cleared his throat. "Well, what I want is, I want you to report any further seditious letters or message from him. Anything that you receive, I want to read, is that understood?"

Donald nodded.

"Jonnie, here, is to be married," Flynn went on. "The Sons don't want to see no strain on him and his bride, you follow me? We don't want nothing to stand in Jonnie's way of taking over for you when—when that time comes, if you follow me."

Donald nodded.

"Well, then. That's what I wanted to say. Not that I'm casting no aspersions agin you nor your wife there. You done good work for the cause and will do more, I know. But one bad apple in the barrel, as they say. You know what they say." He looked at one and then the other, and when the silence in the room dragged out he cleared his throat and said lamely, "We got to keep the barrel clean."

Donald shrugged. Flynn folded up the letter and put it in an inner pocket of his coat.

"Can't we have the letter?" she said hesitantly.

Flynn shrugged himself deeper into his overcoat. "I'll have a copy made for you," he said. "This here is evidence."

Flynn and the third man stood uncomfortably for some seconds and looked vacantly about them. "Well, then," Flynn said at last, and, pulling his collar up, he shuffled his feet and moved toward the door. Jonnie Morse sprang to open it and went out after them and stood talking in the thin snow and then watched them walk down the hill, their lantern a point of light in the windy darkness.

He came back into the kitchen and stood just inside the door. His father was still sitting there, eyes on his Bible. His mother moved toward him.

When she reached him, she stood an arm's length away, looking intently into his face. Her cheeks were very red and she was breathing harshly. Her hand came swinging toward him and landed with a painful smack on his left cheek and tears came into his eyes. When he glanced aside at his father, he saw that Donald was nodding, nodding, as if to confirm that all of his fears had proved right.

"And do you accept the protection of his majesty, King George the Third, and of his majesty's government in America, and of his governors and such officials as shall be appointed, including officers of his majesty's military establishment?"

"I do."

"And do you swear loyalty to the Crown and proclaim yourself a loyal British subject?"

"I do."

"And do you abjure and reject and abhor all rebellion and all disaffection and disloyalty with all your heart and mind, and affirm your hatred of all who rebel against the Crown and its government?"

David Morse hesitated. His unhappy face turned to Ferguson, who was standing next to him.

"He has relatives among the rebels, my lord."

"Aha. Ah, I see." The judge shuffled through his papers. "This is the smith, is it?"

"Gunsmith, yes, my lord."

"Aha. Hum, I see." He peered at David through vagrant strands from his wig. "Mr. Morse, you are putting yourself under the protection of his majesty and accepting the condition of General Howe's proclamation, a wise course of action; in your case, however, given your admitted history of manufacture of weapons to be used *against* his majesty's army—"

"Under duress, my lord—a form of duress," Ferguson murmured.

"Yes, yes, I quite understand that! Nonetheless, we must not make dangerous precedents." His eyebrows arched. "Perfect forgiveness is an attribute of Almighty God; I am not at all sure that we can hope that it will be an attribute of his majesty's government. Mr. Morse, has Captain, um, Ferguson, yes, spoken to you of enlisting in his company?"

"Well, sir—my lord—we've talked of it, but—"

"Then I will accept your enlistment as earnest of your loyalty; indeed, I shall take it as the sponge that will wipe away the chalk mark of an earlier disloyalty." He smiled at his metaphor. "Conditional upon your enlistment, I accept your oath to his majesty and will place you on the list of loyal citizens. Do I make myself clear?"

"I—yes, my lord."

"Excellent. Then I need not listen too carefully to that part pertaining to hatred of your relatives, and so I ask you again, David Morse, do you abjure and reject and abhor all rebellion and all and so on and so forth"—he waved a hand— "so help you God?" His mouth open expectantly, he looked up. "Well?"

"I do."

"Who vouches for him? You, Captain Ferguson, and—"

"Captain Hanger, my lord."

They peered down the room. "A German?" the judge said doubtfully.

"English, my lord. One of our finest officers."

"Indeed! Hum." He waved at David. "Sign the oath, if you please. Tell my clerk to send in the next one, captain."

Outside the courtroom, David was quiet. Ferguson, walking next to him, carried his right arm crooked with the hand against his waistcoat buttons. Dr. Lamb had cured the septic poisoning, but he had been able to do little with the shattered bone and torn muscle, and the arm could no longer be straightened, having healed in a permanent crook that allowed Ferguson to handle a rifle and a sword after a fashion, but not with his old ability.

"Any regrets, Morse?"

"No, sir."

"We'll dally a bit with the enlistment until I see what is to happen with my company; I don't want you sent off like any foot-slogger to the West Indies. However—you are committed, you do understand that?"

"Yes, sir."

Ferguson got into a coach and was taken back to Dr. Lamb's; even such small exertion as the morning's tired him. David walked, too, like a sick and weary man.

Chapter Twenty-eight

With the February snows lying deep over the Connecticut Valley, the life of the farms seemed as dormant as that of the plants buried under two feet of white, and of the orchards whose bare branches whipped in the winter wind and broke under the loads of ice. Jonnie Morse looked over the winter fields and dreamed of where a new building would go—"the manufactory," he called it, when he was bragging in the Bunch of Grapes. Across the valley, Felicity Gough was planning her wedding and trying to decide what furniture she would take to her new mother-in-law's house, even though Jonnie's mother hardly spoke to him. It was the money she would bring that would put up the new building, if Jonnie could ever persuade his father to build it.

"Don't need a new forge," Donald said. "I built one only four years ago, and look what it got me!"

"Yah, I don't mean only a forge, Dad; I mean a new grinding mill and a casting shed, too. Put 'em all under one roof, make better use of the workmen."

His father did not respond to "workmen." He and Jonnie and one other smith were the only ones regularly at work now. He had contracted with a joiner in Greenfield to stock the guns, now that David was not there to do it; Jonnie, without telling him, had been spinning dreams to one of the Sons who had some carpentry experience and who could come in permanently. The gun works—for so Jonnie called it, and the name would stick—was to be an expanding business, wartime and peacetime, its workmen interlaced with the Sons of Liberty and the Masons. Iron would be got from a Masonic brother in Salisbury, wood from another in Springfield. No matter that the quality might fall off; Jonnie Morse had found the value of brotherhood, and he would make the most of it.

"Jonnie's just so *get-on-with-it*," his father sighed into the night.

"Jonnie's hard," his wife said, nestling against him. "I think it's this war done it to him. He's hard."

He rested his forehead against her bare shoulder. "What if Jonnie's right?" he groaned. "What if Davie's a traitor?"

She was silent. Her hand moved, rasping against the coarse sheet, slid over his buttock and pulled him against her. "I don't care what he is," she said. "When I see the lot Jonnie's running with, I guess I'm a traitor too."

"Don't even say it!" He rolled away from her and lay on his back, breathing like a man pulled from the water. "Dear God, will there never be an end of our squabbles and our troubles?"

Grinning, arms and legs hopping with every bounce, the figure sailed along over the wet brown field like the antic figurehead of a crazed ship. Under and behind it, a crowd of men sang and shouted and pushed, several running ahead to look back and revel in the fine spectacle they made. Over the last fifty yards to the Morse house, they all broke into a trot and then into a run, none of them so quick to reach the gate and throw it open as Jonnie Morse. He tried to snatch the pole the figure rode on, but others wanted it, too, and he had to be content to close his hand around the peeled pine trunk and bounce and raise it with the others.

"Here's Davie Morse!" Flynn bellowed. One of his lieutenants ran to the house door and pounded.

They raised the pole higher. The figure rose up on it, its foolish grin seeming to show great pleasure in its bizarre ascent. A parody of man, it was disturbingly like a human being and mockingly unlike one, its movements jerky and unpredictable, its grin perpetual and pleased. Looking from the window of her front room, David's mother was reminded stabbingly of her son Samuel, now totally bedridden, his control of his legs and his bowels gone, the same grin on his child's face.

"Here's Davie Morse the traitor!" Flynn shouted.

Donald Morse came out of his house. The girls huddled behind him; at a corner window, Old John tried to see, but his raddled eyes could make out only the dark of the March earth and the gunmetal of the sky and blurred movement where the two met.

"Donald Morse, you spawned a traitor!"

"Read it!" somebody shouted. "Go on, read it!"

"From Philadelphia!" Flynn cried. He waved a bit of paper. "Names on the list of those accepting General Howe's proclamation and affirming loyalty to the bloody King George the Third. On this list, the name—David Morse!" Somebody

264

made a sound like a fart and men laughed, and others turned and pulled down their breeches and repeated the sound.

"From Philadelphia!" Flynn bellowed again. "We got news of an enlistment in His Majesty's Loyal American Shitheads—David Morse!" More sounds, more catcalls and laughter. "He took the king's shilling—his thirty pieces of silver, Judas Iscariot Morse!"

They dipped the pole. Catching the end of it, Flynn pulled it down until he could wrench the straw-stuffed figure from the wood. Another man ran up with a rope, the noose already tied; he dropped it over the cloth neck and pulled it tight, grinning and making a sound halfway between a scream and a strangled death rattle. They tossed the other end of the rope over one limb of a maple tree that stood opposite the door, and then Flynn put a sign on the figure's chest, "David Morse Traytor," and they hoisted it up so that it dangled with its cloth heels six feet off the ground, blowing in the wind like drying laundry, smiling happily at its lack of self-control.

"Take that down!" his mother screamed from her window. "Take that down!"

"That stays there for three days for you to see and understand the truth of!" Flynn shouted.

"You take that down," she said, "or I'll—I'll—!" She began to sob. She looked futilely at her husband, around whom half a dozen young men were capering in a manic Indian dance. Jonnie Morse would not look at her.

"Take it down," she groaned. Her sobs sounded almost like laughter as she rushed from the window. Her two girls came out and stood looking at the figure, and seconds later she was between them, holding the tightened fist of each in one of her own big hands.

"The town got to look at this," Flynn roared. "The Sons of Liberty make it a duty for every right-minded man to get hisself up here and look at this! Now you all heard me say it—spread the word! The Sons expect every patriotic man and woman to get hisself up here and look at this traitor hung!"

The body ballooned away from the tree, borne on the wind, sailing, smiling, at peace with itself.

When they were gone, Jonnie escaped into the cowbarn. Donald Morse stood in his front yard with the effigy of his son sailing over his head. His wife came out of the house with a big kitchen knife in her hand, the knife she had butchered hogs with in the fall, and Donald Morse, seeing her, roused himself and snatched the knife away and rushed to the tree;

he hacked at the rope until the figure fell, collapsing in the winter-flattened grass, and then he slashed its clothes and the paper sign until there was nothing left but rags and a bird's-nest of straw to be scattered by the March wind.

And then Donald Morse went down to his forge and pumped the bellows madly until the sparks shot up and the charcoal spat, and he took a piece of iron and began to pound it. He worked the metal for forty minutes, pounding and pumping, his face contorted and red and his breath gasping, and then he doubled up like a man hit a great blow in the belly, and he fell forward over his anvil with his hand gripped into the muscle above his heart, victim of all the torment and troubles of his forty-nine years; and he died there at his forge.

When they found him, he had on his face a look of pain and utter astonishment, that even at the very end, the last thing he was to know was hurtful.

Chapter Twenty-nine

"Ice is out, Grandfather."

"Who's there?"

"Jonathan."

The old man turned his filmy eyes. He grunted, as if to say, *Oh, you.* Jonathan had been holding his breath, as if— *as if what? As if I was waiting for him to change toward me.* The old man was still bitter. He still blamed Jonathan for seeming to have betrayed his brother. *That ice ain't out. That ice will never go out.* His grandfather, he knew, wished that it were David who was there on the farm and Jonathan who was away fighting—on either side.

"Thought I'd tell you, is all. Spring almost here."

His mother was in the kitchen with his sisters. The room was steamy; he could smell baking. There was laundry boiling in the room behind, and he could smell that. *Smell of women.* The sight of them almost melted the icy vision of his grandfather's contempt. Jonathan loved women—his mother and sisters, the whores of Boston and Greenfield, the farm girl he was going to marry.

"Ice is out, Ma."

She turned a quick smile to him. "Ain't that good! You hear what Jonnie says, you girls? Be time to plow, soon."

"Time to marry!"

Jonnie laughed at himself with them. He and Felicity Gough would marry in the summer. No date had been picked; Jonnie, aware of his responsibility to the farm, felt that he would have to choose a time when there was no work to be done. *Self-important of me,* he thought now. But it was better to err on the side of responsibility.

His mother had accepted his father's death with what he thought was great courage, turning away from the bitterness of which his grandfather was such an example. She had accepted what life offered: a son, Jonathan, who would take over for his father, despite his youth; two daughters to support her emotionally; cheerful, afflicted Samuel; and the absent David, that hurtful mystery that they all had to bear. The girls followed her example.

He touched his mother's waist; surprising both of them, he kissed her cheek. She was flustered, and she seemed grateful when one of his sisters screeched that he was "only keeping in practice for *Miss* Gough!" But she was pleased.

He and his mother were getting to know each other. They had spent the night of his father's death in beginning the process as they sat in the candlelit room with the body. Neither had understood how much Jonathan had lived in the shadow of David all his life, even in their mother's eyes. She had been honest enough to accuse him of betraying his brother; he had tried to explain, honestly, that he had thought he could make himself a buffer between David and the most violent of the Sons. They had held hands—two strong, hard people who were not accustomed to touching.

He could kiss her cheek now, touch her waist. *The ice is out.*

"I thought I'd go over to the—to Davie's place and have a look about."

"Thinking of taking Felicity there to live?"

"That miserable place? Loneliest spot in the valley. Nah, I want to live here, like we talked."

"You can live over there if you want, Jonnie. A woman wants her own house, often as not." She dried her red hands on her apron. "Look how that poor Sara took on, living here."

"Yah, Sara!"

"Now, Jonnie—"

"She's no good, Ma, why not say it? Best thing that ever happened to Davie was the day she run off. When—when the war's over and Davie comes home—or whatever happens—he can take up again without her. I'm going over there just to look around, see what damage winter's done."

She gave him part of a new loaf and a fist-sized lump of soft cheese curd in a cloth. He wanted to get away by himself, and she knew it. The year was changing; there was always excitement in that. Ice was gone from the river; the black earth was almost free of frost. Soon the fish would be moving in the warming waters—salmon would go down to the sea, black now and lanky; birds would flock in the trees; he would turn the soil of fields that his father had cleared.

"Want I should bring Davie's things back here?"

"Why—" She looked at the distant mountains through the steam on the windowpanes. "Sara might come back yet."

"I surely hope she don't!"

"Jonnie, Jonnie. Just leave their things as they be." She

would not give up. If the house was cleaned of David's presence, it would be more admission that he was not coming back. What Jonathan really wanted to do was rent that house out, but he dared not suggest it.

He rode to the hillside high above the farm so that he could look over it and over the whole of the valley. The smoke of the forge was like a newly painted sign proclaiming *business*. The contract that David had sent from Philadelphia when the Congress fled had been completed; now he had secured another through the Sons. He was a creditor of the Congress; that thought pleased him, made him a bigger man. Unlike his father, he had no deep suspicion of credit. "Credit in Heaven" was a common term enough; credit in Congress must be worth something, then.

Jonnie Morse had ambition. He knew it. He did not want to be a country blacksmith and he did not want to be merely a farmer. He wanted to be—although he had no example of it, and so no word for it—a merchant prince.

He rode toward Davie's house. He filled the valley with forges and fires as he rode; he put outbuildings around the farm; he cut down every scrap of wasteful forest and put up buildings, planted fields, made all productive. He created a line of forged goods: knives, axes, farm tools, wrought iron. Perhaps even light metal wares, whitesmithing work—copper and tin utensils.

He believed in credit and he believed in growth. Instinctively, he knew that when the colonies won the war, growth must follow.

A figure was coming along the road toward him, black against the dark springtime earth, a long cloak flapping around its legs. The man carried a pack basket on his back, a smaller one on his chest. *Peddler*. Even in wartime, the peddlers were on the roads. Jon touched his hat.

"Your pardon, peddler. I got a question for you."

"Ayeh?"

Jon leaned down from the saddle. "Where do you find your wares—your knives and needles and the like?"

The peddler grinned. "Sheffield."

"What, in England?"

"Ayeh. Ain't made here, mister."

"But Sheffield goods must cost very high, even when there's peace."

The man grinned toothlessly. "Better to pay high than not have 'em at all, mister."

Peddler's wares. Jon rode on. Not so romantic as military guns, perhaps, but there would be a steady market for such goods. When the war was won and men pushed out beyond those artificial boundaries that the English had set to the West, there would be even greater demand for such goods. *How do they make needles, I wonder?* Jonnie marveled every day at how much he had to learn—but then he set about learning it.

Like almost everybody who approached Davie's shuttered house down the long hill from the north, Jon felt the gloom of the setting and could not whistle himself out of it. The sun was always blocked by a steep hillside that was crisscrossed with standing and fallen trees, which rested in their turn on earth that always seemed dank. Moisture oozed from this hillside in the form of trickling springs and snowmelt, which dripped and trickled down beards of ice that were still two feet thick in the hillside shade and that ended, finally, in a runoff stream that gushed along beside the road. In places, it even spilled over the road itself, and the horse had to splash through the chill water. Jonnie shivered. The dark little house lay below him, and there, behind it, was the black water of the swamp, collector of all this icewater that coursed beside him.

Nothing seems so cold as a house shut up in winter. For those with a mind so inclined, it seems a foretaste of the grave. There is no moving air; the only smells are mildew and damp; everything is of the same pitiless cold, and the familiar things of the house are like the furnishings of a mausoleum.

Jonnie walked quickly through this dead atmosphere. The house had been closed for a year and a half; he or his father had visited it only to see that it was secure. A pile of hulls in a corner gave evidence of mice. In an upstairs bedroom, a dead bird lay on the coverless bed.

He was glad to step outside. The sun had found a corner of the yard; he stood in it, welcoming the pale warmth. More cheerful, he looked into the barn, then walked the property line, first along the road, then at an angle to it toward the swamp, following the rail fence that Davie had rebuilt to keep in his horse.

At the corner nearest the swamp, the ground was springy, and he realized that water must run under it to reach the swamp. On an impulse, he straddled the rail and walked out several feet. He wondered that there were never trout in that water, or none that he had ever heard of; this cold, black water should hold small, dark brook trout that would be perfect for eating. Surely trout would not care for the gloom of the setting; surely—

A vagueness in the water caught his eye. It was as if the water was less black for a moment, clouded with murky white, as if milk had been spilled into it. *Trick of the light.* He searched the surface. *Yes, there it is.* The water was like frost fingers on his feet; it had seeped into his boots. He tried to keep to the tussocks, but his feet got wet anyway. *Cold, bloody cold—*

It was a white something in the water in a miniature bay no more than ten feet across. Its shape seemed to change, like the wispy white of an egg dropped into boiling water, like gauzy draperies stirring in a wind. It was still ten feet from him, but he could see it—its size, its nature. He felt as if he were choking. He had thought at first it might be a dead cow, a dead deer that had frozen on the ice and fallen in when the swamp had thawed. *That White Beast Grandpa natters about.*

But this white beast was human, he knew. There was no mistaking it: there, sticking from the white draperies, was a shriveled, yellow, but unmistakable human hand.

"Sara." He said it aloud. He was sure that he knew what had happened. She had drowned herself in the swamp. *Oh, thank God.* His first thought was that Davie would be free when he came home. The body revolted him, but he was glad for its existence. *No worse than some I seen at Saratoga,* he told himself.

He had to get a pruning hook from the barn and splash out into the swamp, waist-deep in icewater before he could reach it, and then he could hook the white cloth with the tool and slowly, slowly draw the burden in. He saw the black swirl of her hair, for she was floating face down. *Sara, Sara. Done it while she was drunk. Maybe she come back here in the winter, fell through the ice or somewhat.* He pulled the body out, careful to touch only the cloth that wrapped it (*Jesus she's tied up in this*) half rolling it in the water, steeling himself against the sight of the face (*It'll be the worst, one look and it won't be so bad*) turning it without daring to touch the flesh until the leathery, yellow, waxy, horrible face looked up at him through two inches of water—

"Oh, Davie!"

The bullet hole was a little puckered, but it was very clean,

271

even after a year and a half under the water. Cold, pure, acid water.

"Oh, Davie, how could you!"

He understood it all. Later he would know that it could have been suicide, or it could have been the work of somebody else, but at that moment, as if the dead woman herself had screamed it in his ear, he knew that his brother had murdered his wife.

He looked around him at the gloomy hills. *Nobody.* He brought blankets from the house to wrap the awful thing in, looking over his shoulder as if he had done the killing himself. *Nobody.* There was an old stoneboat by the barn; it would do to drag her in, with his saddled horse pulling. *Nobody.*

He buried her in the cellar, under the huge protrusion of a granite ledge that formed the east wall of the foundation. It curved under just at the cellar floor, like the underside of a huge chin; by tunneling down and back he put her in under the stone itself, as if he feared that she might rise up straight one day; if she did, she would find a granite roof over her head and rise no higher. He worked like a lunatic, like a man racing a hurricane; he dug, sobbing, cursing, stopping to listen for footsteps. Halfway through his task, he ran outside and raked fallen branches and leaves and rotten barn boards into a huge pile and set fire to it; then he ran down and stripped off her wrappings and her clothes, even her petticoats and her undermost breeches until the corpse was nude, and he burned them all. *Could burn the corpse; no; bones left, too much left—*

More guiltily, more anguishedly than David ever had, he went over the house, the cellar, the weedy yard. He piled dirt over her and stamped it down; he got three big pieces of granite from the hillside and tumbled them down the cellar stairs and planted them over the hole he had dug. *Stay down! Stay deep!*

He rode home in funereal twilight. His one thought was to protect what he had—his mother, the farm, the business. *Nobody must ever know.* Not for Davie's sake. For the Morses' sake.

His mother was shocked to see him. "Jonnie, you look a sight! Where have you been, you're all muddy, you're—what's *happened?*"

"The place was a mess."

"You've got ash all over—and the mud!"

"There was something dead in the house. I had to bury it.

Built a fire of sticks and all. As long as I was there—I thought—clean the place up—"

"You must have worked like a Trojan, you been gone all day! Well, there's hot water; you go wash, now—it's good of you to take such care of Davie's house."

After he had made a show of eating with them, he sat alone at the table, sipping apple brandy. After an hour, he went quietly into the kitchen where his mother was sewing.

"I've changed me mind, Ma. I'm thinking I'll take Felicity to yon gloomy little place to live."

"Well, but—it's Davie's, and—Sara might come back."

"Sara won't come back." He said it very flatly. "Somebody ought to be living in that house."

"Well, then—all right. But we could rent it out."

"No. I don't want anybody else there. I'll live there with Felicity." He would give her no explanation.

Later in the spring of that year, the Congress decided to punish the Indians who, they believed, had been tormenting the settlers of parts of Pennsylvania and New York, and they commissioned General John Sullivan to raise a force and take it into the western Iroquois country. Those Indians were old allies of the English, it was believed; they should be disciplined.

"Burn," was the order. "Starve them out."

During the second half of the summer, Sullivan's army moved slowly, sinuously north and west from the Chemung River to the Finger Lakes and west to the Chenusee, reaching that river in September. The Senecas, retreating before them, called the army "the Snake," for so it seemed to them as it wound through their valleys and around their lakes. Orchards and cornfields burned; villages burned. The army brought artillery and five thousand men. The Senecas were two thousand people altogether.

Jonnie Morse was asked to go with Speke's company, for Sullivan was a New Hampshire man and it was thought there would be good pickings. But Jonnie married Felicity Gough and went to live in the house that had been his brother's, and he said that he would fight to defend the valley, and he would fight to defend Liberty, but he wouldn't go out of his way to burn out a pack of savages. A few men from the valley went.

The Snake crawled through the Seneca country and made a desert of it. Two hundred and fifty thousand bushels of corn were burned. Seventeen villages. Kanandaque; Little Beard's

Town; the little town where the black man, Sunfish, was a war leader; the castle on the Chenusee. The Senecas hardly fought back; after a defeat at the place the whites called Newtown, when the Senecas were under heavy artillery fire for the first time in their history, they fell back—and back, and back.

Message-bringer sat on the west bank of the Chenusee and watched the Snake crawl back toward the settlements, its work of destruction done. He was fifth in the line from Snow Elk, an orator, a leader who had not been able to save his people. The smoke of burning corn hung over the Chenusee Valley for days, and the smell of it was in their nostrils like a mockery of food; they would remember it when they were starving that winter.

"Where are the riches of the People now?" he asked in his grating voice.

"Where is the war that will make us rich again?"

With him were the green-coated Major Butler, the brilliant Tory guerrilla fighter who made his winter camp among the Senecas, and a red-coated officer from Niagara.

"Where will the People ever find their riches again?"

The officer was embarrassed. Butler tried to say something about raids of vengeance, but he, too, fell silent.

"There is nothing to say any more." Message-bringer pulled his blanket, which had been made in England, tight about him. "It is all over," he said.

He walked upstream for a day and a half to the highest falls of the Chenusee, there in the narrow gorge where the water falls hundreds of feet over eroded shale shelves, and he stripped off everything that had come from beyond the ocean—his silver arm bracelets, and the silver gorget that Johnson had given him when he had signed the treaty that was to guarantee the Senecas their lands forever, and his white shirt, and his gun and his metal ax, and even his scarlet blanket; and he jumped into the creamy thunder of the waterfall and had his head broken like a bird's egg on the shale, and his body crashed down over the ledges and was driven deep into the pool below by the hammer of the water, where it rose and fell, circled, churned with the active bubbling of the water, until it drifted free and floated slowly down the river to rot.

The Snake wound out of the Seneca country and back to the settlements; the men went home. Those from the valley came back all in health and pleased with themselves, and

274

they sat in the taverns and told all the stories that they had been told to tell by their officers, for General Sullivan was no fool, and he understood the power of having good things said about him. They told all the things they had been told about Seneca atrocities and brilliant strategy and heroism.

"And the land!" they said. "Christ Almighty! The land! Them Indians was growing more corn per acre than you ever seen here in Massachusetts! And apple orchards, and plums—and they fatten their cattle like barrels. And the milk—it comes out half cream!" They meant what they said, for they had seen it, and this part was true.

"It's all black dirt, I swear it, deep as you can dig, and rich as money. That land is rich, boys, I don't mind saying—I'm going out there when this war is over, I swear I am! It's rich, boys—rich—rich!"

In October, because it was pleasant weather, Mr. Arthur Morrison ordered his coach to drive south and west because there was a sight he wanted to see, a sight such as no man in England had ever seen before. Mr. Arthur Morrison—"old Mr. Arthur" now, for he was nearing seventy—took his son, William, along; together, they were the brains of Morrison and Pittsden of Birmingham, for Pittsden had been a fool to start with and was getting more senile by the day.

They drove over roads blessedly dry for the season, through a landscape of glorious color. "Second summer," William Morrison called it. His father smiled. William was something of a poet, was old Mr. Arthur's view—a poet among merchants, at any rate, for William showed all the signs of continuing his own leadership of the firm and of expanding it even beyond its present status as the leading iron manufactory of Birmingham.

"There!" old Mr. Arthur said. He rapped on the underside of the coach roof with his stick, and the coachman braked to a rattling halt.

"Remarkable," William said.

"More than remarkable, surely," old Mr. Arthur said. He was hoping for a small flight of fancy from his fanciful son.

"Why, it's—poetry in iron, Father!"

Old Mr. Arthur smiled. "Just so." His son had not disappointed him. William never disappointed him. William was an excellent son to have.

They got out of the coach and walked slowly to a better

vantage point a few yards above the road. The object of their wonder stood below them in all its newness: the Iron Bridge. It was the very first of its kind, a single, graceful span across a river, linking shore with shore as stably as stone ever had—and built entirely of iron!

"It's the beginning of a new age, Father!"

"You think so? So do I!"

"A new age, sir! Why, it's wonderful—an act of creation that puts man the ironworker on a level with—the Romans. The Greeks! Praxiteles could not have wrought more wonderfully!"

Old Mr. Arthur beamed. Education was a splendid thing; he did not regret a penny that he had spent on William.

"The Age of Fire and Iron, Father! Wonderful!"

In the pitiless Massachusetts winter, the little house in the gloomy cut between the hills was cold, cold as a tomb. Jonnie and his wife warmed themselves at each other's bodies; by day, he cut cords of wood and stoked the fireplaces so that they roared. He insisted that Felicity keep a servant, who slept over the kitchen; it made company for her, he said. He insisted that she must never be alone in the house, although she said she would not have minded.

He brought people to the little house—business friends from up and down the valley, friends from the Sons of Liberty, friends of his parents. He was always bringing a sister or his mother to stay the night or for a few days. At Christmas, he insisted that they keep candles lighted and hang boughs at their door and on their mantels. In all, the house was a happy place, and his young wife never had reason to think it anything but a warm, pleasant home.

Jonnie Morse hated the house. But he never said so.

Chapter Thirty

Jonnie Morse dreamed of death. He knew he was dreaming of death. Not his own death; he knew that, too. He had seen death in battle; he had seen Davie's murdered wife. He knew death well enough to know when he was in the midst of a dream of it.

He was mounted. Davie was behind him, his hands wrapped tight at Jonnie's waist, as tight as that last morning when they had embraced in the cowbarn, two strong young men letting themselves show that they were brothers. On a white horse, they were galloping through a landscape of horrors and were yet safe from them, as if the dying men, the hands that still clutched sabers, the puffs of cannon smoke, were only ghosts across whose unreal world they galloped in all the strength of life. The horse pounded on; he could feel the wind of its passage on his face. The cannons roared. Men rose up, swords in hand, then fell back.

Ahead, turmoil. A horizon, blood-red: sunset. A tangle of struggling men. The horse strained forward, as if it was toward that point they had been hurrying. He felt Davie's hands loosen and knew that Davie was preparing a weapon. The horse was an unstoppable energy that bore them, out of control. The horse was running away. They plunged into the midst of the struggling men, the half-naked, brutal figures who chopped at each other—and he heard a cry behind him; the touch on his waist loosened, the horse reared—

"Davie!"

He woke, sweating. There were too many blankets on him. Felicity's hip was plastered against him with his sweat. "Davie!"

"You been dreaming again. *Jonnie!*"

He pushed the great weight of the blankets away and lay naked in the cold room. "I'm sorry."

"It's all right, I always tell you it's all right, don't I? It's all right. You was screaming."

"I was dreaming about Davie."

"Yes, same as always. You screamed out."

"I'm sorry." He lay naked on the sheets, panting. The

motion of that horrible, ungovernable horse was still insistent between his legs; still, he had the realization of his brother's loss of his grip, his sudden slipping away. *Davie!*

"I could rub your back," she said.

"No. Just stay awake a little. It's only a dream. Only that same old dream."

When David dreamed of death, he dreamed always of potatoes stored in his father's cellar for the winter, potatoes too long kept and gone soft, their eyes sprouted into long, white tendrils like blind serpents. Why such a picture flashed to mind he could not understand, but it was always there when the dream of death was, a picture of an ugly and obscene excess of nature. Sent down into the cellar to fetch potatoes for his mother, he had cringed as a child from these strange creatures that put out their growth in the dark; once, reaching into the potato barrel and feeling the white sprouts brush his fingers, he had closed his hand on a rotten one that was wet and slimy, and he had cried out aloud. That was death.

Now, sitting on a stone on a little hill called King's Mountain, eight hundred miles from the valley, he waited for that death. The wintered potatoes came to mind, but he did not flinch. He had seen death now, caused death, and he knew that the vision meant a return to earth, to growth, to life of a kind. He had been in other battles—Cold Harbor, Stonypoint, Charleston—and had seen men die, had been wounded by a ball and known the astonishment and the resentment that *he* could be hit and that his blood could run. He had killed at least one man with a rifle and had stuck another with a bayonet. Death and his missionaries, the gun and the bayonet, were very real. But now he did not flinch; he did not pray for a reprieve. He looked down the little wooded hill that was called a mountain in the Carolinas—so much less than a mountain in the Berkshires, even less than the high hill behind his father's forge—and thought for once of death, and was calm.

It was a warm October day, a day plucked out of early summer and given him in autumn. At that quiet turning of the day when evening is on the way and the wind drops, when the birds are quiet and the sun slants across the treetops, he found a sudden and astonishing serenity. The blue of the sky deepened; the greens of trees and grass down the mountainside turned rich and translucent; the voices of other men became a low and melodious murmur on the silent afternoon.

278

A horse whinnied. David Morse looked to the west and saw the next wooded hill, and beyond it, bluer and more promising, another; and beyond that others still, and always others farther away, bluer and beckoning, as real as earth and as glorious as dreaming.

A breath of wind brought a sound. He turned, his senses sharpened; he looked at men around him, but no one seemed to have heard. The sound came again, a hymn carried on a breeze from somewhere to the north, its individual voices, its dissonances muted by the distance; and he thought that these might be his enemies singing before they came on. He smiled, listened again, but the vagrant music was gone.

Toward five o'clock, the chaplain passed from man to man and from group to group; coming to David Morse, he stopped, his usually severe voice hushed, and said, "Have you made your peace with God?"

He stared at the man's face, trying to understand what the words could mean. "Yes, sir," he said at last. "I hope I have."

He had relatives among his enemies. He did not know it, and they did not know it. They were hard-faced, brutalized, self-righteous men from the mountains of the Carolinas, men who had brought God and hatred with them from Scotland and who would give both that God and that hatred to the future. As surely as London shaped the future of Boston, so Scotland shaped the future of the American South: it bred good haters. These were men who could know without question that God had made women and blacks inferior; these were men to whom God had given the gun as a token of their manhood.

There were four Morses in the thousand men who surrounded the English force on King's Mountain. They were all grandsons of Duncan Morse, that bitter clergyman who had sired Old John on Magdalena Gottshalk; like Old John, they had come to America after the debacle of Culloden. But they had come to the Carolinas, not to New England. Now they stood as enemy to their kin, waiting with hard faces to kill him.

They carried long guns that had been made at rude forges back in the steep and uneven valleys of their razorbacked mountains. Some of them were rifled; many of them were not. A Morse had made a number of the guns that were carried at King's Mountain—both the long woods guns of the mountaineers and two or three of the Ferguson rifles that were carried up above.

They had prayed with the chaplains, and now they stood in the woods and waited to start the killing. Their chaplains waited with them, armed, ready to kill. Theirs was the God of ancient Israel who ripped the garment of His nation from Saul for the sin of leniency. They would not make the mistake of being compassionate.

The signal was given. The Morses looked at each other and nodded. Old Duncan Morse was long since dead, but his narrow-minded sense of justice lived on in his grandsons. After the killing was over, they would call it not narrow-mindedness, but Liberty.

An hour later, it was over.

A thousand rebels ringed the little mountain like a snake coiled around its base, preventing their escape, then began to push up the slope in sectors, pushing up and falling back, coming up through the big trees and firing from their cover and running pell-mell down it again when the British regulars and the King's American, who were as good as regulars now, thrust back until they were overextended and uneasy in the woods, and then they would withdraw to the top again and the rebels would come on.

The hilltop was bare of trees, fish-shaped. There were no safe places up there, not even among the wagons at the tail. There were places in the rocks where a man, two men, five men could hide for a little time, but there were no citadels. The rebels came on, firing rifles, most of them, slow to load and middling accurate of fire, but there were a thousand of them and they came on like hunters who have driven game into a ring and are closing it up, killing as they come.

Ferguson was not sane by then. David Morse knew he was not sane; some of the other men who had been with him from the beginning thought so, too. Gaunt, driven, unable to see truth any longer, he had become a butcher and he had turned his men into butchers, and now they were caught on a mountaintop that he had chosen for them, madly declaring it impregnable. He raced his horse along the ridge, shouting, cursing, driving them to be as insane as he; when his horse was shot, he flung himself into the saddle of another.

When he fell, he was still promising them victory, his voice a hoarse croak, a hawker's voice, a crow's voice; when he fell, the rebel riflemen continued to fire at his body, and afterward, when it was over and they had won, they put three more balls into his corpse and one hacked at it with a brush ax, because he was one of the butchers who had made them killers.

David Morse did not see Ferguson fall, but he heard a shout from the far end of the line, the shout coming down to him with one voice and then another until he understood that Ferguson was dead. Somebody put up a flag of truce then, but it was no good; the rebels were in the fringe of the trees, still shooting, and there was no stopping them. He fired his musket and snatched up one of the Ferguson rifles from a lung-shot veteran who was gasping and swearing and begging for somebody to help him; he took the man's cartridge box and tried to return the fire that was growing now as more and more of his enemies came to the edge of the trees and poured shot at them. He fired three times, and each time the rifle was harder to load. He knew those cranky guns; he had been repairing them for two years. He knew what would happen. He spit into the breech and got another shot from it, and that was all; there was no closing it after that. He had lost his own musket by then.

Rebels trotted from the woods toward him and the little cluster of green-coated Loyal Americans who were with him. Somebody to his left fired; somebody else waved his white shirt for a flag. It was too late for that. The breech-loading rifle was useless and his bayonet would not fit it. He threw the impotent gun away and waited by the man who was waving the shirt. He had the steel pistol in his right hand, loaded and primed, but he had never fired it, never in all the time since he had murdered Sara back in their gloomy little house.

One ball hit him in the belly and another in the left eyebrow and he went down on his back, dying, knowing nothing but the fading buzz of nerves and blood like the sound of bees in the apple blossoms; and then he was dead, dead as his father, dead as Ferguson, dead as anybody who had died of cholera or gunshot or bayonet or a sick heart in all of that miserable war.

When they had rounded up the prisoners and rifled the bodies for what could be carried away, they made some small attempt at decency by saying a prayer and piling brush and rocks over the corpses, and shooting three men who were too far gone to be saved and too much alive to leave, and then they walked down the mountain with their prisoners and celebrated the only battle in the whole war where the rifle had mattered a damn, the battle when Patrick Ferguson had been destroyed by the weapon he had lived for.

For two weeks after, nobody went up on King's Mountain, but the hogs and the wild dogs and the wolves were there, and pious people in the neighborhood would not eat hog that winter because of what they'd fed on.

When Lieutenant Colonel Banastre Tarleton got the news—too late to help, because he had malaria and was delirious when Ferguson and David Morse were dying—he rode out with his legion, split into two wings with Major George Hanger commanding the other, and chased some of the rebels up and down the countryside for ten days and killed whatever ones he caught, because it had become that kind of war. One of them who was chased down by two of his dragoons had the steel pistol with the scenes of Death engraved on the butt, and one of the dragoons took it as his prize while the other took the man's rifle and his meager stock of coins. Because the dragoon was a Scotsman, he treated the pistol properly, wrapping it in an oiled cloth and putting it in his wooden box of personal property.

"Can we go back now, Gran?"

"Soon. Don't complain so. Take me to the top of the hill."

"Oh, Gran!"

Yet, dutifully, the child led him up the road through the opening into the hayfield and along the half-completed stone wall that the Morses had been building out of the stones that were plowed up in their hard fields. There, on the highest knoll on the Morse farm, the old man stood in the May sunshine with the faint scent of apple blossoms still in his nostrils, his apple with its white flowers still in his hand like a staff of office.

"Is it a clear day?" he said.

"Yes, sir." The boy became impatient again. "Can't you see *nothing?*"

"Light and dark, is all. Light and dark. Is there smoke coming from our chimney?"

"Yes, Gran."

"And from the forges?"

"Yes, Grandfather."

"And our cows are in the west meadow."

"Yes."

"And all my apple trees are in blossom."

"*Yes.*"

"And you can see over the river, and beyond that to the far hill, and to the mountains beyond."

"Yes, sir. They're blue."

"I know."

The old man stood with the warm sun on his face and looked with his sightless eyes at the Morse farm and the Connecticut Valley. The child, relenting, slipped his hand in Old John's and looked in the same direction, seeing and yet not seeing the same things, vaguely conscious of the pity of his lost vision, entirely unconscious of the glory of what he saw. The old man looked—and saw, not the things themselves, but the replica engraved upon his mind: the hayfield and the hedgerows, and then the roofs of the Morse house and barns and the Morse forges; the grassy road and its avenue of trees, white, blossoming mounds like clouds; then the steeply declining, wooded hill and the twist of river at the bottom; and the far side ascending, wooded, green with budding hardwoods; and beyond, the Berkshire hills, blue and misted. In his mind's eye he saw it all.

"Is there a White Beast?" he said.

"A *what?*"

"Never mind. There wouldn't be."

He let the child lead him down through the engraving of his imagined landscape, back to the house. He felt old—so old! He had broken old fingers and an old, old gunshot wound in his back; he was so old that he no longer was sure if he remembered things or if they were things told to him from history. Had he really been at Culloden? At Carlisle? Had he really loved a woman who was his sister, so very, very long ago?

The child led him down across the meadow toward the forges. It was time to die.

Chapter Thirty-one

When the war had been over for some years, and nobody care
so very much any longer about who was a Tory and who wa
a rebel, a man of unmistakably arrogant bearing appeare
at the Morses' gate. He hesitated, then bent to loosen the rop
and let his horse move through; clearly an accomplishe
horseman, he had no trouble fastening it again and ridin
slowly up the curved road to the barns before he dismounted

He looked at the grave little boy who was studying him.

"Is your name Morse, young fellow?"

"Yes."

"Is Mr. Donald Morse about, young fellow?"

"Me father's here."

"Fetch him for me, there's a bright lad."

The gentleman stretched his legs, having been riding fo
some distance, and he eyed the new buildings down the hill
side below him. Two forges were at work; the sounds of meta
being worked came clearly up to him.

"Is there something we can do, sir?"

He turned to find a tall, handsome woman of fifty standin
behind him. There was an instant understanding betwee
them, for both were strong personalities. "I have not come o
a happy mission, ma'am. I wished to tell Mr. Donald Mors
of the circumstances surrounding the death of his son David."

Inadvertently, she glanced toward a plot beyond the hous
that was fenced with a neat, newly painted wood rail. "M
husband died during the war."

"I am so sorry." The conventional phrase sounded in hi
mouth as if it had genuine meaning. He had removed hi
beautifully brushed hat. "Forgive me, ma'am. I am Majo
Hanger, late of the Brunswick Jaegers and His Majesty'
Army of the South. Now that all that unpleasantness is over
I hope I do not offend you by coming here."

"No. No, major!" She turned away slightly toward the road
his eyes lingered on the small graveyard, where he saw a
very new grave and a makeshift wooden marker. *John
Morse—1701–1786.* "My son is coming up from the works
major."

284

He sat with them in their, to him, impossibly stiff and useless front room, a glass of some local brew at his hand, untouched. His manner was quite perfect, however, for he was serious about his mission. A rakehell and a profligate he might be, and so history would judge him, but he believed in these forms as between soldier and soldier, and hoped that somebody would do as much for him one day.

"David Morse," he said carefully, his clipped, slightly Irish accent falling in that rather pretentious room like the echoes of England's hopes, "was an excellent soldier. I regret to tell you that he is dead, but he died well, as befits a man. With him was his commanding officer, one of England's finest younger soldiers and an acquaintance of my own, Major Patrick Ferguson. It is painful to say these things, painful to hear them, but our war is over and these men are beyond our factions; therefore, believe me when I say that I grieve, as I know you do, for their death, no matter which side they espoused."

Hanger unwrapped a small bundle that had been carried in a leather case. "I believe this belonged to your son and brother." He held up a steel Scots pistol, heavily engraved. "Do you recognize it?"

"My grandfather made it!"

"I saw the name 'Morse' on it, and, knowing the gun's provenance, thought it might belong here." Hanger smiled slowly; his pouchy drinker's eyes closed up almost sleepily. "I should have written you long ago, had I but known, but those who perished at King's Mountain lost their officers in so many cases that it was extraordinarily difficult to puzzle out who was lost there. And then, to inform the families—" He spread his hands. "It was rather outside my own command, of course. But, returning to England in 'eighty-two, I found this pistol in Henry Nock's shop. He'd bought it from a dragoon who'd been with Ban—Colonel Tarleton. They'd chased down the—forces—who had been victorious at King's Mountain, and so the dragoon had acquired the pistol. I spoke to him, and guessed at its history."

"But how did you know it was my brother's?" Jonnie's voice was hoarse.

"I knew him slightly. I had seen the pistol, as a matter of fact—had rather admired the workmanship in Philadelphia. There was no question of the ascription."

Donald Morse's wife stirred. Her voice was steady. "And you're sure my son is dead, major?"

Hanger's head inclined. "Yes, ma'am. All those who wer with Ferguson are accounted for—or dead. You have my deep est sympathies, ma'am."

"We are very grateful, major."

"Not at all, ma'am." Hanger's debauched face showed th greatest seriousness. "This is the debt we pay to each othe ma'am. In death, we are all comrades," he said pretentiously

When he was gone, she paced up and down in the yar behind the picket fence for some minutes, beating her hand together soundlessly. Jonnie held his young son back so h would not run to her; he would not answer the boy's question At last, she turned away from her pacing and came towar him, scuffing aside the dry leaves that littered the grass. " would like to put a stone in the cemetery, Jonnie."

"All right, Ma. It was good of the major to come."

"I thought you'd be that angry, him being English."

"The war's over, Ma."

They walked together to the kitchen door, the small bo trailing at his father's side, silent, tired. When she was abou to go in, Jonnie said, "I'd like to move up here to the bi house, Ma. Me and Felicity and the children. Build a win on the place, make it our home."

She flushed with the idea of it, but habitual caution mad her say, "What about the little house? It can't go to waste."

"Maybe I'll rent it out." He was thinking of the old busines in the cellar. He was thinking that he would creep dow there, some autumn night, and set fire to it. It would bur to the ground and he could plow it under; then the dead woul be dead.

"You must do as you think best," she said. "You're th man of the family now."

He had a second note coming due on the Congress in eigh months. Contrary to what people had thought, those note were worth money. The honeybee had been right: notes o a government were always worth something. He rode hom through the twilight with his son on the saddle in front o him, thinking of Hanger's visit, of Davie, of the money tha existed for him in the future. He had not seen Davie in- *Good God, ten years!*—and he could think of him only as th impetuous, hot boy of that day. He had passed Davie by, fo Davie had been dead, a boy, while he had been growing olde

After his supper, he sat in the front room that served hi as an office and figured up his profit and loss. The work would make money, no doubt about it; then there were th otes coming due—and two new contracts through his old riends in the Sons of Liberty, well, that was like money in he bank for two or three years from now. And he had the works making tinware now, and hoes, and axes. The business f peace could be as profitable as the business of war.

Next year, the arbitrary line that had been drawn along he western boundary of settlement would be opened, and hen men could push into that rich country that the men had seen n the Sullivan campaign. It was said to be good farmland, lmost empty now. There were land companies advertising or investment in those lands; he marked a sum down in his ccount book, the amount he would put into such a venture.

"Dad?"

His son was at his elbow. He moved the candle so the boy, leepy-eyed, would not bump it. "Well?"

"Who was that man who was up to Gran's today?"

"He was an English officer from the war."

"Why didn't you shoot him, then?"

"The war's over."

"Is he a bad man?"

"No. Quite a good one, I thought. He brought back something from your dead Uncle David."

His son had never seen Uncle David. Uncle David was nly a name, a sound, a puff of smoke.

"He brought that pistol." The boy nodded at the gun, which ay on the back of the desk next to its twin. David's gun was icked a bit, and a trifle discolored, perhaps from something n the cloth in which it had been packed; still, the two were nmistakably a pair.

"Did you make them guns, Dad?"

"No. My grandfather did."

"Did you ever shoot anybody with them guns, Dad?"

Jonnie hesitated. He took a deep breath. "Maybe somebody id, once long ago."

"Don't you know?"

"No. We make guns, child; how people use 'em is something lse. We're the gunmakers, is all." He hugged the sleepy boy o him, feeling the warm, animal body. "Do you want to make uns when you're grown, boy?"

The child nodded, too sleepy to speak.

"Then we will! Morse and Son—hey? How will that be—Morse and Son?"

Felicity came and took the child away and put him to bed, eaving Jonnie Morse with his books and his contracts and

his dreams. He touched the two pistols. He took down th
book that Jan Morse had given to his son Archie, and tha
each Morse in turn had written in. He looked at the famil
tree, the mysterious words about the White Beast, whic
embarrassed him because he had had dreams that seemed
be about a white beast, but he was a man of practicality an
he did not trust old scribbles in a book.

He turned instead to the page of marks. He could unde
stand those. They represented material accomplishment, th
realization of dreams. He took up a pen. Under the last entr
he wrote:

J. Morse and Son. 1787.